Praise for *Blue Springs*

"This book is nothing short of brilliant, and so full of suspense and surprise, that it is hard to put down. *Blue Springs* takes the reader on an emotional rollercoaster ride to the world of 1955 America. The action moves swiftly, and the despair of alcoholism leaves the reader cheering for the counterbalancing effects of honesty, integrity, and the power of a friendship that bridges generations. Any reader will enjoy this fast-paced page turner!"

Round Table Reviews (Tracy Farnsworth)

"In this wonderful read, we meet a delightful young boy named Charlie and his dog, Taffy. Charlie is like any other boy with all his fears, hopes, and dreams, but Charlie has a problem, and his life is about to change—forever.

"A real page turner with not one but two evil characters, family conflict, a wonderful child with his loveable dog, and an elderly man with a heart of gold. The author pens the characters to perfection. This book has mystery, adventure, hatred, greed, and love. It is layered with conflict, spiced with loyalty, splattered with adventure, and ends with joy. Exceptional and worth every moment of your time."

Book Review.Com (Shirley Johnson)

"*Blue Springs* is an entertaining and exhilarating mystery, with captivating, often charming, characters. The cast covers the spectrum, from the intense evil of a bible-thumping hired killer, to the sweet innocence of Charlie Nash, and the innate moral virtue of Quill Purdue. The plot never lets the reader down, filled with exciting foreshadowing and thrilling drama, as we are carried along Charlie's journey, ever aware of how close his stalkers are. The writing is descriptive, intelligent, and colorful. *Blue Springs* is a brilliant book, and I strongly recommend it as a wonderful way to spend some well-earned leisure time."

All Books Review (Nancy Morris)

"A great book! Truly enjoyed *Blue Springs*! It was a poignant read—with terrific characters that I admired greatly."

Once Upon A Crime Bookstore (Pat Frovarp)

"On the heels of *French Creek*, *Blue Springs* might be his best novel yet! It is truly wonderful—a joy to read! More than that, it's a page-turner! This really is an extraordinary novel in every way!"

Alice 'n Ink (Alice Peppler)

"*Blue Springs* quickly snowballs into a fast-paced, gripping story full of unexpected twists and turns. Rennebohm still skillfully manages to keep the reader guessing about what will happen next—right down to the very last page.'

"This story . . . will leave the reader coming back for more and eagerly waiting for Peter's next novel."

Absolute Write (Brandy Y. Foster)

"*Blue Springs* is well-plotted, intertwining and exploring a network of thoughtful asides with poignant sensitivity, as family relationships, alcoholism, forgiveness, and life's tragedies. What is noteworthy about the author's writing is the subtlety with which he embeds these complex ideas into the novel. The most absorbing parts of this book concern the intimate moments shared between Charlie and Quill, wherein the compassionate character of Quill illuminates the dark world that Charlie had been subjected to. On the other hand, with a little help from Charlie's innocent prodding, Quill comes to terms with the ghosts of a personal tragedy."

Book Pleasures.Com (Norm Goldman)

"Delightful! *Blue Springs* is more than a mystery—chock full of suspense, it's a story of secrets, trust, and forgiveness. This tale delves into familial relationships and healing from the perspective of an eleven-year-old boy. Peter Rennebohm has written a compassionate and heartwarming story that weaves through a compelling, tension-filled mystery. If you can't resist a story about a boy and his dog, then you'll love this read."

Word Museum (Carolyn Smith)

Praise for *French Creek*

Winner of the CG Choice Award—given to the BEST cover artwork.

"*French Creek* cuts straight into the action, which is really rare. It's an imaginative story and setting, with extremely well-drawn characters. The cover art is gorgeous. It's a really solid product, and for a first novel, quite exceptional."

Writer's Digest

"Peter Rennebohm's masterpiece lacks nothing: the character development is flawless, the descriptions of the players are crisp, clear and allow the readers to all but feel the breaths of the pursuers on their own necks. A page turner from the very beginning, the author leaves nothing to chance, but promises experience to the avid reader, mystery aficionado, and anyone in the market for an evening with a good book."

Round Table Reviews

"Taut with tension and frighteningly real, readers who love the huge adrenaline flow will find their anticipated thrills in this terror-driven tale."

Crystal Reviews

"A new voice in mystery fiction, Peter Rennebohm, a Minnesota writer, has created an exciting, fast-paced mystery set in Minnesota and South Dakota."

Once Upon A Crime

"Award-winning author Peter Rennebohm presents *French Creek*, a suspenseful novel about an ordinary Minneapolis salesman whose trip to a junkyard quickly entangles him in a lethal struggle—with his life as the prize. Against ruthless and experienced killers, he must weather a severe winter storm amid the rural farmland of central Minnesota and the prairies of the South Dakota borderland. A gripping saga of personal defiance, ingenuity, and courage—compelling to the last page."

Midwest Book Review

Peter Rennebohm is the author of:

Be Not Afraid: Ben Peyton's Story (ISBN: 0-87839-205-X) Non-fiction.
French Creek—a thriller. (ISBN: 0-87839-211-4)
Blue Springs—a suspense novel. (ISBN: 0-87839-227-0)

www.prennebohm.com

Blue Springs

A Suspense Novel

Peter Rennebohm

NORTH STAR PRESS OF ST. CLOUD, INC.

St. Cloud, Minnesota

Cover art by Mark Evans
www.cloudmover.net

ISBN: 0-87839-227-0

First Edition
October 2005

Printed in Canada
by Friesens

Published by
North Star Press of St. Cloud, Inc.
P.O. Box 451
St. Cloud, Minnesota 56302
<northstarpress.com>
<nspress @cloudnet.com>

1 2 3 4 5 6 7 8 9 10

In memory of two great,
best friends who made us laugh and cared about all the right stuff.
Both left much too soon.

Steve Clausen
Never had the opportunity to live his dream.

Steven Kenneth Gebert
Somehow lost his way—but not his friends.

Acknowledgments

After forty years of marriage, I have finally learned to trust my wife, Shari's, instincts. She has been right about so many things—not the least of which was the tone and feeling this novel should convey. Somehow she has endured me and my sometimes stubborn ways, and I love her for that. Our daughters, Emily and Jenny, are fortunate to have inherited their mother's best qualities, and they too have been wonderful advocates of my work.

I would be remiss if I did not thank my cadre of "first" readers whose opinions I value and encouragement I feed on: Tom Carlson, Becky Planer, Dale Mayer, and Alice Peppler—who also provided much needed editing and critical comment. Many, many thanks for all you have done.

At some point in the writing process, after countless revisions and deletions, the manuscript is ready for public scrutiny. I have been fortunate to have a great number of close friends who not only have taken an interest in my second life, but have provided much needed support and interest. Thanks to all.

And, finally, to a special friend and mentor, an accomplished author himself, whose writing I could never hope to emulate, Michael O'Rourke. I'm not certain I could have progressed without his guidance. Thank you, Ory . . .

Prologue

T HE FIRST MIGRANTS of autumn, a team of green-wing teal borne by a strong north wind, collectively collapsed their wings. Parents and brood dropped from the gray clouds, circled the small lake, and lifted—not quite ready to settle.

A juvenile separated. With adolescent exuberance, it flicked one wing, then another, and parted. Over the narrow spit of straw grass, slightly above the line of cattails, it wove and jigged, soaring and jubilant, happy to be what and where it was.

Satisfied, the venturesome fowl splashed down, dived, shed droplets, and briefly rubbed and straightened errant feathers with its grayish bill. The setting sun cast remnant light on the barely visible, rust-colored topknot while briefly highlighting faint patches of green on each feathered arm.

Then all was still. The flock had long since departed, and the impish, imprudent fledgling paddled silently and alone. It peeped—twice, anticipating return notes of reassurance—but there were none.

The impetuous youngster had chosen a course fraught with danger.

PART ONE

The Hunting Trip

One

A T 11:30 A.M., Charlie ran out the school's front door, jumped, and cleared all six concrete steps. He tore down the walk as fast as he could, his Red-Ball Jets slapping the pavement all the way to the street. It was Friday, October 4, 1955, Charlie Nash's eleventh birthday. He had left school and his sixth-grade classmates early.

He hoped he wasn't late, for, just as he was about to leave class, he had endured another of the all-too frequent, unannounced "atomic bomb" drills. At the blare of the warning, he had raced from the door to his desk, scrambled beneath, and covered his head with both hands. He and his pals agreed the whole exercise was stupid, and Mrs. Witherspoon failed to explain how half an inch of pine could possibly protect their little heads from the devastation of an atomic bomb.

"It's a joke," his buddy, Phil, whispered.

"I know. Wish they'd blow the 'All Clear' so I can get out of here!" Charlie muttered.

Miss Witherspoon had reluctantly accepted the note from his mother, made a comment about his missing a spelling test, and told him he had to take it on Monday. Charlie didn't care. He didn't like Miss Witherspoon and didn't care what she thought.

3

She's just an old battle-ax, he thought. *I'm going hunting this weekend with Dad and Taffy!*

That was all that mattered to the boy. He stopped in front of the school and looked around. There was no sign of his father, so he began to worry.

What if he forgot? What if he decided not to go? What if . . . ?

Charlie paced the sidewalk in front of the school, running his hand idly over the fence's metal links. He stared at it, then turned and stood as tall as he could without cheating. Putting his hand flat on top of his head, he stooped, twisted, and looked at his fingers, then carefully counted the rows of links to the ground.

Seventeen! he thought. The last time he had measured was a little over sixteen. *I must've grown an inch!*

He hated when his father stood him beside his mother. He much preferred devising his own, private forms of keeping track—like the chain-link fence. Mom was a small woman, barely five-feet tall, and Charlie's blond head almost reached her nose. That was a weekly ritual the boy dreaded, because nothing seemed to change until now . . . maybe. Charlie was eleven today, and he felt he should be at least as tall as his friends, even though he was the youngest boy in the class.

Forgetting the fence, he stepped closer to the curb and looked up and down the street.

Maybe he stopped at the drugstore. No. I'll bet he went to buy groceries. Charlie nibbled his lip and frowned.

Both stores were around the corner from the school. Charlie walked toward them, hoping he was right. He carefully avoided the cracks on the sidewalk, thinking, *Step on a crack, break your mother's back.*

His father had not only promised to take him to the duck shack for his birthday, he also said he would let Charlie shoot his shotgun. Charlie smiled, picturing himself carrying the over-and-under with Taffy, his golden retriever, at his side. He turned and looked back at the windows of his class-room.

Johnny Peyton's face appeared in the window. *He must've lifted himself up from his seat to peek out.* When he saw Charlie looking, he waved.

Charlie waved back, knowing Johnny wished he were going with him. Not only was Charlie going hunting, he was also missing half a day of school with the dreaded Miss Witherspoon. Suddenly, Johnny's head jerked up from his chair, and his face twisted in a grimace as the redheaded teacher grabbed the back of his collar.

The old bat must've caught him looking, Charlie thought. He hoped his friend wouldn't be hauled into the cloakroom. It was a dark, narrow room that smelled of gym shoes and rotten bananas—not a place that Charlie or any of his friends relished visiting, especially if alone with Miss Witherspoon.

Charlie slunk around the fence, recalling times when he had misbehaved and had been yanked from his desk like that. Absently, he rubbed his left ear. He hated his teacher for the abuse she meted out in that evil room.

He watched as Johnny was hauled from the window. Then Miss Witherspoon peered out and saw Charlie. She glared. Her lips formed a cruel, crooked smile that looked like the tread of Charlie's tennis shoes. That wasn't something Charlie wanted to think about, because it meant, *I'll see you Monday, smart boy!*

Good luck, Johnny, Charlie thought.

When he reached the end of the fence surrounding the schoolyard, Charlie again looked up and down the street without seeing his father's black Buick Century sedan. Disappointed, he leaned against the fence and waited.

Just when he thought his father had forgotten, meaning the trip to the duck shack was canceled, his father pulled up and stopped in front of him.

Charlie looked up and realized his father had remembered. *They were going, after all!* He smiled and waved.

His father waved back and beckoned Charlie to the car. Charlie glanced in the rear window and saw Taffy, with her black nose pressed against the glass, ears back, tail wagging vigorously.

Charlie felt relieved. Everything was working out fine. He opened the front door and said, "Hi, Dad." Jumping in, Charlie landed on the seat and faced his happy dog. "Hi, Taff. You ready to go hunting, girl?"

"Hey there, Slugger. You all set?" His father put the car into gear and drove away.

"You bet. How do you think Taffy'll do?" He turned to let her lick his chin.

"I guess that depends on how well you trained her, Slugger. You sure spent lots of time working with her this summer. I never did get you that pigeon I promised, did I? You were going to work with her on a real bird."

"No, but that's okay. Uncle Tom shot one and showed me how to use it. She didn't like it much at first, but, after I tossed it in the water, she went after it. I'll be she'll be a great duck dog. What do you think, Dad?"

"Huh? Oh. I don't know. The guy we got her from said her parents hunted, so that's a start. The best dogs I ever saw, though, were big, old tough, ornery males." He glanced at Taffy. "I dunno. She might be too gentle."

Charlie was disappointed. Not only was Taffy his best friend, but she was always there when he felt sad or lonely. He didn't care what his dad thought. Taffy was still the best dog in the world. Charlie was certain she'd do just fine.

When he turned back and settled in the seat, he noticed the bottle of beer between his father's legs. Charlie turned away, determined not to let anything spoil his day.

"Your mom fixed some lunch for you," his father said. "It's in the brown bag on the floor."

Charlie leaned over and reached for the bag.

"Not that one. The other one!" The tone of his voice startled the young boy.

Charlie stopped, fumbled a bit, and grabbed the other sack. He opened it and found a bologna and cheese sandwich, made with his favorite Wonder Bread—with the crusts removed. He unwrapped the waxed paper and silently ate his sandwich.

Taking out a bottle of Coke, he asked, "Can I use your church-key, Dad?"

His father handed him the opener without comment. Charlie opened the bottle and sipped.

His father drank from the long neck and asked, "Did your teacher give you any guff?"

"Naw. As long as I had a note, she couldn't say much. She's mean, though. Everybody hates her."

"Maybe, but if you keep lippin' off to her all the time, she'll make your life miserable. Why can't you learn to keep your mouth shut?" He glanced over at his son—heavy brows raised as if by some miracle Charlie might respond with an answer that would appease him.

"I don't know. Most of the time, I'm not doing anything, and she still drags me into the cloak room."

His father picked up the other bag and placed it on the floor between his legs. He pulled another beer from the sack, opened it with one hand, and put the empty bottle in the bag. "Who'd you get to take over your paper route?"

"Jimmy McCarthy."

"Does he know what he's doin'?"

"Yeah. He's done it before. It'll be okay."

"Better be. I don't want you to lose that route. Otherwise, you go back to delivering evening papers on Mount Curve, and I don't want to have to drive you around on Sunday mornings."

It took Charlie a full year to earn his current route of three blocks around his home. It was a morning route, which meant the papers weighed less. He didn't want to deliver evening papers any more than his father.

"Jimmy's okay. I'm payin' him two bucks if no one complains."

Charlie finished his sandwich and looked in the bag for his second-most favorite food, Hostess Twinkies. His mother thoughtfully included them with lunch. He finished his dessert and turned to play with Taffy. She was excited to be with him, prancing back and forth on the rear seat. He tousled her ears, gently held her muzzle when she tried to shake loose, then scratched her slender chest.

Charlie smiled. "You just love that, don't ya, girl?" He waited for the expected smile from his friend. As predicted, a few seconds later, the young retriever stretched her lips, half-closed her brown eyes, and gave him a toothy grin.

She's the smartest dog in the world, Charlie thought.

He had first choice of the litter when he chose her. Knowing what he wanted, he promptly selected the smallest female, the runt.

"Why her, son?" the litter's owner asked.

"I read that the runt is the smartest. She has to be to get her share of food and keep the bigger puppies from picking on her."

Taffy hadn't disappointed him. She was a willing pupil and patiently tolerated his zestful attempts to train her. She seemed very willing to please her young master.

Charlie felt content. He was with his dad and his dog, and they were going hunting. He wouldn't think about school and old Miss Snaggle-Tooth for the rest of the weekend. If they arrived at the lake in time, before dark, Charlie fervently hoped his dad would let him shoot the shotgun—just as he had promised.

They drove without further conversation. Charlie's father listened to the radio, thinking hard on something that didn't involve Charlie. After a while, he pulled over on a side street in one of the many small towns they passed through, and stopped.

"You and Taffy wait here, Slugger. I have to stop to visit a client. I'll be right back." He finished his beer, dropped it into the paper sack, and got out of the car. Leaving his son and dog alone, he walked around the corner and out of sight.

Charlie tried to remain upbeat. He figured that his father had work planned for the trip, although he wasn't entirely convinced. He stared out the window, counted the passing cars on the highway, and played with Taffy. After thirty minutes, his father returned and got into the car. Charlie detected a faint smell of Chlorets. He turned away and looked out the window.

"That wasn't so bad, was it, Slugger?" his father asked.

"I guess not," Charlie said. The boy's small voice wasn't convincing, but it fell on deaf ears.

"When do we get the groceries, Dad?" Charlie knew his father had been given the responsibility to buy food for the weekend, but Charlie worried he might forget.

"Ah . . . we'll stop in the next town."

His father stopped three more times to visit additional clients. Each stop was longer than the ones before. Between each break in their trip, Charlie was assigned the task of opening more bottles of beer. By now his father couldn't quite manage to open a new brew and drive at the same time. Charlie squirmed as he watched the road in front of the Buick.

Charlie reluctantly complied with each request for a fresh bottle, because he knew it was the wrong time to challenge his father. The mood in the car slowly became as sour and foul as his father's breath. The mints failed to hide the stale smell of both bourbon and beer.

As the sun set above the two-lane highway ahead, Charlie asked, "How much farther, Dad?" With each passing mile, the small boy grew more and more worried about his father's ability to negotiate the narrow blacktop.

His father looked around, having lost track of their location but not wanting to admit it. "Nah mush farther. Grab me another beer, will ya?"

Charlie looked in the bag, but he knew there weren't any more bottles. He feared admitting the truth to his father but knew he had to. "It's all gone, Dad." His voice was barely audible above the radio and rumble from the big car. Summoning a last bit of courage, he asked, "Shouldn't we stop for groceries?"

"Whaddya mean it's gone? Damn! No! Someone else is buyin' the food . . . I think."

Charlie tried again. His voice trembled and he slid closer to the door. "I don't think so, Dad. Mom said Uncle Tom asked you to, uh . . . stop and get groceries." He realized his mistake the moment he spoke.

"I don't give a damn what she said!" his father shouted. His face was red and a splatter of spittle flew out towards Charlie.

Charlie fell silent and slunk down into the deep seat, facing the window and looking at the reflection of his sad, blue eyes. They clouded briefly, and Charlie inhaled, fighting back tears. That would just make his father angrier.

Instead, he climbed over the seat to be with Taffy, who cowered in a corner. As with her master, Taffy had been witness to the big man's outbursts on more than one occasion.

"Where you goin'?" his father whined, looking in the rearview mirror at his defeated son sitting with his head against Taffy's shoulder.

After a few seconds, he grunted, "Ah, the hell with you." Turning his gaze back to the road, he fought to keep the Buick on the right side of the highway.

Charlie put an arm around Taffy, who slid down and rested her head on his lap. Charlie closed his eyes, wishing he was in his bed at home, the covers pulled over his head. That was what he always did when injured by his father's cruel words. All he could do was pretend he was anywhere but in the back seat.

He leaned over and rested his head on Taffy's warm, tan back. The heat emanating from her comforted him briefly.

It was soon dark, and they passed through the last small town before reaching their destination. Slowly and inexorably, the boy's heart was breaking.

It had been for a long time.

Two

THE BUICK CONTINUED on an unsteady course through the night. Soon, the small town of Lockhart appeared out of the gloaming. Charlie averted his gaze through the windshield and looked out the side window. He had returned to the front seat, not because the dark mood in the auto had improved, but for a better view of the road ahead. It was pitch black, and few lights showed. He turned and spotted the moon rising in the east, slowly inching its way into view. Charlie pointed at the orange crescent and closed one eye, measuring the growth of the moon against a spot on the glass.

"I'll bet it takes thirty seconds to reach that spot," he said out loud.

"Huh? What'n hell're you talkin' about?" his father asked.

Charlie was embarrassed now and wished he hadn't spoken what he thought was a rather clever observation. "I'm watching the moon come up and counting how long it takes to grow."

"Who cares? Cripes almighty, you're spooky sometimes. Hey. We're gettin' close. This is my old stompin' ground, ya know."

"Yeah, you told me that before."

"I did? Huh. Well, I grew up just north a here—good old, Long Prairie. You know . . ."

11

A bright pair of lights appeared behind them, startling both. Charlie's father glanced at the rearview mirror and squinted as the lights grew brighter. "What the hell? Turn your brights off!"

Charlie turned and peered over the seat. It seemed as if the car behind them would smash into them, it was so close. Charlie couldn't look into the lights, so he turned back. He watched as his father rolled down his window and stuck his arm out with middle finger raised.

The car backed off just enough, then pulled out to pass the Buick. Frank withdrew his arm as the car pulled alongside. It was an older model car, dark blue. Father and son caught a quick glimpse of a leering face staring through the side window. The passenger raised a bottle of beer towards the Buick, and then took a long pull as the blue car sped away.

Charlie noticed the back of his father's neck redden. He knew he was steaming mad. "Please don't do anything, Dad." At that moment, two arms appeared from either side of the car in front—both held empty beer bottles. Charlie's father couldn't react fast enough as each arm tossed a bottle up in the air. The first one landed on the Buick's hood, the second thumped on the roof. The car sped off into the darkness as the Buick slowed momentarily.

"Bastards! Wait'll I catch up to 'em."

"Dad? Don't, please? I'm scared." Charlie shook from fear.

Frank Nash had never backed down from a confrontation, and he was not about to ignore this humiliation. He was angry. Very angry. He stomped on the accelerator and clicked his bright lights off and on.

Charlie gripped Taffy tightly. Suddenly he feared for his life. He had seen his father's anger before, but never like this. He was terrified—so scared he had to pee. As if he were observing a movie in slow motion, the boy watched the bigger Buick creep closer to the dark car. He guessed what his father was going to do and closed his eyes.

But Frank had miscalculated. His intent only had been to nudge close to the car—to irritate and pester the driver inside. Too late, he realized his mistake. BANG! Then, a second bang! He couldn't stop what he had set in motion.

The Buick slammed into the back of the blue car. Charlie's head jerked with the impact and smacked the dashboard. Taffy was thrown against the back of the front seat.

Frank hit the brakes! But the Buick didn't stop. It skidded, and Frank was thrust first right, then left. His head hit the side window! He lost control of the wheel! The Buick spun in lazy circles down the center of the road.

Charlie was groggy. He looked up, trying hard to make sense of what had just happened. He felt dizzy, and could only catch brief glimpses of the dark car ahead of them. Taffy whimpered and dug into the seat cover with her claws. Charlie shouted at his father, "DAD! LOOK OUT!"

He saw his father shake his head from side to side—once, twice— then again, like a prize fighter struggling to regain awareness. Then his father grabbed the wheel and spun it—hard! The tires scrabbled against the shoulder. Charlie looked down into a deep, dark ditch that would surely tip them over.

Suddenly, Charlie heard, and then felt, the rear tires gain traction as his father hit the accelerator. They sped past the blue car, and once the Buick straightened out, he again applied the brake.

Charlie turned and watched the other car fishtail from right to left, raising dirt and dust. CRACK! Its front tire exploded! Again, the boy closed his eyes, afraid to watch what would happen next.

Finally, after what seemed a lifetime, the slewing blue car slid sideways back across the highway and settled just off the tarmac—its rear end slanted down toward a deep gully.

Charlie's father shook his head. The Buick spun one last time before Frank gained control and skidded to a stop just ahead of where the blue car slipped into the ditch. The Buick was on the other side of the road now, facing east. Frank stared through the windshield. His heart pounded in time with his head. His throat had parched, and he couldn't catch his breath. His breathing quickened as the shock of what had just transpired took hold. He closed his eyes and lowered his head.

Charlie saw a large man climb from the driver's side of the other car and stumble out on to the pavement. He fell to one knee, then rose—holding his hand over his mouth.

Frank looked up at that moment. Both father and son clearly saw blood dripping from between the man's fingers. There was no movement from the passenger seat.

"Dad?" Charlie imagined the worst and was convinced the other man had been killed.

"Damn! We have to get out of here, Charlie!" Without waiting to check on the condition of either man, he threw the gear shift into drive and stepped on the gas. His window was still down. He glanced left at the man standing in front of the blue car.

"Shouldn't we stop and see if—?"

Frank cut him off, "NO! WE SHOULDN'T!"

Father and son watched as the large man took a bloody hand away from his mouth long enough to make a fist and wave it in their direction.

"I'll find you, you sonofabitch, and when I do . . ." The man's angry words were lost in the roar of the Buick's engine.

The Buick sped off into the darkness. Charlie's father reached for his bottle and took a long pull as he headed back down the highway. Frank's nerves were shot. He gripped the steering wheel until his fingers ached. "Gotta go back and find the road to the shack, Slugger." His voice shook as he spoke.

After a five minute drive retracing their original route, the car slowed for the left turn to the hunting shack. "Those guys di'n't know who they're messin' with, did they, Slugger?"

Charlie was still too terrified to reply. He was shaking, and his father's weak attempt at bravado did little to calm the boy. Even Taffy trembled. By now he had lost interest in the hunting trip and wished he were anywhere but in his father's car.

His father drove down the narrow road for half a mile. "There's the lake, Slugger." His father pointed. "See? Ya c'in aahmost see the point where we're gonna hunt tamarra."

14

Charlie peered out the window but didn't respond.

His father stopped in front of the tarpaper shack and honked. "Here w-are . . . Parker's Lake Gun Club. Better not say ana-thing 'bout what jest happen—'kay, Slugger?"

"Sure, Dad."

The shack door opened, and Charlie's Uncle Tom stepped out. Charlie immediately opened the door. Taffy leaped over the front seat, and both ran toward his mother's brother—his father's friend.

"Hey!" his father said. "Where'n hell you goin' so fass? Come 'ere."

Charlie stopped and walked back. A weak, "What?" was all he could muster.

"Take tha' bag on the floor and dump it someplace."

"Oh. Okay." He opened the Buick's front door, leaned in, and pulled out the large bag of empties. He carefully held the sack in both arms as he backed from the car, kicked the door shut, and walked toward the shack. "Hi, Uncle Tom. Is Tommy here, too?"

"Hi, Charlie. Yep. He's inside with his cousin John and your Uncle Dick." Tom glanced at the bag and heard the rattle of bottles. "The can's by the door, Charlie. Then go inside and look around. I'll help your dad with the groceries." Tom glanced at the Buick as Charlie's father tried to step out. "Hey, Frank. How's everything?"

"Pretty . . . damn . . . good." Frank's foot caught on the door sill, and he tripped. "Oops. Firss step's a doozy." He laughed as he grabbed the open door and staggered a bit.

Tom shook his head as Frank tumbled from the car.

Charlie entered the cabin.

"Hi, Tommy. Hi, John. Wow! This is really cool!" He looked around the shack.

The main room, which also served as the kitchen, had a stove, ice-box, sink, and large wooden table in the center. Two sets of bunk beds stood against the far wall. Just inside the door were a series of wooden pegs for coats and hats. A large gun rack hung on the wall beside the pegs.

The room was lit by three bare bulbs mounted in white porcelain fixtures. The floor was constructed of heavy pine planks. The second room had an overstuffed, faded, red couch, two more bunks, and a pot-bellied, cast-iron stove in the corner. The air was still—the room filled with the combined odors of pipe tobacco, wood smoke, and pine sap.

Charlie's other uncle, Dick, Tom's brother, sat at the kitchen table cleaning his shotgun. Charlie ran over and stood beside him.

"Hey there, Charlie," Dick said. "How are you, young man?" He held out his hand.

Charlie eagerly clasped his hand and shook it. "I'm fine. I brought my dog, Uncle Dick."

Taffy stood beside Charlie, wagging her tail as Dick held out his hand for a warm, wet greeting. "I see that. Think she'll be any good?"

"I bet she will. I worked her pretty hard. I even threw an old, dead pigeon for her."

"Guess we'll find out tomorrow, won't we? Lake's down what with the drought and all, but there's still plenty of ducks around, Charlie. A big north wind blew in here yesterday and brought a bunch of new ducks with it."

"Really? How many? Thousands?" Charlie's face flushed and his heart pounded as he finally allowed himself to experience the thrill of his first duck hunt.

Dick laughed at the boy's enthusiasm. "Probably all of that. We took Tommy and John out this evening. I think we shot seventeen or so. Isn't that what you counted, John?"

"Yep. Seventeen, Charlie," John replied. "That was in just one hour. You shoulda been here. What kept ya?"

Charlie hesitated and looked at his boot tops. "Uh, my dad had some calls to make on the way."

Dick, looking at him sympathetically, changed the subject. "Well, then, young Master Nash, let's get your stuff in here and start dinner." He noticed the boy's worried expression. "What's wrong, Charlie?"

Charlie didn't want to answer, but he had to. "We . . . we didn't bring any food, Uncle Dick. My dad forgot, I think."

"Hmmm. Okay. Wait here and I'll go see." Dick left the cabin.

Tommy walked over to Charlie. "I thought you'd be here in time to hunt this afternoon." Tommy was one year younger than Charlie. Though they weren't close friends, they were cousins and saw a lot of each other, because of their fathers' relationship.

John, Charlie's older cousin, was bolder and disinclined to let Charlie off the hook. "I'll bet your old man was drunk again." He smiled cruelly.

At first, Charlie didn't know how to respond. His ears burned, and blood rushed to his face. "You don't know anything, John."

"Oh, yeah? Tommy and I heard our dads talking. They knew you guys were late because your old man had to stop at every bar along the way."

"That's a lie! He was . . . was, uh, calling on clients."

"I'll bet. He was getting drunk, that's what."

Taffy, sensing the tension, stepped between Charlie and the older, bigger boy.

"My dad says your old man has a drinking problem but won't admit it," John said, challenging the smaller boy to respond as he knew he would.

"He does not!"

"Does, too!"

Charlie stepped forward, pushing Taffy with his knees. He was breathing rapidly and could barely speak, but he said, "Take it back!" His fists clenched, and he stared up at the bigger boy.

Taffy stood rigidly between the boys, the hair on the back of her neck rising.

"I won't take it back!" John said. "Make me!" The cruel, taunting smile returned.

Charlie leaped at John and wrestled him to the ground. Small for his age but strong, he quickly put John in a headlock, though he knew it was just a matter of time before the older boy got loose and hit him. Charlie didn't care. He wasn't about to let another kid talk about his dad like that.

Tommy felt sorry for Charlie so he tried to pull them apart. Taffy pranced around, barking furiously, nipping at John's pant leg.

"Let go, Charlie!" Tommy yelled, pulling on the two combatants. "John, stop it!"

John broke loose and rolled over. He sat on Charlie's chest and pulled back his right arm, fist clenched. "You're an idiot! Everyone knows your old man's a drunk except you. What a dummy."

"Take it back!" Charlie bucked, kicked, and tried to break free. Taffy mouthed John's arm, tugging at his sleeve.

John shook his arm free, shoving Taffy against the table leg. "Get out of here, you stupid mutt!" He drew back again, ready to punch the smaller boy in the face.

John's epithet and rough treatment of the dog incensed Charlie even more. He punched John's chest hard.

"Ow!"

Uncle Dick walked into the shack. "Hey! What's going on? Break it up!"

Both boys stopped. Taffy kept barking. Dick picked up his son by the collar and turned him around. "What started this?"

John hung his head. "I . . . I dunno. I guess I said something that made him mad."

"Like what?" Dick asked, with a fistful of his son's plaid collar.

John didn't want to answer, but he knew his dad wouldn't stop until he knew the truth. Reluctantly, he said, "I called his dad a name, I guess."

"What name?" He gave John a firm shake.

"Uh . . . a drunk."

"You apologize to Charlie right now. What's the matter with you?"

"Sorry, Charlie," John said in a small voice. "I didn't mean it."

Charlie got up, sniffed a few times, and walked to the door. Embarrassed and spent, he wanted to be alone—didn't want the others to see. "Come on, Taff."

"Charlie, why don't you stay here for a minute? Your dad and Uncle Tom are talking outside," Uncle Dick said.

But Charlie had to get out. He opened the door and immediately heard his father and Tom arguing. Their loud words stabbed at the still night.

"What do you mean, you forgot?" Tom asked. "You were supposed to get the food."

"I forgot. Big deal. I'll go and get—"

"You're in no shape to go anywhere. I can't believe you drove here in that condition—especially with Charlie in the car."

"I'm fine," Frank said. "Mind your own damn business and leave me be."

"You're hopeless. You're out of control. I've had it with you! I have a good mind to—"

Charlie closed the door and turned back inside, not wanting to hear anymore. His shoulders slumped as he shuffled to the table and sat down. Taffy sat beneath the table, pressing against his legs. He looked down, stroking her ears. She laid her tan head on his knees and looked lovingly into his face, her brown eyes glistening. Embarrassed and despondent, Charlie wanted to be anyplace but where he was right then.

I should run away somewhere, he thought glumly. *He's always yelling at me . . . acts so crazy sometimes . . . I hate being around him when he's like this . . .*

Tom returned to the shack carrying Charlie's bag, slamming the door behind him. Charlie, looking at his face, saw he was angry.

Tom set the bag on a lower bunk. "Here's your bed, Charlie. There's a sleeping bag already laid out for you, okay?" He took a deep breath, trying to calm himself.

Charlie, grateful for any excuse to move, walked over and sat on the bed. "Thanks, Uncle Tom." Taffy followed and sat down next to the distraught boy. She rested her head on his knee—her tail swished across the dusty wood floor.

Tommy sat beside Charlie without speaking.

"Dick," Uncle Tom said, "I have to run to town for food. I hope the store's still open. Otherwise, we'll have to eat some of those ducks for dinner."

He tipped his head toward the door, where Frank still waited outside. Dick nodded in agreement. Tom left the cabin just as Frank stumbled in lugging his duffel bag.

No one said anything as he dragged the bag to where Charlie and Tommy sat. He stopped, turned, and asked, "Which bunk's mine?"

"Take the lower one next to Charlie," Dick said. "Tommy, you take the one above Charlie, okay?"

Charlie watched his father shuffle to the bunk, sit, and collapse on the bed without removing his shoes. He began snoring heavily, ready to sleep through the night.

Charlie looked across the room at Dick and smiled sheepishly, then he said, "Come on, Tommy. Show me those ducks." John joined the younger boys as they left the shack to check out the fowl hanging on the outside wall.

Dick stood in the shack and shook his head. *Something bad's going to happen . . . I can feel it. I wish the boys weren't around to hear all this. Shouldn't have invited Frank . . . only did it 'cause of Charlie.* He stepped closer to the bunks and looked down on Frank. *I've seen your act far too often, Frank.* He pulled an old army blanket from the end of the bed and threw it over the big man. He stood only a moment longer—long enough to watch Frank's mouth open and close. He was gurgling and chucking air like a small engine at full choke. He shook his head and turned away.

TOM RETURNED THIRTY MINUTES later with a meager amount of food. As he feared, not much was open at that time of night. The boys came inside, and Charlie fed Taffy.

"Uncle Dick, would it be okay if Taffy slept on my bed tonight?" Charlie asked.

"Sure. That'll be fine."

The five sat down to a meal of hot dogs and potato chips. The boys also had cocoa. As they ate, Charlie asked, "What kind of ducks did you shoot today, Uncle Tom?"

"Let's see. I'm sure you recognized the mallards. The little ones are teal, both green and blue. We also got a couple of wood ducks, some gadwall, and the ones with the fat bills are spoonies. Your uncle Dick shot those by mistake." Tom chuckled and pointed an accusatory finger at his brother.

They all laughed, knowing that spoonbills were not considered edible by anyone's standard.

"See any canvasbacks or bluebills?" Charlie asked. His eyes sparkled as he envisioned the big, silver-backed birds prized by every duck hunter.

"Nope. It's too early for the diving ducks. Later, that lake will have thousands of 'em out there, along with bluebills, redheads, and golden eye. That's when a duck hunter is really tested."

"Why?"

"'Cause that's when it's colder than a well-digger's ass," Tom replied.

The boys giggled hysterically at sharing an adult ribald comment.

"Hey," Tommy asked with a twinkle in his eye, "what's for dessert?"

"We'll, I'll be darned. I almost forgot." Tom left the table and walked across the kitchen. "It seems to me some that some young fellow here has a birthday. Who do we think that is?" He looked at Charlie and scratched the top of his head.

Charlie blushed and smiled. He watched Tom remove a small chocolate cake from the icebox. He set a single candle on top, lit it, and carried the cake to the table.

He set the cake directly in front of Charlie and affectionately squeezed his shoulder. "Happy birthday, son. Aunt Susan made the cake for you. Now make a wish and blow out the candle."

Charlie closed his eyes and thought hard. There was only one thing he wanted more than anything else in the world. *I wish my dad would be like other dads . . . like my uncles.*

He opened his eyes, turned, looked at his father, then blew out the candle. "Thanks, Uncle Tom, and thank Aunt Susan too."

"You're welcome, lad," his uncle said. "Now cut pieces for all of us before we get so old our teeth fall out, and we can't eat it." Tom rustled Charlie's short blond hair and returned to his chair.

Charlie cut the cake into thick slices and passed them around. "Thanks again, everyone."

The five hunters ate their desert in silence. Frank's loud snores echoed around the room. "We'd better hit the hay," Uncle Dick said, standing and stretching. "Five o'clock comes awful early. We want to be up before sunrise."

Charlie took Taffy outside to relieve herself before bed. He unzipped his pants and peed in the long grass outside the shack rather than take a trip to the spidery outhouse. He shivered in shirt sleeves as he looked up at the starry sky. In just a few hours, he'd walk out that same door again with his dad and Taffy and head for the blind to shoot ducks! He zipped up his pants and whistled Taffy back inside.

Charlie removed his jeans and shirt and crawled into his sleeping bag, noticing that his father hadn't moved. Taffy jumped up on the bunk, spun twice, and settled with Charlie. Tom turned out the lights, and Charlie closed his eyes. With some effort, he willed himself to sleep. The sooner he slept, the sooner morning would come.

He squirmed under the sleeping bag, gave Taffy one last pat on her soft head, and, after a brief prayer asking God to help his dad, he fell asleep dreaming of canvasbacks, mallards, and bluebills.

Three

C HARLIE WAS THE FIRST to wake up the following morning. The alarm clock that would rouse the others ticked rhythmically. Taffy had crept close to the boy's head and at his initial stirring, she opened her eyes and licked his chin. "Hi, girl," he whispered. He looked at his father, still snoring, the drab blanket snarled around his father's legs. He still lay on his back, one heavy forearm draped across his forehead as if sheltering his eyes from some unknown vision.

Charlie threw back the covers, dressed hurriedly, fed Taffy and went outside to pee. It was chillier than the night before, but still not as cold as previous Octobers. He shivered and went back inside, stoked the barrel stove and decided to put on his long underwear. By the time the alarm went off, he was dressed and ready for his first hunt.

He looked at his new Red Wings, a gift from his mother. The leather was spotless, without a scratch anywhere. *Should've oiled 'em myself, he thought. But, dad said he'd do it . . .*

The others awoke slowly, and the interior of the shack came to life. Tom started breakfast. Charlie went to wake his father, shaking his shoulder three times without a response. Finally, after the fourth hard shove, Frank showed signs of life.

His father stirred, rolled toward him, and mumbled, "Huh?" He opened bloodshot eyes toward his son. "Oh. Hi there, Slugger. Time to go hunting?" He rubbed a meaty hand over his bristly stubble, smacked his lips, and looked around the shack.

"Yep. Breakfast is almost ready, Dad." Charlie couldn't wait. Maybe he'd be allowed to shoot the gun.

They sat down to a breakfast of scrambled eggs, bacon, and toast, all except Frank. He went to the icebox and removed a quart of fresh milk. Charlie watched as he hurriedly flipped the pleated paper top off the bottle, then fumbled with the cardboard stopper. His hands trembled as he tried to pry up the paper tab.

Once it was removed, he poured half a glass of milk, set down the bottle, then unscrewed the cap from the bourbon on the counter and added three inches of that to the glass. Frank's morning pick-me-up looked like Charlie's favorite Bosco or Ovaltine, but it wasn't.

"A little early for alcohol, isn't it, Frank?" Tom asked.

Frank opened a bottle of aspirin, dropped half a dozen pills into his hand, threw his head back as he popped the medicine in his mouth, and downed the drink. "Just a little something to jump-start the day," he mumbled. When finished, he walked to the table and sat across from his son.

Charlie watched his father as he ate. Eating always helped when he was drinking. His hands shook, and each forkful of food reached his lips with care. He ate very little, then pushed himself away from the table to return to his bunk. While the others ate, he rummaged in his duffel bag.

Charlie finished eating and took his and his father's plates to the sink. Then he found his Roy Roger's thermos so he could fill it with hot cocoa. "Do you want me to fill your thermos with coffee, Dad?" he asked hopefully.

"What? Oh, yeah. Sure, Slugger. Thanks."

Charlie's spirits rose.

"Let's get moving," Uncle Dick said. "It's getting light out."

CHARLIE WAS READY, and he was glad to see his father was, too. Charlie donned his father's old hunting coat that was too big, but he didn't care. He put on the new hunting hat his mother gave him for his birthday and waited patiently by the front door. Taffy pranced and jumped.

I wonder if she knows where we're going? Charlie considered.

One by one, they left the warm shack and gathered outside. As they prepared to walk to the lake, Frank said, "You guys go ahead. I forgot something inside. I'll be right back."

Charlie's uncles looked at each other and shrugged. "Watch what you do with your cigarette butts, Frank. It's dry as tinder around here," Dick called back. The two men walked off with the other two boys while Charlie waited with Taffy. He was eager to leave, eager to follow the others, but he remained behind—loyal to his father.

After five minutes, his dad left the shack, and they walked through tall switch grass to the point. Overhead, Charlie heard whistling sounds and something whooshing through the dark sky.

"What's that noise, Dad?" he whispered.

"Those are ducks, Charlie. Lots of 'em."

Charlie shivered in anticipation. A huge smile crossed his face. He followed his father's footsteps until they heard Uncle Tom's soft voice. They had reached the first blind, the one closest to the shack.

"Take Charlie to the last blind on the end, Frank. We'll fill these blinds closer in," Tom said.

"Okay. Keep going, Slugger."

They hiked a good distance until they reached the last blind. Daylight was just breaking as Charlie and Frank stepped inside. Charlie heard, then saw, hundreds of ducks flying overhead and on both sides of them. Their dark silhouettes darted every which way against the pale, morning, sky.

"Look at all the ducks, Dad!" Charlie exclaimed. "When can you start shooting?"

"As soon as we know what we're shooting at, Slugger. Right now, I can't tell what's flying over. We'll wait a few minutes, I guess."

25

Charlie stood beside his father, while Taffy sat just outside the blind's door. She looked back expectantly. Charlie hoped she could see the ducks.

Dawn broke. Immediately, Charlie witnessed a spectacular sight! Hundreds and hundreds of ducks flew everywhere, overhead, to the left, to the right, some diving just above the tops of the cattails, some splashing carelessly into the water on either side of their blind.

The blind they were in was nothing more than lengths of snow fence on two sides, supported by iron posts. Clumps of weeds—bulrush stalks and cane—were woven between the slats. The blind was open on both ends, and sat forty yards from the far end of the point. Charlie, peering over the edge of the blind, saw that the lake was kidney-shaped. The point was barely thirty yards wide, running east to west into the lake, tapering to an abrupt end. A narrow channel snaked around the tip, connecting both sides of Parker's Lake.

The Carlson brothers had purchased the twenty acres two years earlier from a farmer who had pastured his cows on the property. The lake had long been a natural resting place not only for local ducks, but for migrating birds as well. Now, flock after flock flew from one body of water to the other, directly over the point.

Suddenly, they heard a loud BANG! A moment later came another shot, then two more.

Charlie looked up at his father. "Who was that, Dad?"

His father didn't reply. His back was to his son, and his head was tipped up as he drank from a metal flask. He screwed the top on and said, "That's Uncle Tom and Dick, Slugger. You watch north, that way," he pointed, "and I'll watch south. If you see any ducks coming towards us, you yell, 'Mark!' Then I'll know something's coming. That's your job, okay? Oh, and your other job is to get all the ducks I'm gonna shoot."

"Sure, Dad. Taffy will pick 'em up, I bet." Charlie, facing north, didn't have to wait long. "Mark, Dad!"

A flock of twelve mallards flew toward them. Just before they were overhead, Frank raised his gun, aimed, and fired twice from his double-barreled over-and-under.

26

Charlie watched in fascination as one of the birds crumpled. Following its original flight path, it slowly dropped into the cattails south of the blind.

"Send your dog, Slugger," Frank said. "Let's see what she can do."

Charlie left the blind, sat Taffy down at his knee, pointed toward the fallen bird, and said, "Taffy, go fetch!"

Taffy disappeared into the tall weeds. Charlie heard her tail beating against the stiff stalks. Soon, her head popped out, and she had a young drake mallard in her mouth. She ran back to the blind, her head high, ears flat against her head. Charlie had never seen her look so happy or so proud.

"Wow!" was all the boy could exclaim.

Taffy entered the blind, sat beside Charlie, and waited with the prize in her mouth. Charlie held out his hand and said, "Drop, girl."

The mallard fell into his palm. He grabbed it by the neck and held it up triumphantly. "Look, Dad! It's a greenhead! You shot a greenhead, and Taffy found it!"

"Yeah." Frank laughed. "How 'bout that? Looks like all the time you spent working with her finally paid off."

The words barely left his mouth before he looked up, jerked the gun to his shoulder, and took a quick shot at a passing trio of widgeon that flew across the point. One of the ducks fell.

"Send the dog, Charlie!" Frank said as he broke the gun in two and reloaded.

The golden retriever bounded off and returned with the downed bird.

Charlie held it up and looked at it. "What is it, Dad?"

His father glanced at it. "Looks like a widgeon, a young one." He set down the gun and reached inside his coat.

Charlie looked away. More shots came from the other blinds.

"Charlie!" Tom called. "Bring your dog over here! We've got a couple ducks down and can't find 'em."

"Can I take her over there, Dad?" Charlie asked.

"Sure. Go ahead. I'll wait here."

"Come on, Taff." He led the dog to Tom's blind. Out of breath from the hard run, he stopped and looked at his uncle, a broad grin spread across his flushed face.

"Take her into those weeds over there, Charlie," Tom said, pointing at heavy cover near shore. "Let's see how good her nose is."

Charlie marched toward the weeds with Taffy, feeling confident she could find the downed bird. "Taffy. In there, girl." He led her into the tall rushes but realized he was asking a miracle from such a young dog. The cat-tails were so thick they were almost impenetrable. He could hardly thread his way through and was almost immediately turned around.

Charlie was confused. He looked around, pausing to get his bearings.

The rushes were six feet tall and thick as a plate of day-old spaghet-ti. Then he heard a shot behind him. That gave him the direction he need-ed, and he breathed easier. He couldn't see the dog, so he decided to walk back out.

As he left the jungle of rushes, he stopped in amazement at the sight of Taffy sitting on the edge of the cattails, with her tail wagging. She had the duck in her mouth. "Good girl, Taff!" He took the duck, hugged Taffy, and sent her back for the second one.

He listened intently for the sound of her movements. First she was on his left, then the right. Next, he heard her straight ahead but farther away. Splashing, then silence, then more splashing farther away.

Come on, girl, he thought. *You can do it.*

Charlie waited a long time. Finally, he couldn't hear her anymore. His heart raced at the thought of losing his best friend. He almost called her back but hesitated because he wanted her to find the second bird.

"Charlie, you might as well call her back," Uncle Tom said. "She'll never find it now. The scent's gone."

Charlie hated giving up. He knew she could do it. *Come on, Taff!* He looked and listened, but there was no sound of her. Now he really began to worry. What if she got lost in the marsh? What if she drowned? Blood rushed to his head, and his chest heaved in panic. *I never should've sent her in there. It's all my fault.*

28

Paralyzed with fear, he didn't know what to do.

"Charlie!" Tom called. "Come here, quick!"

Charlie ran up the incline to Uncle Tom's blind. He and Tommy pointed out over the lake. Charlie stood on his uncle's wooden shell box and strained to see over the bulrushes. He was barely able to see above the tall cover, but, far in the distance—seventy yards from shore—Taffy was swimming, chasing the crippled bird.

"Will she drown, Uncle Tom?" Charlie asked, eyes wide with fear. His lower lip trembled.

"No, but she might become disoriented and lose track of where she is. Let's watch and see what happens. She's a strong swimmer, but that duck's got a lot of life left." Tom feared they might have to haul out one of the boats and row after the young dog.

Charlie faced the water, his eyes never leaving Taffy. By then, Dick and John, caught up in the drama on the lake, watched Taffy with interest. Time after time, the dog approached the crippled duck, only to see it dive below the water's surface.

Taffy spun like a bobber, raising her head and rotating in place to locate the duck. It surfaced just in front of her, and she lunged with a splash. To everyone's disappointment, the duck escaped again.

"I don't know, Charlie," Tom said. "Maybe we better get the boat and row out there to get her. She's been out a long time, and she's going farther from shore."

Charlie had never been so frightened in his life. If she drowned he'd never forgive himself.

They watched as Taffy rotated once more, spotted the cripple, at least its head as it lay low on the water, and paddled toward it. Just as the duck dove, so did the dog. Charlie and the others could only see Taffy's tail for what seemed an eternity.

She surfaced in a rush, water spraying from her head, holding something in her mouth.

"I'll be damned," Uncle Tom said. "She caught it, Charlie! Look! She's coming back! She's got the duck!"

Charlie saw Taffy had something in her mouth and was on a direct path back to their blind. He wanted to shout with happiness. *She did it! She never gave up!* He looked toward his father, wishing he'd seen it, too.

Charlie ran down to the rushes where he hoped Taffy would emerge from the water, and then he waited. There was no sign of her. Just as he was ready to charge into the tangled weeds to find her, he heard a sound like someone slapping his thigh with a gloved hand. It came from his left.

Taffy appeared from the rushes. Breathing heavily and covered in mud, she held the duck by its neck, and one wing beat soundly against her chest. The small, brown, female mallard was still alive—its legs kicking, and its head moving from side to side like someone waving a finger.

Taffy trotted the ten yards to where Charlie stood, dropped her blackened rump to the soggy grass and waited for Charlie to take the bird. He was so proud of her, he wanted to scream. He accepted the bird from Taffy, gave her a big hug, and whispered, "Good girl, Taffy. I'm so proud of you. You never gave up, did you?"

He stood and held the duck high for all to see.

They all cheered and clapped. It truly was a memorable retrieve.

Charlie walked to Uncle Tom and handed him the mallard. "It's still alive."

"I know. That's why she had so much trouble finding it. Ducks naturally move toward water when they're wounded. She chased this bird a long time, Charlie. I've seen other dogs dive like that, but they usually don't learn how to do that until they're older. You've got a special friend there, young Master Nash."

Charlie's eyes filled as he stared down at his friend. He was very proud of what she had just done.

Uncle Tom held the mallard's head and swung the bird several times to break its neck. "It's not pretty to watch, boys, but it's effective. Thanks for your help, Charlie. You should be proud of that dog. She did a terrific job."

"Thanks, Uncle Tom. Come on, Taff. Let's go get some more ducks for Dad." He couldn't wait to tell his father about Taffy's great retrieve.

He and Taffy ran back to Frank's blind. Breathless, Charlie said, "Dad, you should've seen Taffy! She chased a cripple way out into the water and dived for it! Uncle Tom said she worked just like a much older dog."

If Frank was impressed, he didn't show it. "I was wonderin' what took you so long over there. Ducks have been flyin' by, but I couldn't shoot, 'cause you're over with Tom, getting *his* ducks." He turned away.

Charlie looked at his father's slumped form and wondered what he had done wrong. Why was his father mad at him?

Frank shot seven more ducks. The lifeless waterfowl lay in a pile on the ground inside the blind. "Three mallards, a wood duck, and three widgeon. That's pretty good, isn't it, Dad?"

"I guess." His father seemed preoccupied—disinterested.

"Are you as good a shot as Jimmy Robinson?" Charlie felt certain of it, and wanted to raise his father's spirits. Jimmy was one of Charlie's latest heroes—a renowned bird hunter who had personally signed his book, *The Art of Duck Hunting,* just for Charlie. It proved to be one of the boy's favorite birthday presents from his mother.

"Who? Oh, Robinson? Hell, I don't know. Who cares?"

Charlie tried hard not to let his father's mood ruin his day. He had seen him miss a few shots in the past thirty minutes, but he excused those, telling himself the ducks were too far away.

Then his father began missing even more. A pair of low-flying widgeon came over that Charlie felt he could've hit with his hat, but both flew through, untouched by his father's errant shots. A flock of six mallards passed them barely thirty yards off the ground. Frank fired twice, but not a feather was ruffled.

Charlie watched all six fly off. It seemed his father couldn't hit anything anymore.

"Crap!" Frank said, missing another easy shot. He reached for the flask in his pocket.

"Want me to pour you some coffee, Dad?"

"No! I don't want any damn coffee! These crappy shells are probably no good, that's all it is."

At ten o'clock, the shooting slowed, and Tom walked over with Tommy. "I'm going to town to get groceries."

Frank immediately perked up. "Aw, hell, Tom. I'll go. It was my fault we didn't have any food. Besides, there's a guy in Lockhart I want to see. I . . . I told him I was coming down here and might stop in. I didn't get a chance yesterday, 'cause we were late."

Tom eyed him skeptically, then decided it wasn't worth an argument. "Okay." He took out a scrap of paper. "Here's the list of stuff we need. Try to get back by noon so we can eat, all right?"

"Yeah. Sure. It won't take long at all." He picked up his gun.

"You want me to come with you, Dad?" Charlie asked without enthusiasm.

"No," Frank quickly replied. "You say here. I'll be back before you can shake a stick. Then we'll shoot some more ducks, Slugger."

Charlie hesitated, but comforted by his uncle's presence, dared to ask, "When can I shoot your gun? After lunch?" He didn't want his father to forget his promise.

"Don't worry you're head about it. You get to shoot the damn gun when I say so." Frank's face purpled, and he glared menacingly at his son, daring him to respond.

Charlie, hanging his head, pulled Taffy closer.

Tom looked at the crestfallen boy. Deeply moved, he said, "Charlie, why don't you come with Tommy and me and hunt with us for a while? We sure could use Taffy's help."

"Yeah, Charlie," Tommy said. "I want to watch Taffy work some more. It's really neat the way she finds our birds. You can help sort the ducks we shot."

Charlie had little choice, but he felt glad for any sort of relief. "All right." He followed Tommy from the blind. "See you later, Dad." He glanced at his father who by this time was hurriedly gathering his gear for the trek back to the shack.

"Yeah. Right." Frank mumbled.

After the boys left, Tom turned on his friend. "Did you have to treat him like that? He worships the ground you walk on. It's his birthday, for pity's sake. This is supposed to be fun for him. You promised you'd let him shoot your gun, didn't you? What's the matter with you, anyway?"

"Iss none of yer concern. Look out." Frank tried to push past his friend. "I gotta get the damn food," Frank said angrily. "He's my kid, an' I'll treat him any way I damn please. I'm not raising babies."

"He's barely eleven years old, Frank. He can't stand up to you. You keep this up, and you'll break him into pieces. Can't you at least stay sober for one weekend?"

"I don' need you ta tell me . . . about . . ."

"The hell with you! Make sure you're back by noon so we don't starve!" Tom said and turned away.

Just as Frank prepared to leave, he bumped his shotgun. It fell over and slammed against a metal post, rebounded, and hit the ground. Tom had taken only two steps when he heard the loud, *clang!* He froze and hunched his shoulders—waiting. Then came a smaller, muted thud.

Tom turned and saw Frank lean over to pick up his weapon. He pulled it close to his face to examine it. When he saw a dent in the upper barrel, he shouted, "Son of a bitch!" Frank picked up his shell bag and stumbled from the blind, tucking the still-loaded weapon under his arm. He took one last drag on his cigarette and flipped it into the dry grass. Without a word, or a wave, he stomped away and headed back to the shack.

Tom quickly stepped on the smoldering butt and ground his heel on the burning ash just as a small flame erupted in the grass. "Dammit, Frank! I told you to watch what you do with your butts."

If Frank heard Tom's words, he did not acknowledge it. He just kept plodding away.

Charlie watched his father weave his way unsteadily along the path and disappear from sight. Maybe tomorrow he'd be permitted to fire the weapon.

Four

CHARLIE HUNTED WITH TOM and Tommy for another ninety minutes. His keen-eyed uncle shot nine more ducks. Charlie happily watched his dog retrieve all but one that fell far out into the lake.

"She's a tired, happy dog, Charlie," Tom said.

Charlie's chest swelled with pride. Taffy's efforts and obvious enjoyment provided a much-needed boost to the boy's deflated psyche. "This was really fun, Uncle Tom. Taffy probably had more fun than anyone."

Tom laughed. "She sure looked like she had a good time. She made life easier for Tommy, I can tell you. Without her, he'd have been out in the weeds looking for ducks all morning."

"Yeah," Tommy said. "She saved me lots of work, Charlie."

"You'll have many great hunts with her over the next few years," Uncle Tom said.

"I hope so," Charlie said, wishing his dad agreed.

Charlie leaned against the snow fence. He gazed out over the point and saw a canoe with two hunters paddling across the channel and pointed at them. "Who's that?"

"I don't know, but I can probably guess." Tom replied. "Be the same guys we've been having trouble with ever since we bought the place." A puzzled, worried look planted on his face. "This is private land. We have it post-ed down there. Those guys surely couldn't have missed seeing the sign we put up. They can't hunt over here. I guess Dick and I'd better have a chat with them."

He turned toward his brother. "Dick! Come here!"

Dick lay down his gun and together with his son, John, traversed the short distance to his brother's blind.

"We'd better talk to those guys again," Tom said, directing Dick to look out over the point at the new group of hunters.

"Are we going to have trouble with them?"

"Guess so. Old Myron told me those guys used to hunt and trap over here all the time—ever since they were kids, I guess. Said they were nothin' but trouble—still are, I'm afraid. Tommy, you, Charlie, and John stay here. We'll be right back."

Charlie and the other two boys watched the brothers walk to the end of the point to confront the trespassers. When the two men approached the boat, they saw Tom wave and point to a sign posted nearby.

Without being able to hear the ensuing conversation, the boys could tell that everyone involved was angry. The slight breeze blowing from the east brought the sounds of cursing and shouting. They watched Tom take his brother's arm and pull him away from the intruders.

The two men stomped back to the blind.

"What happened, Dad?" John asked.

"The jerks won't leave," Dick said angrily. "Said they had every right to hunt there as long as they were standing in the water." Dick looked back across the channel to the other shore. At one time the pasture had been fer-tile and full of cover for nesting waterfowl. Now, as he scanned the land-scape, he noted it was overgrown with noxious weeds and dotted with bro-ken down cars, trucks, and various pieces of useless farm equipment. Dick couldn't understand how anyone could let their land turn so sour.

"Can they do that?" John asked.

Dick looked at his brother. "I dunno. Tom, they might be right—legally. So long as they aren't on dry land, there isn't much we can do."

"Maybe, but they'll certainly spoil our hunting. As soon as they start shooting, the birds won't come near us. If they stay, it'll be a mess. Maybe they'll get their limit and leave. I hope so. Come on, let's pick up our stuff and head to the shack. Charlie's dad should be back by now, and I'm hungry. Who else wants to eat?"

"I do!" all three boys said.

They picked up their ducks, and the five hunters hiked back to the shack. Charlie was relieved to see that his father must've returned, because the big Buick was parked in front of the building.

They hung their ducks on the wall, and Dick suggested, "Charlie, why don't you take Taffy down to the lake to wash off some of that mud?"

"Okay, Uncle Dick. Come on, girl. Let's go for a swim." Charlie ran down to the beach in front of the shack.

Picking up a piece of driftwood, he waved it under Taffy's nose. "Go fetch, girl!" He tossed it into the water as far as he could.

Taffy bounded after it, swimming out and grabbing the stick, then returning to shore.

When Taffy was washed clean and had a couple of vigorous shakes, Charlie brought her back to the shack. As he approached Tommy and John who were waiting outside, he heard the men arguing inside.

"You know the rules, Frank!" Dick snapped. "No loaded guns in the shack!"

"Aw, give it a rest, will ya? It was jest a slight . . . oversight, tha's all." Frank said.

"No, we won't give it a rest," Tom said. "You broke the rules, Frank. I cracked the gun open, and it still had two shells in it."

"Big deal. So I made a little mistake. No harm done."

"It is a big deal. Besides, Dick and I aren't stupid. We know where you were."

"Mind your own damn business. I told ya I had a call ta make."

"That's a crock, and you know it," Tom said. "Dick and I talked it over, and we think you should stay here this afternoon."

"Why?"

"You know damn well why. You need to sleep it off. Charlie can come with us."

"No. Hell with you two. I'm huntin' with my son!"

"You're in no condition, Frank," Dick said.

"I've had enough of this crap!" Frank shouted. "Charlie, come in here!" he yelled.

Charlie glanced at his two cousins, lowered his eyes, and reluctantly opened the door and went inside. *Why does he have to spoil everything? I hate him!*

He stood inside the door and looked at the three angry men. The tension in the room was palpable. Charlie saw his father's gun on the kitchen table, with two fresh shells standing beside it.

"Hey, there, Slugger. Ready ta go huntin' with yer old man?" Frank took a step, knocked over a chair, and stumbled toward his son.

Charlie put out his arms to catch his father.

"Oops." Frank tried to straighten up. "Who the hell left that there?" He nodded toward the offending chair, and promptly kicked it back under the table. It banged against the edge and settled.

"I'm kinda hungry, Dad. Can we eat first?" Charlie didn't know what else to say.

"Sure. Let's do that. Come on. I'll make ya a sandwich." He put his arm around his son roughly, shook his shoulders, and used him as a crutch as he shuffled toward the counter.

"Charlie, why don't you sit with your dad?" Dick asked, "And I'll fix us all something to eat."

Charlie guided his father to the table and both sat down.

The other two boys entered the shack. After glancing briefly at Frank's slumped form, they sat at the table.

"Pour me a cup of coffee, will ya, Charlie?" Frank asked.

Eager to please, especially if he didn't have to get beer, Charlie got up, poured the heavy brew into a cup, and set it before his father. Tom made lunch. By the time they were ready to eat, Charlie had poured a second cup and gratefully watched his father drink it.

"I'll jus' lie down a bit," Frank muttered. "I'm bushed. "Wake me up before you go out, okay, Slugger?" He lurched toward the bunk bed, knocked both shins against the rough wood, turned, and collapsed on the bunk. His legs dangled over the edge.

"Sure, Dad." Charlie went to his father, raised both legs, and unlaced each boot. With practiced care, he swung his father's legs onto the bed and turned away. Anxious for something to do, he took his father's gun from the rack, checked the barrels, and took out the cleaning equipment. He spent the next thirty minutes carefully cleaning every inch of his father's Browning. The dent in the barrel disappointed him; then he saw the front sight was missing, too.

He wondered how the gun had been damaged, as the last time he had looked at it, the gun was unblemished. Charlie was saddened. His father's double-barrel was a thing of beauty to the young boy—something he coveted and treasured almost as a work of art. He rubbed at the dent, hoping by some magic that it would disappear. The scar remained.

Tom and Dick stepped outside to clean ducks while John and Tommy settled on the old couch to read comics.

The bright, sunny day that had offered hope and promise earlier that morning slowly gave way to thickening clouds. The wind rose until it blew steadily from the east. Dead leaves from the giant cottonwood that hovered over the small shack smacked against the little window on the east wall. Charlie finished cleaning the gun, put it on the rack, and went outside.

Tom and Dick, busy cleaning ducks, lowered their voices as Charlie approached.

"Hi," Charlie said.

"Hi, Charlie," Dick said. "Want to help?"

"Sure, but I don't know what to do."

"Come here and stand beside me. We have only a couple left to clean. I'll show you how," Dick said.

Charlie pulled an old, wooden Winchester shell box to the table and stood beside his uncle. Emulating the men, he rolled up his sleeves then watched as Dick cleaned and gutted a mallard. Charlie was an apt student.

Dick handed him the knife, and he cut into the breast of one of the remaining birds.

His uncles watched as he carefully sliced skin from the breast. Feathers lifted on the breeze and flew into Charlie's face. His mouth was open—tongue worrying against his lower lip as the boy concentrated on the task before him. He wanted desperately to get it right the first time. Before long, he had feathers on his lips, stuck to his bloody hands, and clinging to his red flannel shirt.

"How ya doin', Charlie?" Dick asked. He smiled as he observed his nephew.

"Okay, I guess."

"You're doing jest fine, son. Slice away the breast filets on either side of the ridge. That's it. Good job, young man."

Charlie dropped the two slightly mangled filets into the pot of cold water, looked at his bloody hands, and then wiped feathers from his face with the back of his sleeve. "Got any more?"

"Nope. That was the last one," Tom said. "Thanks for your help. Next time we'll get you involved much sooner, though. You have a knack for cleaning ducks, Charlie."

"You know, Charlie," Dick said, "You'll be a great hunter someday."

Charlie, beaming, stood tall on the wooden box. His two uncles towered over him, even at his adjusted height. With a smile, he said, "Thanks, Uncle Dick." Jumping down, he went inside to wash his hands.

At two-thirty, it was time to return to the blinds. The sun hid behind thickening clouds as they dressed for the evening's shoot. Charlie went to his father's bunk, hesitated, and shook his shoulder.

"Dad? Wake up. It's time to go hunting. Dad?"

Frank slowly awoke, rubbing his face with shaking hands. "Huh? What time is it?"

"It's two-thirty, and we're all ready to go."

"I'll be there in a minute. You go ahead with the others, and I'll be right there."

"That's okay. I'll wait. I don't mind."

Frank sat up so fast he hit his head on the upper bunk. "I told you to go! I'll be right behind you."

Charlie stepped back quickly. Frightened by his father's tone, he stared at the man he had worshiped for so long. Then he left the shack.

Charlie fidgeted with his belt buckle only briefly to hide his face before joining the others. The five hunters left the shack in silence. He and Taffy stopped at the second-to-last blind with Dick and John. Immediately, they heard gunshots coming from the far end of the point.

"Is that those guys again, Dad?" John asked.

"I'm afraid so. Looks like they decided to stay."

"Can't you kick them off?"

"I'm afraid if we try, it'll lead to more angry words. Your grandpa taught me long ago that guns and short tempers don't mix. We'd better leave 'em alone for now."

He looked at the boys. "Besides, there are plenty of ducks around for everybody. See? Here comes a pair of mallards. Mark!" He pointed north.

They crouched as the birds approached. When they were in range, Dick stood and fired two quick shots.

BANG! BANG!

Charlie watched both ducks fold and drop into the weeds.

"Send out your dog, Charlie," Dick said.

"Great shootin', Uncle Dick! Taffy, go fetch!"

Taffy, seeing the ducks fall, ran toward them. Within minutes, she returned with the first one, a large greenhead with curly tail. She held it for Charlie and waited for his command.

Charlie took the bird as if the two of them had been doing the same thing for years, and said, "Go fetch, girl! Get the other one now."

Taffy scampered off as Charlie held up the large mallard for all to see. Taffy took a little longer to find the second bird. Just as she broke from the weeds, more shots came from the point.

The sound of gunfire faded. At that moment, Frank walked up and asked, "Who the hell's that?" pointing to the far point. His threatening tone startled all three.

"Oh. Hi, Frank," Dick said. "Well, unfortunately, we have company over there. They own the property across the bay. We've had trouble with them before. Come over in an old canoe. They grew up on that old farm over there and apparently have hunted this point for years—somehow feel it's still their right to come over here." Dick observed his friend's reaction and immediately regretted involving him in their problem. "Tom and I asked 'em to leave, but they refused. Not much we can do about it as long as they're in the water, I'm afraid."

"Oh, yeah?" Frank said angrily. "I'll get rid of those clowns. Hell's bells. This is private property. They'll spoil our hunting!"

"Let's not have any problems, Frank." Dick stepped in front of his brother-in-law. "I'll put up more signs next weekend."

"Nuts to that. Signs don't mean diddly-squat to jerks like that. I'm going down there." He pushed past Dick, and left the blind. "Charlie, you stay here. Dick, you coming?"

"No, and I don't think you should go, either. I don't want any trouble, Frank." Dick stepped close to his friend and pulled him away from the boys.

"Look, Frank, Myron told me . . ."

"Who's Myron?" Frank asked.

"You know, the old farmer we bought the point from—Myron Jimson. Anyway, Myron said that this guy lives in that old farmhouse up on the hill over there," he pointed to the weather beaten, faded white, two story barely visible in the distance across the channel, "and is one of the meanest bastards he ever met. Story goes that when the kid was fifteen or so, he snuck out to the pasture one night, roped an old cow and broke all her legs with a mall! Then he left her to die!" Dick gazed across the channel.

"Yeah? So, wha's your point?" Frank asked.

Dick looked at his brother-in-law intently and replied, "After his daddy died, the guy came back home to take over the farm and the first thing he did was shoot all the cows—didn't even bother takin' them to the slaughterhouse. Just marched into the dairy barn and shot all of 'em—one at a time." Dick paused to let his words sink in. "This is not someone we should mess with, Frank!"

"I don't care. He and his pal are trespassing and it's time to get rid of 'em once and for all." Frank turned away and trudged off, his gun cradled loosely in his left arm.

Dick paused, unsure whether or not to follow his friend.

Charlie listened to the conversation, but said nothing. *Please, don't do anything, Dad. You're mad . . . again . . . and . . . and, drunk! Stay out of his way . . .*

He watched his father march off. *I hope he doesn't . . .* Charlie shuddered.

Five

ICK DECIDED HE HAD better accompany Frank. As they approached the end of the point, two hunters turned in the shallow water to face the pair.

"Weren't you guys told to get the hell off this land?" Frank shouted.

The larger of the pair took one step in the muddy water and replied, "We're not on your land, pal. Checked with the warden before the season—long as we stand in the water there's nothin' you can do about it." He pushed back the brim of his long-billed cap, revealing a deep indentation just below the hairline. His upper lip was swollen, and one eye was blackening.

"Why don't you two clowns go back across the bay where you belong and hunt on the other side?" Frank asked.

"'Cause we don't want to, that's why. Been huntin' over here all my life, and you guys ain't gonna chase me off."

"I don't know about this, Virg—maybe we should leave," his smaller companion said.

"Hell, no! Got as much right to be here as these guys."

Frank had heard enough. With his loaded weapon still cradled, he sloshed into the water and stood toe to toe with Virgil.

The large intruder pushed Frank away, as if an imaginary line had been crossed. Frank stepped back and stuck a gloved finger in the man's face and said, "Listen, butt head, I'm only gonna tell you once more—get the hell outta here 'fore you've got more trouble'n you can handle!" He dropped his hand and shoved the man back—hard!

"Who you callin' a butt head?" Virgil edged closer. As if a switch had been thrown somewhere behind the dent in his forehead, he swung at Frank's face. Instead of striking flesh as intended, Virgil tripped on a sub-merged tangle of weeds, stumbled past his antagonist, and fell face first into the mud. Virgil's shotgun planted in the mud, barrel down.

Frank backed up to dry land and looked down at the fallen figure that by now was soaking wet and spitting muddy water.

"Dammit, Frank! That's enough." Dick said as he pulled Frank far-ther inland. "Look, mister, we don't want any more trouble."

Virgil was standing now and looked as if he wasn't through. He glared at Frank with a look of pure venom. His friend, Lenny, reached out and grabbed Virgil's arm.

"Come on, Virg. Let it go."

Virgil wiped his face and said to Dick, "You better drag that drunk-en bum back if you know what's good for him!"

"Who are you calling drunk, you piece of crud?" Frank lunged, rais-ing his gun as if to club the man.

"Frank, cut it out!" Dick shouted. "Let's go." He turned Frank around and pointed him back toward the boys.

"If you jerks know what's good for ya, you'll haul ass outta here!" Frank said over his shoulder.

VIRGIL PISANT STAGGERED in the muddy water and caught his balance. His face was a strange reddish-blue color. He again wiped his face, and withdrew his gun from the mud. Then, in a split second, something snapped in the big man! His brown eyes turned yellow! His lower lip quivered! His breath came in rapid, short staccato-like bursts! His whole body shook with rage!

Lenny Cathcart had never seen Virgil in such a fury. The top of Virgil's head looked like it might explode! He asked, "You okay, Virg? Maybe we should pack it in—we got plenty of ducks. Come on. Let's go home."

In a steady, even voice spoken between clenched teeth, he replied, "We're stayin'." He glowered at the retreating pair. Once he stopped hyperventilating, he said, "You know what, Lenny? I've seen that guy before somewhere. He look familiar to you?

"Nooo . . . can't say as he does. Where you think you seen him, Virg?"

"Don't know for sure, but it wasn't long ago, I'll tell ya that. It'll come to me though."

Virgil grabbed a stick and cleaned the mud from the end of his shotgun. He wiped the barrel down with a rag from the canoe, and gazed off toward the assembled hunters farther inland.

"Tell ya what, though . . . when I do remember, that guy's ass is grass!"

CHARLIE WAS SHIVERING. Even from a distance he knew how angry his father was. He squatted and put both arms around Taffy. Reluctantly, he decided to be with his father. He called Taffy and walked slowly toward his father's blind.

As he drew close, he heard Dick asking, "Are you out of your ever-lovin' mind, Frank?"

"They're trespassin'," Frank shouted. "I shoulda knocked the stuffin' outta that guy when I had the chance."

"With a loaded gun? Are you that far gone?" Dick turned toward Charlie. "I'm sorry you had to see that, son. Your dad lost his temper, but he's all right now. Aren't you?" He faced his irate friend.

"Yeah, yeah," Frank said. "They're still a bunch of turds—AND THEY'RE TRESPASSING!" he shouted in the intruders' direction.

"Leave 'em alone," Dick said. "I'm warning you." After taking a deep breath, he patted Charlie's shoulder and walked off.

Charlie's father set down his gun and reached in his pocket. "What are you looking at?"

"Nothing." Charlie turned away and leaned against the fence. Any faith in that day becoming fun or pleasantly memorable for the eleven-year old was long gone.

Frank saw the hurt on Charlie's face and in a brief flash of concern, said, "I'm sorry, Slugger. Those guys really made me angry, ya know?" Once said, he slipped back into an accusatory vein. "It wasn't my fault. They're trespassing, and your lilly-livered uncles are gonna let 'em stay. They'll ruin our hunting. You watch! If we don't boot 'em off, they'll be back tomorrow. I have a good mind to—"

"Mark, Dad! There's a flock coming this way," Charlie said, relieved for the distraction.

Seeing the small flock coming toward them from the north, they both crouched. The birds came closer. Then Frank stood, his weapon raised. But before he could fire, a volley of shots echoed from the two tres-passers at the point. The flock flared at the noise, turned, and retreated over the lake.

"Sons-a-bitches!" Frank said.

"It's okay, Dad. I'll bet another flock comes by."

"Nope! Those guys'll keep shooting, and I'll never get another shot." He reached into his coat for his flask and took a long pull.

THE TWO CARLSON BROTHERS and their sons were getting shots farther inland. The intruders, Virgil and Lenny, were too far away to affect their hunting very much.

The pattern continued. Ducks approached Frank and Charlie's blind but flared when shots were heard. Frank had few chances to shoot during the next hour.

Charlie leaned against the fence, watching a small, solitary duck circle the lake. *He looks like he's lost,* he thought. *A teal, I bet. He's small and alone. The poor thing's probably looking for his family.* The small duck dove, feigned as if about to land, then jerked skyward—beating its small wings to gain altitude. Charlie heard a plaintive, "*Peep, peep,*" carried on the wind. Was the bird calling out to him? The tiny duck looked as lonesome and forlorn as Charlie felt.

Charlie stood, not wanting to alert his father. He felt sorry for it and wanted it to fly away—safely. He remained silent as the tiny bird came closer. *Keep going, little guy!*

Just as it flew overhead, just as it reached optimum shooting range, just as it dipped even closer to the small boy, Charlie heard his father's gun fire. BANG! The bird was thrust skyward by the shot's impact, then immediately spiraled back down to earth. It landed a short distance from the blind with a pronounced *thump!*

"Why didn't you yell?" his father asked. "Might've missed that one."

Charlie sent Taffy after the downed duck without answering his father. She ran to the fallen bird eagerly, but as she approached, she stopped and stood over it without picking it up. Taffy glanced over her shoulder at her master—confused, and reluctant to mouth the still thrashing bird. Charlie stepped from the blind and walked a few paces to his dog's side.

The small green-winged teal was on its back alternately kicking both legs—as if it were pedaling a bike upside down. Charlie observed the duck's heart beating as its fluffy chest rose and fell. All of a sudden, it flopped over on its belly, spread both wings, and attempted to scrabble to the safety of the surrounding bulrushes. Taffy jumped at the bird, made as if to retrieve it, but did not. "That's okay, girl. I know how you feel. Wish he hadn't shot this one, don't you?"

Charlie picked up the still struggling teal with both hands, tucked its wings along its body, and stroked its rust-colored head. He stared at the brilliant green patch on each wing, and then shifted his gaze to the duck's dark, blinking eyes. Warmth spread through Charlie's palms. He watched as the faint pulsing of the bird's heart faded.

"Hey! What the hell ya doin' over there? Come on! Git back here before some more ducks fly by."

It's still alive, Charlie thought. *I can feel its little heart beating.* He looked into a coal-black eye. He's looking at me. The teal blinked once, then the eye went blank, and the lid closed forever. The beating heart stopped.

Heartsick, Charlie stared at the bird for a long time. His blue eyes filled with tears. He didn't think that shooting teal was the same as shooting the other, bigger birds. He wished the small bird were still alive, still free to fly away, to escape and seek a happier place. To join its family perhaps. But, it was too late.

Instead of casually tossing the dead duck onto the pile with the rest, he gently laid it alone in the grass.

"What the hell are you doin'?" Frank asked.

"Nothing." Charlie took one last look at the teal and decided he had seen enough of death.

After a few minutes, Charlie asked, "We've had a pretty good day, don't you think, Dad, even if we don't shoot any more ducks?"

Frank's mood had grown increasingly nasty. "You think so, huh?"

It was four o'clock, and they had another hour of daylight left before it would be time to quit. Charlie wanted to shoot his father's gun as promised, though not at a duck, but he didn't know if he dared ask. Looking at Frank's bloodshot eyes and flushed face, he decided tomorrow might be a better time.

The hunters at the end of the point fired sporadically. Each time they did, Frank cursed under his breath, "Bastards! Jerks!"

Another small group of ducks appeared over the bulrushes on the south side of the blind.

"Mark!" Charlie called, pointing.

Frank raised his gun. A moment later, gunfire from the end of the point scared the group away.

"All right! That's it! I've had it with those bastards!" In one quick, unthinking moment, he turned and raised his shotgun. Without hesitation, he aimed over the men's heads and fired twice. BANG! BANG!

Two rounds of number-two lead shot, approximately four hundred pepper-sized pellets, traveled toward the trespassers at a high rate of speed.

Charlie looked up, wondering where the ducks were. Seeing an empty, gray sky, he turned and gasped when he saw how low his father's gun was aimed. "Dad?"

The hunters fell into the weeds as pellets rained around them.

Oh, no! Charlie thought. He killed them!

"HOW'D YOU LIKE THAT?" Frank shouted. "NOW, GET THE HELL OUT OF HERE!" He raised his fist at the hunters.

Charlie watched for movement. *Were they both dead?* He breathed heavily, unable to speak. Tasting bile, he wanted to vomit, but couldn't.

As the wind rose, it brought with it angry shouts from the point.

"Son of a bitch!"

"You trying to kill someone?"

"Crazy bastard!"

Charlie stared at his father. He didn't know what to say—or do.

"I jus' tried to scare 'em a little, that's all. No big deal," Frank said, attempting to downplay his reckless act. "It worked, didn't it? Look, I think they're leaving. AND DON'T COME BACK!" he shouted.

Dick and Tom rushed over.

"Frank?" Dick asked. "What are you thinking?" His face was flushed, and his voice shook.

"We saw the whole thing," Tom said. "You could've killed one of 'em."

"Yeah, but I didn't," Frank said. "I just wanted to scare 'em a little. They'll be leaving soon." There was no remorse in his voice.

"Charlie," Uncle Tom said, "Take your dog over to Tommy and John. We need to talk to your dad." There was no mistaking the anger in his voice.

Charlie looked at his father.

"Go ahead, Slugger." Frank tried to reload his shotgun, but the shells fell from his fingers. He bent to pick them up, and the barrel swung toward Charlie.

Tom stepped forward and quickly redirected the weapon away from the boy.

Charlie flinched. Calling Taffy to his side, he left his father. *I wish he hadn't done that,* he thought. *What'll happen now?*

He felt very alone.

Tom and Dick verbally lambasted their friend. Some of the one-sided conversation drifted to Charlie.

"We've had it! This time you've gone too far."

"Unload that gun right now."

"What if they bring the sheriff?"

"We could all be arrested. No more second chances for you, Frank."

"Aw, come on. I just tried to scare 'em," Frank said.

"No, Frank. It's over. You aren't welcome here. Pack up your stuff and go home. Leave Charlie with us. We'll bring him home tomorrow."

"The hell with you two!"

Charlie reached the other blind.

"What happened, Charlie?" Tommy asked.

"I don't know. I guess my dad shot too close to those men. He didn't mean to. I guess it scared 'em."

"Did he really shoot at those guys?" John asked.

"No. It wasn't on purpose! It was an accident." Charlie looked back where his father still argued with his friends. *Please, Dad, don't get mad at Uncle Tom and Uncle Dick.*

Charlie watched his father angrily pick up his shotgun and shell bag and stalk off. Charlie felt relieved the shouting was over.

Without stopping as he passed the blind, Frank said, "Charlie, come 'ere. We're going home right now."

"Home? Why, Dad?"

"'Cause I said so. Move!" His face flushed with anger and embarrassment.

"I gotta go, you guys," Charlie told them, fighting back his disappointment and hurriedly gathering his possessions.

"See you, Charlie," the other boys said.

Tom and Dick returned to the blind. "Charlie, why don't you stay? We'll take you home safely tomorrow."

"I'd better go with Dad," Charlie said. "Thanks for everything, Uncle Tom. You too, Uncle Dick." He waved good-bye. With Taffy trailing, he trudged after his father, his head down.

I hope he's not mad at me, Charlie thought. *Why'd he have to ruin everything again? He's acting crazy!*

His father walked quickly, mumbling and swearing. "What the hell do they know? That's the thanks I get. I chased 'em off, for cryin'-out-loud! Who needs 'em, anyway? Come on, Slugger. Let's git the hell outa here."

They reached the shack. Frank stormed inside, almost slamming the heavy door in Charlie's face.

Charlie stared at the door, wondering if he should go in.

"Charlie! Get your butt in here!"

Charlie opened the door and entered. Frank carelessly tossed clothes into his duffel. Charlie walked to his bunk and gathered up the few things not already in his bag. He picked up Taffy's dish. Without a word, he walked to the car, put his bag in the back seat, let Taffy in, and waited for his father.

He didn't wait long. The door slammed again, harder than before, and Frank rushed to the black Buick, tossing his bag and gun into the back seat. Holding a brown paper bag under one arm, he got behind the wheel.

Charlie climbed into the front passenger seat as his father reached into the bag, unscrewed the cap, and took a long drink. Suddenly, Charlie felt cold all over.

His father stuck the bag between his legs, turned the key, and stepped on the gas. All eight cylinders roared. He put the car into gear and slammed his right foot to the floor. The Buick spun its tires in the loose gravel, kicking up an angry cloud of dust. The car slid back and forth across the two-lane path as it raced away from the shack.

Charlie turned and looked back. The sun popped out from behind the clouds, touching the horizon. Rays of bright, reddish light filtered by the settling dust highlighted the shack.

I hope I can come back someday, he thought. *Maybe when I'm older, and when Dad isn't so angry. Maybe I'll come alone. Or maybe I'll be someplace else— far away . . .*

Six

B ACK ON THE END of the point, as Frank and Charlie were leaving, Virgil's mind was racing. Something about the man who tripped him seemed familiar. The shots over their heads were intended as a warning, and even though the pellets slapped their canvas coats and stung a bit, they were never in any danger. Yet the confrontation triggered a remembrance, but of what? *What was it about that guy?*

Pisant touched his tender, swollen lip and then, in a flood of anger and realization, everything fell into place. "That's it! I got it!"

"What's that, Virg?"

"You remember that guy in the Buick . . . last night?"

"Yeah, what about him? Still say we shoulda called the sheriff."

"Right! You dumbass, I'm on parole, and we were both three sheets to the wind. How smart would that a been?"

"So, what about the guy in the Buick?"

"Jest so happens it's the same guy that jest pushed me in the mud— same guy that . . . that I had a problem with . . . ah, I'll tell ya later."

"He didn't push ya down, Virg, you slipped . . ." Immediately, Lenny regretted correcting his friend.

Virgil flared and grabbed the front of Lenny's coat. "What'd ya say, ya little twerp?"

"Uh, nothin', Virg. I meant to say, uh, well you know—"

"Shut up, Lenny! I'm thinkin'." His eyes still shining with delight, Virgil released the smaller man. "Finally, after all these years . . . guy turns out to be nothin' but a drunken slob. Whatta ya know about that?"

Wisely, Lenny remained silent.

Caught in his hateful memories, Virgil continued, "Yep, finally I git my chance. This is gonna be sooo easy it ain't even funny." Virgil slipped his bare thumb over the safety on the old shotgun and twitched the raised knob back and forth.

"What the hell you talkin' about, Virg?"

"Never you mind, little man . . . let's see, how's that go? Oh yeah, 'Vengeance is mine,' or some such crap." He turned and looked inland, inhaled deeply, and kept thumbing the safety.

FRANK DIDN'T SAY MUCH as he drove. Mostly, he mumbled, cursed, and blamed everyone but himself for his misery. "Lousy, ungrateful bunch of twits. That's what they are. Some friends I've got. Screw 'em."

Charlie, trying to tune it all out, thought of anything but the events of the past twenty-four hours. His father was in a particularly foul mood, and he wondered if he'd ever calm down.

The boy stared at the road ahead. The car drifted to the right, then hit the shoulder. Alarmed, Charlie jerked to attention and glanced at his father. He was ready to speak up when Frank finally straightened out the car's path.

Frank's erratic driving continued for over an hour. Charlie watched in horror as the car crossed the centerline directly in front of a pair of headlights. He was certain they were going to crash and all three would be dead. He looked at his dad, whose head sagged to his chest.

The approaching vehicle honked. Frank jumped, turning the wheel barely in time. The big Buick skidded briefly, then regained traction.

Charlie watched him carefully and realized he was nodding off. He didn't know what to do. He knew that if he shook his father, chances were excellent he'd wake up angrier than ever.

Cars honked as Frank sped past.

Charlie realized he had to do something—quick!

He gingerly shook his father's arm. "Dad? Wake up!"

Frank opened his eyes. "Huh? What's the matter?"

"You're falling asleep. I'm afraid we'll crash." He shrunk back, waiting for the inevitable venomous flow of words.

"Don' worry, Slugger. I'm okay. I won't let anything happen to you."

Charlie wasn't reassured. "Maybe we should stop to eat."

Frank tested the bottle between his legs. "Yeah, maybe we should." He wiped his lips with the back of one sleeve. "Tell ya what, I know a place in Montrose where we can get you a cheeseburger and some fries. How's that sound, Slugger?" His mood improved noticeably. "I guess I need something to wake me up. We have a ways to go."

They slowed and stopped in front of the 12-Hi Bar and Grill.

"Lock the door, Slugger." Frank said as he stumbled from the car.

"Will Taffy be all right here?"

"She'll be fine. Come on."

"I'll fill her dish with food."

Frank waited impatiently while Charlie filled the dish. He reached over and slammed the door just as Charlie set Taffy's dish on the backseat. They walked into the saloon together. It was seven o'clock on Saturday night, and the place was filling up with local residents. The smoke and odor of stale beer made Charlie choke and squint as he crossed the room. He climbed onto a barstool next to his father and put his elbows on the bar. He spotted a pinball machine across the room as his father waved to the bartender.

"How 'bout a shot of Jack and a beer chaser?" Frank asked. "A Coke for my son, here. We want some food, too. How about a cheeseburger and fries, Slugger?"

"Sure, Dad."

"Make it two cheeseburgers and one order of fries."

"Can I play the pinball machine?" Charlie asked.

"Sure. Let's see what change I've got." Frank handed Charlie coins from his pocket and turned away.

Charlie hopped down and went to the pinball machine. He remembered when he first played the machines, he was barely tall enough to see over the edge and use the flippers on either side, but he had refused to stand on a chair because that was for little kids. He had occasion to play them a number of times since because his father often took him into bars.

He played two games with limited success. When he returned to the bar, Frank was talking to a man on his left. Charlie climbed back onto the stool and heard the men discussing football. The man had apparently recognized his father and wanted to discuss the Gopher team of twenty years ago.

"I remember that Pitt game," the man said. "Greatest game I ever saw. Six to nothing as I recall. You recovered a fumble and ran in for the score, right?"

"Yeah. That game won us the title that year. After we beat Wisconsin, we were National champs. That was in '35, our second National title in a row!" Frank noticed Charlie was back. "This is my son, Charlie."

"Hello, Charlie," the man said. "You gonna be a football player like your dad?"

"Hi. I dunno'. Maybe." Charlie averted the man's gaze, hoping their discussion would turn to something else.

"Sure he will," Frank said. "He'll probably be a running back. Kid runs like the wind. Maybe be a quarterback. He can really wing the ball. Can't you, Slugger?"

"I guess." Embarrassed, Charlie blushed. He'd heard it all before, and it made him uncomfortable. He knew he'd never be as good as his father— nor would he be as big. Charlie preferred hockey. His dad never played that sport, had never been on skates. As proud as he was of his father, he hated conversations like the one he now heard.

"Your dad was quite a football player, Charlie. Do you know what his nickname was? Fearless Frankie Nash. I saw him in every home game he played." The man said.

I know. Fearless Frank. Not afraid of anybody or anything, Charlie thought. He thought of the unpleasant incident at the lake.

"Looks like you'll have to grow some, young fella, but you got time, I guess."

"Hell," Frank said. "He'll probably be bigger than me. Look how big his hands are. Show 'em, Slugger. Hold up your hand. Come on, don't be bashful."

Charlie did as requested, holding up his small hand to press against his father's large, warm palm. Knowing his hand was smaller, he didn't bother looking.

"See? Look at that. He'll have a big pair of mitts for sure, won't ya, Slugger?"

Charlie hated that name. He wished his father would stop bragging and call him Charlie.

Thankfully, the cheeseburgers arrived, and Charlie hid behind his food as he ate. The two men moved on to discuss more football.

Frank's new friend ordered another drink for the ex-football player, and they continued chatting.

Charlie watched to see if his dad ate his burger. He took only a few bites, leaving over half of it. Charlie's heart sank.

He wondered how long they would have to stay at the saloon. Bored and tired, he was anxious to get home. He also worried about his dad's continued drinking. This wouldn't help his driving. Charlie glanced at the clock over the bar and saw it was eight o'clock, but other men were coming over to talk, and he realized that he might not be able to pry his father loose from the gaggle of admirers. Especially if they bought him drinks.

Charlie watched his father in the mirror behind the bar. He looked about as happy as he ever got. He loved the attention. Charlie wondered what it would be like to be that famous.

I'll never know. That's for sure. Especially not by playing football, he thought, feeling small and insignificant. He wanted to go home.

Fifteen minutes later, he tried to separate his father from his new friends. "Dad?" He tugged on his arm. "Dad?"

His father turned and looked down at him as if seeing him for the first time that evening. "What? Oh, Charlie. What do you need, Slugger? Another Coke?" Frank turned and raised his hand to the bartender.

"No thanks, Dad. I think we should go. It's getting late."

"Sure, Slugger. We'll leave in a little while." He turned back to the assembled gathering of admirers.

Charlie knew what that meant. "Can I have the keys to the car? I want to let Taffy out and get her some water."

Frank fumbled even as he reached into his pocket. Without looking at his son, he handed Charlie the keys and kept his attention tuned to the conversation surrounding him.

Charlie left the bar and went outside. He opened the Buick's door and let Taffy out. Together, they walked down the street. He watched her find an appropriate spot on the boulevard, squat, and pee.

They walked back to the car. Charlie put her in back, then took her dish inside the bar to fill with water.

As he crossed the noisy, smoke-filled room, he saw his father surrounded by two more men, one of whom occupied Charlie's abandoned bar stool. Charlie went into the bathroom, filled the dish from the sink, and went outside.

After Taffy drank her fill of the tepid water, Charlie dumped out the rest and got in the back seat with his dog.

He sat with Taffy's head on his lap, gently stroking her ears. "You're still my best friend, girl. No matter what, I've always got you."

Charlie fell asleep wishing he were another person in another life, in another place far, far away. A lone tear slipped unnoticed down to his jaw and vanished.

BANG!

Charlie bolted upright, his eyes wide and heart pounding. Taffy sat up, ears alert.

BANG! There it was again!

For a moment, Charlie felt as if he were back on the point. He was frightened by what sounded like shotgun blasts.

He looked out the window and saw an old pickup across the street. It chugged and jerked, then backfired again, trailing blue smoke. He felt relieved.

Relaxing, he leaned over the front seat and looked at his Babe Ruth watch. It was nine-thirty, and his father still hadn't returned.

He wondered if he should go inside. His father wouldn't want to leave, but Charlie knew they had to—soon, or it might be too late.

He opened the door and left the relative warmth of the car. The wind was up, and the temperature had dropped. Leaves rustled and swirled around his boots as he went back into the bar.

Frank sat on the same stool as before, with at least seven men crowded around him. Charlie timidly approached, trying to slip between the hangers-on. When he was close enough, he tugged on his father's arm.

"Dad?"

Laughing, Frank turned and looked down. "Slugger. Where you been?"

"Out in the car with Taffy. It's late. I want to go home."

Frank tried to pull back his shirtsleeve to check the time, but he failed, so he studied the clock on the wall. "Holy cow! Sorry, fellas, but we gotta go. Charlie! Why didn't you come an' get me sooner?"

He reached for his wallet to pay for his drinks, but his newfound friends wouldn't hear of it.

"Don't worry about it, Frankie. We got it covered, don't we, boys?"

"Thanks, Fellas. Tha's real kind of ya. Charlie, go start the car. I'll be right there." He turned back to his new buddies.

Charlie stepped back and left the bar. He climbed into the Buick again, this time in front, put the keys in the ignition, and turned the engine on. He waited for the interior to heat up.

True to his word, Frank left the bar. Charlie watched from the passenger seat as he approached, walking unsteadily and carrying a small brown sack. Frank fumbled with the door handle, and then settled behind the wheel. He set down the package, put the car into gear, and sped off without bothering to check the mirrors.

Neither one spoke for a while. Charlie watched the road, glancing frequently at his father to make sure he was awake. Before long, after a few more sips of bourbon, Frank's eyes grew heavy. The car wandered over the centerline, then back.

"Dad!"

"Wha . . . ? What's the matter?"

"I'm scared. You almost hit that car!"

"Yer gonna have ta keep me awake, Slugger. I'm pretty tired. Don' let me fall asleep. Promise?"

Charlie was terrified. His father was drunk, and it would be up to Charlie to keep him awake. He slid across the seat closer to his father.

Nothing happened for twenty minutes, but then the car drifted to the right. Charlie put both hands on the right side of the steering wheel and carefully guided the big Buick back to its lane.

"Dad! Wake up!"

"Yeah . . . right. Yer doin' good, Slugger. Should be home soon . . . ."

A car passed them, honking angrily.

He's mad and scared, too, I'll bet, Charlie thought.

He looked at the speedometer. Somehow, his father maintained a steady fifty miles an hour.

Soon, the car slid toward the left. Once more, Charlie grabbed the wheel and redirected the automobile. It was difficult to steer the car from where he sat. He'd be able to see the road better if he was in the back seat behind his father.

"Dad!"

"Wha . . . ?"

"I'll climb in back and watch from behind, okay?"

"Huh. Sure, Slugger. Good idea."

Charlie quickly slid to the back seat and stood on the floor behind his father, reaching around his head with both arms. Frank quickly nodded off again. Charlie leaned forward, his small head alongside his father's, grabbed the wheel with both hands, and tried to steer.

They drove that way for a while, with Charlie helping and nudging his father awake as he watched the road.

When they approached a small town or intersection, Charlie shouted, "Dad, slow down!"

His father awoke with a start, raised his right foot, and even braked to a stop when needed.

"Getting close . . . now . . . Slugger. Home . . . soon . . ."

As they neared Minneapolis, traffic increased. With more cars on the road, it was all Charlie could do to keep the big car in its lane. *I can't do this,* he thought. *I'm too scared. Please, Dad, wake up!* He breathed hard. The interior of the car was no longer warm, it was stifling! Charlie cranked down the rear window with his left hand.

Occasionally, his father opened his eyes and controlled the car briefly, but he always drifted off again.

Cars honked at them frequently. *I can't help it. I'm trying!* Charlie did his best to ignore the irate drivers. He was tiring. The brief periods when his father was awake didn't last long enough.

He began to hyperventilate. He couldn't catch his breath but didn't know why. The new Buick wandered all over the road. By now, Charlie was convinced they were going to crash. He had reached the limit of what he could do to keep the big car on the road.

Suddenly, Charlie recognized a few familiar landmarks. They passed Porky's Drive Inn and the Prudential Building. Seeing the Basilica of St. Mary's, he realized they were almost home. His spirits soared! Soon he'd be tucked in by his mother and everything that had transpired would seem like a bad dream.

"Dad, we're almost home!" he shouted, taking one hand off the steering wheel to nudge his father awake.

At that moment, a car pulled up alongside. Charlie spotted it from the corner of his eye. Suddenly, a bright light shone through the side window, right into Charlie's face. Blinded by the intense light, he squinted and tried to avoid looking at the beam.

"Dad!" he shouted.

"Huh? Wha . . . ?" His father opened his eyes and threw up his hand to shield his face. He glanced left and immediately saw the black-and-white cruiser. The spotlight went off, and a flashing red beacon came on. The Buick's interior filled with an intermittent red glow.

Seven

O H, NO!" WITH SUDDEN CLARITY, Frank realized what was happening. He threw his arm back in a gesture of disgust, hitting Charlie's head and knocking him into the back seat.

Charlie rubbed his head, sat up and watched his father grip the steering wheel with trembling fingers and white knuckles.

Frank slowed the car and pulled over to the side of the road. They were on Highway 12, two blocks before their turn off at Parade Stadium. They were only twelve blocks from home.

"Damn it, Charlie!"

"Yeah, Dad?" he answered quietly.

"I told you to keep me. . . . Aw, geez! Damn it to hell! Here! Take this and hide it someplace." He took the brown bag from between his front legs and passed it between the seat and the door.

Charlie took the bag and hid it in his own duffel bag, wondering what would happen next. His father was angry with him, but Charlie felt he hadn't done anything to deserve his ire.

Taffy trembled along with Charlie. Frank muttered incoherently. Charlie was too petrified to speak.

After a short wait, two officers approached the car on either side. Charlie and his father were blinded by their flashlights. The cop on the left tapped Frank's window and waited as it rolled down.

"Sir, we've had several complaints tonight about you. It seems you've been weaving all over the road." He leaned closer. "Have you been drinking?" He wrinkled his nose in distaste.

"I mighta had a couple back in Montrose. Tha . . . was a long . . . time ago."

"I'll have to ask you to step from the car, sir. Bring your driver's license with you." He stepped back from the door.

Frank fumbled for his wallet. He couldn't see it very well and had trouble removing his license, so he handed it to Charlie and said, "Take it out for me, Slugger."

The cops noticed the gesture. The one on the right tapped the back window after Charlie handed Frank his license. Charlie scooted over and rolled down the window on the right as Frank left the car. Charlie didn't know what to say, so he remained silent.

"Son, what were you doing in the back seat?" the cop asked.

Charlie, paralyzed with fear, didn't want to get his father into more trouble than he already was. "Nothing. I was just sitting here with my dog."

"Are you sure that's all you were doing? It looked like maybe you were helping your dad steer the car when we pulled up behind you. Is that what you were doing?"

Charlie hated to lie. He couldn't admit to steering the car—he was certain he'd be arrested. "No. I was just standing up to keep my dad awake. He's pretty tired. That's all."

The cop clearly didn't believe him. "What's your name, son?"

"Charlie Nash."

"How old are you, Charlie?"

"Ten. No, eleven. I just had my birthday."

"Happy birthday, son. I need to look through the car, Charlie. You can stay there with your dog, or you can get out, whichever you like."

"I'll stay here if that's okay. I don't want Taffy to get hit by a car."

"That's fine." The cop opened the door and searched the car's interior, looking under the front seat and in the glove box.

He climbed into the back seat with Charlie and Taffy. "What's in the two bags, Charlie?" He pointed at the duffel bags.

Once again, the boy was driven to lie. "Just our hunting stuff. Me and my dad were duck hunting. That's why he's so tired." Charlie's voice wavered as he spoke.

The cop eyed him carefully but didn't press the matter. He stepped away from the car, closed the door and returned to where his partner stood with Frank.

Charlie turned and peered over the edge of the seat. Frank stood between the cops, his back to Charlie. They watched him extend one arm and bring it slowly toward his face with one finger out.

What are they doing? He wondered.

Frank was clearly having trouble standing. The two cops edged away to observe him as he tried to stand on one leg.

As Charlie stared, his father almost tipped over.

Satisfied by what they observed, heard, and smelled, they took Frank's arm and escorted him to the cruiser.

Time passed very slowly for Charlie. He almost slept, but he was too scared and confused. Taffy snuggled closer to Charlie's thigh and sighed. The boy felt tired, sad, and alone. His only remaining source of comfort laid her head on his thigh.

Abruptly, the door opened—interior lights illuminated the inside of the car. Charlie's father slumped into the passenger seat dejectedly, slamming the door.

"Dad? What's going to happen? Where are we going?"

"Home, that's where. Damn it, Charlie. I tol' ya ta keep me awake. Now look what happened. Sons-a-bitches. They couldn't jus' let us go home. Damnation, Slugger! You had a job to do, and you didn't get it done."

Charlie shrank back and collapsed against Taffy, holding her tightly. He believed it was all his fault, that he should have somehow forced his father to stop and nap. Accepting the blame, Charlie was convinced his father would never forgive him. *I just wanted to go home . . . just want to run away someplace and get away from Dad . . .*

The driver's door opened, and the older of the two cops got in and started the Buick. The Minneapolis cruiser pulled in front of them.

"Where are we going?" Charlie asked.

"I'm driving you and your father home, son," the cop said.

It was only twelve blocks to their house, but Charlie felt it took forever. The Buick arrived at their house and stopped. Frank got out and slammed his door loudly. Charlie jerked and stiffened. The cop got out, and stood beside Charlie's door.

The police cruiser was parked in front of them at the curb. One of the officers helped Frank up the steps to the house, while the other opened Charlie's door.

"Come on, son. You're home now." He held the door for the boy, seeing moisture on his cheeks. "Don't worry, lad. You're safe now."

Taffy jumped out and walked to a familiar spot on the lawn to pee. Charlie grabbed his bag and got out of the car, accompanying the officer up the steps. When Charlie reached the front door, he called, "Come here, Taff. Come on, girl."

Running to him, she slipped past and through the door.

They crossed the front porch and opened the interior door. Standing just inside were Charlie's mother, father, and both policemen. Charlie looked at his mother and saw her mouth open in alarm. The cop quietly explained what happened.

She looked at her husband, supported by the other cop, with a combination of disgust and concern.

Glancing at Charlie, she said to the men, "Let's go in the kitchen and talk."

The two cops led Charlie's father into the kitchen, but his mother held back and hugged Charlie briefly. "Are you all right?" She removed his cap and tried to smooth the boy's unruly, blond hair.

He looked up at her face and thought she seemed older. She was fighting back tears of her own, and he felt sorry for her. "Yeah, Mom. I'm

65

okay." He dared not say anything more for fear of revealing his true feelings and growing plan for escape. "I'm pretty tired, though."

"Do you want something to eat, honey?"

"No. I'll just feed Taffy and go to bed if that's all right."

"Sure. Why don't you bring in your father's bag and gun? I'll feed Taffy for you. When she's done, I'll bring her upstairs."

"Thanks, Mom." Charlie went back to the car and dragged out his father's bag. He picked up the gun, looked longingly at it for a moment, and then he carried both to the house, leaving them in the front hall. He was ready to climb the stairs when he stopped to listen.

"You know, Mrs. Nash, if it weren't for the fact that I recognized Frank," the older cop said, "we'd have hauled him off to jail tonight. I watched him play football." His voice trailed off.

Charlie picked up his bag and ran upstairs. He desperately wanted to forget all the bad things that had happened and go to sleep, but knew he couldn't. His mind was racing as he formulated a plan to leave home as soon as possible. He went to his bedroom and closed the door.

When he unpacked his bag, the brown paper bag hidden earlier slipped out and fell to the floor. He picked it up and removed the bottle. Transfixed, he stared at the bottle of whiskey.

He wanted to smash it, throw it out the window, that bottle and every one like it. Instead, he took it to the bathroom, poured the amber liquid into the toilet bowl, and replaced the empty bottle in the bag before setting it on the tank. A strange, undefined sense of satisfaction briefly visited the boy, as if somehow he could eradicate the vileness of his father's drink. But, the brief second of relief lapsed and faded away like a spritz from his mother's atomizer. He pressed the lever and watched it all disappear. The empty bottle and bag he left on the tank.

He returned to his room, put on his pajamas and climbed into bed. Voices still came from the kitchen. Then he heard light, soft footsteps on the stairs—his mother's.

The door opened, and Taffy bounded in to leap on the bed. His mother followed and sat on the edge of the bed.

She'd been crying, and her face was red. Charlie looked at her and said, "Uncle Tom and Uncle Dick made us leave, Mom. What'll happen to Dad? Why does he get like that?"

She took a deep breath. "I'm sorry, Charlie. I don't know why. He's sick, though. Someday, he'll get better," she said without conviction. "Go to sleep now. We'll talk in the morning." She kissed his forehead, left the room, and gently closed the door.

Charlie and Taffy were safe. They were together, and nothing more could hurt them that night.

Charlie closed his eyes. *What'll they do to him?* He wondered.

He remembered his father standing on the highway with the two cops. For the first time in Charlie's life, he saw his father as a small, defeated man. His all-too-familiar belligerence and intimidating voice had vanished for a while back there on the blacktop.

Charlie didn't know what the following day would bring, but he knew that once again, his father had broken his promise. And on top of everything else, his father had blamed Charlie for all that happened. *If I stay, nothing will ever change . . . I have to leave as soon as possible.*

Silently, Charlie wept. He had a decision to make. *Tomorrow. . . .* Tears ran down his cheeks, mingling with his dog's long hair. *He promised . . . . He promised . . . .*

The young dog raised her head and looked lovingly at her master's face. In the darkness of the small room, she sensed his unhappiness, fear, and pain. She edged closer, placing her head just under his chin, and breathed deeply. After slapping her tail twice against the bed, she fell asleep.

At last, Charlie drifted into a troubled slumber . . .

Eight

VIRGIL PISANT AND HIS FRIEND, Lenny, paddled back across the channel on Saturday afternoon. By the time they reached shore, beached the canoe and walked back to Virgil's dilapidated farmhouse, Virgil was muttering and swearing incoherently. "Swear to God . . . if it's the last thing I ever do . . . gonna make that bastard pay . . . I'm gonna git you, Nash—and when I do . . ."

"What's that, Virg?"

"Nothin'. Come on. I'm gonna git some dry clothes on. Then let's go to town and have a few beers."

"Sounds good to me, Virg."

Once inside, Pisant dug out a pile of phone directories he had accumulated over the years to handle his shady dealings and searched for Frank Nash's address. He wasn't in the St. Paul directory, so he tossed that one aside and opened the Minneapolis book. He knew that the black Buick had come the way most people from the Cities came. His blood was boiling by the time he actually saw his adversary's name in print. As if by fate, he reasoned, the one man who represented all that he hated and despised in the world, fell into his lap. The same guy who had embarrassed him in high school; the same guy who had run him off the road the night before; the same guy who not only pushed him into the mud and slime out on the point, but took shots at him and Lenny—that man had popped back into his life.

Pisant's anger had turned to a silent rage once he realized just who his tormenter was, and the twisted pieces of the demented puzzle rattling around in his head began to fall into place. He ripped the page from the phone book and stuffed it in his pocket.

"What's that, Virg?"

"Never you mind. I'll tell you later. Let's go." They left the old house, climbed into the Packard, and headed for Lockhart—their destination, the Comfy Corner Bar.

Once seated at the bar, Virgil withdrew the yellow page from his pocket and re-read the address. "2300 Oliver Avenue—Minneapolis."

"Huh? What's that, Virg?" Lenny turned to look at his friend.

Pisant didn't reply. He had to check something out. He stomped to the back of the bar and lifted the pay phone receiver off its cradle. He plopped in a few coins, studied his piece of paper and dialed. He didn't speak, but he had an evil grin on his face when he returned to the bar. He stared at the scrap of paper for over two minutes, and then said, "I ever tell ya about when I went out for football back in high school?"

Lenny looked at his friend. "Nope. Didn't know you did."

"You didn't live around here back then, but another friend of mine told me that if I ever wanted to get close to this little cheerleader—cute blonde doll—I had to join the football team. So I did . . . my junior year."

"Yeah . . . so?"

"Well, I wasn't nearly as big back then . . . didn't really grow much 'til my senior year." He paused to rotate his head and flex his thick neck as he straightened on the bar stool. A large man with an over-sized, pumpkin-shaped head, he kept his well-greased hair swept back into a ducktail. The long hair failed to conceal two very small ears, one of which—the left, was missing its lobe—the result of a bloody fight with a larger boy back in grade school. The ear looked like a dried, shrunken apricot. Now, his brown, ferret-like eyes scanned the bar looking for the bartender.

"Anyway, I signed up, and they gave me a bunch of pads and stuff to put on." Virgil looked for the bartender. "Hey! We're gettin' kinda dry down here, Mal!"

Pisant waited for the beer to arrive before continuing. "Anyway, I heads out to the practice field at the old high school on the hill and the dumb-ass coach looks at me and says, 'Linebacker!'"

"Supposed to be pretty big to play linebacker, ain't ya Virg?"

"I guess. Anyway, coach shows me where to stand, and the next thing I know this little guy comes bustin' through the line carryin' the ball . . . headed right for me."

"What'd ya do, Virg?"

Pisant took a long pull on the Grain Belt and said, "What ya think I did, stupid? I stuck my leg out, pounced on the guy, and slammed my fist in his mouth. Knocked out two teeth! Blood all over the place." Pisant chuckled at the memory.

"Wow! You musta really clobbered the guy good, Virg."

"Yep!" Pisant studied his reflection in the bar mirror. The slight smile was soon replaced by a dark glower. "Next thing I know, that piece of turd coach is all over my ass . . . screaming about a cheap shot or somthin'."

"What'd ya do?"

"Nothin.' Jest stood there for a while until the next play. I see the coach huddlin' up with the other guys and he's pointin' at me to one of his all-stars. I can see 'em all laughin' like crazy, and one a the bigger guys calls out, 'Hey, Pisant! Better keep yer head up!'

"So the ball gets hiked, there's a big hole in the line, and some other guy comes running at me with the ball."

"What happened?"

"Don't know. I was told later that some big hero in the line pulled out and hit me from the side—never saw him coming." Pisant fingered his nose. "Broke my nose in two places and knocked me out. When I woke up, I had a headache that wouldn't quit, but I wasn't going to let that piece of shit run me off." Virgil fingered the dent in his forehead and remained silent.

Lenny had consumed a sufficient quantity of beer by now to screw up enough courage to ask, "Say, Virg? Ya never tol' me how ya got that, uh . . ." he pointed at Pisant's forehead, and continued, "that dent up there?"

Virgil dropped his hand and closed his eyes. He took a long pull from the beer bottle, belched, and replied, "A bitch cow my old man wouldn't get rid of did it."

"No, kiddin'? How old were ya?"

"I dunno, six, I guess. It was that damned Gypsy—old man's favorite cow—hated milkin' those damn cows . . . old man said I shoulda listened to him about not comin' up on her from the rear. What the hell, Lenny. I was only six fer crying out loud!"

"So . . . she kicked ya?"

"Yeah. I dropped the milk pail, I guess. Scared the crap outta her. And when I bent to pick it up, that's when she clipped me." Virgil fingered the old wound once again.

"So, what happened?"

"Don't remember much. I was outta it for eight—nine days. Guess my head was all swole up. Doctors had to drill a hole to let summa the fluid out." He pointed to a spot on the side of his head. "Right here's where they bore a hole in me like they was gonna tap a maple tree."

"Cripes, Virg! You're lucky to be alive, ain't ya?"

"Yeah, I guess." Pisant waved at the bartender for more beer, and continued, "Old man blamed me for everything after that."

"Whatta ya mean?"

"Dumb ass di'n't have no insurance! Whatta ya think over a month in the hospital costs?"

"Dunno. A buncha dough, I guess."

"Yeah—more than the old man made in a lifetime. He never could get outta the hole after that. Blamed me for everything—as if I wanted to git kicked by that bitch, Gypsy!" Pisant's face flushed and his voice rose as his anger mounted. "Hated those damn cows! Guess I finally got even, though."

"Why? Whatta ya mean, Virg?"

Pisant chugged the remainder of his beer and said, "Nothin'. Never mind. Anyway, the doc said I had to be careful about getting' whacked in the head after that. Shouldn't have gone out for football, that's for sure." Two fresh beers arrived.

Now he shook his head, and continued. "After that guy blind-sided me, I remember being dizzy as hell and sick to my stomach . . . shoulda left the field . . . coach shoulda taken me out. But he left me in there so the all-star and his buddies could keep whackin' on me."

"Geez, Virg! Are you sayin' this was the same guy from today—from last night?"

Virgil nodded his big head. "Always promised myself I'd get that sonofabitch. And now the guy walks back into my life a drunken slob—God hands him to me on a platter, so to speak." He reached in his pocket and pulled out a seven-inch switchblade.

"Virg?"

"Huh? Oh. Yeah. Same guy. Fearless Frankie Nash. Big shot senior—All State in football and all that crud. And, guess what?"

"What?"

"He's the same guy ran us off the road . . . same guy sucker punched me and took those shots at us." Virgil's voice lowered in a threatening tone.

"No kiddin'? Really? The same guy?"

"Yep."

"Why didn't ya git him back then, Virg?"

"Well, had to let my nose heal. Then got in some trouble and got kicked outta school that winter. Left town for a while with some guys."

"Still, musta had a chance to git him sometime . . ."

"Shut up, Lenny! Don't ya think I planned on gittin' him? Problem was, before I could, he goes off to college—on some big football scholarship—and that summer I git caught hot-wiring a Studebaker. Got hauled to court, and the judge says, 'You got two choices: join the Army or it's JD Hall in Glenwood for a year.' Old man hauled my ass into Minneapolis to the recruiting station and signed me up for a four-year hitch. Bastard!"

The small bar was filling with locals who dropped in for a cold beer before returning to their afternoon chores. The bartender leaned over the bar at the far end—talking to a couple of farmers.

"Hey, Mal! How about takin' care of yer paying customers down here instead a chattin' up those ladies down there!" Virgil yelled, holding his empty bottle high and twitching it back and forth.

The bartender said something to his friends and walked down the length of the bar. "Shut your mouth, 'Piss Ant.' I don't need any trouble from you today."

If there was any one thing that was guaranteed to send Virgil into a rage over the years, it was being called Piss Ant. "Go to hell, Mal! Give us a couple more! Then you can go back to those ladies down there that smell like pig crap. But, you call me that once more, and you and I are going to go at it, Mal. And I don't think yer club is big enough to slow me down."

Mal reached down and fingered the baseball bat beneath the bar, but resisted the temptation to use it. He'd seen Pisant in action before and didn't relish having to deal with the man on a Saturday evening. Instead, he slid open the cooler and pulled out two more Grain Belts. He snapped the caps and slammed both on the bar. "I don't want any trouble, Virgil . . . understand?" He stared up at the larger man.

Virgil's face reddened as he drew the bottle to his lips. His eyebrows dropped and met. He set down his beer and placed both hands on the bar. Other conversations ceased—the tension was palpable. Just as Pisant readied to launch himself over and grab Mal by the shirt, a voice behind him said, "You causin' trouble again, Piss Ant?"

Without turning, Virgil knew who had spoken. He studied the image in the mirror.

"Asked you a question, Piss Ant. You and the Weasel gonna give me the opportunity to throw you in jail again?"

Virgil eased back into his seat.

The bartender relaxed, seeing the big man behind Virgil. Tensions eased. "It's okay, Sheriff. Me and Virgil here was just having a few words, is all." Mal said.

Virgil was big at six-foot-one and a hundred and ninety pounds, but Sheriff Gil McIlheny dwarfed him at six-foot-four, and he weighed a very muscular two hundred and forty pounds. No one in their right mind ever messed with the sheriff. Ever since grade school, Virgil and Gil had been adversaries. If there was any one person responsible for Virgil's hated nickname—"Piss Ant," it was Gil McIlheny.

"What happened to your face, Piss Ant? You're a mess—eye all discolored and lip puffed up. Decided to fight someone yer own size for a change?"

Virgil fingered his swollen lip but didn't reply.

"How many beers you had, Piss Ant?" McIlheny asked.

Virgil took a deep breath, settled back on the vinyl stool and replied, "Jest a couple, Gil. Me an' Lenny was jest about to leave."

Sheriff McIlheny had arrested Virgil more than once over the years—first for car theft, then cruelty to animals from repeated cock fights held at the Pisant farm, and finally for beating up a girlfriend two years earlier. "Ya know, Piss Ant, all it takes is one more offense, and they're gonna lock you up for good. Nothin' I'd like better than to be the one sends you off to Stillwater for ten years or so."

"We ain't done nothin', Sheriff. Ya got no right bustin' our ass like this. We ain't done nothin'."

"That so? Seems to me that if I was to ask most of the good citizens around here who they'd most like to see disappear for good—it'd be you and the Weasel. Now finish your beer and git the hell outta here." McIlheny removed his short-brimmed duty cap, brushed a meaty hand through his short-cropped, graying hair, and adjusted his Sam Browne belt a notch higher. The gun on his hip creaked in its holster.

"You hear me, Piss Ant?"

"You don't have to call me that, Gil," Virgil replied, his voice low.

"Why not? Everyone else does!"

"Not to my face, they don't," Virgil replied with head bowed.

"What's that? What'd you say? That's yer name, ain't it? Oh yeah, I almost forgot . . ." A broad smile plastered his face as McIlheny moved clos-

74

er to the bar. He rested one elbow on the worn mahogany, and looked sideways at Virgil. In a voice meant to include anyone near, he said, "I ever tell ya about the time ol' Virgil here tried to change the spelling of his name, Mal?"

"Nope. Don't believe I heard about that, Gil," Mal replied, now enjoying Pisant's discomfort.

"Seems like it was what, Virg, fourth or fifth grade? Right after you came back from the hospital . . . after that old bossy kicked ya in the head. Yep, Virg tried to convince everyone that his name was spelled with a Z instead of an S. What a dumb ass!" McIlheny laughed and poked Virgil in the ribs.

Virgil was visibly enraged at the memory. He rose to leave—having heard enough.

McIlheny pushed him back down. "Stay awhile, Virg. I'm jest gettin' to the best part!"

Pisant lowered himself and focused on the flashing Grain Belt Beer sign over the mirror.

"So, here's this pathetic little kid with a big dent in his forehead . . . actually I think that old cow kinda scrambled yer brains, Virg, but that's another story. Anyway, Mal, he tries to change the spelling of his name on all his schoolwork, but the teacher won't let him. She finally gits fed up and writes his name in big letters on the blackboard—PISANT."

"What happened?" Mal asked.

"All hell broke loose, is what! Piss Ant tips over his desk in the back row . . . scatters stuff all over the place and runs to the front of the room. He was kind of a runt back then, but grabs an erasure and jumps up to scrub off his name. Teacher gives him a lick along side his head, and he hauls off and kicks her in the shin. She goes down like she's been pole-axed." McIlheny howled at his description.

"Come on, Lenny. Let's git," Virgil said.

"Not so fast, Piss Ant." The sheriff said, his tone instantly dark. He placed a heavy hand on Virgil's shoulder and pushed him down. "I haven't finished my story. Ole' Virg was suspended for two weeks, Mal, and the teacher had to use a crutch for a month. Lordy, you were a piece of work, Piss Ant." The sheriff and bartender chuckled as Virgil's face turned purple.

"Leave it alone, Gil. I mean it!" Virgil said through clenched teeth.

The sheriff became all business again. "What's that, Piss Ant? Jest give me an excuse to haul you in. I'd like nothing better."

Virgil dismissed the sheriff with a wave of his hand and chugged what was left of his beer. "We ain't doin' nothin' wrong. We're almost done." Virgil turned back to Lenny.

Sheriff McIlheny sauntered down to the far end of the bar where he could watch the pair from a distance.

Virgil drew a deep breath and turned to Lenny. "Where was I? Oh yeah, so I got shipped off to boot camp at Fort Leonard Wood for basic . . . then to Fort Dix. Never forgot about Nash, though."

"Why di'n't ya come back here after the Army, Virg?"

"Oh, me and a couple guys cooked up a neat little play that made us a lot of money. Besides, couldn't stand the old man, hated the cows, and knew that sooner or later, I'd run into Nash again. And guess what? I did." Virgil smiled, exposing a row of discolored teeth.

Lenny was afraid to ask his friend about his next move, but knew he should. "So . . . uh, what's next, Virg?"

"Ever see me skin a coon, Lenny?" Pisant snapped open the blade beneath the bar for Lenny to see.

"Yeah, but hell, Virg, you don't mean yer gonna . . . ?"

"What do you think, pea brain?" His voice dropped and he continued, "Besides, wouldn't be the first time . . ."

"What's that, Virg?"

"Never you mind. Finish yer beer while I take a leak. Then we're gonna git the hell outta this dump. Pay Mal, Lenny. I'll get ya back later." Virgil slid from the stool and headed for the bathroom.

When he returned, he and Lenny walked slowly toward the door.

"Hey, Piss Ant," Sheriff McIlheny called.

The pair stopped and turned to face Gil. "Yeah, what now?" Virgil asked.

"Better let the Weasel drive, Piss Ant. Looks to me like you had a few too many." McIlheny stared at both, waiting for a reply.

Virgil nudged Lenny, and they left without saying a word. But Virgil was thinking, *I'm gonna git all these bastards . . . sooner or later. First on my list is the hero.*

Pisant tossed the keys to his friend. "Here, you drive for a while, Lenny."

"Where we goin', Virg?"

"The farm. We're gonna get something to eat and pack the car. Might be gone for a while." He glanced at the large fresh dent in the old Packard. *Damn you, All-State! You not only ruined my car, you tried to kill me too! I'll get you for that! And soon!*

He slammed the door so hard the rear view mirror rattled. "Come on! Let's go!"

PART TWO

Leaving Home

Nine

CHARLIE DIDN'T SLEEP VERY WELL that Saturday night. His parents' loud voices kept intruding. Even with his door shut, their angry words drifted from the kitchen below and eventually from the bedroom across the hall. His mother and father fought continuously for over two hours while Charlie wept.

The boy woke early. Taffy had her head on his pillow and watched her friend sit up and knead sleep and fog from his swollen eyes.

A chilly breeze slipped beneath the cracked window on the south wall of his bedroom. The model airplanes hanging above his bed slowly rotated on thin threads of fishing line. Charlie knew he had to get up, but he didn't want to. He felt safe in bed. The airplanes overhead spun and waved in the early morning light. *Wish I could fly away in one of those and never come back,* he thought.

With great reluctance, he flipped back the covers and left the warm bed. He dressed hurriedly and went downstairs. After he let Taffy out for her morning pee, Charlie fixed a bowl of cereal for himself and fed his dog. By the time he finished, his mother slipped quietly into the kitchen. Charlie looked up and noticed her reddened eyes. "Mom?"

"It's okay, Charlie." But her voice trembled, and her words failed to convince the boy that she was anything but distraught and frightened.

Charlie glanced at the doorway to be sure his father wasn't coming in before he asked, "What's gonna happen, Mom?"

His mother took a deep breath, wrapped her robe tightly, straightened a stray strand of auburn hair, and replied, "Oh, I don't know, Charlie. You father knows he made a mistake last night and he's . . . well, he's promised that—" She never finished the sentence, for at that moment her husband's shadow loomed in the doorway.

Frank glowered at his wife, leaned against the door jamb, and asked, "What are you two yappin' about?"

Charlie knew from previous episodes that the morning after was possibly the worst time for his father. It was always best to remain quiet and slip away at the earliest opportunity. That Sunday morning proved to be no exception.

Charlie didn't dare look at his father. Instead, he rose from the small table, picked up his cereal bowl, and stepped towards the sink. Just as he was about to lay the bowl down, his father reached out and grabbed his arm. The bowl slipped from Charlie's fingers and dropped into the cast iron sink. It shattered on impact and pieces of china rattled around the sink basin.

"And you, you little twerp! You were supposed to keep me awake last night, weren't ya?" He shook Charlie's arm roughly. The boy's slight frame vibrated. His teeth rattled, and his head threatened to break from his skinny neck and fly across the kitchen.

"Frank, don't! It wasn't his fault and you know it! Leave him alone. I mean it!"

The diminutive woman stepped between her son and husband and pried Frank's large hand from Charlie's arm. She bent her head back and looked up at her husband. "What's the matter with you? Haven't you done enough?"

"Aw, be quiet. Kid knows he messed up . . . don't ya?" Frank raised his arm as if preparing to smack the boy.

Charlie stepped back quickly and slid around the edge of the counter—well out of range. Taffy rose from beneath the table and trotted to

Charlie's side. She nosed his hand and licked him gently. Charlie couldn't help what happened next. He was beaten down and completely drained. Tears welled up and slipped down his reddened cheeks.

His father brushed past the boy and reached for an upper cabinet door. "Git outa the way!" He withdrew a bottle and went to the refrigerator.

"Frank, don't. Please?"

Without acknowledging his wife's plea, he pulled out a quart bottle of milk, stepped to another cabinet for a glass, and mixed the amber fluid with a shot of milk. Then, without pause, he turned away from his family and downed the concoction in one long chug. After wiping his chin on the back of his robed sleeve, he replaced the whiskey bottle, slammed the glass and quart bottle on the counter top and left the kitchen.

Mother and son avoided each other's gaze, but only for a moment. Charlie went to his mother and folded into her arms. "Oh, Charlie! I'm so sorry," she said, weeping.

"That's okay, Mom." Charlie snuffled, turned and left the kitchen.

Charlie spent the balance of the morning raking leaves from the front and back yards. Once he had hauled numerous loads into a huge pile in the street, he went into the house to get a book of matches. This was the fun part of his chore—lighting the fire. He loved the smell of burning leaves, and being something of a firebug, he enjoyed poking around in the ashes and creating trails of burning leaves over the tarmac.

A gust of wind blew against the smoking pile. Charlie coughed and turned away. New flames shot up as more leaves were exposed from within the smoldering pile. Charlie stared intently—lost in the moment of flickering flames. As suddenly as the flames erupted, they died and the pile returned to a smoking heap. The brief flare-up served as a reminder to the boy about his almost-made decision. He had to gather up the items needed so he'd be prepared to move on short notice.

After he gave the ash pile one last sweep with the steel tines, the pile exploded into the street. Each minute piece of ash soon died and blew down Oliver in the October breeze. Charlie called to Taffy, who was busy stalking a gray squirrel next door in the Bowmans' yard, and then walked past the house down the short driveway to the garage.

"Charlie! Where are you?" his mother called. "I've got to drive your father to the train station."

"I'm out in back, Mom. I'll be in, in a second."

When he arrived in the kitchen, his mother explained that his dad had to leave on a long business trip that very day. Charlie was to spend the afternoon at his grandmother's house, six blocks away. He looked forward to spending time with her—she was always comforting, and they had great fun playing cards and going down to the tracks to watch the steam and diesel engines in the train yard.

"Come on, Taff! Let's go, girl." Charlie was anxious to leave and would not go out of his way to say goodbye to his father.

CHARLIE SPENT SUNDAY AFTERNOON at his grandmother's house, returning home at 6:00 P.M. After he and his mother ate a quiet dinner, Charlie took Taffy for a walk up and down the block. It was a warm evening—unusual, but consistent with the warm weather Minnesotans had experienced over the previous three months. The drought had brought down curled leaves from the deciduous trees much earlier than normal, but residents didn't complain as the uncharacteristic warmth delayed the bitter cold of winter.

Charlie returned home in time for the start of the Ed Sullivan Show.

"Would you like some popcorn, Charlie?" Marsha Nash asked.

"Sure, Mom," Charlie replied as he kneeled in front of the twelve-inch Admiral console. He flipped on the power and waited for the small screen to light up.

Marsha came back into the large living room with a tray containing two bowls of popped corn and two large glasses of milk. "Here you go, Charlie."

The boy rose, retrieved his bowl and milk, and sat cross-legged in front of the television. A grainy, black-and-white image appeared of the host. Sullivan was in the midst of introducing his first entertainer, a young rock and roll singer named Elvis Presley. Mother and son watched and listened—occasionally giggling at the weird gyrations on the screen. At the Nash house, important discussions were seldom, if ever, pursued—especially if the topic was at all emotional. Together, mother and son avoided the one topic foremost on each of their minds and, instead, watched the young singer in relative silence until he was done singing a song called "Blue Suede Shoes."

"I don't think that young man has much of a future, do you, Charlie?" Marsha asked.

"Huh? Oh. Yeah, I guess not, Mom. I've heard some of the older girls say they think he's pretty cool, though."

"Really? I can't imagine what they see in him. I think he's quite repulsive."

Elvis was followed by a brief skit from Abbott and Costello. Charlie normally would have laughed out loud at their silliness, but he wasn't in the mood. When the show was finished, Charlie rose, took the tray with bowls and glasses to the kitchen and returned to the living room.

"I'm going to bed now, Mom." He leaned over and kissed his mother.

"Don't forget to take a bath first, okay, Charlie?"

"I will. Good night."

"Good night, Charlie. Sweet dreams."

Charlie whistled for Taffy and climbed the stairs to his bedroom. As was his custom, he counted each step, eight on the first rise, six on the second around the corner. With three bedrooms and two baths upstairs, a den where the family business operated, and a full attic, the house was generous by 1955 standards and similar to others in the Lake of the Isles neighborhood in Minneapolis.

He went into the bathroom and turned on the water to fill the tub. He closed the door, quickly undressed, and checked in the mirror to see if a few early sprouts had miraculously appeared under either arm. Peering closely, on tiptoes, Charlie looked for some, any, sign of growth of hair on his chin or upper lip. Failing to spot even a single sprout, he made a face, and looked down at the other area of concern—his diminutive boyhood. What he saw looked anything but what he continually hoped for.

Charlie envied those of his friends who proudly displayed their first, dark curls of pending manhood. Unfortunately, it wasn't his time just yet, and he wasn't too sure when it would be. Somehow God, or Nature, or both, had dealt him a cruel blow—at least for the time being. Still, he was disappointed. *Maybe next month. Sure wish it'd hurry up, though.*

He slipped into the warm water and lay back—almost totally submerged. The warmth felt good. The tub always had a soothing, safe feeling for him, and, as was his custom, Charlie soaked until the water chilled. Taffy lay on the mat next to the tub—familiar with her master's routine. Finally, Charlie rose, quickly soaped, rinsed, and pulled the plug. He dried himself, slipped on his pajamas, and went into the bedroom.

Without intending to, he allowed himself a brief moment to consider what had transpired over the weekend. Saddened and worried, he hugged Taffy tightly.

Within minutes, having made up his mind to leave home, he was fast asleep. Taffy curled tightly next to him—his only ready source of comfort and relief. With her head on Charlie's pillow, the retriever's breathing matched the boy's. The big house was quiet—blessedly so.

THE FOLLOWING MORNING, Monday, Taffy thumped her tawny tail against Charlie's leg, rolled over, and licked his cheek. The brief movement of outside air across the room reached her nostrils—carrying with it perhaps the faint scent of one of the resident bunnies in the bushes near the house. "Hi, girl. Guess we better get moving, huh?"

The eleven-year-old boy threw back the covers and quickly dressed. Even though the autumn temperatures had been unusually warm, Charlie shivered as he stepped from his small bed. He was late and had to get moving. He didn't want customers calling to complain about their paper being late. Breakfast, as always, would wait until he finished delivering the sixty-nine papers on his route. Taffy led the way downstairs to the front hall. Charlie threw on a light jacket, his New York Yankees cap, picked up the paper sack, and quietly opened the door. Taffy slipped out ahead of him on to the porch.

NEITHER BOY NOR DOG noticed the car parked across the street. It sat in front of the neighbor's house, up the slight incline of the street. The dark blue, 1949 Packard coupe sat beneath the towering elm trees on Oliver Avenue. At first glance, it appeared to be just another automobile nudged against the curb on the quiet Kenwood street. Unlike the other cars parked up and down the curved pavement, however, the Packard was not empty.

Two figures slouched against the worn fabric of the front seat. The small man on the passenger side was asleep. Mouth open, lips twitching like a beached pickerel, he was snoring loudly. A larger man, fully awake behind the wheel, was rubbing one large hand against the other methodically—over and over, palm against palm, as if attempting to wipe away some evil stain or foul substance. His head turned to the side, and he fixed his gaze on the boy as he left his house.

"Lenny! Hey, Lenny! Wake up!" Virgil Pisant turned back and poked a heavy elbow in the other man's ribs.

"Umph . . . what the hell, Virgil! What'd ya do that for?"

"Quiet! A kid jest came out!" Virgil's voice lowered to a whisper.

Two pairs of sleep-deprived eyes followed the boy and small dog. The first rays of dawn provided just enough light for the two men to observe the activity outside the front porch, but the interior of the beat-up coupe remained in deep shadows. A small golden retriever bounded out and immediately squatted. Following close behind was a small boy. The two men watched as the boy climbed onto his bike and pedaled away from the darkened house, down the sidewalk in front.

"Nuts! It's just a kid," Virgil muttered.

"Where's he goin' so damn early, Virg?"

The big man behind the wheel rubbed two fingers across the dent high on his forehead. "See the canvas bag he's totin'? Kid's gotta paper route," Virgil whispered.

"Start the car, will ya, Virg? I'm freezin' my ass off here. Why don't we jest go home and fergit this whole thing, anyway? This is crazy."

"Shut yer pie hole, Lenny. I'm tired a listening to you whine. That big Buick is still in the garage. Besides, ain't time to go to work yet." From their vantage point, the men could not only spot anyone coming or going from the front door, but they had a clear view down the driveway next to the house directly to the garage in back.

"I'm gettin' hungry, Virg. How long we gonna wait, anyway?"

"Until we grab him, that's how long." Virgil started the car and let it idle in neutral.

"What if he don't show? Then what—huh, Virg?"

Pisant stared after the retreating boy and dog. "Don't really matter, Lenny. I have another plan that's guaranteed to draw him out—one way or another." A cruel smile formed as Pisant watched the boy pedal down the darkened street. As quickly as the smile appeared—it vanished. The big man fingered his swollen upper lip, and then carefully wiggled two loose teeth. *I'll make that sonofabitch pay!* He gripped the worn steering wheel with a vise-like grip—bending and pulling the wheel toward him.

AFTER TAFFY BOUNDED out the door, Charlie boarded his shiny black Schwinn Phantom. He had purchased the bike that summer with money earned from his paper route. Charlie was proud of the bike and was the envy of the neighborhood.

The boy pedaled down the sidewalk with his dog loping next to him. Before long, she found a convenient spot for her morning dump, spun once, and did her business. Charlie stopped to wait. *Hope Mrs. Watson doesn't step in that. Have to remember not to hit that pile with my bike.* Charlie concluded that the neighbor would more than likely blame the black lab from across the street—leaving Taffy guilt free. They continued down the block scattering dry elm leaves on the concrete sidewalk. Once they reached the corner, he stopped next to the two wired bundles containing the October 7th, 1955, edition of the *Minneapolis Tribune*. With a practiced move, Charlie withdrew a pair of pliers from the sack and twisted the wire back and forth repeatedly until the wire snapped.

Charlie knelt down and began folding each paper into thirds, then tucking one end into the other to form a perfect rectangle. This was the boy's third route in as many years, and he finally had garnered enough seniority to select a much sought-after delivery route that included three blocks around his own home—Newton Avenue, Lake of the Isles Boulevard, and his own street, Oliver Avenue. He was an accomplished paper boy who prided himself on getting the morning paper to his customers early enough to be read at the breakfast table. Charlie often thought he could almost deliver the papers blind-folded—imagining himself as a fully-masked Lone Ranger who had to finish his deliveries within forty-five minutes or his sidekick, Tonto, would be killed by a gang of thieves.

Charlie Nash was proud of the letters of excellence he received from his district manager. Form letters, each spoke of "An absence of complaints during the period, February-July, 1955." He made certain that each letter of commendation was placed where his father couldn't miss seeing them. Regrettably, the letters went unnoticed.

The small boy sped up and down each block pitching papers to each doorstep with deliberate skill and accuracy. Only in a few instances did he have to dismount and climb steps to reach a convenient throwing distance. As long as the weather was decent, as long as there was no snow on the ground, as long as he could whip around on his Schwinn, the papers were normally delivered within forty-five minutes.

He had to get moving now, however. He was late and knew he had to make up time. He loaded the sack with half the papers and took off. Within twenty minutes, the bag was empty, and he was back at the corner to fold and load the second half. Taffy was panting as Charlie skidded to a stop, kicked down the stand, and climbed off the bike. The sun crept above the horizon, and the first rays poked through the giant elms. The air was dry, but nonetheless, a sour, pungent odor of fallen leaves blended with the stale smell of ash piles scattered up and down the street permeated the neighborhood.

Charlie knelt once more to twist the wire from the second bundle. After numerous twists, the wire snapped—one sharp end smacked his cheek. "Ow! Darn it, that hurt." He rubbed the sore spot and as he withdrew his fingers, noticed blood on the tips. "Nuts." He took the corner of his jacket collar and pressed it against the wound. Waiting patiently for the bleeding to cease, he glanced down at the front page of the *Tribune*.

He scanned the page in the brightening morning light and was just about ready to fold it up when an article in the lower right corner caught his eye. He unfolded the paper, turned to catch more of the morning light, and pulled the paper closer to his face. *Oh, no!*

He read the article—each harsh word committed to memory like ugly black flies to a sticky fly strip. A drop of blood crept down the boy's cheek and traced a bright crimson line to the edge of his jaw. The paper slipped from his fingers and plopped on top of the pile.

His head pounded. Tears formed in each eye, then broke loose from his long, blond lashes and fell to the paper below. His knees weakened. He stared at each droplet, some pale red, as they blotted and blurred the newsprint.

He bent, picked up the paper, and read the article three times to make certain he wasn't mistaken. There it was, right in the paper where all his friends would see it. He knew how cruel kids could be—especially after years of listening to his bragging. "It's all my fault," Charlie sobbed.

He dropped to both knees and hugged Taffy tightly.

In a daze of confusion and sorrow, Charlie finished folding and packing the remaining papers. He climbed on his bike with the sack over one shoulder, and set off to finish his deliveries. The words that shouted from the front page of the paper scrambled through his head. Scarcely aware of his movements, he tossed each paper with little energy. Many never reached the top step. Charlie finally finished and returned home.

Once he reached his house—the house he grew up in, the house he loved, the house that until recently represented all that was safe and secure, the house he would soon leave—he dropped the Schwinn on the walk with a loud, *clang!* Charlie trudged, head bowed, to the front door. Taffy darted through the opening. The last copy of the morning *Tribune* clutched tightly in one small hand, Charlie trembled as he entered the house.

Across the street, Virgil and Lenny watched the boy and dog enter the house. Neither moved as the green door closed.

It was 6:45 A.M. Charlie could smell bacon cooking in the kitchen. *Mom's up.* He removed his jacket and hung it on the brass hook behind the door. He tossed his baseball cap onto the hall table. On any other morning, Charlie would have welcomed the chance for a private breakfast with his mother—but not this morning. Charlie took a deep breath and entered the kitchen.

"Hi, Charlie. Everything go all right this morning?" His mother wiped her hands on the apron front, turned and waited for a reply. "Charlie? You're crying! And . . . your cheek's bleeding! Honey, what happened?"

The small boy held out the paper without saying a word. He thrust it in her direction as if he were holding a dead rat—his deep-blue eyes searched her face.

She reached for a tissue and approached her son. "Here, let me see your cheek."

Charlie twisted away and jabbed the paper at her again.

"What's this?" Marsha reached for the paper, took one look at the top half, and glanced back to her son. "What? What about it?" She flipped the paper over and scanned the lower half. With trembling fingers, she touched a couple of loose curlers on the side of her head. Marsha inhaled sharply as she spotted the particular news story that she too would dread reading. She pulled out a metal, vinyl covered chair and sat down at the kitchen table. Charlie slid on to the bench seat across from her, his chin resting in both hands. Neither mother nor son said a word as she read the entire story.

When she had finished and looked in the boy's direction, he said, "Mom . . . you . . . lied to me. You said you took him to the train station yesterday . . . that he was going out of town on a long business trip."

Marsha Nash assumed the stoic demeanor that had been both her salvation and curse for the past two years. She rose from her chair and slid onto the bench next to her son. She cradled his head against her small chest and rocked back and forth. "Oh, Charlie. I'm so sorry, sweetheart."

"Why didn't you tell me the truth, Mom?"

"I'm so sorry you had to find out like this, Charlie. We both felt that . . . well, that you had been through enough . . . that it would be better if you thought your dad was away on business."

Charlie moved away from his mother, wiped his eyes with the back of one sleeve, and said, "It's my fault, isn't it, Mom?"

"No, Charlie! You can't blame yourself. What happened to your father had nothing to do with you. He's sick, Charlie, and needs help. Maybe now he'll have time to think about . . . well, time to think about all the mistakes he's made."

To Charlie, his eleventh birthday celebration—the excitement and anticipation of the weekend past—seemed only a distant memory. In spite of his mother's reassuring words, the boy was convinced that he was at fault. And that his father would never forgive him.

OUTSIDE, ONE OF THE TWO MEN in the Packard was losing patience. Lenny yawned and squirmed against the rough fabric of the seat. "My ass is asleep, Virg."

Virgil ran two hands back through his heavy, greasy ducktail. He swept the long hair on each side back behind both ears—then tucked the ends between the backs of all eight fingers and drew a line down from top to bottom. His coal-black hair shimmered and glistened with an over abundance of Brylcreem. He cracked his knuckles and said, "We'll wait another hour, then go grab a paper and pick up a bag of donuts."

Virgil had already decided that if his target failed to appear, the boy would have to suffice. In fact, he now believed that the boy would not only provide the needed bait to lure his quarry out, but enhance his ultimate, desired, demented retribution.

CHARLIE LEFT HIS MOTHER alone in the kitchen and went upstairs to get ready for school. Having made up his mind, he was already planning on what he had to do to get ready to leave. He climbed the stairs to his bedroom and closed the door. He went directly to the closet. Inside, beyond the clothes pole, was a series of shallow steps leading to an elevated platform. This was his private retreat. At the base of the far wall, hidden behind stacks and stacks of comic books, was a small door that opened into a cubby hole beyond. He quickly cleared away the comics, pushed the door open, and reached inside.

In a red hatbox was all that Charlie held dear: including his paper route money which he kept in a Prince Albert can, Taffy's AKC registration, his father's gold 1935 Championship miniature football, Cub Scout badges, his most valuable comic books, an autographed picture of Hopalong Cassidy, a baseball he had caught at a Minneapolis Millers game signed by the player who hit the home run—a player his father said would be a star someday—Willie Mays—and a small penny collection given to him by his Great Uncle Hedwig. He cradled the hatbox, closed the door and climbed back down the steps.

On his unmade bed, he lifted open the cover and carefully removed the contents. As he handled and considered each item, he, ultimately, was drawn to the coin collection. Pushing the other objects aside, he opened the cardboard packet and studied the coins within. An envelope with his name penned on the front fell onto the spread. Charlie ran his fingers over its surface, all the while thinking of the very major decision he had made.

Convinced his father not only hated him for what happened Saturday night, he also knew that Frank Nash would never change—would never forgive him for what had happened or stop his drinking.

Truly saddened by the prospect of leaving everything he knew behind, he opened the envelope and began reading his uncle Hedwig's letter. Soon, comforting words from a once close, now deceased relative, filled his head.

Ten

CHARLIE HATED THE THOUGHT of going to school that Monday, but he knew he had to. His plan depended on everything appearing as normal as possible. He carefully wrapped his coin collection in a paper bag and placed it with his school books. He tucked the letter sent by his great uncle Hedwig in his shirt pocket and ran downstairs.

"Mom? I'm going to school now," Charlie called.

Marsha Nash hung up the phone and came from the kitchen. She had been crying.

"Mom? Are you okay?"

"I'm fine, Charlie. Just feeling kind of mopey this morning. You better get going . . . don't want to be late. Here's your lunch, son."

"Thanks, Mom."

"Remember what I said . . . if any of your classmates say anything about the article in the paper—just ignore them, all right? Kids can be pretty cruel, but remember, 'sticks and stones,' right?"

"Sure, Mom." Charlie knew that some of the kids at school would have been told about the article, but he had no choice but to face the music. "Oh, is it okay if I go downtown after school?"

"What for, Charlie?"

"Uh, I want to show my coin collection to the man Uncle Hedwig told me about."

Marsha hesitated, puzzled by her son's request. "Sure, I guess so. Be sure you're home by supper, though."

"I will." He took the lunch, reached up to kiss his mother, gave Taffy a pat, and left the house.

❖ ● ❖

ACROSS THE STREET, Virgil and Lenny watched the small boy leave.

"Kid's leavin'," Pisant muttered.

Lenny looked up from the paper briefly, stuffed the last of a powdered sugar donut in his mouth and returned to his reading. Suddenly he sat upright and peered closely at an article on the front page of the *Minneapolis Tribune*. "Holy cow!" Pieces of donut flew from his mouth and landed on the dashboard.

"Hey! What the hell! Spit up in your own car, ya little jerk. Oh yeah, you don't own a car, I forgot."

"You ain't gonna believe this, Virg."

"What? What you reading, anyway?"

"Paper says, 'Franklin Nash, former Gopher football great—arrested. He was to report for voluntary lock-up—a sentence of up to thirty days in the county workhouse is expected Monday.'" Lenny paused to let the words sink in.

"What the hell? Lemme see that." Virgil reached over and grabbed the paper from his friend. He found the article and continued reading:

Detained Sunday night on Highway Twelve by a Minneapolis patrol car, Mr. Nash failed an on-scene sobriety test. He and his son were returning home from a hunting trip out west when stopped by the police for erratic driving. Numerous motorists had stopped to phone the police about Mr. Nash's dangerous driving, and the police finally caught up to Nash and his son just inside the city limits. Officer Norwald, the arresting officer on the scene, stated that he and his partner had observed the small boy actually steering the father's car from the back seat for a good distance before being stopped. After driving Nash and the boy home, Nash surrendered his driver's license, and the following day pleaded guilty to driving under the influence. Judge Nesbitt of Hennepin County court sentenced Nash to thirty days at the county workhouse. A particularly severe sentence, Nesbitt stated that, 'as this was not Nash's first offense, the sentence was appropriate and advisable.' Franklin Nash, a former All-American on the 1935 University of Minnesota National championship Football team was not available for comment.

"Damn, damn, damn!" Virgil threw the paper back in Lenny's face.

"Hey!" After re-folding the paper, Lenny said, "Guess we can go home now, huh, Virg?"

Pisant did not respond, but instead looked down the block at the back of Charlie Nash.

"Virg? You hear me?"

"I heard ya, and no, we ain't going home. This don't change nothin'—jest makes things a bit more complicated is all."

"What ya mean?"

"Been thinking what we'd do if the old man never showed—got a plan already formed. We'll snatch that runt kid of his and use him for trade bait."

Lenny had heard enough. "Virgil . . . look . . . you an' I been friends a long time . . . know I'd do most anything . . . but . . . a kid? No way, Virg. I don't want no part a this . . . gone too far . . . I got no stake in this."

Virgil reached over and without looking at his friend, grabbed his collar and yanked him savagely across the short distance of the front seat. "You chickening out on me, Lenny . . . you little piece of grunt?"

"Virg . . . let go! Can't breathe . . ."

Virgil released Lenny and threw him back across the car where he slammed his head against the side window.

"Ow! Geez, Virg! I don't know about you sometimes." He rubbed the side of his head. Undeterred, he continued his pleas, "Look, Virg, I know you got it in for this guy . . . probably deserves everything you want to do to him, but kidnapping kids is a capital crime! I ain't gonna be involved in this. Don't care if you beat the tar outta me, I'm done with this whole thing and if you got any sense left at all, you'll give it up too—at least until the old man gets outta the slammer."

"No way, José! Kid's jest as good as the old man. Soon's he hears I got his kid, he'll find a way out of jail and come runnin' to me to save his kid." Virgil cracked his knuckles and continued, "Then I'll cut him up into tiny pieces. Might jest do it in front of his kid. Ya, I like the sound a that." Pisant continued babbling as he started the Packard, put the big car in gear, and slipped away from the curb.

"Guess we'll take you home, then, Lenny, so's I can get about my business . . ." Virgil's eyes glazed over as he imagined how he was going to make Frank Nash pay.

CHARLIE'S DAY AT SCHOOL was a nightmare. Not only did he have to defend his father to his friends, but he was forced into fist fights with two older boys during recess. He came into the classroom in the afternoon with a bloody nose. Mrs. Witherspoon had little sympathy for the boy—especially after Friday afternoon. She hauled him into the cloakroom by the ear and shook him by the shoulders.

"You're nothing but trouble, Charles! At the rate you're proceeding, you'll turn out just like your father. I want you to sit here for fifteen minutes and ponder your behavior." She slammed the door and Charlie was left alone.

Dad will hate me for the rest of my life, Charlie thought. *It's too late, he won't forgive me. I've made up my mind. I'm running away, tomorrow . . . going to Montana! I've always dreamed about . . . about living on a ranch out west—riding horses and herding cattle will be so cool!*

AT 3:15 P.M. THE SCHOOL BELL rang for dismissal, and Charlie was one of the first to leave school. He ran down the steps to the bus stop, waiting to

catch the 3:30 bus downtown. Just as the bus arrived, a number of older boys spotted Charlie and began shouting, "Nash, Nash—his father's a drunken ASS!"

Charlie quickly entered the bus, dropped a token in the rotating machine and sat down in the back of the bus. The bus pulled away from the curb. Charlie laid his books on the seat next to him, reached in his shirt pocket, and withdrew his uncle's letter.

He opened it up. The letterhead was printed in raised script. "Hedwig Mackey. 4776 Marine Drive, Chicago, Illinois." Charlie reread the letter.

> Dear Charlie: I'll never forget the wonderful time we had fishing down at Lake of the Isles. You took the time to be with me when you could easily have left me with your grandmother to play with your friends. Thank you for your kindness.
>
> You will recall I spoke of my rather extensive coin collection begun when I was a boy about your age. Well, I want you to have a small part of my collection. It is a penny collection, Charlie. Some of the coins have, well, some value. If you develop an interest in collecting, this small collection will get you started. Learn all you can from a coin book available at the library, and keep the coins in a safe place.
>
> Someday, they will be of considerable value, but if at any time you or your family are in need, I suggest you contact a gentleman named, Leonard Massimo, a trusted friend. Show the coins to only him; Leonard will give you a fair and honest appraisal. He is one of the most reputable and honest numismatic dealers in Minneapolis. I strongly urge you to resist showing the coins to any dealer other than he. Leonard Massimo's shop is called Heritage Coin Company and is located at 1201 Harmon Place in downtown, Minneapolis. His phone number is Franklin 4- 8331.
>
> These coins have been very lucky for me over the years, Charlie, and I have every confidence they will ultimately bring you good fortune and success. Think of me when you gaze upon them, my boy.
>
> With great affection,
> Your Great Uncle Hedwig.

Charlie swallowed hard as he re-read the letter. He had only been with Hed a few times, but had enjoyed their time together more than anyone else he could think of. A wealth of stories accompanied the old man—

particularly war stories of his time in France as an ambulance driver during World War I. Charlie had been heartsick when he learned of his uncle's death the previous summer.

He recalled the last time they were together after a day catching sunnies at Lake of the Isles. Just before leaving to return to Chicago, Hed laid a hand on Charlie's shoulder and said, 'Here's hoping that as you slide down the banister of life, Charlie, the splinters are all facing the right direction.' Charlie giggled at the remembrance.

Now, he gazed down at the shiny pennies beneath the cellophane covers with sadness. *I miss Uncle Hed. I wish he was still around. I bet I could stay with him . . .*

Charlie rubbed his fingers over the coins and looked up. The bus slowed as it turned onto Hennepin Avenue. Just a few more blocks, Charlie thought. He refolded the small coin packet and slipped it carefully into his book bag along with the letter.

"Harmon Place," the driver called out. "Next stop, Harmon Place."

Charlie rose from his seat and walked carefully to the front of the bus.

"Getting out here, son?" the driver asked.

"Yes."

The bus slowed, then came to a stop. "Thank you," Charlie said and skipped down the steps to the sidewalk below. He stopped and checked out the street number. He was on Twelfth and Harmon, so he turned left and walked down the block. Before long he reached 1201 and looked up at a sign: THE HERITAGE COIN COMPANY - LEONARD MASSIMO, PROP.

Charlie hesitated, not convinced he should proceed. He peered in the window. Finally, he shrugged his shoulders and entered the coin shop. A small bell tinkled, announcing his entrance. The door closed with another tinkle. Charlie glanced at the interior of the shop in one quick look. Glass cases were lined up on either side of the central pathway. A pair of dusty brass lamps coupled with light from the front window provided the only illumination, and that wasn't much. The smell of the small shop reminded Charlie of his great grandfather's house—stale cigar smoke and the pervasive of age. He wrinkled his nose and stepped toward the high counter directly ahead.

As he approached the ancient wooden counter, he noticed a small man wearing a green shade sitting behind it, hunched over a scarred desk. A bright desk lamp shone directly above his workspace, and he was looking through a magnifying glass at something. Charlie waited for the man to look up—to acknowledge his presence.

The man had coal-black hair swept straight back and plastered to his skull—a style fashionable ten years earlier. His dark, bushy eyebrows appeared as one single line above a pair of squinty eyes. He took a fast peek above his reading glasses at the boy and returned to his work.

Charlie shifted his weight from one foot to another, laid his book bag on the counter, and coughed—politely.

Without looking up, the man behind the counter said, "Can I help you?"

"Yes . . . uh . . . I'm here to see . . . Mr. . . . uh . . . Leonard Massimo."

Again without a direct stare, the small man said, "And what would be the nature of your business, young sir?"

"Are you Mr. Massimo?"

"No, I am not. I am Seymour Wenzel—the proprietor."

Once Charlie had a close look at the man's face, he realized that his skin was the color of some of the mushrooms he learned to pick at Cub Scout camp. It was as if the man had never left the dusty shop to venture into the sunlight. "Uh, isn't this the Heritage Coin Company?" Confused by the man's reply Charlie looked around for a sign.

Wenzel laid down the large optic, covered up the coins he had been studying, and said, "It most certainly is. However, Mr. Massimo is no longer with us. He met with an . . . unfortunate accident two months ago, and I now own the Heritage Coin Company." Wenzel folded his arms and stared across the scarred counter at Charlie.

"Oh, uh . . . what happened?"

"What do you mean, 'What happened?'"

"I mean, what happened to Mr. Massimo?"

"Oh. Well, he had the misfortune to step in front of a passing freight train—no one knows why. The local police ultimately concluded that dear Leonard must have tripped. He was always a bit clumsy and absent minded, don't you know. Very tragic—very untimely." Wenzel sported a pencil-thin mustache that Charlie swore twitched as he described the grisly accident.

Charlie wanted to leave—immediately! Something about the place, the man, and his words made him uncomfortable. He had come a long way, however, and would not have the opportunity to return, so he forged ahead. He set his books on the counter and withdrew his small coin packet, set it on the counter, and opened up the letter. "I was told to show my collection to Mr. Massimo . . ." Charlie hesitated. *I suppose it's all right. If he was Mr. Massimo's partner or something . . .* He spread the letter on the counter.

Wenzel shifted his position and clucked as if he were losing patience with the boy's intrusion. He focused on the letterhead printed in bold type. "I can assure you. Uh, pardon me, but you haven't introduced yourself. You are . . . ?"

"Oh. I'm Charlie, Charlie Nash."

"A pleasure, I'm sure, Master Nash. Now, about your collection. I worked for Mr. Massimo for thirteen years—in fact I was his only trusted employee." Wenzel puffed out his invisible chest and continued, "As such, I learned a great deal from the gentleman. I can assure you with every confidence, that whatever business you intended with Mr. Massimo can certainly be conducted with me—the current proprietor. I am bonded, and my reputation is beyond reproach. Now, time's wasting, young man—what's it to be? Shall I cast an eye on your prized collection, or shall you retreat back through the same door from whence you recently passed, without availing yourself the opportunity to permit my trained eye to appraise your apparently modest packet?" Wenzel eyed the single folder. Then he raised one eyebrow, waiting for Charlie's response.

Charlie hesitated.

"Come, come, Master Charles. Be quick about it. What shall it be?"

Charlie reached for the packet, and slowly unfolded the three cardboard sections of the coin folder.

Wenzel watched with obvious disinterest. He had wasted far too much time with the boy and was anxious to return to more lucrative endeavors.

Once the contents had been revealed, Wenzel reached out and turned the coins around, "May I?"

"Yes, I guess." Charlie waited as the new proprietor studied his collection. He watched as the man's bony index finger hesitated just beneath the first two coins on the left side. Three fingers slid back and forth across the covers.

Wenzel looked at the boy sharply, then brought the bright desk lamp over to the counter. With the same hand, he reached for his large magnifying glass. His finger never left the two coins. Once the lamp was in place, he picked up the glass and bent over the coins.

Charlie's collection consisted of twenty-one pennies—all United States coins. Ever since Charlie had received the collection, he had never taken the coins out of their individual slots or their plastic covers. Most were Lincoln-head pennies in fair to excellent condition. The first two—the ones that had so captivated Wenzel, were a shiny, bright brass color. The first coin was positioned face up, Lincoln's head and shoulders facing to the right. "In God We Trust" arced across the top of the coin—the letters in relief. The word, "Liberty" appeared to the left of Lincoln's neck, and to the right, the date the coin was minted—"1943." There was no mint stamp beneath the date.

Wenzel did his best to remain calm—disinterested even—but he struggled to control his uneven breathing. His heart pounded and a thin bead of sweat broke out beneath his mustache. He gathered himself, and without daring to say a word, he reached under the counter and withdrew a thin pair of cotton gloves. "Ahem . . . an interesting little collection you have here, young man." Wenzel's voice had risen an octave from before, and he cleared his throat.

Charlie had already decided that he didn't like the man, but the dealer's obvious interest had him curious—particularly so as he watched the man study the first two coins. "Can you tell me what the collection's worth?" Charlie asked.

"Just a minute, Master Nash. I need to study the complete assortment. I can tell you that other than the first . . . ah . . . two coins here, the balance is rather pedestrian—nothing special, really. The first two Lincoln heads have . . . ah . . . captured my interest as you may have noted. Do you mind my asking where you got these?"

Wenzel removed his glasses momentarily and fixed a glazed stare at the young boy.

"Uh, my Great Uncle Hed gave them to me . . . along with this letter. I was to show them only to Mr. Massimo." Charlie needed money, as much as he could gather, but now wasn't sure he should even have shown the set to this peculiar man.

"I see, I see. And your uncle is where?"

"He died last summer."

"Oh, dear. I am sorry. Please extend my sympathies to his widow—and her name is?"

"Aunt Marie."

"Of course. Now, let's take a closer look." Wenzel replaced his glasses and looked back at the coins. He reached for the packet and as he did, spun Hed's letter so it faced in his direction. He memorized the name and address. "Mind if I remove these from their slots, Charles? I really must, you see, if I am to give them a fair and complete appraisal." Wenzel held his breath, waiting for Charlie's reply.

"No, I guess not. I've never had them out of the sleeves, though." Wenzel turned away and scribbled a note on a pad sitting on his desk. He hurried back and said, "I can assure you that I handle valuable coins frequently, young sir, hence the gloves." His retort was sharp and cutting.

Wenzel slid back the clear cover on the first coin and gently removed the coin. With great diligence, he turned it over and placed it on a piece of velvet. On the reverse side of the coin, "E Pluribus Unum" arced across the top. In the center of the coin in large letters were two words, one on top of the other: "ONE CENT." Beneath the coin's declaration of value was stamped "United States of America." And to either side were curved wheat stalks that filled out the left and right sides of the coin.

Wenzel picked up a small piece of metal and held it just over the loose coin. He waved it back and forth.

"What's that?" Charlie asked.

Wenzel remained silent. He groped for a logical response. After tossing the metal aside, he finally replied, "Oh, it's . . . uh . . . a dioptric—a common tool utilized by all numismatists." Wenzel didn't bother removing the second coin.

"What's it do?"

"Huh? Oh, it verifies metallic content—uh . . . specifically the presence of zinc and steel. A trained eye, such as mine, can detect a slight change in color on the surface of the dioptric when it . . . uh . . . senses the presence of either or both of those minerals." Without looking at the boy, Wenzel replaced the coin in its slot, slid the cover over it, and said, "Just as I feared."

Charlie was started by the dealer's tone. He tore his eyes from the dioptric and fixed his eyes on the small dealer. "What? What's the matter?"

"Well, young man, for a moment there, I thought perhaps some of these coins fell into a category we term, "Exceptional." But, alas, while in very good shape, and considering that they were from a relatively small minting, they do have some value, but not a great deal."

Wenzel removed his glasses, turned out the light, and refolded the packet. He picked it up and carried it over to his desk, as if he didn't want to let it out of his sight. He opened a book and punched some numbers into a noisy adding machine. After he had pulled the lever a final time, he leaned back in his chair. "Tell me, Master Nash. Why are you in need of funds at this point in your life? Hmmm?"

"I . . . ah . . . well, I'm going away on a trip tomorrow. I have my paper route money, but might need more. Can . . . can you tell me what the collection is worth?"

"Certainly. Because of your need, and because it's been something of a slow day, I'm prepared to offer you, ah . . . let's see . . . ." Wenzel looked at his notes. "Oh, I'd say somewhere in the neighborhood of, let's say, two hundred and fifty dollars—for the complete set."

Charlie didn't know what to say. He had no idea the coins were worth that much. He needed the money, as he only had seventy-nine dollars in his Prince Albert can, but still. . . . He reconsidered Uncle Hedwig's words of caution, "I strongly urge you to resist showing the coins . . ." Charlie was already sorry he had even opened up the packet for this strange little man.

The boy kept his eyes on the packet, which still sat on Wenzel's desk. "Uh . . . no thanks. I think I'll keep them. Could I have my coins back, please?"

Wenzel's eyes blazed. His face reddened. He had to think fast as an opportunity was about to disappear onto Harmon Place. "I'll tell you what, Master Nash. I'm feeling in a generous mood today, let's say three hundred, and we have a deal. Will that suffice?" His hand covered the packet.

"No, I don't think so. I'm sorry for taking your time, but I've decided not to sell them. I think my uncle would want me to keep them. May I have my coins back, please?" Charlie held out his hand.

Wenzel didn't want to let the coins out of his sight. *Think! Quick!* He picked up the coins and laid them in front of the boy. "Why don't you leave me your address and phone number, young man. If, perhaps I can find another, well, more motivated dealer than I, well, I could call you at a later date. How's that?"

Charlie picked up his coins and put it with his books. As he picked them up, however, the front of his notebook lay on the bottom, visible to the coin dealer. "I don't think so. I have to be going. I don't want to miss my bus."

Wenzel noticed Charlie's name, address, and phone number written on the outside of the notebook. He quickly memorized the numbers. "Very well. Good day to you, Master Nash. Take good care of your coins."

"Thank you, I will." Charlie turned and walked to the door. The bell tinkled as the door swung open, but before he could pass through the doorway, Wenzel called out to him.

"By the way, Charles, where are you going on your journey?"

Charlie stopped, spun to face the interior of the shop, located the dealer who by now was off to one side, and said, "Oh, uh . . . Montana."

"I see. Have a safe trip."

"Thank you, I will." The door closed but this time Charlie could not hear the bell. He rushed away, anxious to be out of sight of the strange coin dealer.

Inside, Seymour Wenzel immediately reached for the phone on his desk and spun the rotary. Heart pounding, he tapped his fingers nervously on the desk top with his right hand, and with his left, he opened up one of his many numismatic books—*Strobel's Definitive Book of Coins*—to the section on Lincoln head pennies. His heart pounded as he opened the book.

Charlie left the shop feeling guilty. He regretted showing his collection to the little man inside. His uncle had been specific about Charlie not showing the collection to anyone but Mr. Massimo, and, in his desperation, he felt he had violated a sacred trust.

The boy stood waiting for the bus back to Kenwood. He now believed that he should take the coins with him. Perhaps someday he'd find a more trusting dealer to talk to about the collection. *I have enough money to get started*, he thought. *I can always sell some coins later.*

His bus arrived and Charlie climbed on board feeling sad and very alone.

Eleven

IRGIL AND LENNY DROVE back to Parker's Lake Monday morning after reading the article in the paper. Virgil's plan required revision, but, in his mind, nabbing the boy to lure Fearless Frankie into his web didn't pose a problem. Of more immediate concern was what to do about Lenny. Pisant felt focused and alert. The irrational rage he felt provided motivation and energy he hadn't experienced since he returned from the Army. *Take care of business, Virgil. No loose ends!*

Lenny didn't say a word during the drive. After vocalizing his desire to withdraw from Pisant's plan, Lenny feared his friend's reaction. He looked across the short distance and noticed Virgil silently mouthing indecipherable words. A gob of spit formed at the corner of his mouth and threatened to slip down his unshaven chin. His eyes didn't seem to blink, and he gripped the worn steering wheel as if he'd never let go, as if every muscle in his body were at high alert.

"Virg? You okay?"

Pisant ignored Lenny's question.

"I mean, you're okay with my . . . with my not wanting to go any further with this, right?"

Still no response. Virgil looked almost catatonic. Lenny shivered and licked his lips. "Virg! Virg! What's the matter?"

All at once Pisant collected himself, shook his head, and blinked rapidly. He turned his head very slowly and stared at Lenny as if seeing him for the first time. His expression twisted. "Lenny, you're a wimp! Always were and always will be. Now shut the hell up!"

Lenny shriveled. Virgil's words stung. He crept closer to the door— even put one hand on the handle, fully expecting Virgil to reach over and grab him by the neck. *Why the hell did I ever get involved with this maniac?* "Geez, Virg! I didn't do nothin' except try to point out how . . . how, well, you know . . . how crazy this whole thing has gotten. See, the thing is, I ain't got no quarrel with this guy . . . not like you, least ways . . . so I jest . . . ."

"Shut up, Lenny! I've heard enough from you." Lenny's pleas for a free pass away from Virgil's scheme had done nothing but convince him that Lenny couldn't be trusted. Sooner or later, he'd say something to someone. *He's got a big mouth . . . too big. Can't take a chance.*

He glanced at the smaller man as if to confirm his decision. His eyes narrowed briefly. *Yep, too bad, but you're a pansy, Lenny. And, if McIlheny ever backs you into a corner—for whatever reason, you'll squawk like a stuck pig. Nope, you made your bed, Lenny. Now you'll have to sleep in it!*

"Ah, you gonna drop me at my place, Virg . . . or what?"

Virgil smiled, and said, "Later, little man. I got somethin' to show ya back at the farm first."

"What's that, Virg?"

"Oh, jest sumthin' yer gonna kinda like, I think. Been savin' it for a special day. Seems like today is as good as any."

With a clarity Virgil had never experienced before, he knew exactly how events would proceed from this point on. Once Nash and the kid had been disposed of, he'd contact the local realtor in town and put the farm up for sale. Then he'd head for California. Once there, he'd change his name to Pizant, once and for all—legally—and start a new life. *Yep, everything was going to work out jest fine. Hell, maybe those guys over at Parker's Lake point would buy the farm—wouldn't that be sumpthin'?*

Pisant slowed as he approached Lockhart and just as they passed the filling station on the east end of town, Sheriff McIlheny pulled out and crept up behind them.

"Aw, crap!" Virgil said as he noticed the flashing lights in his rear view. "You keep yer yap shut, Lenny! Understand?"

"I won't say nothin', Virg. Honest!" Lenny considered his options—jump out of the car and run to McIlheny, or sit tight and do nothing, hoping that Virgil would take this as a sign of trust. He opted to sit tight.

Pisant watched the sheriff approach the Packard from the rear. "I should back over the big jerk right now," he muttered.

"Virgil! No! Don't."

Pisant resisted the sudden impulse and relaxed. He rolled down his window and turned to look up at his life-long antagonist. "Sumthin' wrong, Gil?"

McIlheny removed his dark glasses, tucked them in his pocket, and leaned against the Packard. "Where you two nitwits headed this time of day, anyway?" He leaned over and looked directly at Lenny.

Now! Lenny thought. *Move!* But instead, he sat transfixed—frozen by fear.

"Ah, we're jest coming back from a job in town. That's all, Gil."

"Hah! What job? Boost another car, Piss Ant?"

Virgil laughed, attempting to break the tension. "Aw, hell, Sheriff. You know I been clean. Don't do that shit anymore. Started a new career, actually," Virgil said proudly.

"Oh yeah? And what might that be—dog fights instead of cock fights?"

"No. Guy in Minneapolis started a new business cleaning up cars—calls it, 'detailing.' Heard I was pretty good around cars—heh, heh, no, not like that, Sheriff—but you know, cleaning 'em up inside and out so's they look brand new. Then he can get more money for 'em on his used car lot."

Virgil had never held a steady job for more than two weeks. When one of his many, ill-fated money-making schemes fell apart, he'd pump gas at the Phillips 66 in Lockhart, but that was only out of desperation.

"Really? And what's this guy's name, Piss Ant? Just in case I have to track you down someday for one thing or another." McIlheny pulled out a note book and pencil. He waited for Virgil to respond.

"Uh . . . Simpson . . . Mathew Simpson. Got a used car lot on Lake Street—'Quality Motors.'" Pisant was pleased with his quick response.

McIlheny scribbled on his pad and tucked it back in his pocket. "I'll check it out. Say, Weasel, old man Groves said you didn't show up for work at the supermarket this morning. How come?" He bent for a gander at Lenny and waited for the small man's reply. "Said he pounded on your door up in that rat's nest you call home above the store but you didn't answer."

Virgil nudged Lenny with an elbow, "Answer the man, Lenny."

"Uh . . . didn't feel too good this morning, Sheriff. Besides, I wanted to check out this new job of Virgil's—thought I might like to do the same thing. Think I might quit and work there instead." Lenny beamed.

"That so? You two birdbrains couldn't clean yer butts with a toilet brush. Hah! Detailing! That's a crock if I ever heard one. Better stick to baggin' groceries for old man Groves, Weasel."

The sheriff glanced back toward the back of the car. "Looks like someone whacked ya in the back end, Piss Ant. Got one taillight busted out. Hand me your license."

"Aw, hell, Sheriff . . . I'll get it fixed tomorrow, honest!" Virgil hesitated, then passed his license through the window.

McIlheny took the tattered card and wrote out the ticket. When finished, he handed both to Pisant. "Sorry, Piss Ant. Here . . . this ain't gonna land ya back in jail, but it'll cost ya fifteen bucks!"

McIlheny straightened and finished with, "Jest remember, Piss Ant, sooner or later you're going to make a mistake. And when you do, I'll be all over you like a pit bull on a poodle! Got that, Piss Ant?"

Pisant grabbed his license and the ticket. Facing the windshield instead of McIlheny, he said, "I hear ya, Sheriff. Can we go now? We got things to take care of."

"I'll bet. Get the hell outta here," McIlheny said, and then backed away from the Packard.

Pisant put the car in first gear with a loud growl of gnashed gears and slowly pulled away. "God, I hate that guy! Thinks he's so high and mighty in that goddamned Boy Scout uniform he's so proud of. I'd like to stick those crappy sunglasses a his right up his fat rear!"

"Let's jest go, okay, Virg? I don't want no trouble with him."

"Shut up, Weasel!"

Pisant crumpled the ticket and tossed it out the side window.

Once the sheriff's car was out of sight, Virgil stomped on the accelerator and tore through town, leaving a cloud of dust in his wake. It long had been Pisant's signature nose-thumbing gesture—whether coming or going.

"I really don't feel too good, Virg. Think I had too many a those donuts or sumthin'. Maybe I should go home and lie down for a while. You can show me whatever ya got, later. Okay?"

Pisant never slowed down, nor did he respond. He tore out of town and, before long, had reached seventy miles an hour. He bent forward, transfixed by the roar of the eight-cylinder engine.

"Hey, Virg . . . better slow down, that curve is coming up, ya know." Lenny was concerned. He had seen his friend in such a state a few times before, and always it led to his doing something well over the edge—something stupid. "Virg?"

"Not to worry, little man. Virgil's in control of everything." Pisant smiled and looked across at Lenny. All of a sudden he slammed on the brakes, throwing Lenny against the dashboard.

"Ow! Cripes, Virg. That hurt!" He rubbed his forehead and braced against the dash as the Packard skidded to a stop.

"There. See? In complete control."

The car came to rest directly in front of the turn-off to the Pisant farm. He cranked the wheel and drove up the gravel road. Once they reached the farm yard, Virgil headed to the dairy barn and stopped the car. "Come on. Follow me. You won't believe this. Honest."

Pisant climbed out of the car, walked around the damaged rear end, and waved at Lenny. "Hey! Let's go!"

Lenny's hand shook as he pulled the door handle. On unsteady legs, he exited the car and followed Virgil's gesture. When he reached Pisant's side, the bigger man threw one heavy arm over Lenny's shoulders and guided him inside the barn.

In spite of the warm weather, Lenny felt chilled. He felt as if he really was coming down with something and more than anything, wanted to go home and go to bed.

Virgil escorted Lenny into the barn. The few small windows in the dairy barn were covered with matted spider webs and provided little illumination. Virgil led him over to a stall in the center of the barn. "Gypsy" was written in faded, green paint directly above the small area.

"Know what happened here, Weasel?"

"Nnn . . . no. What, Virg?"

"This is where that old bitch of a cow kicked me in the head." He rubbed the spot on his forehead as if by doing so it would vanish—that all the pain might go away.

He nudged the smaller man into the stall. Lenny resisted, but only briefly. "Lemme ask ya sumthin', Lenny?"

"Wha . . . what's that, Virg?"

"You an' I been friends for how long? Seven, eight years, maybe?"

"Yeah, I guess. Listen, Virg. I really am feeling pretty sick—think I might throw up here pretty quick . . ."

"Well, go right ahead. Been bigger messes in here than what's in yer guts, that's for sure."

Lenny stepped forward and attempted to leave. Pisant stuck out his arm and stopped him in his tracks.

"Anyway, where was I?" Pisant looked around the confined space. He spied what he was looking for and fingered the handle. "Oh yeah, friends. Ya know, after that cow kicked me in the head, I never had too many friends—not like you, anyway. Friends are supposed to stick together through thick and thin, or sumthin' like that, ain't they, Lenny?"

"Yeah, I guess so, Virg. Honest to hell, I'm gonna . . ." He lurched forward, intending to leave.

113

Virgil stuck a leg out and tripped the smaller man as he staggered past. At the same time, he shoved him sideways—hard! Lenny sprawled on the filthy concrete and banged his head on one of the ancient iron stanchions. White spots floated in front of his face. Everything appeared in a fog. From a distance, he heard Virgil's voice. "Well, when one friend deserts another, then he's got to pay the price, Lenny. Yer yellow, Lenny! Now you got to pay the price."

Pisant grabbed the mall tucked against the post at the corner of the stall, raised it over his head, and swung it back down on a cruel curve at Lenny's head. Lenny raised one spindly arm to fend off the blow, but the bony limb did little to slow the impact of the heavy, iron tool. The eight-pound sledgehammer smashed his forearm and embedded in the top of Lenny's skull! WHUMPF!

Lenny never knew what hit him. Virgil observed the brief twitching of the little man's limbs, replaced the mall in the corner of the stall, and said, "Friends don't desert friends, Lenny—ever! Ya shoulda known that."

Lenny's eyelids flickered briefly, then stilled.

Virgil shrugged, spun, and left the barn.

LATER THAT EVENING, Virgil returned to the barn and dragged Lenny's stiffening body outside. He placed him in the bucket of the old John Deere along with a chunk of cinder block and length of baling wire.

The tractor chugged out of the yard and through the overgrown pasture to the channel on Parker's Lake. The night was clear. The moon appeared just above the eastern horizon. Virgil dragged the body and cinder block over to the canoe and loaded both inside. Then he wrapped the wire around one of Lenny's legs and fastened the other end to the block of concrete.

The canoe scrapped against the gravel as Virgil launched it and hopped in. He paddled slowly out to the middle of the north bay. Ducks and coots scattered as the canoe creased the calm water. There was no other sound except for the quacking of hen mallards and the cat-like peeps from a flock of redheads.

Satisfied that the canoe now sat over the deepest part of the lake, Pisant pushed the body over the gunnel as if it were a bale of hay. He held Lenny's stiff body close to the canoe, as he lifted the block with his other hand. "Too bad, Lenny. You and I coulda had a good time out in California," he whispered.

Lenny's eyes were open—the glow of moonlight gave them the appearance of still having life. Virgil pulled the body closer to make sure he was only imagining, "Yeah. Whew! Scared me there fer a minute. Hell, he's deadern' a doornail."

Pisant released the block and watched as the corpse slid beneath the surface of the lake. Bubbles rose as the body sunk. Finally, the surface stilled. Virgil knew that the body would never be discovered. It would be assumed that Lenny left town with Virgil, or simply moved away. Either way, he now knew exactly how he would dispose of two other bodies—once he was finished with them.

He turned the canoe around, and paddled back to shore. In no hurry now, Pisant decided to return to the farm, fix something to eat, sleep for a few hours, then get an early start to the Cities. He wanted to be ready to move when the Nash kid left the house to deliver his morning papers. He already had a spot picked out for the snatch—a particularly dark section of Oliver Avenue with no street light within fifty yards.

Virgil smiled as he imagined the look on Nash's face when he worked on the kid as the old man watched. *Oh, yeah. That bastard's gonna pay! And when I'm done messin' up his kid, it'll be his turn.*

Virgil's eyes shimmered like a feral cat poised over its prey.

Twelve

O NCE CHARLIE LEFT THE STORE, Wenzel spun the rotary and dialed a familiar number. He waited for the receptionist to answer. "Yes, Seymour Wenzel calling for Paxton Armbruster. Yes, I'll wait." Wenzel palmed the small magnet on his desk as he waited.

"Pax? We have to meet—right away. What? No, it can't wait and when you hear what I have to say, you'll understand. Huh? No, I didn't! I sent the check two days ago. Some sort of snafu at the post office, I guess. Wait and see if it comes tomorrow. Look, this is small potatoes compared with what I just discovered. Meet me at Murray's? Thirty minutes? Perfect. See you then."

Wenzel locked the safe, turned out the lights, flipped over the OPEN/CLOSED sign in the front window and left his shop. In his growing excitement, he fumbled with the keys as he attempted to lock the door. "Come on," he muttered. Murray's—a popular watering hole famous for good food and privacy—was three blocks away, on Marquette Avenue. He hummed a favorite Perry Como tune as he strolled down the street.

Wenzel reached the restaurant ahead of Armbruster, secured a table, ordered a dry martini, and waited.

PAXTON ARMBRUSTER WAS AN ATTORNEY—specifically, a defense attorney with Minneapolis mob connections. He and Wenzel had grown up together in south Minneapolis and attended Washburn High School. They were an unlikely pair. Wenzel was introverted, small in stature, unathletic, bookish, and a collector of just about anything of value. Armbruster was the high school gadfly and debate champion who made a point of getting to know anyone and everyone of importance. He was also an outstanding three-sport athlete. Armbruster seemed to have it all, and once he graduated from law school, quickly rose to the top of his profession.

Unfortunately, Paxton had been stricken with polio in 1946 and after a period of confinement in an iron lung, was relegated to a wheelchair for the balance of his life. Bitter, full of self-pity, the crippled man willingly succumbed to a lucrative offer from a certain criminal element in town who felt that his paralysis would garner sympathy from most any jury. Paxton became a fierce advocate for the mob and seldom lost a case.

Seymour watched the door and all at once, his friend was wheeled in by a statuesque blonde, almost six feet tall, who was Paxton's constant companion. She guided her charge over to Wenzel. Seymour ran his eyes up and down her lithe body, noting the shapely press of her long skirt. She wore her hair short—curled close and tight. She was obviously fit—*had to be to load and unload Armbruster*, Wenzel thought.

"Mr. Wenzel, how are you today?" she asked, as she leaned down to position her charge's wheelchair.

"I'm just peachy, Madeline, and yourself?" Wenzel's tiny eyes dropped to the swell of Madeline's bosom. He was certain that her provocative pose, exposing a generous portion of white skin from the scooped neck of her dress, was meant for his eyes to feast on.

She smiled coyly across the table and asked, "Is there anything else you need at this time, sir?"

Paxton patted her hand, allowed his fingers to linger briefly, and replied, "That'll be just fine, sweetheart. Buy yourself a drink and put it on my tab. We shouldn't be too long."

"Very well. I'll be at the bar if you need me, Mr. Armbruster." She cast a sideways glance at Wenzel.

Wenzel watched her saunter away, and then reluctantly turned back to his friend.

"Seymour," said the attorney.

"Pax."

"You order me a drink, you cheap screw?"

"No. Order your own damned drink, cripple!"

"Watch your mouth, runt, or I'll sic Madeline over there on you." Armbruster nodded toward his aide.

"I should be so lucky," Wenzel replied.

"Yeah, you should," he replied wistfully.

"Why do you torture yourself like that, Pax?" Wenzel nodded toward the woman.

Armbruster smiled and said, "What makes you think it's torture?"

"I thought you told me you couldn't, ah . . . how shall I put this? That your plumbing didn't quite work . . . so to speak."

"Seymour. Where have you been? Someday I'll fill you in. Suffice to say . . . there are multiple ways to enjoy the opposite sex. All that's required is an adventuresome, willing partner." His wyes twinkled.

"I had no idea! Good for you, Pax. Any chance she'd be interested in a little outside action?"

Paxton smiled. "Sorry. Find your own. All right. Enough chit-chat, Seymour. What's so urgent? And I still am waiting for my check, by the way."

Armbruster waved at the waiter, who promptly trotted over to their table. "Manhattan. On the rocks—with two cherries."

Seymour paused. When the waiter was a safe distance away, he began. "A short time ago, a young boy left the shop with a small penny collection that's worth a small fortune—only he has no knowledge of it's true worth." He waited for his words to sink in.

Armbruster leaned his elbows on the linen table cloth. "So, how does that benefit me—or you?"

"Because we can easily separate the boy from his collection with the help of your friend, you know the one. However, we have to move rapidly, as the boy is leaving town tomorrow—for Montana, of all places."

"What's he got that's so valuable?" Armbruster's cocktail arrived, and he stirred the amber fluid with one finger.

Seymour relished the moment, so he paused and beamed at his crippled friend. "All right, here's the story. In 1942, President Roosevelt ordered that the United States Mint should cease manufacturing coins made of copper. He issued a decree that in essence made it illegal to stamp coins from anything except ferrous metal. The war effort, and all."

"So?"

"Well, unfortunately, or fortunately, depending on one's perspective, the head of the Philadelphia Mint—one Edwin H. Dressel—was a bit tardy, apparently, getting this message to the individual stamping copper pennies on the cut-off day. Either that, or the man intentionally left copper blanks in the machine, because legend has it that twelve—and only twelve—copper Lincoln head cents were stamped before the changeover could occur." Wenzel's eyes flared. He paused for effect.

"Okay, you have my interest. Proceed."

"No one knew for sure at the time, but again, according to stories bandied about, the press guy took the twelve coins and stuck them in his pocket. He effected the changeover to steel—which was then coated with zinc, by the way, and went to lunch."

Armbruster listened to the little man's description with increasing interest. He threw back what was left of his drink and waved for the waiter. If twelve and only twelve coins had been minted . . . and somehow survived circulation? Dollar signs flashed in Armbruster's head.

"Okay, I'm buying into this so far, but workers don't simply walk out of the U.S. Mint with coins jingling in their pockets or casually tossed in a lunch box. How'd he get them out?"

Wenzel smiled, exposing a brilliant set of white teeth. With a grand gesture, he reached over, plucked a cherry from Paxton's drink, tilted back his head, and dropped the cherry into his mouth. Still smiling, he swallowed the cherry whole, wiped his mouth, and sat back in his chair. "The pennies were wrapped in a piece of waxed paper left over from his sandwich—peanut butter and jelly, I believe—and subsequently bound with a string into a tight, little envelope."

"What? He ate the package?"

"Yes, indeed. Of course, sometime later, when it was time for his daily defecation in the privacy of his home, out popped the coins, safely ensconced and protected from acidic stomach fluids by the wax paper."

"Son of a bitch! And, you mean to tell me—?"

At that moment, a new waiter approached their table with menus in hand. He stood quietly to the right of Armbruster waiting for the appropriate moment to interrupt.

Armbruster sensed his presence, turned, and said, "Yes?"

"Would you gentlemen care to order dinner?"

Armbruster looked at his watch. "It's only 5:15 P.M., but I skipped lunch. How about it, Seymour? Shall we order?"

"Yes, I could probably eat."

"Very well, I'll have a club sandwich—hold the mayo. Tossed salad and coffee," Armbruster replied.

"Very good. And you, sir?"

"That sounds excellent. However, I'll have mine with mayo and horseradish, please."

"Perfect. Another round of drinks, gentlemen?"

"Sure—why not?" Armbruster replied.

Wenzel leaned over the table—his voice dropped. "Whatever happened to the coins is not known—except that one, and only one, appeared in 1947. It was sold, privately, to a collector in France for $125,000."

"Okay, so I suppose you're going to tell me that this kid walked into the store with the remaining eleven?"

Wenzel chuckled. "No, I'm afraid not, dear boy. However, I can tell you with certainty that within his piddling collection, he did have two of them. A 'double', Pax! A matched set! Do you have any idea what a 'double' is worth?"

"No. But before you tell me, and I'm sure you're just dying to do so, how do you know they're authentic? Not that I am questioning your veracity, you understand."

"Of course, of course. I, too, was skeptical at first. But please understand, because there were only twelve minted, and legally they could not exist, there was never any mention of the coins in any of the most reputable and reliable numismatic books. I checked *Strobel's Numismatic History*—not a word is mentioned. According to Leonard Dressel and the Philadelphia Mint, no copper pennies were minted after the die change in 1943."

"So?"

"Any copper penny minted before 1943 is virtually worthless—same goes for 1944."

Armbruster looked puzzled.

"All right. First of all, the Lincoln head penny . . . here, let me show you." Wenzel reached in his pocket and withdrew a similar coin with an earlier date. "Look here, on the obverse side—'heads,' if you like—we have in the center, Lincoln's bust. At the top, the legend simply reads, 'In God We Trust.' 'Liberty' appears to the left—see? And the exergue, the date and origin of engraving, is stamped just here. In this case, the capital letter 'D.' See the 'D' below the date? That means it was minted in Denver. If it had an 'S,' it was minted in San Francisco. Philadelphia has never stamped a letter on pennies."

"What does our coin's, uh . . . 'exergue' read?"

"Just the date—1943—without a mint mark."

"Let's see if I have this straight. All the pennies minted prior to the die changeover were copper, stamped 'D,' 'S,' or blank if it came from the Philly mint."

"Correct."

"So the guy puts the new 1943 die in the machine, leaves the copper blanks in place, and stamps out twelve, 'by mistake'—the copper ones. Then he puts steel blanks in the hopper, and runs those. Is that about it?"

"Yes."

"So, according to this guy Dressel, the only coins minted after the die change were zinc-coated steel, dated 1943 without a mint mark."

"Correct."

"Okay. And the other side of the coin?"

Wenzel flipped the penny over. "The 'tails' side has as its legend at the top, 'E Pluribus Unum.' 'ONE CENT' is stamped in the center, with 'United States of America' beneath. And, as you can see, on either side are the conventional—wheat stalks arcing down each side."

"All right, thanks for the lesson. Now what makes you so sure the kid's two coins are the real thing?

"Pax, I don't think these coins have ever been in circulation. The edges were perfect. The milling, and reeling showed no signs of wear. The flan areas—those areas of the coin without any printing—shone brilliantly. This double has probably never been out of their sleeves—until I removed one of them."

"But still, there has to be some test you can perform?"

"Yes, indeed. There is, and was—and I performed it without the boy being aware I had done so." Once again, Wenzel reached into his pocket and withdrew the small magnet.

"Know what this is, Pax?"

"Looks like . . . here, let me see it." He reached over and took the magnet from his friend. "Looks like a small magnet."

"Correct. Now take this penny and hold it against the magnet."

Armbruster did as instructed. Nothing happened. The penny remained separated from the magnet. "And?"

"I did the same thing with the boy's pennies—nothing happened. Because it's made of copper! If the coins had been counterfeit, if they had indeed been steel with an artificial coating made to look like copper, the magnet would have pulled the coin away from my hand like it was covered with honey."

Armbruster shifted in his wheelchair. "So they were real?"

"Oh yes! They most certainly are genuine—no doubt about that."

"Well, once you applied the magnet, didn't the kid figure it out?"

"Paxton! My dear man! The boy is maybe ten or eleven—a mere child. I told him the magnet was a . . . what the hell did I say? Oh, yes, I told him it was a 'dioptric.'"

Armbruster chuckled. "And what was that supposed to test?"

"Oh, some silly nonsense about the coin changing color. At any rate, he accepted my deception as the truth and has no idea that the double in his possession represents one of the greatest numismatic finds in recent history."

"Well, why didn't you buy the damn things from him?"

"That is real the tragedy in my story, Pax. I offered the young man three hundred dollars, and he declined. Said he thought he'd hang onto the collection. However, I managed to secure his name and address without his knowing I had done so."

"You cheap screw! Why didn't you offer more?"

"I didn't have the same advantage of hindsight as you, Pax."

Their meals arrived and both remained silent as they began eating. After a couple of mouthfuls of food, Armbruster asked, "Where'd the kid get the coins, Seymour?"

Wenzel took a bite, chewed at the morsel exactly seven times, wiped his lips, and replied, "From a great uncle who recently passed away."

"You don't suppose the old guy had more than those two pennies, do you?"

"Ah, the sixty-four dollar question! Imagine if you will, that young Master Nash's Uncle Hedwig somehow purchased all twelve from the original owner. Intriguing, yes?"

"Did the kid happen to mention whether or not the old guy had any other family? A widow he might have left more coins with?"

"Yes, indeedy! Dear Aunt Marie. I can certainly imagine that a certain, well-connected attorney such as yourself could easily ascertain that bit of information . . . and perhaps solicit your services to the dear lady. But, first things first. We need to get those two coins from the boy before he leaves town."

"All right, Seymour. I'm sure you've saved the best for last. Let's have the dessert, if you please. What is a double such as this worth?"

"I thought you might never ask. I made a few phone calls, to, ah, verify my appraisal." Wenzel paused again, for effect.

"And? Come on, Seymour. What're they worth?"

Seymour withdrew a scrap of paper from his pocket, jotted down a number and slid the scrap across the linen to his partner.

Paxton studied the scribbled figures and said, "Holy mackerel! You sure?"

"Oh, yes. I have a standing offer from a gentleman in Albany. If any coins such as these were to surface, he'd pay top dollar. A bona fide offer, Paxton."

The waiter cleared the dishes and left coffee. The restaurant was full by now. Downtown executives stopping by for a cocktail before heading home gathered in small groups.

"How do we get our hands on them?"

"Seems to me, Pax, that this is a job for your friend—the nameless one. The same gentleman we employed to create that unfortunate accident for dear old Leonard."

Armbruster studied his friend. "I was afraid you'd say that. We got away with that once, but I don't know about tempting fate twice." He squirmed in the chair.

"Look, Pax. Remember how easy it was to change Leonard's will? Yes, we were lucky that his wife preceded the old man, but it wasn't much effort to rewrite his will. I assure you, this will be just as easy. He's a child! How difficult can it be to create another such accident?"

"But the kid has family, surely? What if our guy's got to enter the house to get the coins and runs into his parents?" Armbruster imagined a worst case scenario.

"So? Maybe the furnace fails? Maybe someone leaves a burner lit on the stove? Any numbers of accidents happen to families every day. Perhaps a simple car accident is all that's required. One thing I know with certainty is that if the lad leaves for Montana as planned, he might take his collection with him. If we allow that to happen, it presents a number of problems. No, we must act fast—tonight, actually, if we are to secure the double!"

Armbruster reached in his jacket and withdrew a small notebook. "You're a heartless little bastard . . . you know that don't you, Seymour?"

Without a moment's hesitation, the little man replied, "Yes, indeed, especially when considerable sums of money are involved."

"Okay. What's the kid's name?"

"Nash, Charles."

"Address?"

"2300 Oliver Avenue—Kenwood. Know the area? Near Lake of the Isles."

"Of course. Lots of money around Lake of the Isles. How old?"

"Ten—maybe eleven. Hard to tell . . . kid's kind of runty looking. Blond, short-cropped hair. Blue eyes. Few freckles."

Armbruster turned toward the bar and waved at Madeline. "I'll make the call. Be right back." He spun his chair away from the table just as she arrived. "Take me over to the phone booth. You have a dime, Sweetheart?"

Wenzel fingered the penny, glanced at the image of Lincoln, and slipped it back in his pocket. He sipped his coffee as he waited for his friend and partner to return.

At the Bell Telephone booth near the restrooms, Paxton asked, "Madeline, will you phone this number for me?" He handed her a slip of paper.

She slid into the booth, deposited the coin, and waited for the operator to come on the line. "Franklin 9—8765, please." She handed the receiver to her boss.

Armbruster took the phone and gestured for her to wait over by the coat room. He faced the booth. "Armbruster, here. I need you to get hold of your man—right away. Yes, it has to happen tonight or early tomorrow morning. What? Yes—an accident. No, we don't care."

He lowered his voice to a whisper and looked around to be sure he wasn't being overheard. "A boy. Ten or eleven. Armbruster described the boy. "Name is Charles Nash. Lives at 2300 Oliver Avenue. Kenwood. Don't know. Maybe. Best to do him alone if possible. He has a coin collection—pennies. About twenty or so in a folded packet. Kid leaves for Montana in the morning. Don't know about the parents. Yes, if it's required. We want the coins—all of them. I'll wait."

Armbruster rested the phone on his shoulder and smiled at Madeline. Before long he was back on the receiver. "What? Whatever it takes. Five thousand? Done. Tell him no mistakes—another accident like . . . you know. Yes, if need be, but I'd rather it was just the boy. No, if he doesn't get in the house before he leaves, he'll probably take the collection with him. Yes. Call me when he's secured the coins. Great! As always, I can count on you. You too. Bye."

Armbruster waved Madeline over. She crossed the short distance, replaced the phone, and wheeled him back to Seymour.

Madeline left them alone once again. "It's all set. He'll check the house out this evening then decide how to proceed. He'll try and separate the boy from the coins. If other family members get in the way . . . well . . . only as a last resort."

Wenzel rubbed his hands. A broad smile filled the lower half of his face. "Wonderful! And once we complete this transaction, we can think about the balance of the collection and how best to secure those. I may be able to close the shop and retire after this, Pax. You as well."

"One thing at a time, Seymour. Let's not get too far ahead of ourselves. A lot can happen between buttering the bread and tasting it. Let's wait to hear from our man tomorrow."

"Yes, yes, I know. But can you permit me just a slight wave of euphoria, if you please? It's not every day that fortune smiles on a person as it seems to have just now."

"Yeah, I know. Val's guy is good, but things happen—you know."

"At least let's have a little toast, shall we? Why not bring your handsome friend over for an after-dinner drink before we leave, eh?" Wenzel stared across the room at Madeline.

Armbruster noticed his friend's leer. "Find your own entertainment, Seymour." He waved at Madeline and laughed. "You better wander over to Hennepin Avenue and stop at the Gay Nineties on your way home . . . buy yourself some action."

"Not a bad idea, my good man. Not a bad idea at all. I might just follow your sage counsel." He stood and reached back to pull his trousers away from between his sweaty cheeks.

"Had my eye on a new girl over there—legs like Betty Grable. Come to think of it, she looks a lot like your sweet Madeline." A broad smile creased his narrow face as he studied Paxton's assistant and considered how the balance of the evening would play out.

Thirteen

ONCE ARMBRUSTER MADE the call to his mob contact, Val, that man, in turn, picked up the phone and called one of his most reliable independent contractors. A man known for ruthless attention to every detail—a person whose background gave little indication of the man he would ultimately become.

AS A BOY, JOSEPH TENAVIE endured a childhood that was not normal. While others his age played ball, cowboys and Indians, or mumbly-peg, Joseph's spare time was consumed by his father's passion—the Bible and the Lord's teachings.

"'He that gathereth in summer is a wise son: but he that sleepeth in harvest is a son that causeth shame.' Proverbs, Chapter 10, Verse Five, Joseph."

His father's words stung as never before. His head drooped in a familiar pose as he stood before the imposing, dark-clad figure of his father, Zachariah.

By the time he was eighteen, Joseph had been nowhere; he had spent his entire life living with his father, mother, and two sisters near Storm Lake, Iowa. The boy's view of the world was bleak and one-dimensional.

Zachariah Tenavie was a Pentecostal minister who believed that children should be seen, but seldom heard. When they did speak, their sinful babbles required corporal punishment—especially almost anything uttered by his only son, Joseph.

The youngster quickly learned that it was in his best interest to speak little, and when he did, make certain his father was absent. He found consolation and peace with his Bible, which he read constantly—not because he had to, although his father would have been pleased had he known—but because he wanted to. Joseph was convinced there had to be a better life for him—away from his father.

He had few friends, and as the Great Depression reduced the number of parishioners to a mere handful, and, with his father's future in the parish equally as bleak, Joseph decided that was a good time to leave.

He clung to his Bible and turned his back on his family. He found the courage to leave in Mathew: *Provide neither gold, nor silver, nor brass in your purses, Nor scrip for your journey, neither two coats, neither shoes, nor yet staves: for the workman is worthy of his meat.*

Few tears were shed by either Joseph or his family as he took the few belongings he had accumulated, and joined the Army.

Always something of a loner, he kept to himself and made few friends. Before long, however, his multiple skills with firearms came to the attention of his battalion commander. No other soldier had scored as high on marksmanship as did Joseph. He was assigned to an advanced weapons unit where he completed his high school degree. Soon he had advanced in rank to staff sergeant. Proficient with every weapon used by the infantry soldier in 1943, Joseph had found a home in the Army.

Still without many friends, he was most at home learning all he could about pistols, rifles, and submachine guns. Every night he'd study the Bible for inspiration and guidance.

In late summer of 1943, when Joseph was the lead instructor in weapons training at Fort Hood, Oregon, he was called to the office of his battalion commander.

"Sergeant, how'd you like to ship overseas—see some action, finally?"

"I guess I'd like that just fine, sir."

"About time you put some of your skills to work," the colonel stated. "What I'm about to tell you can not be repeated, is that understood, sergeant?"

"Yessir. I understand."

"Good. The Army is in need of snipers for . . . well, let's just leave it at that, for now. You'll find out more about your assignment, later. Your skill with the rifle is unequaled, sergeant, and the Army is forming a new unit that requires skilled marksman." The pending Normandy invasion was being formulated, and the Allies required a company of sharpshooters to be dropped into France ahead of the invasion.

"Where'd you learn to shoot, sergeant?" his commander inquired during the interview.

"Back home, sir. Pretty much grew up with a rifle. Sometimes all we had to eat was what I could bring home."

"The Twenty-fifth Infantry will be your new unit, and after a brief training period, you'll be shipping out."

"Yessir."

"Think you could kill a man as easily as a rabbit?" The colonel studied his weapons instructor, closely.

"Don't see why not."

"Very well. Go back to the barracks, collect your gear, and report to Headquarter's for further orders. Nothing we've discussed here is to be repeated, sergeant. Is that clear?"

"Yessir." Obedience was something he had learned well at home. He was conflicted, but only briefly. His Bible would once again calm his troubled mind. *No man can serve two masters: for either he will hate the one, and love the other, or else he will hold to the one, and despise the other. The wisdom of Mathew,* thought Tenavie. He vowed to always pledge allegiance to his only, true master, The Lord.

Joseph spent three months training with the Twenty-fifth Infantry. He was a willing pupil and, before long, rose to the top of a select unit of snipers. He was rushed through advanced paratrooper school and shipped to England in December of 1943. Within another two months, he and his small company were air-lifted over France. On a dark, moonless night, he parachuted into the French countryside.

Joseph was to join up with the local resistance and immediately acquire his first target. His weapon of choice was a M1903 Springfield, bolt-action, thirty-caliber rifle with a Weaver telescopic sight.

Joseph Tenavie killed his first German officer from a distance of eight hundred meters and never felt as alive or fulfilled as he did at that moment.

When he returned from that first kill, he opened his Bible and read from John 8:10. *Then took they up stones to cast at him: but Jesus hid himself, and went out of the temple, going through the midst of them, and so passed by.* The words of John provided validation and justification. Before long, he felt he had found his true purpose in life.

Joseph had no equal when it came to concealment and camouflage. The French partisans praised his talents, and before long he became something of a legend. The French underground press soon realized that it would serve their purposes to herald each and every "kill" Joseph made—specifically, to the Germans. They reasoned that if Jerry could be kept off balance—nervous, fearful that any officer, or group of officers might be targeted—it would divert their attention from the real purpose of the allies—to invade Normandy.

Joseph executed thirty-nine, high-ranking German officers in a span of six months. The Germans soon referred to him as "*Ausgeburt des Teufels*"—"Spawn of the Devil."

The French resistance picked up on Joseph's dubious nickname and plastered posters throughout the countryside warning the Nazi's of "Der Teufel."

A highly skilled squad of German marksman was brought to France to set a trap for Der Teufel and bring an end to his reign of terror. Joseph not only eluded their efforts, but relished the challenge and killed each marksman sent to find him, as well.

Before long, Joseph began to make a game of his daily killing. To challenge his skills, he varied the distances from 100 to 1,000 meters—depending on his mood. Like a dog left in the wild, Der Teufel developed an insatiable taste for blood. He was being paid to kill Nazis in any manner he chose, and the French considered him a hero.

After each mission, Joseph would return to a tunnel the partisans had established as their headquarters and curl up on a filthy mattress with his Bible. The Gospel according to John became his favorite book. "John wrote as a poet might," he told more than one admirer. "He could communicate to the masses as no other."

Whenever the grateful French gathered around him, he could not resist spouting passages from his book of faith. "Listen to the beauty of John's words: 'Jesus went unto the mount of Olives. And early in the morning he came again into the temple, and all the people came unto him: and he sat down and taught them. And the scribes brought unto him a woman taken in adultery. Now Moses in the law commanded us, that such should be stoned: but what sayest thou? He lifted up himself, and said unto them, He that is without sin among you, let him first cast a stone at her. When Jesus had lifted up himself, and saw none but the woman, he said, woman, where are those thine accusers? Hath no man condemned thee? She said, No man, Lord. And Jesus said unto her, neither do I condemn thee: go, and sin no more. The word of God.'"

WHEN THE ALLIES INVADED Normandy in June, Staff Sergeant Joseph Tenavie had become a highly efficient killing machine. Like a stray dog living by its own wit and skill, Joseph required little in the way of companionship. Even the idolizing, passionate French women of the resistance could not compare to the sublime feeling of pleasure he experienced after a kill. He ate minimally—just enough to provide needed nourishment. He did not drink liquor, wine, or beer—alcohol dulled his senses.

He lived to kill. He relished the stalk, the set-up—the wait. Joseph seldom missed his target, and when he did, his depression and sense of failure could not be relieved until the next assassination.

Once France was returned to the French and the Germans were routed, however, Joseph's skills were no longer required. He was a craftsman without a market in which to trade. Before long he was eating too much, drinking too much, and wanted nothing more than to be left alone. Even the French women who still considered him something of a matinee idol couldn't satisfy his lust.

When he returned to the States after the war, Joseph discovered he no longer wanted to make a career out of the Army. He missed the action—missed tracking a man, lining him up in his scope—missed pulling the trigger and watching the results from great distances. He chose not to re-enlist, was mustered out with an honorable discharge, and given numerous medals and ribbons, which he threw in the first garbage container he came across.

Joseph came back to the Midwest. He spent six months moving from one unfulfilling job to another. He drank too much and after a particularly gruesome barroom fight that left his adversary hospitalized, he moved to Minneapolis. Within days, he met a man in a saloon on Hennepin Avenue who listened with interest to Joseph's rambling, slurred stories of what he had done in France.

Joseph and his new friend met a second time, then a third. Finally, the man was convinced that what he had been hearing was more than likely, the truth. This was a skilled marksman, a killer who, with just a little attention, could be of value to certain elements in the Twin Cities.

"Joseph, I have a proposition for you. Interested?"

"Maybe. What do you have in mind?"

"Let's go over to a booth where we won't be disturbed."

Once the two men were seated, Joseph's new friend said, "Listen. I know a guy who might be interested in a man with, uh, your particular skills. Get my drift?"

Joseph listened eagerly, and before long, was introduced, by phone, to a man Joseph knew only as "Val." Joseph never saw his friend in the bar again, but it didn't matter. Val became Joseph's contact with the Minneapolis mob—an intermediary, an agent—who took ten percent of every "job" Joseph contracted for.

Joseph never learned Val's real name—nor did he want to. The arrangement suited his purposes perfectly. He could operate anonymously with plenty of distance between himself, his various employers, and Val. Money was left in an envelope at an agreed-upon safe drop. Joseph had a partner, and their partnership succeeded because of extreme caution and anonymity.

Val suggested he acquire a contact name. Joseph turned to the Scriptures for inspiration. After two days of study, he found what he was looking for in Revelation 4:7. *And the First Beast was like a lion, and the Second Beast like a calf, and the Third Beast had a face as a man, and the Fourth Beast was like a flying eagle.*

During his stay in France, Joseph had come to not only appreciate what the French were doing to free their homeland, but he also grew to love the French language. Unlike German, which sounded harsh and guttural, French was almost lyrical—pleasing to his ear.

He considered the passage from Revelations and decided on "The Third Beast—man," or, "La Troisième Bête." He shortened it to "LaBette." He was pleased with his choice. The name carried the connotation of a fearless killer who lived by its wits and guile. A loner—a man of many masks. LaBette would have no equal when it came to carrying out swift and certain death.

Before long, LaBette had his first job. A union representative in Chicago needed to be dealt with. He received an envelope detailing the man's address and description, the preferred method of execution, a train ticket, and a thousand dollars. LaBette took the Hiawatha Limited to Chicago. It took two days of stalking before he was ready to move on the target. It was almost too easy. He waited outside behind a bowling alley on the South Side. The target stepped outside, lit a cigarette, and leaned against the brick wall. LaBette stepped from the shadows, took three steps, and put a bullet in the back of the man's head.

LaBette was on his way. Before long, he gave up booze, exercised regularly, and made certain his senses were as sharp and alert as humanly possible.

Der Teufel was back in business.

Fourteen

CHARLIE STEPPED OFF THE BUS just as a reddish, hazy sun set behind Kenwood School. Forest fires in the West had been burning for weeks, and the warm chinook carried remnants of the massive burns for thousands of miles.

Because it was unseasonably warm, Charlie had tied his lightweight blue jacket around his slim waist. He trudged past the school, crossed the street, and turned in to Milt's Supermarket. Once inside, he grabbed a cart and made his way up and down the aisles, gathering supplies for his trip. Once he finished, he stopped at the checkout counter.

"Hi, Charlie." Mr.Gutkin called. "Going away someplace?"

Charlie hadn't thought about what his selection of snacks, candy, and soda might reveal to the storekeeper, but it was too late now. "Uh, no . . . some of this is for my mother." He lowered his head so Gutkin wouldn't spot his deception.

"Cash or charge, Charlie?"

He hadn't intended to charge the food, but now he knew he must, "Charge, please."

Gutkin bagged the snacks, filled out the charge slip, and handed it to Charlie to sign.

He picked up the pencil, signed his name, handed the slip to the storekeeper and picked up his bag. "Thank you."

"You're welcome, Charlie. Say hello to your mom for me, okay?"

"Sure. Bye."

Charlie left the store and walked the short distance to Oliver Avenue. All at once he realized that, if his mother spotted him coming into the house with the grocery bag, she would surely ask questions. He stopped —wondering how to hide the evidence. He set the bag down on a short wall, removed the contents, and stuffed everything in his jacket pockets. The brown bag he folded and stacked with his books. *There, that should work.*

He hefted the books and started up the street. Head down, he carefully avoided each deep crack in the sidewalk.

He was anxious to get home, anxious to see Taffy, anxious for the following morning to arrive and to be on his way. When he was halfway up the street, he spotted Taffy lying on the front stoop, and whistled.

Her ears perked—then she spotted his small form walking up the street. She leapt from the concrete steps and tore down the sidewalk.

Charlie knelt and waited for his friend. As soon as she reached him, Taffy put both paws on his shoulders and knocked him down. Her tongue covered his face with kisses.

Charlie giggled and rolled over on his back. "Hey, Taff! Miss me, girl? Sorry I was so late." He scratched her soft under-belly, rose, gathered up his books and ran toward his house. "Come on, Taff. Bet I beat you home!"

The two raced back up the street and finally halted by the front door. Charlie gave her one last pat and opened the porch door. Once inside the house, he yelled, "Mom! I'm home."

Without waiting for a reply, he ran up the stairs to his room. Taffy galloped at his heels. Once safely in his bedroom, he dropped his books on the bed and pulled out the coin packet. He stared at it for a moment—still concerned that he had done something wrong, that he had betrayed a confidence—and silently asked for Hedwig's forgiveness. At least he hadn't sold any of the coins and had walked away from the strange man in the coin shop without giving him more than his name.

Marsha Nash appeared in the doorway. "Hi, Charlie. Johnny, Shelly, and Michael stopped by earlier to see if you'd play football with them."

"Oh! Hi, Mom." He tried to act as normal as possible, though he made a quick glance at his jacket to make sure none of the snacks showed. "Uh—maybe tomorrow we can play."

"How'd it go at the coin shop?"

Charlie averted his eyes, not wanting to look directly at his mother. "Oh, okay, I guess. The man Uncle Hed told me to see was gone, and the new owner was kinda strange."

"How do you mean, strange?"

"I don't know—just funny, is all."

"What'd he say?"

"He said it was a nice collection . . . that someday it might be worth more money than it is now," Charlie lied.

"You didn't sell any of them, did you? Hed was hoping you'd hang on to the coins until you were much older."

"No. I still have them all." Charlie was uncomfortable with the conversation. "When's dinner?"

"Well, let's see," Marsha glanced at Charlie's alarm clock. "It's 5:30 now, and your father said he'd call at 6:30. How about waiting until after he calls—say seven o'clock?"

"Yeah, that's okay." Charlie said. This would give him an opportunity to pack—without being disturbed.

"Your grandma is coming for dinner and she's bringing a hot dish."

"Good."

"Be sure and wash your hands before you come down."

"I will."

Marsha left the room and went back to the kitchen.

Charlie silently wished he could leave at that moment—wished he could put his plan into action immediately. The house was so quiet without his father around, but he knew that sooner or later, when he returned, all the noise and anger and stress would return—much of it directed at him. The thought of his father's anger made his heart race.

Taffy jumped on the bed, spun twice, and plopped down. Charlie closed the door, set his books on the floor, and went into the closet. He climbed up the short, slanted ladder, opened the cubby-hole, and withdrew the hat box. On his bed, he sorted through the contents. He opened the Prince Albert can, took out his money, and stuffed the bills into his Roy Rogers wallet. Next, he took the Swiss army knife given him by his grand-mother and laid it on the bed. Then he took his canvas newspaper bag, selected a change of clothes from his dresser, and stuffed everything—including his coin collection—into the generous bag.

He knelt by the bed, leaned down, and reached under to pull out his flannel sleeping bag. With great care, he opened, then rerolled the bag in a tighter bundle. Everything fit in his paper route sack.

He looked at Taffy and suddenly realized that he had to make sure he had food and a dish for her. He looked around the room, and finding nothing light enough to carry, realized he would have to lift a lightweight dish from the kitchen. *One of the picnic dishes! That will work. A single dish would work for both food and water. No room for two . . .* Taffy ate dried dog food along with table scraps. He'd take a small bag from the kitchen and pur-chase additional food as he needed it.

He sat on the bed and ran his fingers through Taffy's long, golden hair. All of a sudden he questioned his decision, imagining for the first time just how difficult, how scary, how bold his leaving home really was. He buried his head against Taffy's neck. "I hope . . . I hope everything will be . . ." *Wait! I almost forgot! A note!*

He hopped from the bed and went to his small desk. There he opened a spiral notebook and picked up a pencil stub. Charlie stared at the picture above his desk of the Lockheed jet banked against a blue sky. He wondered what he should say to his mother.

After two or three minutes, he bent down and began writing. It didn't come easy and he had to stop more than once.

Dear Mom,
I have to go away for a while. I think Dad hates me now, so it is bet-ter if I go. Don't worry. Taffy is with me and she is real good at pro-

139

tection. Tell Grandma Goodbye. I will come home some day so don't look for me now. I will be far away. Love.

Charlie.

He ripped the note from the book, folded it four times and addressed it on the outside to his mother. By the time he had finished, he was filled with sadness. Tears brimmed each eye. A single drop settled on the rough paper. The word, "Mom" blurred as he tried to focus. He could still change his mind but knew he wouldn't. It was too late. He had to go.

It was dark in the boy's room. He lay down on the bed and heard the phone ring downstairs. *I wish everything was different. I wish I could . . .*

A SHORT TIME LATER, Charlie heard the doorbell ring. He threw both bags in the closet, opened the door, and went downstairs. Taffy barked as she always did.

"Taffy! Hush," Marsha said, reaching the door before Charlie.

She swung the door open. "Hello, Mother."

"Hi, dear," the gray-haired, rounded version of his mother replied. "Charlie? Are we going to play gin rummy after supper?"

"Sure, Grandma. That'd be fun."

Taffy sidled close to their visitor. Her heavy tail beat steadily against the older woman's green dress.

She reached down and scratched the dog's ears. "Hello, Taffy. Seems as if I just saw you at my house . . . of course I did! That was the day before yesterday. I swear I must be losing my mind, Marsha."

"No, you're not, Mother. Let's go in the kitchen and eat. It's getting late."

Shortly after the three began eating, the doorbell rang.

"Charlie, will you see who that is, please?"

"Sure, Mom." Charlie slid off the vinyl bench and went to the front door. Taffy was barking at the door. "Shhh. Quiet, girl."

He opened the door and faced a tall, angular man who wore a fedora and horn-rimmed glasses and carried a large satchel. "Hi," the boy said.

Taffy growled and backed behind Charlie.

"Taff! Cut it out! What's the matter with you?"

She continued to bristle, and her eyes never left the stranger's.

The man removed his hat. His white hair was cut short. He smiled and said, "Is your mother or father home, young man?" His eyes were pale blue, the color of the sky on a hot summer day.

"Uh, well . . . my dad's not . . . but my mom's here."

"Excellent! And your name is?" He leaned down and smiled again—displaying a perfect set of snow-white teeth that matched his mustache and hair.

"Charlie."

"Ah, yes. And this is the Nash household, am I correct?"

"Yes. Just a minute. I'll get my mom."

Taffy remained stiff legged, but kept her distance.

Charlie and his mother returned to the front hall. Marsha wiped her hands on an apron and asked, "Yes? Can I help you?"

"Mrs. Nash, please pardon the intrusion. I hope I'm not here at a bad time?"

"Well, we were just in the middle of supper. What do you want?"

"Ma'am, my name is Jenkins. William Jenkins. I work for the Encyclopedia Britannica Company. I'm certain you have heard of our fine set of reference books?" Instead of looking at Marsha, his eyes darted over her head and quickly scoped out the interior of the house.

"Yes, but—"

"Oh, I know, I know, you've undoubtedly considered the markedly prudent investment in our product before, particularly as it will apply to your fine son here . . . you know, high school work and college preparation, and all. However, as I am in the neighborhood this evening, I thought you might—"

"I really don't think so. My husband's not home, and I wouldn't make such a purchase without his approval first."

"Yes, of course, but let me at least offer you the opportunity to reserve a set at a very special, reduced price that I'm certain will fit your budget. You see, the Britannica Company is prepared to finance the full purchase price for a period of—"

Taffy growled once more and that gave Marsha her opening. "Look, we really must finish our supper. Why don't you come back some other time?" Marsha's irritation over the interruption was evident.

"Of course. I've come at a poor time. My apologies." LaBette had seen and heard all that he required. Time for a quick exit.

He replaced his hat, picked up the satchel, and said, "I'll try another time—when your husband is home." He turned to leave, stopped and asked, "And when might that be?"

Marsha had her hand on the door handle. "He's away on business. Why don't you come back in a month?"

"Excellent. Good evening, Mrs. Nash. Good evening, young sir." LaBette smiled and left the house.

Marsha closed the door, and Taffy ran to the living room window. She stood on the sill and watched the man leave.

"Goodness, gracious. I thought he'd never leave."

Mother and son returned to the kitchen to finish their now chilled dinner with Charlie's grandmother. When they finished, Charlie and his grandma went into the den and played gin at the card table.

As was always the case, she let Charlie win. He knew she did, and loved her for her kindness. *Maybe someday . . . someday when I come back . . . she won't have to . . .* The boy couldn't complete the thought.

They played for an hour. Then all three watched the Sid Caesar Hour until it was time for bed. Charlie walked his grandmother to her car. He stood on the passenger side, opened the door, leaned in, and said, "Goodbye, Grandma." His eyes glistened and reflected back across the interior of the Oldsmobile.

"Charlie? Are you crying?"

"Uh, no, Grandma . . . got something in my eye is all."

She looked as if she wasn't sure whether to believe him or not. "Don't worry, Charlie. Everything will work out. Remember, you always know where you can come when you need to get away for a while."

"Thanks, Grandma. I'll, uh, see you later." Her words echoed through his head: *away for a while.*

He watched her pull away from the curb and drive down the street. He waved much longer than he normally did. After clearing his throat and sniffling a couple of times, he took Taffy for a quick walk and then came back inside. It was late. The day was drawing to a close—faster than the boy imagined it would. Now, once again, he was unsure of his decision, but he felt it was too late to turn back.

"Turn the front light out, will you, Charlie?" His mother requested. "And lock both doors too?"

"Sure, Mom." Charlie locked the front door and went into the kitchen. He heard his mother's footsteps as she climbed the stairs. Once the back door was secure, he opened the cupboard and took out the bag of dog food. When certain his mother was in her bedroom, he turned out the lights and hurried upstairs—the bag held behind his back.

He quickly stuffed the bag in the *Star Tribune* sack, changed into his pajamas, and went into the bathroom. He abandoned his nightly ritual of checking for pubic hair, quickly brushed his teeth, peed, and took toothbrush and paste with him back to his bedroom. Once the brush and paste were stored, he sat on the edge of the bed waiting for his mother to kiss him good night.

Charlie looked around the room and took a quick mental inventory. He was certain he had everything he needed except for a heavier coat, a stocking hat, and gloves. He'd grab those on his way out in the morning. Of greater concern now was to be sure he didn't cry when his mother came in and he saw her for the last time. *Don't, Charlie. Think of something else . . . Taffy! Think of Taffy and how well she did hunting . . .*

Before long, his mother came in. She had her quilted bathrobe on and her hair in curlers. "Ready for bed?"

"Yes."

"Okay. Get under the covers, and I'll tuck you in."

"Aw, Mom. I'm too big for that."

"Yes, I know. You're eleven now, but it makes me feel better to know you're safely tucked in for the night." She tugged and straightened the bedspread, tucked the edges in, and leaned over her son.

"Sleep tight, Charlie. Don't let the bed bugs bite!" She smiled and turned out the bedside light.

"Goodb . . . uh, good night, Mom," Charlie replied weakly.

She walked to the door and glanced back. "Door open or closed, son?"

Charlie could hardly talk. "Closed, please," he murmured.

The door shut, and the room became pitch dark except for a small ray of moonlight coming from the south window. Charlie turned his face into the pillow and, finally, had to let everything out. He sobbed for a long time. A very long time. *Why couldn't dad just . . . ? No, it's hopeless . . . dad'll never change.*

Charlie had no idea what lay ahead, but he had to escape the hurt that weighed on his small frame like an anvil—the pain caused by his father was just too much to endure any longer.

Finally, the crying stopped. Charlie, exhausted, hugged Taffy tightly and slipped away into sleep.

Fifteen

A T 3:00 A.M., A GRAY DeSoto Diplomat cruised up and down Oliver Avenue. The lone occupant looked for any sign of movement—anything out of the ordinary. If someone was arriving home late or was out for an early walk, he needed to know. Satisfied none on the quiet street were up and about this early, he drove down the alley behind 2300, returned to the street, and parked two houses up. He reached up and removed the cover for the dome light, popped out the bulb, and stuck it in his pocket. He slipped on a pair of thin, black, leather gloves, took one more look around, and stepped from the silent DeSoto.

He was dressed in black, including a watch cap pulled low on his head. The white hair and mustache were gone, as were the glasses—LaBette's hair was dyed black now. He allowed the door to close only part way—not enough to create a sound.

With the target house in sight, he walked across the street, sauntered over to the Nash driveway, and, as alert as a cougar on its stalk, went up the drive. His rubber-soled shoes were soundless in the still night air, but he intentionally picked up his feet with each step. A loose stone or a piece of gravel could accidentally be scuffed. Someone might hear.

LaBette walked around behind the house and approached the back door. After testing the handle, he paused to consider his options.

The dog presented his biggest problem. Breaking a window would surely be heard by the animal. He could pick the lock on one of the two doors, but there again, once in the house, and without knowing where the dog was, it was risky. No, he'd just have to wait for the right opportunity.

He was puzzled by what he had been told about the boy's trip to Montana. He had read the article about Frank Nash in the previous day's newspaper, and now that he knew all the facts about why the father was away—and for how long, he needn't worry about an unexpected return. That also explained the presence of the black Buick in the garage. What he couldn't grasp, however, was who, besides the boy, was taking the trip?

If the mother was leaving also, then he could wait, follow the pair as they drove west, and pick them off at his convenience. If the coins were left behind, he could safely return and scour the house without interruption, for the dog would also be absent.

LaBette made up his mind. He'd wait to see who left. If the boy was being driven to the train station, or driving with someone else, he'd know how to react. It made no sense to break in to the house at this time. Silence was his friend for now. Any sort of noise or commotion would create unwanted inquiry.

He returned to the driveway and quietly slipped into a row of arborvitae along the foundation of the neighbor's house. From that position, he could see and hear both the front and back doors of the Nash house, as well as keep an eye on the street. A patient, cautious killer, LaBette knew how to wait.

Like a hawk poised on the branch of one of the giant elms, the tall, contract killer took up his vigil. At the same time, he rested. He slowed his breathing, folded his arms, and leaned back. Every sense was still alert—nothing would escape his notice. A whippoorwill called in the distance. A small dog barked from a block away. The heavy smell of old smoke filled his nostrils. Time passed.

From some distance away, LaBette picked up the sound of small pieces of asphalt being crunched beneath tires. He stepped from the evergreens and glanced up the street. The dark shadow of an older model car slid down the street and stopped directly across from his position. LaBette focused on the make—a Packard, older. *Who the hell's that? Neighbor sneaking home after a night on the town?*

He watched and waited for the driver to exit. There was no movement. Five minutes passed—then fifteen. Still no sign of movement from the Packard. Suddenly a match flared as the driver lit a cigarette. LaBette caught a quick glimpse of a large shape, large head—nothing more. He was certain the man was parked to watch and wait. LaBette had an idea that the guy was watching the same house as he. *But for what?* The same reason as LaBette? He felt the first stirring of anger building.

LaBette required complete and total knowledge of every situation he contracted for—right down to the last, minute detail. Someone had failed to relay an important piece of information. He was certain of it.

CHARLIE OPENED HIS EYES. His heart pounded. He'd had another bad dream. The identical nightmare that plagued him for so many nights had returned. *It's just a dream . . . Mom will be okay . . .*

Wide-eyed, he waited for his eyes to adjust to the darkness. The moon had set moments earlier. Charlie's room was a black void. He rubbed his eyes, patted Taffy, and wiggled from beneath the covers. It was time. This was the day. He switched on the bedside lamp and glanced at the clock. 5:00 A.M.—the same time he always rose when he had papers to deliver.

He gathered everything needed for his journey, opened the door, and went into the bathroom. He returned to his bedroom and slipped on his long underwear, jeans, flannel shirt, and red sweater. He took one last, sad, glance around his room, switched out the light, hefted the newspaper sack to his shoulder, and walked into the hall. His mother's door was closed. A sudden urge to open it and run to her bed swept over him. He stopped and stared at the closed door. *No! It won't work . . . you know it won't. You have to leave—now!*

Charlie heaved the strap higher on his shoulder and whispered, "Come on, girl. Let's go."

Taffy and the boy crept downstairs to the kitchen. He fed the dog, ate a bowl of Cheerios, gobbled a cinnamon roll and drank a large glass of milk. It was time to go. *Wait! I forgot!* "Taffy, come here, girl." He whispered.

Taffy came close to his side, and Charlie knelt. He reached for her name tag and untied the short piece of rawhide attached to her collar. Once he had it off, he slipped the tag into his pants pocket. "There, now no one will know where we came from, girl." Saddened by the finality of this small action, he stood, took a deep breath and left the kitchen He stopped in the front hall to put on his fleece lined, blue canvas jacket, and left the house.

Once outside, Taffy took care of her morning business while Charlie mounted his bike. A warm breeze blew from the south—from down the street—the direction Charlie and Taffy were going. Had the breeze been from the other direction, or if the air had not been as saturated with the smell of smoke from distant fires, the dog might have caught the scent of the man hidden in the shadows next door. But she did not.

Charlie pedaled across the lawn and down the sidewalk. Taffy ran ahead.

LABETTE WAS GROWING CONCERNED. If the man in the Packard didn't leave soon, the coming dawn would expose his position, and he'd be forced to find a way back to his car in the daylight. Above all, he wanted to avoid detection. He was just about to exit the bushes and walk back behind the house and up the alley when he heard the front door of the Nash house open. He froze as the tan dog bounded out. *Oh, no! That cursed dog!* He reached in his jacket pocket and fingered the Luger thirty-eight. A small weapon fitted with a sound suppressor, the deadly German pistol had served him well over the years. If the dog came close, gave away his position, he'd have no choice but to shoot and run.

Across the street, Virgil watched the boy leave. He smiled as he thought of how easy this would be. Once the boy and dog were halfway down the block, he turned the key and started the Packard. He put the car in gear, and without turning on the headlights, pulled away from the curb.

From where LaBette was hidden, he observed the boy hoist a full canvas bag, climb on his bike and pedal away from the house. He released the air in his lungs as the dog ran ahead of the boy. Before long, the engine of the Packard fired. He heard the transmission shift and saw the car pull away from the curb—its headlights off. Once the boy and car were almost at the end of the block, LaBette stepped out of the arborvitae. He was confused and more than a little perturbed.

He hated surprises. Hated sloppiness. In his line of work, the slightest oversight could spell disaster for not only the contract, but for his own safety, as well.

Something was clearly wrong. *Who was in the Packard? Why was he tailing the kid?* With no time or way to phone his contact at that moment, all he could do was trail the Packard and the boy from a safe distance and wait to see what transpired. At the earliest opportunity, he'd make the call and find out what was going on.

LaBette raced across the street, opened the car door, and sat behind the wheel of the DeSoto. He started the car, left the lights off and slipped away form the curb. His mind raced as he attempted to figure out where the boy was going. More important, who was in the Packard? *Should have passed on this one . . . not enough information . . . not enough time to prepare . . . best thing I can do is pull the plug now and leave . . . but still . . . five thousand is a lot of money.*

LaBette wondered if the man in the Packard was some sort of backup, or hit-man-in-training. Sooner or later—one way or another, he would have to find out. This concerned him, but he was not surprised. His—theirs—was a ruthless business, with little room for mistakes or weakness. LaBette vowed to be especially alert on this job.

He kept the Packard in view but stayed well back to avoid detection. If the man was, in fact, his replacement, he would be an adversary of skill and repute—a killer, like himself, and probably much younger. *Pay attention! No mistakes!*

Suddenly he noticed in the distance that the Packard had turned right without slowing, while the boy went left. LaBette applied the brakes and slowed to a stop. Both the dark Packard as well as the boy were out of his sight. *Damn! Now what?* LaBette waited a few seconds, and decided he had to keep the boy in sight. He pulled away from the curb.

CHARLIE SHIFTED THE BAG around and pedaled down the block. When he reached the corner, he slowed, turned left and, after peddling a few yards, stopped. Jimmy McCarthy was crouched over the paper bundles, folding each paper and placing them in a bag identical to Charlie's.

"Hi, Charlie."

"Hi, Jimmy."

Jimmy stood and looked at his friend as he dismounted from the Schwinn. "Looks like you're all set. Still can't tell me where you're going?"

"Naw, I better not."

"Any idea when you'll be back?"

The reality of what Charlie was doing suddenly hit the boy like a mule's kick. Then he pulled out his coupon book and thrust it at his friend. All he managed was a brief, "Uh, uh." He cleared his throat. "Here's the collection book, Jimmy. Don't forget, the manager's name is Mr. Grisvold, and he's pretty fussy about no sick days."

"I'll remember, Charlie. Thanks for giving me your route. I can sure use the money . . . like to get a bike like yours."

"Tell ya what, Jimmy. I, uh . . . won't be needing mine. Why don't you pick it up at my grandma's later today?"

"You sure?"

"Yeah, I'm sure. Who knows when I'll be back? You might as well use the bike."

"That's great, Charlie. I'll take good care of it—promise!"

"Well, I better get going. See ya around, I guess." Charlie stared at the ground, reluctant to leave his good friend.

Jimmy returned to his bundling and said, "Yeah, see ya around. Bye, Taff." He rumpled the dog's ears briefly.

Charlie remounted and pedaled away. Taffy bounded ahead. He had a six-block ride to his grandmother's house, where he'd leave the bike. It only took ten minutes to travel the short distance. When he reached her house on Sheridan Avenue, the sun was just beginning to appear.

He hurried to park the bike in her small garage. He closed the door, then walked past her house and down the street. Once at the end of the block, he turned right and headed for the railroad yards down the hill. When he reached the first set of tracks, he called Taffy over and clipped a short leather leash to her collar. "Sorry, girl. That's just in case you get scared of the trains."

Charlie had some experience hopping freights. He and his friends frequently used that method of travel to the swimming beach at Cedar Lake during the summer. They always picked the slower starting steam engines rather than the big new diesels and found an empty car, while paying special attention to any nearby brakemen. They seldom had trouble because the distance they had to travel to the beach was less than a mile and the steam engines could never attain high speeds in that short a distance.

Now, however, he had a different problem to deal with: how to get Taffy into one of the box cars. She was not very heavy—Charlie had lifted her up before—but the floor level of the car was about equal to his chin. He also had to be certain that the train he was about to hop was going west— soon—and the car had to be empty. Again, Charlie was inclined to look for the engines rather than the diesels. He had a better chance of getting on board with the slower moving trains.

He held Taffy close and studied the waiting trains in the switchyard. Freight cars shuttled up and down the tracks. As each was released, it coasted until it slammed into the car ahead with a loud *clang!* The noise was unsettling. Charlie's nerves were already on edge.

One train captured his attention. Its engine was stoked with coal and heavy, acrid smoke billowed from the hour-glass shaped stack. The amount of steam coming from the smokestack and the sound of the steam engine indicated it was preparing to pull out.

Yes, that's the one we want—about forty cars. He selected as his target a car in the middle—a safe distance from both the steam engine and the caboose. That one! With the door half shut! He looked left, then right. He would be hidden for a short distance by a lone caboose and a couple of boxcars on adjoining tracks.

He took one last look up and down the tracks, and said, "Come on, Taff! Let's go!" She hesitated, but then stood to trot beside her master. Charlie jumped multiple sets of tracks and raced toward the train. The heavy shoulder bag made running difficult, and he stumbled over loose rock. He caught himself and continued. When he reached the partially open door, he stopped, took a quick look inside, and then leaned over. He picked up Taffy before she could resist, and with great effort, lifted her up to the deck of the freight car.

Suddenly aware that she was entering a strange smelling, forbidding space, she thrust both legs out in an effort to retard further entry.

"It's, okay, Taff. Please! We have to hurry, girl." Every moment he and the dog were exposed invited detection. He was terrified that they would be seen before ever mounting the train. He stepped back, turned sideways, and heaved her into the car.

Charlie removed the strap from around his neck, threw the bag in after Taffy, and then placed both hands on the wooden floor. He swung his legs up, banging one shin on the scarred plank flooring in the process. "Ow!" He sat and rubbed his shin as Taffy licked his face.

"Quick! Come on, girl." They ran to the front of the car where a dozen bales of hay were scattered, and sat down. He was breathing heavily and his heart thumped. He waited—certain they had been seen.

Taffy stood off to one side, her nose in the air, and her tail held high. One ear cocked in alarm. She was looking at the opposite corner of the bulkhead where they now sat—staring intently at a mound of loose hay.

"What's the matter, girl?"

Sixteen

IRGIL PISANT HAD A PLAN for grabbing the boy, but once he turned the corner and saw the boy chatting with another kid, he didn't know what to do. He sped around the corner in the opposite direction. He was worried that the boy would slip away for some unknown reason, and his sure-fire plan would fall apart.

He turned on the car's headlights, turned left on Lake of the Isles Boulevard, and hung another quick left on Franklin. He sped to the end of the block, and took one more left on Penn Avenue. He raced down the street in front of Kenwood School and slowed.

It was still quite dark, but as he coasted to the corner and glanced left, he could see both boys and the dog standing together. Virgil pulled over, killed the lights, and inhaled deeply. He was puzzled, however, and was unsure of his next move. He had planned to snatch the boy at a certain, dark section of Oliver once the boy started delivering his papers, but now. . . . *Nuts! Looks like the other kid's deliverin' the papers.* All he could do was watch.

Once Charlie remounted his bike, he rode to the corner of Penn and Twenty-first Street. He looked quickly in Virgil's direction, then zipped across the street and continued on up Twenty-first. Virgil started the car, left the lights out, and followed the boy all the way to Sheridan. He never noticed the car trailing him some distance behind.

Virgil observed the boy ride through the yard of a two-story brick house half-way up the block. *Maybe he's goin' to visit someone? Nope, here he comes . . . walkin' now.* Before he could react, the boy and dog came down the sidewalk directly toward Virgil.

Now! Grab the kid right now when he's next to the car! Virgil couldn't believe his good fortune. He ducked below the dashboard and peered through the steering wheel. He lifted the door handle and heard it click. *Get ready, he's almost . . .*

Just before Charlie and Taffy reached the car, they crossed the street. In seconds, the pair were running down a side street—toward the freight yards down below.

Pisant rose up and stared in disbelief at the retreating form of the small boy. The short street ended in a turnaround. *You jest blew yer chance, bone head . . . why di'n't ya jump out . . . Damn!* All Virgil could do was watch and wonder what the boy was up to. *Pretty heavy lookin' bag he's got . . . don't s'pose he's gonna . . .*

LaBETTE WAS EVEN MORE CONFUSED than his adversary in the Packard. What started out as a simple contract to snuff a eleven-year-old kid with a coin collection had taken more turns than a snaky, mountain road. The kid was leading them on a wild goose chase, and now it appeared like he was going to hop a freight! *This kid can't intend to ride a freight all the way to Montana . . . can he? Judas H. Priest! What the hell have I gotten into, here?*

Daylight broke through the elms. LaBette was exposed and suddenly wished he had not agreed to the contract on such short notice. He hated all of the unknown elements involved. *I should pop this other guy right now and get him out of my way!* He fingered the Luger. It lay on the seat near his thigh. *Do it! Now!*

Just as he was about to exit the car and walk ahead a hundred yards to the Packard, he realized that such an impetuous move was precisely what he prided himself on not doing. *No! Think! Whoever is in the Packard probably has more information on the boy . . . knows where he's headed . . . than I do.* LaBette concluded that Packard Guy was his for the taking any time he chose. Better to wait, follow, and act when all the odds were in his favor. He relaxed, let go of the Luger, and stared ahead. *A stone is heavy, and the sand weighty; but a fool's wrath is heavier than both . . .* LaBette thought.

VIRGIL STARTED THE CAR and turned left on to the side street. Charlie was still in view, but if he kept going toward the freight yard, as soon as he reached the high grass, he'd vanish from view. Pisant crept ahead until Charlie slipped into the weeds. He parked, opened the door, and left the security of the big car. He crept ahead until he reached the area where Charlie disappeared. He parted the grass and observed boy and dog crouched alongside the first set of tracks.

Virgil scanned the area—straining to locate the boy and dog. The massive freight yard covered an immense area set well below where he now stood. The air was heavy with the nauseating odor of burning coal and diesel. Combined with the already smoky atmosphere, the effect was a heavy blanket of smog that hung over the entire yard. Virgil worried that if a brakeman spotted the boy, he'd nab the kid and whatever opportunity Pisant might have had that morning would be lost. There was no one in sight, however, other than one man far off to the right climbing into a caboose. He spotted the switch house some distance away. *If the kid isn't careful . . .*

All at once, Charlie and the dog darted across three sets of tracks. He watched the boy stumble and catch himself. Before Virgil could react, both were inside a box car in the middle of a train. *I'll be damned! Kid's hopped a freight somewhere.* Virgil stood and waited but the boy never reappeared.

The sun was up above the horizon, and he could almost see all the way into the interior of the boxcar. His mind raced. If the train pulled away and headed west, when would it stop for water and coal? He had to find out where the train was going—when it would make its first stop. *Could be any number of small towns or whistle stops west of the Cities*, he thought.

The long freight train jerked ahead, and began to pull out of the yard. *Aw, geez! Now everything's gettin' too, damn complicated.*

He ran down the slight incline and raced across the tracks toward the switch house. He had to find out where the train was headed . . . where it would stop first.

Virgil approached the side door of the switch house, paused to catch his breath and opened the door. A tall three-story tower, the building was positioned directly in the center of the yard where it commanded a broad view up and down the tracks. Once inside, Virgil climbed a set of stairs to the glassed-in control room. Two men were hunched over a long counter. Neither sensed his presence.

Pisant collected himself, and said, "Say, excuse me, gents."

Both men turned at the sound of Pisant's voice. "How'd you get in here?" One asked.

"Oh, the door was open, so I jest came on up." Virgil decided to forge ahead before they could really question his motives. "I was wonderin' about something?"

"Yeah, what's that? We're kinda busy here, bud . . . gotta train jest pullin' outta the yard . . ."

"Yeah, I know," Virgil interrupted, "See, what I was wonderin' was, I was out walkin' jest now . . . uh, with my missus . . . an' . . . uh, well, we got a bet about when a train like that makes its first stop. So, I says to the missus, 'Heck, I'll jest run down there and ask the fellas inside.'"

He paused to catch his breath, " See, this bet we got, well if I lose, I gotta do the dishes for a month see, but if I win—well, I get to go huntin' with my buddies next weekend."

The taller of the two smiled, and said, "Hell, mister! We sure wouldn't want you to lose a bet like that, would we, Merle?"

Merle chuckled and said, "Hells-bells, buddy, we'll tell ya whatever ya need to know."

"Great," Pisant replied. "I bet her the train's first stop would be Litchfield—she says it's gotta be Howard Lake. Which is it?"

Merle and his co-worker laughed together. "Aw, hell, bud, looks like you're outta luck. That train that just pulled out is headed to South Dakota, but it's scheduled to pull over at a siding west of Hutchinson to wait for an eastbound passenger train. Looks like neither one of you wins."

"Aw, nuts!" He chuckled and added, "Guess I'll jest have to tell the missus' a little white lie, eh, fellas?" Pisant smiled.

Both men laughed and prepared to turn back to their switching, "We better get back to work now," Merle said. "Have a good time with your buddies."

"Oh, yeah . . . I will. Thanks a bunch for the information. See you boys again," Virgil said. He turned around to leave, and added, "When you think it might reach that siding?"

Merle replied, "'Bout 10:30 or 11:00 this morning, I expect." The switch master never questioned why Pisant required this last bit of information.

"Thanks."

Pisant made his way down the stairs, out the door, and back across the tracks toward his car. Now he knew where to intercept the train—and the boy. *But, how do I get the kid out without being seen?*

Virgil had plenty of time to figure out his best approach on the drive to Hutchinson. Fortunately, the small town was situated along State Highway Seven, which ran parallel to State Highway Twelve—the road through Lockhart. Once he had the boy, it would be a short drive back to the farm.

It was 7:00 A.M. by the time Pisant reached the Packard. He started the engine, lit a cigarette, and put the car in gear. He never noticed the gray DeSoto he passed on his way out of Kenwood.

LaBette put the binoculars back in the leather case, set the case on the seat, and started the car. He shifted into reverse and backed away from the embankment overlooking the tracks. He stopped, shifted to first and slowly edged from the curb. He had no choice now but to continue to follow the Packard and hope the man had knowledge of the boy's destination. He missed seeing the boy through the binoculars and had to assume he either crossed the yard and continued walking or jumped a train.

He had managed at least to get a good look at his adversary. A big man, dressed like a mechanic—or farmer. Long, greasy hair. Some sort of old wound high on his forehead. Clumsy looking, black eye on the left side—as if he'd been in a fight recently.

Something else he couldn't quite put a finger on—the guy looked, well, very strange, was all he could think of. LaBette had learned to read body language over the years, and something about this guy's posture left him questioning whether or not he was a pro. He looked awkward—clumsy even. When the man returned to his car, he focused the binoculars on his face. The man's small eyes had a demented sort of look to them. *Better be careful—mental cases are unpredictable. Might not be playing with a full deck . . .*

He hated the way the morning had played out—too many uncertainties, too much he didn't know about. He wished he could get to a phone and find out what was going on, but that would have to wait. All he could do was to stay behind the Packard. Sooner or later, he'd have his chance.

TWO AUTOS DROVE out of the Lake of the Isles area early Tuesday morning. Caught in the morning traffic, they both blended in with all the other cars heading for work. Virgil led the way, oblivious to the DeSoto following him at a safe distance. Pisant's plan had taken a detour, but now he was certain that once he reached the railroad siding, everything would fall into place as he desired.

LaBette had no idea where they were going, and he was tempted to give up the chase, call Val, and hand back the contract. He resisted, however, and drove out of town a fair distance behind the Packard. The five thousand dollar fee awaiting him would go a long way toward securing his retirement. *Hang in there, Joseph. Your turn will come . . .*

Seventeen

TAFFY BRISTLED. Tufts of hair stiffened just behind her ears. Her black nose flexed as she tried to decipher what was hidden in the near corner. She stood to her full height—all fifty pounds alert and tense.

"Taff? Come here, girl."

The train lurched, and Taffy lost her balance. Charlie tugged at the leash to pull her toward him. She refused to budge.

Suddenly, the pile of hay shook. Taffy saw a scuffed, black boot appear from beneath the pile. Then another. She growled a deep, guttural sound that frightened Charlie.

"Taffy?" Then he too noticed the legs protruding from the pile. Soon, the hay parted and the arms and torso of a man appeared—brushing stalks of grass from his unshaven, dirty face.

Taffy barked and stood stiff-legged.

Charlie froze. Too late to jump from the slow moving train, all he could do was sit with his dog and hope the man intended to get off.

"Hey! What the hell you doin' in my car, kid?"

Charlie's heart pounded. The man presented a frightful sight. Dressed in tattered clothing, the stranger brushed hay from a dark green, full length, wool, army coat. A black watch cap covered his head. When he opened his mouth, Charlie noticed that the few teeth he had were the color of oatmeal. When he spoke, the mouth was nothing more than a large, gaping, jagged hole. Charlie could see he was about his father's age, only he looked . . . well . . . unhealthy.

"I asked you a question, kid! What the hell ya doin' in my car?"

"I . . . I didn't know anyone was in here."

"Well, there is. Now you and that mangy dog a yers can git the hell outta here!"

He pointed toward the half-open door.

Charlie knew he couldn't leave the car—not without risking both his and Taffy's life. "Uh . . . I can't. The train's moving." He was trembling and his voice shook.

The stranger stepped toward the boy but was halted by Taffy, who was barking and snapping her teeth. "Keep a good grip on that lead, kid." He walked around the boy and dog toward the door, reached outside, and pulled the heavy door closed. Darkness filled the large space.

Charlie blinked—waiting for his eyes to adjust. Shafts of light streaked through gaps in the doors, as well as cracks in the wooden side panel. He tightened his grip on Taffy's leash and said, "Hush, girl! That's enough."

Taffy's barking ceased, but a low, menacing rumble continued to echo in the large chamber.

The filthy stranger leaned against the wall nearest the door, pulled a cigar stub from one of many pockets, struck a match, puffed twice, and said, "Oughta pitch the both a ya off right now. Anyone see ya climb in here, kid?"

"No. I don't think so. I looked pretty good to make sure no one was around."

"That's good, cause if one a those bulls down here sees ya, yer ass is grass! Ever see what they do with them big ax handles they carry?"

"No."

"If they catch a rider like you or me, they whack ya over the head and toss ya on the tracks. If another train don't run ya over, yer lucky. This here's my car, got it? First time we stop, you and that mutt's leaving—unnerstand?"

"Yes. I'm sorry."

"You should be—brat kid and a mutt intrudin' on my space. World ain't the same no more. Used to be a man could ride from one coast t'other and never be disturbed. Now I got to put up with a runt and a mongrel." He puffed at the cigar one last time, dropped it and ground it into the planking with the heel of one boot while he continued mumbling to himself and returned to his pile of hay. Once seated, he reached in his trundle and withdrew a bottle of wine. After a long drink, he screwed the cap back on and turned his attention back to the boy.

Charlie noticed his stare and edged closer to the corner. Taffy lay down between Charlie and the hobo.

"What's yer name, kid?"

"Charlie?"

"What ya got in the bag there, Charlie?" His eyes shone as he eyed the boy's sack.

"Oh, nothing much. Just some clothes and a sleeping bag . . . and some food for my dog." Charlie told him. He dragged the bag to his other side—out of sight of the mean-looking man.

The train gained speed, and as it did, the box car rocked and shook. The noise soon became deafening—a combination of metal and wood rattling along with the wind blowing through and around the car. The air chilled.

"That so? Don't suppose ya got any liquor in there? Naw, yer jest a kid. How about food?" he asked eagerly.

Charlie was not about to reveal anything in his sack to this man. He was still frightened by the strange man. "No . . . I, uh . . . had to kinda leave in a hurry. Don't have much."

"Left in a hurry, did ya? How come? Cops after ya?"

"Uh . . . no. I'm . . . well, I'm leaving home to go to Montana." Charlie immediately regretted telling the man the truth. *Have to lie . . . don't tell anyone the real reasons . . .*

"That so? An ya mean to tell me ya don't got no food—or money?" The bum shifted on his butt, pulled his knees up, and leaned closer.

Charlie wanted to get away from this man but knew he couldn't. His only hope was to continue to lie and keep Taffy between himself and the hideous hobo. "Nope."

The bum looked at the boy closely. "Anybody see ya leave—parents, friends? Anyone know yer here?"

Charlie was terrified as he thought he knew what the man was considering. "Uh, yes. My friend, Jimmy McCarthy . . . he came to the yard and watched me hop the train . . . he's probably still down there now."

"That so? Well, this here train's now five miles away, kid. Near as I can tell, ain't nobody around to see where yer at—'cept me, that is." He rose to one knee and reached in a pocket of his coat.

Taffy noticed the movement—her eyes had not strayed from the man for one second. She stood and bristled once more.

"Aw, settle down, ya ugly bitch! I ain't gonna hurt no one. Ya keep a tight grip on her. Hear me, kid? She comes after me she's gonna git a size ten in the head, an' that'll be all she wrote—that's fer sure. Mutts! Hate them sonsabitches!" He stood and leaned against the bulkhead.

Charlie jerked and Taffy barked. "Taffy, be quiet."

"Taffy, Huh? Like the candy? Ya know, kid, not too long ago me an' some a my friends ate a dog 'bout that size—didn't taste like no taffy, but it wasn't too bad." He laughed and coughed up a gob of phlegm. With a quick motion, he turned his head and spit on the worn floor. "Yep, when yer hungry and poor, a guy'd eat jest about anything . . . but ya wouldn't know bout that, would ya, kid?"

Charlie wanted to vomit. Eat a dog? He swallowed hard and stared at the ugly man. He felt helpless. And terrified!

"Yep, I seen it all, kid. Hell, been riding the rails since I was fifteen." He paused, leaned over and withdrew the wine bottle. After unscrewing the cap, he took two long pulls, checked the remaining level of wine, and put the cap back on. He slipped the jug in a side pocket and edged closer to Charlie.

"Say! We ain't been formally introduced, have we? My name's Willy. Railroad Willy. What's yours?"

"I already told—uh . . . Charlie."

Willy took two steps, reached out one hand, and said, "Well, put 'er there, Charlie!"

Taffy snapped at his outstretched hand.

Willy jerked his hand back and said, "Whoa there, bitch! I've a good mind ta give ya a whack alongside yer head, ya mangy mutt!" He pulled out a wicked looking, black club and waved it at the dog. "Know what this is, kid?"

"Nnn . . . no." Charlie heard a roar in his ears that had nothing to do with the other sounds in the car.

"It's a billy—took it off a railroad dick back in St Louie. Any idea what one a these things kin do to a man's head . . . or a dog's?"

Charlie couldn't answer. Visions of the ugly man hitting him and Taffy on the head flashed through his mind.

"Split yer skull like a rotten melon! That's what!" He slapped the billy into an open palm with a *crack*. He suddenly lunged at Taffy but not close enough to be bitten.

She leaped toward him and snarled and snapped. She was at the end of the leash.

Charlie pulled on the leather with all his strength. "Taffy! Taffy! No!" Tears formed and pooled in both eyes.

Willy stepped back and chuckled. "Goddamned mutt!" He slipped the billy in his pants pocket and took another swig from his bottle.

Charlie felt like he had to say something to make the bum leave them alone. "Listen, mister . . . me and Taffy'll get off as soon as the train stops, honest." His voice sounded squeaky, and he was afraid that the man never heard him.

Willy sat down, heavily, into the hay. He was mumbling again. His head drooped and fell to his chest. A thin line of spittle escaped and ran down his chin. As the freight rocketed down the tracks, Willy's head rolled from side to side. He slipped into a drunken stupor.

Charlie watched the man closely. When he was convinced that Willy was asleep, he wiped his eyes, and pulled Taffy close. "Come here, girl." He lowered his voice to a whisper. "Good job, Taff! We need to keep this guy away until we can get out of here." He wrapped both arms around her and rested his head on her shoulder.

Charlie knew he was trapped and defenseless, except for the fierce protectiveness displayed by his dog. Even though Taffy was of average size for a female golden, Charlie feared that the two of them were no match for the man in the corner. *My knife!* He reached in his pocket and slipped out the pocket knife with built-in compass.

After glancing over at Willy to make certain he was still asleep, he opened the blade and tucked it into his coat pocket. Satisfied that if he needed to, he could quickly show the knife to Willy, he relaxed—but just a bit. He didn't dare fall asleep—even with Taffy's vigilance.

He looked around the car. Small pieces of alfalfa and dirt swirled across the scarred floor in miniature whirlwinds. Even smaller flecks of chaff were air-borne and drifted around the interior of the car. Shafts of sunlight from the shallow arc of the October sun poked through the slats, creating parallel bands of bright light. Each looked alive with perpetual motion as the tiny fragments darted in and out of the light. Charlie thought, *the streams of light looked like stairs—with tiny people—or what were those called? Escalators. That's what they were—escalators.* The dry, dusty fragments were everywhere, and all of a sudden he had to sneeze. He pinched his nose before the sneeze erupted and cut it short.

The steam locomotive barreled through the countryside. Every now and then, the whistle blew and its sound—a measured *whoo, whoo*—drifted back on the swift-moving steam and smoke. Charlie was hungry and thirsty, but he chose not to do anything that might cause the man in the corner to wake up. As hard as he tried, he couldn't keep his eyes open, however. The rhythmic swaying of the train lulled him asleep.

Taffy's brown eyes never left the man asleep in the corner. She finally slid to a prone position after Charlie lay his head back against a hay bale. She continued to stare into the corner, ready to react to the slightest movement from then man huddled in the hay.

VIRGIL DROVE OUT HIGHWAY SEVEN toward Hutchinson. He had decided not to stop by the farm as he didn't want to run into McIlheny. He couldn't afford any delay in meeting the train. He had to reach that siding west of Hutch before the train pulled over.

He had spent the past couple of hours berating himself for not memorizing either the words or numbers stamped on the outside of the car the boy had climbed into. Nor had he counted the cars from either end of the train. Now he could only guess which car he was after. *At least I know it's in the middle of the train. Guess I'll jest have to open all the ones I can 'til I find him.*

He stopped in the small town of Mountain Lake for gas. The village sat alongside the railroad tracks and contained a filing station, grocery store, post office, and two grain elevators.

Virgil sat and waited. Before long, the attendant appeared at his side window. He rolled down his window and said, "Fill 'er up, mac."

"You got it. Check the oil?"

"Yeah. Say, that freight that normally comes through here been by yet?"

"Nope." He glanced at the Pepsi Cola clock above the door. "Should be coming through any time, I'd guess."

Perfect. I'm ahead of it. "Say, would ya mind cleaning the windshield, mac? Never seen so damn many bugs on the road."

"Yeah, funny year, isn't it? We should have a couple inches of snow on the ground by now, and instead we're swattin' mosquitoes."

"Got that right. Ain't complainin', though. Rather have this than cold weather." Virgil added. He was feeling particularly friendly this morning. His plan was still going to come together.

"Looks like you got whacked pretty good in the back end here, bud. Grill and bumper are all smashed in, and the taillight is busted!" the attendant called. "Gonna cost plenty to fix that, I'm afraid."

Virgil's former good mood dissipated like a vapor of steam on a hot day. The reminder of how everything had started crystallized all at once. He leaned his head out the window. "Yeah. Some guy ran me off the road the other night."

"No kiddin'?"

"Yep . . . know who done it, too."

The attendant finished gassing the car, replaced the hose, and screwed the cap back on. "Did you report him?"

"Hmmm? Oh. No, not yet. I'm kinda in a hurry, mac. Here ya go."
He handed a five-dollar bill to the attendant.

"Be right back with your change."

As soon as the attendant returned, Virgil left the filing station and
drove over to the grocery store. After purchasing a loaf of bread, a quart of
chocolate milk, a jar of mustard, lunch meat, cookies, and two six packs of
Pabst, he climbed back in the Packard.

He knew he had plenty of time, so he fixed himself a sandwich. Just
as he was mouthing the first bite of bologna and mustard, he noticed a county sheriff's car speeding past—going east. *McIlheny! That piece of crud! Like to
take care of that bastard while I'm at it,* he thought. He watched to see if the
sheriff slowed. He did not.

Fortunately for Virgil, a large milk truck coming the other way had
blocked the sheriff's view of the front of the store just as he was passing. He
never saw Pisant's dirty Packard.

After eating half the sandwich and gulping a couple of slugs of
chocolate milk, Pisant pulled back out on the highway.

A SHORT DISTANCE DOWN the highway, from a spot next to two grain elevators, LaBette observed Virgil's movements with interest. He checked his gas
gauge—a quarter of a tank. He'd have to fill up pretty quick. *Doesn't look like
the guy's in too much of a hurry—I wonder if I have time . . .*

As soon as the Packard drove off down the highway, LaBette hurried over to the filing station and quickly hopped out of his car. He met the
attendant at the door.

"Say, that guy that just left in the blue Packard—he happen to mention where he was going?"

"Nope. Sorry. Why the interest, if you don't mind my asking?"

"Oh, I'm a private investigator—insurance. Checking out a few
things is all. He say anything else?"

"Nope. Asked about the westbound freight that's due to pass any
time."

"Got any idea where that train's headed?"

"Nope—somewhere in South Dakota, I'd say. Need any gas?"

"Yeah, guess I have time. Fill it up, will you?" LaBette decided that if the guy in the Packard was interested in a train, then it could only mean he had seen the kid climb aboard. If he was right, all he had to do was stay ahead of the train and keep an eye on it. Sooner or later the kid would appear, or the guy in the Packard—or both.

LaBette stood next to his car as an older model Ford Super-Deluxe station wagon pulled up to the pumps and stopped directly opposite LaBette's car. He watched as an older man opened the door, stepped out, and stretched.

The man was wearing a beaten up, frayed, smallish Stetson. It was sweat-stained, and the brim drooped. The old man's face was lined and deeply tanned—as if he'd been working outdoors most of his life. Bowlegged and somewhat stooped, he stretched both arms over his head, yawned and noticed LaBette.

"Howdy," the man said. "Beautiful day, isn't it?"

"I guess. Depends on your point of view, I'd say," LaBette replied.

"Now, how can anyone complain about a day like this? In October? In Minnesota?" He smiled a friendly grin waiting for a response.

LaBette ignored the old man and climbed back in his car. The attendant finished pumping gas and said, "Let's see. That'll be three twenty."

He paid for the gas and said, "Thanks."

"My pleasure. Stop again."

He gave one last glance at the old man, put the DeSoto in gear, and pulled out onto the highway. He shoved the accelerator to the floor and sped away.

"These young folks are always in such a hurry, aren't they?" the old man said to the attendant.

"Yeah . . . funny guy. Some sort of insurance investigator, he said. Trailing a big Packard with the back end bashed in."

"That so? Fella didn't seem that talkative to me," the old man replied. He stared after the retreating DeSoto briefly and asked, "I do need gas, my friend, and if you could suggest where I might get a decent meal around these parts, I'd be grateful?"

"You bet," the attendant said. He cranked the handle on the gas pump, found the gas cap hidden in the wood siding of the old Ford, unscrewed the cap, and began filling the tank. "Let's see . . . I say your best bet is the Chat 'N' Chew Café in Hutch. Next town of any size west—about twenty miles from here. Tuesday is meat loaf day—best meat loaf in these parts. Check the oil?"

"Please."

The attendant leaned against the old Ford and said, "This was a great car. I always loved the way they blended the wood sides into the body. Real wood, too. Green's a nice color with this wood. Had the wagon long?"

"Yeah, bought her right off the showroom floor in 1947. Got almost two hundred thousand miles on the old girl," he said proudly.

"Still say old Henry knew how to build a better car than anyone else. You ever think of selling this, you let me know, ya hear?"

The old man chuckled, and gazed across the horizon. "Afraid that won't be possible . . . where I'm going . . ." He never finished the sentence, but reached into his pants for his wallet, and handed the attendant a ten.

"Let me just check your oil real quick."

"Oh, yeah. Right." The old man waited while the hood was popped and the oil checked.

"Looks like she's down about a pint. Be okay for a while." He dropped the hood, wiped his hands on a greasy rag, and said, "Be right out with your change."

The old man removed his hat, wiped his brow with a red kerchief, and waited for the attendant to return. He looked up and watched as a high flock of Canada geese flew overhead. Their honking drifted down as they moved in a southeasterly direction. "Headed home, eh, fellas? Me too . . ."

"Here you go, sir." The attendant handed back the change.

"Thank you. Have a good day, now. I'm looking forward to that homemade meat loaf," the old man said.

"Take care, old timer. And take care of that old wagon of yours—she's a beauty."

"I will. So long now." He replaced his hat and, as he prepared to climb into the station wagon, he heard the distant sound of a train whistle.

"That'll be the westbound . . . right on schedule," the attendant called.

The old man waved to the attendant and settled behind the wheel. He started the engine, put the car in gear, and pulled away.

Eighteen

CHARLIE COULDN'T MOVE. He knew he had to get away but his feet were too heavy. He looked down—his new boots were buried in mud. If he didn't lift his feet from the muck—a large man with no teeth towered over him. He had a club in his hand, and he swung it over his head. *Move, Charlie! Hurry!* He couldn't. It was too late . . .

His heart pounded. From far away, he heard what sounded like . . . like, a motor, or . . . growling. Charlie opened his eyes and looked around. He was breathing hard. His nose was plugged with dust and debris from the boxcar. Taffy, leaning against his knee, had stiffened. A deep, throaty snarl rose from her slender chest.

"Taff? What is it . . . ?" He looked around the car. Railroad Willy, the man in the corner, was standing up. His long, wool Army overcoat flapped open and Charlie noticed the billy tucked in his black, wrinkled belt. Charlie's bag had shifted near his feet—the contents open and visible.

"Hey! Who the hell are you? What you doin' in my car? Git outta here—hear me?"

"I, we . . ." *What's the matter with him? He's crazy . . . or drunk!* Charlie trembled. He couldn't speak. His legs wobbled as he stood and reined Taffy closer to his side. The dog's teeth were bared, and her tongue darted from between four large, canines. Her upper lip curled—a warning to the large man to stay clear.

"This is my car . . . not yours!" Willy said. He turned to his left and swayed across the car to the far bulkhead. Turning his back, he brushed the coat flap aside and unbuttoned his pants. A long, yellow stream splashed against the wall. Willy's piss seemed to last forever. After a long while, he adjusted himself and shuffled over to the door instead of going back to his corner. A new, raw stench permeated the space.

Charlie wrinkled his nose. His teeth were chattering. Taffy didn't budge from her threatening posture.

"That yer mutt, kid?" Willy said as he slid the door open a few feet. He stuck his head out and glanced up and down the length of the train.

"Yyy . . . yes, her name's Taffy. I'm Charlie, remember?"

"Remember what?"

"We met before . . . before you went to sleep."

"We did, huh. Well in that case—where the hell are we? Ya got any idea, kid?"

"Uh, no."

Willy eyed the bag at Charlie's feet. "Say! What's in the bag? A jug? You got any booze? Any money?"

"No. I told you . . ."

"You pay the toll yet, kid? Don't ya know when ya come ta another man's car, ya gotta pay a toll? Les see what ya got in that bag." He reached out as if to grab the bag.

The train lurched. Willy spun around the edge of the door and fell back against the side wall. "Aargh! I need a drink," he muttered. Patting his pockets, he found the bottle. After a long pull, he held the bottle up and studied the small amount that remained. "Crap . . . say, lemme see that bag. You gotta jug, don't ya?" He stepped toward Charlie and Taffy.

"No. I . . . I'm too young . . ." Charlie nudged back the open bag with his foot. Smaller, heavier objects spilled into the loose straw.

"Bullcrap! Don't hand me that!" Willy's eyes widened as he spied something in the straw. "Course you do. What's in that bag? You holdin' out on me, ain't ya? Where's my toll? Huh?" By now he was within arm's reach of Taffy. He opened the coat and withdrew the short, ugly oak club.

He waved it in front of Taffy's face—taunting her. She snapped at the billy and snarled in defiance. He was baiting her.

Charlie held fast to the leash with both hands, but his boots skidded on the dusty floor. "Please! Don't hurt her! Taffy! Taffy!"

Willy raised his arm as Taffy edged closer. Realizing that the club was in the wrong hand, he moved to exchange the bottle for the billy.

Taffy was too close, and Charlie couldn't pull her back. She was snapping continuously! Spittle flew from between her teeth. He watched in horror as Willy completed the switch and raised the club directly over her head. "NO! TAFFY!"

Just as Willy prepared to strike the dog's head, the train rounded a curve. Willy fell forward, tripped, and landed on his face! The wine bottle flew through the air and hit the floor. *Clang!*

Taffy barked and leaped as Willy attempted to scrabble away. Charlie was losing strength. His hands were numb. No matter how hard he tried, he couldn't keep from skidding on the floor toward Willy. Taffy snapped again. This time she caught a corner of Willy's filthy coat. She shook it in her mouth, back and forth, as if killing a rat. With all four legs braced, her nails dug into the soft wood. She tugged and pulled.

"Hey! Leggo!" Willy released the club to grip his coat with both hands. Taffy hung on. The club rolled near his foot. He freed one hand and reached for the weapon.

Charlie felt faint. Helpless, sick with fear, he could only watch as Willy stretched for the club. *He'll kill her!* "Taffy! No!" Charlie yelled.

He pulled against the five-foot leash with every ounce of energy that remained. Taffy's claws dug into the plank flooring. Charlie's feet slipped once more on loose dirt and hay. Taffy was slowly pulling him toward Willy. Nothing Charlie could do or say checked her determined tugging.

Willy missed the club by inches. It rolled away toward the center of the car. He reached back with his free hand and hung onto the door frame as he struggled to escape the menacing dog. The train jerked as if braking. The door slid open its full width.

Charlie saw Willy pull himself erect, and with one huge jerk, yanked at his long coat. Taffy suddenly released her grip.

Willy stumbled backwards. His head hit the door frame. His dark eyes glazed. His mouth fell open as if in a scream, but no sound came from the hideous, brown hole. Willy's arms hung limp. For what seemed to Charlie like an eternity, the hobo hung on the edge of the car. He swayed back then forward. Finally, his legs buckled, and he fell through the open door—backwards.

Willy stared at Charlie—his eyes wide, mouth open, brown teeth exposed—and then he was gone.

Thud. Willy's body struck a metal signal pole seconds after falling away. The rush of wind through the car masked the boy's own heavy breathing. Taffy stopped barking and sat down. She was panting heavily but her eyes never left the open door—as if she feared the large man would somehow reappear.

Charlie walked over and with the toe of his boot, kicked the billy through the opening. He pulled Taffy back to the hay and sat down. He was trembling, and he couldn't catch his breath. He was exhausted and in shock. Soon Charlie began to cry. He put his head on his knees and sobbed for a long time.

Finally, realizing he and Taffy were safe and unharmed, he sniffled, patted Taffy and scratched her ears weakly, and said, "Thanks, girl. I think . . . I think . . . you . . . saved my life." The words spoken out loud brought on a fresh bout of weeping. *Shouldn't have come . . . a bad dream . . . that's all it is . . .*

Taffy licked at the salty tears streaming down her master's flushed cheeks.

"No more freight trains, girl. I promise," Charlie mumbled. He inhaled deeply, and said, "As soon as the train stops, we're getting off. I'd rather hitchhike than do this again . . . wouldn't you?" He hugged the dog tightly and scratched her chest.

Charlie pulled back one sleeve and looked at his wrist watch. Babe Ruth smiled at him from the watch face. The watch had been a birthday gift from his grandmother, and it reminded him again of home . . . of all he had left behind. *Too late. We can't go back. Stop being such a baby . . . it's over.* "It's eleven o'clock, Taff. If the train doesn't stop soon, we'll have to eat some of the stuff in my bag. Sure would like a hamburger and a malt, though." He hurriedly searched through the straw and stuffed everything he could find back in the bag.

He sat back and stared at the open door. A rush of warm, dry air swirled around the car. Charlie heard the train whistle as it approached another crossing. *It's gotta stop pretty soon, I think.* He stroked Taffy's long, silky hair and waited for his opportunity to escape the vile boxcar.

Virgil drove through Hutchinson and slowed. The railroad siding began just west of town. He pulled off the highway on the north side of the road at a spot he figured was about half the length of the train, turned off the ignition, and opened a bottle of beer. After the first long swig, he positioned the bottle between his legs and lit a cigarette.

Pisant flicked the lit match out of his window and took a long, deep drag. What he had noticed out the window was like a slap in the face. He gasped as he exhaled. The smoke caught in his throat and made him cough again—then gag, as well. His eyes bulged and teared, but finally the wrack of coughing ceased.

He looked over his shoulder and peered up and down the tracks. "Sonofabitch! The tracks! They're on the wrong side of the road!" It hadn't occurred to the big man that if the railroad tracks and siding ran parallel to the highway on the south side of the road, he would be unable to spot the open car door. More than likely, if the boy left the train, he would exit on the same side as he had entered.

You're an idiot, Pizant! Besides . . . look around. What'd ya see? Nothin'! That's what. The flat landscape was empty. For as far as he could see, there was no relief—no cover—for miles in every direction. Wilted corn, lost to the drought, hung limply just beyond the tracks. Other small grain crops had all been harvested—the fields plowed.

Now what? he wondered. *I can't just wander up and down the tracks looking for the kid's car . . . guys in the caboose or engine will spot me sure as hell.* He chugged the Pabst, chucked the empty out the window, and opened a second bottle. From behind, he heard the long, low whistle of an approaching train. He spun around and saw its white plumes of smoke chuffing into the blue sky from the other side of the small town.

Once he realized how badly he had miscalculated, all he could do was sit and wait. *If the kid gets out on the other side, I'll spot him as he walks to one end of the train or the other. Then . . . I wait for the right time to nab him. Don't worry, Virg, ol' boy. Everything's still gonna work out jest fine.* "I'll git you, you rat . . . but first that runt of a kid of yers!" *And, if he doesn't get out?* Virgil chose not to consider that possibility.

CHARLIE LISTENED TO the whistles. They seemed different from all the rest he had heard along the way. The train was slowing. "Maybe now, Taff?" His heart leaped as he anticipated escape from the smelly boxcar.

The train crept through town. Charlie couldn't see any of the buildings from his view out the car door, but he caught glimpses through the slats on the other side. "It's a town, girl. And I bet they have a restaurant." He was excited. Taffy sensed his change of mood. Charlie grabbed her leash and picked up his bag.

The train diverted to the siding and kept rolling for a short distance. After one, final lurch, it stopped. Charlie hurried over to the still-open door and looked out. He glanced up and down the train. "Okay, let's go."

He hopped down to the rock bed. Taffy jumped down to the ground, eagerly. Once they were both clear of the car, he picked up his bag and slung it over his shoulder, stepped away from the train, and hiked back toward the town. Taffy stopped to pee. She wanted to run, to investigate all the new smells carried by the warm breeze, but Charlie didn't let her off the leash. The deadened, yellow cornstalks adjacent to the tracks rustled like dry news-paper as they walked.

They reached the end of the train and passed by the red caboose. He started running when he realized that the men inside were not at the win-dows. "Hurry, girl. Let's go!"

"Hey! Kid! Where'd you come from," someone yelled. Charlie didn't stop but turned as he ran and saw two brakemen standing at the railing on the rear deck of the caboose. "Hey! Come back here!"

Charlie ran. The bag slapped against his side and slowed his progress. He didn't dare look back . . . didn't know if the men would give chase, or not.

LaBette had followed the Packard until it showed its brake lights just west of town. He pulled over and stopped on the edge of Hutchinson.

When the train arrived and stopped on the siding, LaBette observed the boy and dog leap from one of the cars and race back in his direction—a train man chased them for only a short distance. LaBette tensed, sensing that the boy might pass close. He waited with his left hand on the door handle—his right fingered the Luger. There was no movement from the blue Packard farther out on the highway. He was a step closer than he had been all day and had both the boy and the Packard guy in sight. *It's just a matter of time.*

Charlie didn't stop running until he reached the first small house on the outskirts of Hutchinson. He ducked behind a lilac hedge and leaned over. He was breathing heavily. Taffy panted. Charlie stuck his head out and looked back. One of the men had given chase but now was walking back to the caboose. "We made it, girl. No more yucky trains, right, Taff?"

He gave her a hug and walked through the small yard to the street. He was in a neighborhood of two-story homes with few outbuildings, and eventually reached the main street. As he did, he paused before darting across to let a State Patrol car pass. Once clear, Charlie and Taffy ran toward a gray DeSoto parked on the far side of the road. As they ran past, Charlie heard a car door close behind him.

DAMNATION! LABETTE THOUGHT. *Kid was so close . . . I almost had him! Would have, too, if that cop hadn't driven by.* That would have been a stroke of luck, but LaBette knew better than to count on luck in his business. Besides, he was in full view of others in town as well as the Packard guy, who by now had turned around and was approaching Hutchinson.

Now all LaBette could do was wait again for the right moment to act. He felt that his time would soon be at hand.

CHARLIE AND TAFFY PASSED a filling station, grocery store, drugstore, a Woolworths, and stopped in front of the Chat 'N' Chew Café. He paused and wondered what to do with Taffy.

An old man reached the front door just ahead of Charlie. He opened the door, looked at the boy, and said, "After you, young fella." He removed his hat and waited for the boy's reply.

Charlie didn't know what to do. "Uh, I don't know if they allow dogs in here or not."

"Hmmm. I see your dilemma. What's the dog's name, son?" He turned his hand over and offered the back of his hand to Taffy.

She didn't hesitate but licked his wrinkled skin with a warm, dry tongue.

"Taffy," Charlie said, surprised that she hadn't resisted his offer of introduction. "She likes you. I can tell."

"Hello there, sweetheart. You're sure a beauty, aren't you?" The man edged closer and stroked her head. Before long, Taffy was leaning against the old man's thigh as he scratched just behind her ears. "Let's see . . . I'll bet you a dollar to a donut that she's . . . wait, don't tell me . . . hmmm, got it! She's a golden retriever. Right?"

Charlie laughed. For the first time all day, warmth filled his chest. "Yes. Purebred, too," he added proudly.

"Oh, I can certainly see that she's a purebred, all right. You're a lucky, young man to have a classy friend like that."

"Thank you."

"You're welcome. Now, about your little problem. Why don't you just go inside and ask the owner if it's okay for Taffy to accompany you while you eat. You were intending to eat, correct?"

"Yes, sir. I was. I'm pretty hungry."

"Well, come on, then." He held the door for the boy and dog and all three walked inside.

PISANT HAD SPOTTED THE BOY and the dog, but not until long after they passed the end of the train. He heard the brakeman yell, and saw the boy and dog running toward town. He started the Packard, made a U-turn, and sped back down the highway. By the time he reached the center of Hutchinson, he noticed the boy talking to an old man outside the café.

"Nuts! Now what?" he muttered. He pulled over to the side and parked directly across from the café. *Patience, Virg.* Out of habit when anticipating action, Pisant fingered his switchblade. He hit the button, and the blade sprang open. The knife twitched in his palm. *Sooner or later, ya little twerp . . .*

Charlie, Taffy, and the old man entered the café. As soon as the door closed, they were greeted with delightful smells coming from the kitchen. Fried onions, fresh baked goods, strong coffee—all filled the air.

The café was small, with only a few tables near the window but a long counter with stools.

Charlie walked over to the cash register and waited. Soon a large, ruddy-faced woman walked down the length of the counter and stopped at the register. "Can I help you, son?" She wiped her hands on an apron printed with red apples. A nameplate on her chest said BERTHA.

"Yes, I uh . . . is it okay if my dog is in here with me?"

The woman leaned forward and looked down at Taffy. "She won't tear anyone's leg off, will she?" A broad smile spread across Bertha's ample face.

"Oh, no! She's trained and everything." Charlie eyed the woman hopefully.

"Well, we never turn anyone away if they're well trained—including pretty, golden dogs. Find yourself a seat, young fellow."

The old man hung his hat on a rack to the right of the door and limped down the length of the counter. He sat at an open stool at the far end and smiled as he overheard the conversation between the woman and boy.

Charlie dropped his bag beneath the hat rack and made his way to the only other vacant stool and hoisted himself up on the red, vinyl seat. He looked down and said, "Taffy. Lie down, girl." She sat, and then slid to her stomach, directly beneath Charlie.

Bertha reappeared. "What'll it be, son?"

"I'd like a hamburger, no . . . a cheeseburger and a chocolate malt, please."

"You want fries with that? No extra charge."

"Yes, please. And could I have a bowl of water for my dog?"

"Certainly. Be right back." She lumbered down the counter to the old man.

"Howdy. Nice place you have here," he said.

"Thank you. What can I get for you?"

"I heard that today is meat loaf day, and it's a specialty of the house."

Bertha laughed. "Well, I don't know how 'special' it is, but we don't get many complaints."

"Wonderful! That's what I'll have, then."

She scribbled on a pad. "Mashed potatoes? Gravy?"

"Hmmm. Potatoes, yes, but I'm afraid the gravy will be a bit rich for me."

"Hold the gravy. No problem."

"Perfect. And a cup of coffee, if you please—black."

She finished writing and said, "I'll bring the coffee right away."

The old man looked around the room. Pink curtains framed the two large windows. Various stuffed birds dotted the knotty-pine paneling. The old man focused on a large cock rooster pheasant. Its tail was at least eighteen inches long. He smiled, as if remembering other times—other places.

He blinked, turned back, and observed the boy. *Nice kid*, he thought. *Well mannered. Wonder where he's going with that heavy bag? Young fella shouldn't be out on the road alone.*

His coffee arrived. He dipped a spoon in the sugar bowl and dumped three large spoonfuls into the coffee. He continued to watch the boy.

Charlie's malt arrived along with a large bowl of water. He took two big sips through the straw and picked up the water bowl. He carefully slid off the stool. Taffy stood up, and he placed the water on the floor. She immediately lapped at the fresh water. Charlie waited until she had finished, and then picked up the empty bowl.

Bertha returned and said, "Boy! She was sure thirsty, wasn't she? Want any more?"

"No thanks."

She took the bowl and said, "I'll bring your burger right out."

She returned immediately, and Charlie hungrily bit into the hot cheeseburger. He thought he'd never tasted anything so good. He dumped a big mound of ketchup on his plate and dipped a wad of fries in the red pile. Soon his mouth was stuffed, and he chewed eagerly. Every now and then, he broke off a piece of the burger and handed it to Taffy. He waited for the fries to cool and gave her some of those, as well.

Charlie finished his meal and slowly slurped what was left of the malt. He felt happy—contented. The café was a welcome relief from the nightmare in the boxcar. A shiver went down his back as he recalled how frightening the entire episode had been. Without Taffy there. . . . He didn't even want to consider what might have happened without her.

At the far end of the counter the old man wiped his mouth, folded the napkin, and declined another cup of coffee. "No, thank you kindly, Bertha. The meat loaf was wonderful."

"No dessert?"

The old man laughed. "No, I'm afraid I've had enough. Might fall asleep while I'm driving if I eat anything more." He placed a quarter on the counter and stood up. After adjusting his red suspenders and rolling down blue flannel sleeves, he waited for the bad hip to settle and then stepped away from the counter.

A large hand tapped Charlie on the shoulder. Charlie turned to face the old man. "Gotta be on my way, young man. Take good care of Taffy, now. She's a real special friend."

Charlie beamed. "Yes, I know. Goodbye."

The old man walked to the front, paid his bill and left the café.

Charlie suddenly felt alone again and didn't know why. He'd have to get going again—soon—but was reluctant to leave the friendly café. After waiting as long as he could, he glanced at his watch and decided it was time to leave. Charlie rose from the stool, left fifteen cents for Bertha, and with Taffy alongside, walked to the register where he paid his bill. "Thank you for the water, and for . . . well, for letting her in here."

"You're very welcome. You can both come back, anytime." She handed him his change and smiled.

Charlie pocketed the coins, heaved the sack high on his shoulder, and left the café.

Once outside on the sidewalk, he paused. *Now what? Hitchhike I guess. Wonder if anyone will pick me up with Taffy?*

Nineteen

A S SOON AS THE BOY entered the restaurant, LaBette started the DeSoto and turned around. He cruised past the front window and saw the boy slipping onto a stool at the counter. He turned his head away as he passed the Packard and pulled into a Standard Oil Station. A phone booth stood on the corner.

LaBette parked and left the car. With one eye on the front door of the café, he picked up the receiver, dropped a dime in the slot, and dialed. After a few seconds, he deposited additional coins as requested by the operator. He gave her the number and waited.

The Packard was half a block down the street, directly across from the café. LaBette turned into the booth and said, "It's me." He paused and continued, "You holding out on me? Because it seems there's another player involved. Who? I thought you might have hired a back-up. No? Then who's the other guy? Yes, the target is in sight. A long way from home, that's where. I can . . . any time I want. And the other player? Okay. Find out. Might be more to the contract than you know. Okay . . . two o'clock . . . at the other number." LaBette replaced the receiver.

Hmmm. Seems Val doesn't know any more than I do. He returned to his car and started the engine. He had already decided that the "other player" could be eliminated now that the boy was in sight. *Doesn't matter who he is, I guess.*

LaBette pulled away and parked on the other side of the street in front of the Ace Hardware store. He had a clear view of both the café door and the Packard. He waited. He opened his Bible and turned to John. *In him was life; and the life was the light of men . . .*

After a while the old man who had opened the door for the kid appeared, limped over to a wood-sided station wagon and drove away. Labette gave him a quick glance and returned to his reading.

SOON AFTER THE OLD MAN left, Charlie followed. Once outside, he had to shade his eyes from the bright sun. He put on his ball cap, hefted the paper-route sack, and with Taffy leading the way, started walking down the side-walk. A gust of wind blew towards him, and a piece of paper slapped against his leg and hung there—wrapped around his dungarees. He reached down and plucked the handbill from his pants. It was dirty, but legible.

Charlie stopped to read the small poster. "A rodeo, Taff! There's a rodeo coming to town . . . oops! Guess not." He noticed the date. "Aw, shucks. The rodeo was here in August. Too bad . . . that would have been something to see, wouldn't it, girl?" He folded the handbill and tucked it in his back pocket.

When he reached the end of the concrete, he stepped onto the high-way and kept walking west. Whenever a car appeared from behind, he piv-oted and stuck his thumb out. Some of the cars and trucks slowed, but it seemed to Charlie that as soon as they spied Taffy, they sped up.

They passed the freight train still parked on the siding. In the dis-tance ahead, Charlie heard the whistle from another train. Soon the east-bound freight appeared and quickly passed. Once it cleared the siding, the halted train edged ahead and merged with the main line. Charlie stood and watched the train gather speed.

The red caboose swung out and a solitary figure stood on the rear platform. Charlie thought about his close call and wondered briefly what might have happened if Taffy hadn't been with him. He waved at the departing figure, but the man didn't return the gesture.

Charlie had walked two miles from Hutchinson, well past the railroad siding, when he heard a car slow behind him. He turned around and stuck out his thumb. The car pulled over directly ahead of Charlie and Taffy.

Charlie ran to the car. The passenger door swung open, and he heard a voice yell, "Get in, kid!"

"Thanks, mister." Charlie pulled Taffy close, but she resisted. She had caught a scent from the open car door, and she pulled back, stiff-legged. "Taff? What's the matter?"

Charlie looked in the car at the man behind the wheel. He had a funny looking ear—like part of it was missing. One eye was all discolored. The skin around it different shades of yellow and black. The car smelled like beer. The man leaned over even farther, and Charlie noticed a large dent in his forehead. Uh, uh . . . if Taffy doesn't want to get in . . .

"Hey, kid? Come on. Ain't got all day!"

"My dog doesn't want to get in, so I guess we'll keep walking. Thanks anyway, though." Charlie swung the door closed and stepped away from the Packard. He heard the man yell but couldn't tell what he said.

Pisant knew he had to move fast. He checked for cars on the highway, saw it was clear in both directions, and opened his door. He jumped out and hurried around the front. "Hey, kid! Sure you don't want a ride?" He towered over the boy and dog.

Taffy curled her upper lip and stepped between Charlie and the big man. A deep growl rose in her throat. Charlie stood still and tightened the leash.

Pisant took one more look up and down the highway. Then in a swift movement that caught Charlie by surprise, he reached out and grabbed him by the front of his jacket. At the same time, with his other hand, he pulled the leash from his small fist and kicked Taffy in the side. Hard!

She yelped, flew down into the ditch, and rolled over. Stunned and injured, she could only lie and whimper.

Before Charlie could react, Pisant had the door open. He pulled the front seat forward and threw Charlie into the cluttered back seat. His head slammed against the far window, and he lost track of time.

Pisant closed the door and ran around to the driver's side. The highway was still mostly empty as he clambered behind the wheel and stepped on the accelerator. The blue Packard tore down the highway leaving a trail of dust in its wake.

Charlie shook his head. His nose was bleeding and a dull roar echoed in his head. When he finally realized what had happened, he turned to look for Taffy. She was nowhere in sight. He panicked and yelled, "Wait!" He was more afraid for Taffy's well being at that moment, than his own.

"Shut the hell up!" Pisant said. "Stay right where you are, kid, and you won't get hurt."

Charlie knew he couldn't escape. The car was moving too fast, and by the time he reached the front door handle, the man would stop him for sure. After a few more minutes, he managed to say, "My dog . . . what about my dog?"

"What? Mutt's probably dead by now. Caught her pretty good. Too bad. Now shut up!"

Charlie's head ached, and he was trembling. All he could think of was Taffy lying in the ditch—*in pain, scared, maybe . . . maybe dead?* His head hurt and there was a constant buzz in his ears. *What's happening? Why does he want me? I need to get back to Taffy.*

Virgil drove for a while until he spotted an abandoned farm on the north side of the road. *Gotta git the kid tied up and stuffed in the trunk.*

A large grove of cottonwoods and a shelter belt of cedar trees would hide him from the highway. The farm was set back far enough from the highway that Pisant decided it was perfect for his purposes.

He slowed and turned in on the gravel road. He passed through a barb wire fence and over a grated livestock guard. A large herd of Black Angus cattle were grazing in the distance beyond the farm. Pisant continued up the drive.

Charlie looked out the side window. They passed a small pond surrounded by cattails. A flock of green-wing teal swam from cover and gathered in the center. Heads erect, alarmed, they bobbed nervously. Once the big Packard was abreast of the flock, they all sprung in the air and flew away. A few ripples spread across the pond and disappeared. Charlie swiveled his head back and stared through the glass.

Pisant pulled into the clearing. The farmhouse had been torn down years earlier. All that remained was a large barn and a windmill with a stock tank beneath it. The grass in the clearing had been grazed and was covered with cow pies.

Virgil stopped the car, opened the door, and climbed out. He leaned against the side and lit a cigarette. He flicked the match and watched as it landed and continued to burn. A piece of straw caught fire—then another. Pisant stamped them out.

Charlie huddled in the back seat. He wiped his bloody nose with his handkerchief.

Pisant scanned the area as he finished his cigarette. The cows north of the farmstead had heard the car pull in and were edging closer. *Dumb bastards . . . probably think I'm here to feed 'em.* He snuffed the butt and reached for the door.

As soon as the door opened, Charlie slid to the far side of the car.

"Come 'ere, kid." He waited with the door open. "Don't make me come in there after you."

Charlie slid back and stepped from the car. "What . . . what are you going to do? Why am I here?" He edged backward along the side of the car.

"You're bait, kid. That's all. Now come 'ere!" Pisant took off his jacket and laid it on the hood of the car. Then he reached inside his pants pocket and pulled out his switch blade. Leaning over and picking up a long strand of twine left from a broken hay bale, he said, "Gotta tie you up with this twine . . ."

Charlie stood still. He was so frightened his knees wobbled. His breath came in short bursts. Feeling faint, he eyed the knife as the blade flipped open.

Pisant cut the twine in half and set the knife on top of his jacket. He reached for Charlie, spun him around, and pulled his arms behind his back.

Charlie resisted. He tried to pull away, but he was no match. *What's he gonna do to me? What about Taffy? What if . . . what if she's . . . dead? Please, God! I have to get away before it's too late!* Panicked, now, he broke free and started to run toward the barn.

Virgil took two steps and caught him by the back of the neck. His large fingers dug into the boy's skin. "Listen, you! Now you done it! Guess I gotta teach ya a lesson." With his other free hand, he reached down and unbuckled his wide black belt. The belt had a heavy metal buckle with the shape of a naked girl stamped on the front.

He spun Charlie around, smacked the side of his head with an open hand and threw him to the ground. The belt snaked out of the loops and hung from his filthy hand. He waved it back and forth over the boy's head.

Charlie closed his eyes. *Please God . . . please don't let him hurt me.*

Pisant stepped over the boy and straddled him. Charlie didn't dare open his eyes. He felt the man's boots pressing against his thighs. He heard the rattle of something metallic. *Don't look . . . Maybe it'll be quick . . .*

Twenty

WHEN THE OLD MAN LEFT the restaurant, he pulled out onto the highway and drove west. He felt good. His stomach was full and without pain. The temperature outside had to be at least sixty degrees, and the sun was as high in the sky as it could get for an early October day. He hummed an old tune and scanned the countryside.

Five miles passed. He looked around the front seat and realized that something was missing. "Dog-gone, it! My hat! I plumb forgot about my hat." He stepped on the brakes, slowed, checked the rearview mirror, and turned around. He pressed the accelerator and zipped back the same way he had just come from. He passed three or four cars on the way back, and a dark blue Packard parked along side the road. He barely glanced at it as he whizzed past. He reached Hutchinson in fifteen minutes.

He parked in front of the café, hurried inside, and was relieved to find his hat still hanging on the hook. He waved at Bertha as he stepped through the door. Soon he was back on the highway, retracing his earlier drive. He settled back and stared through the windshield.

All of a sudden he bolted and straightened. Some distance ahead, he saw a blue car speed away leaving a trail of dust in the still air. The old man slowed. Just as he passed the section where the car had left, he noticed a movement from the ditch. He drove past and watched in his rear view mirror as Taffy struggled up the embankment, tested the wind, and hobbled down the road—dragging the leash.

The old man slammed on the brakes. "What in the world?" He backed up a short distance, turned off the ignition, and edged out of the car. He walked behind and stopped as Taffy limped toward him. She was obviously in great pain, but seemed determined to continue walking west—her head was down, but she kept going. "Taffy? What happened, girl? Where's your master?"

The old man knelt and without hesitating, Taffy slid between his knees. She immediately dropped, fell to her side, and groaned.

"Oh, no!" He patted her flank and stroked her neck. She lifted her head and managed to lick his hand once, then twice. The old man twisted his head and tried to catch a glimpse of the speeding blue car. "What's happened here? You don't mean to tell me . . . come on, girl. We have to get going!"

He stood and opened the rear door, then bent to pick up the dog. He slid both arms beneath her body and quickly lifted her up. Taffy did not resist, but moaned as pressure was applied to her stomach. With great care, he laid her on the cloth seat, slammed the door, and hurried around to the driver's side. Once inside, he restarted the engine, threw the shift into first, and sped off after the retreating blue car.

Before long the old station wagon reached seventy miles an hour. Another car, gray colored, appeared—just ahead. The old man never paused. He cranked the wheel and pulled around the DeSoto. He couldn't see the blue car. "No! No! Not again . . . please, Lord . . . not again?" His fingers ached from gripping the steering wheel so hard. From the back seat, he could barely hear Taffy's moans.

And what are you going to do if . . . if you are right? What if you're out-numbered . . . think! I need something. . . . And then he remembered. He could pull this off. *Hurry, hurry!*

The old Ford vibrated. The entire wagon shuddered. *Easy, old man . . . wouldn't do to pile this baby up. There! What's that?* Just over the horizon, he caught a flash of blue. The car had stopped momentarily. Now it made a right turn and drove through a fence.

The old man maintained his speed until he approached the driveway of the old farm. He turned in, drove a short distance, and stopped. The other car vanished beyond a grove of cottonwoods. Thick cedar trees surrounded the property. He jumped out and went to the rear of the wagon. He swung the tailgate out and rummaged through various piles. His hand touched the object he was looking for. After another thirty seconds, he was ready. He went back to the driver's side, took a deep breath, and crept up the gravel road. *Careful . . . don't get too close.*

The old man noticed a number of Black Angus cows crowding the clearing as he slipped beneath a giant basswood. He hesitated a moment, then left the safety of the large tree. He tried to hurry, but his bad hip slowed him down. All at once, he spotted the car. It was parked in the middle of the opening. The door on the driver's side was open. The old man looked around but didn't see anyone. He leaned over and shuffled closer until he was behind the Packard. He raised and peeked through both sets of glass. He saw the back of a man's head—bending over something.

It's now or never, old man! He stood and stepped sideways. What he witnessed chilled his blood. Bile rose in the back of his mouth. The boy was on the ground. A large man straddled the boy—his back toward the Packard. The man's arm was raised as if to strike the boy with a black belt. *Move! Now!* Just as the man's arm flexed as if to strike, the old man hurried forward.

"Hold it right there, fella!" the old man said in a low voice. As he spoke, he jabbed the end of the shotgun behind Pisant's right ear, then quickly scanned the clearing. "You alone?"

Pisant froze. The belt swayed back and forth next to his head. "Whaa? Yeah, I'm alone."

"Good. Now, if you make one little move that I don't like, this ear will look just as ugly as the other one—you catch my drift?"

"Yeah."

"Good! Step away from the boy—slow as can be. This old double barrel has a hair trigger."

Virgil did as he was told. He kept his right arm above his head. His mind raced. *Who the hell . . . ? I didn't see anyone . . .*

"Now, take three steps and turn around," the old man commanded. As soon as Pisant moved, the old man said, "Son! Son! Can you hear me?"

Charlie's eyes were open but they were blank. He heard another voice and blinked. The weight against his legs eased. He blinked again and spotted the old man from the restaurant. Charlie rolled over and rose to his knees. "Who . . . ? Oh, it's you . . ."

"Stand up, young fella. Good. Now step around this big galoot and come over here by my side." The shotgun was aimed at Pisant's midsection. "Hurry, son!" The old man was losing his strength. He was breathing too hard. Before long, he could easily black out just as he sometimes did when he overextended himself.

Charlie did as he was told.

The old man reached out and pulled the boy close. "My car is back there a ways. Run as fast as you can, climb in, and lock the doors. I've got your dog in there. Got it?"

"Yes, sir." Charlie started to run and stopped. "Wait!" he said. "My bag!" He ran to the Packard, opened the door and pulled out his sack. He ran as fast as he could back to the wagon, hopped in, and locked the doors. His head was ringing, but he heard a faint whimper from the back seat. He turned and shouted, "Taffy!" He climbed over the seat, pulling his bag with him and threw both arms around his dog. The newspaper bag, full as it was, caught on the front seat, then flopped into the back, spilling some of its contents. Charlie paid no attention in his hurry to hug Taffy.

THE OLD MAN FELT an all-to familiar pressure building in his stomach. Soon, the pain would hit like a mule kick. Waves of nausea would follow. He leaned

191

against the hood of the Packard. The shotgun drooped, and he closed his eyes.

Pisant noticed the old man weakening for some reason and dropped his arms. He edged closer, waiting for just the right moment to jump and grab the weapon.

"Hold it! One more move will be your last," the old man said through clenched teeth.

Virgil sensed a wounded animal. If he could keep the old man talking, he might have a chance to jump him and grab the gun. "Listen, mister. I wasn't plannin' on hurtin' the kid . . . honest, I was jest—"

"Shut your mouth, you filthy pig! If I had one ounce of sense, I'd blow your good ear plumb off! Hell, I think I just might do that, anyway." He raised the shotgun to his shoulder and pointed it at Virgil's good ear.

"No! Please. You can't shoot an unarmed man!"

"Is that right? And who's around here to stop me. Maybe after I trim your ear, I'll use the second shell to blow your balls off! Yeah, I think I like the sound of that!"

Pisant's face turned white. His lower lip trembled as he realized the man was serious.

"Walk over to that watering tank. Now!" The old man tracked Virgil with the end of the shotgun.

Virgil trudged toward the stock tank beneath the windmill. He stopped when he reached the edge.

"Now, take your clothes off down to your skivies and toss them away," he commanded.

"Aw, geez, mister . . . please don't"

"Shut up! Do as you're told!" The old man watched as Pisant removed his clothing.

"Now, climb in the tank. Face the other way."

Pisant dropped his shirt and stepped into the tank. The cold water struck hard. He gasped as the shock took his breath away.

"Now listen carefully. I'm taking your keys . . ." He walked to the Packard, reached inside, and pulled out the keys. He tossed them deep into the underbrush. "Stay put!" Another sharp pain filled his gut. He laid the gun on the hood of the car. With great effort, he dug in his pants and pulled out a small bottle of painkillers. He quickly unscrewed the cover and stuck one in his mouth. He replaced the cover and put the bottle back in his pants.

Pisant's teeth rattled, but he didn't have the courage to move from the deep tank.

The old man went to the front of the Packard and raised the hood. He quickly reached in and pulled off the distributor cap. He straightened and tossed the cap away, as well. The switchblade slid to the ground. He picked it up. "What were you going to do with the knife, mermaid?"

"Hhhhuuh?"

"Never mind. Stay put! If I see you twitch just a little, I'll come back and do what I should have done in the first place. Got it?"

"Yyyyeeahhh! But, I'mmm gggoonna ffreezee . . ." His voiced trailed away.

The old man slipped the knife into his pocket, took one last look at the figure in the stock tank, and walked back to the station wagon. He unlocked the doors, ejected the shells from the shotgun and climbed in. He started the car, turned around, and headed down the drive. When they reached the highway, he spun the wheel and headed west.

"How's Taffy, son?"

"I don't know. She doesn't look too good. That guy kicked her pretty hard . . . I . . . I'm afraid she's all busted up." Charlie's voice cracked.

"Don't worry, son. There's another town about fifteen miles from here. There's bound to be a vet there. We'll get her fixed up, I promise." He grimaced and clutched his stomach.

Once the old man caught his breath, he said, "By the way. We haven't been properly introduced. My name's Purdue. Quillan Purdue—but my friends all call me Quill. What's your name, son?"

"Charlie. Charlie Nash." The words came out before he had a chance to think. He thought he should invent a new last name to hide his identity, but now it was too late. "You have a, uh . . . 'different' sorta name."

"Yes, I know. Father had a sense of humor, I think. Well, it's a pleasure to meet you, Charlie Nash."

"Me too, Mr . . . er, Quill." Charlie stroked Taffy's soft cheek. She opened her eyes and tried to lick his hand. "I think Taffy's hurt pretty bad." His eyes clouded. The day had gone from bad to worse for Charlie and more than anything, he now wished he had never left home. "I'm sorry, Taff," he whispered. "We never should've left."

Quill tilted the rear view to watch the boy. "Charlie? Listen, to me. You can't blame yourself for this. That man was evil, and you just happened to be in the wrong place at the wrong time. We'll get your dog fixed up. Don't worry." Purdue wished he felt as confident as he sounded. *She doesn't look too good . . .* He pressed the gas pedal another half inch. The old Ford responded and shot ahead.

The old man glanced in the mirror. The boy had his head on top of Taffy's. He had a thousand questions to ask the boy, but they'd all have to wait. *Time enough for all that later . . .*

Twenty-One

LaBETTE WAITED UNTIL the Packard was a mile out of town before he followed behind. He was disturbed about Val's apparent lack of knowledge as to the other player he was now chasing. Nothing about this contract made sense. *Either Val's lying, or something else is going on. Could be the guy's after the kid for some other reason entirely and has ho idea about the coin collection. Or . . . maybe he knows all about it. Either way, I have to find out and get to another phone by 2:00 P.M.*

LaBette slowed and stared through the windshield. The Packard was parked on the shoulder. The kid and his dog were standing next to the car. *Looks like he's ready to make his move. Good!*

He applied the brakes and stopped, pulling far off the road to be hard to spot should the guy look down the highway. Before long, the other player got out, kicked the dog into the ditch and tossed the kid in the back of the car. He sped away, and LaBette followed at a safe distance. He glanced into the ditch and saw the tan dog lying on her side, but he kept going. *One less thing for me to worry about.*

Soon, LaBette caught sight of another car rapidly approaching from the rear. Before he could react, the green, wood-sided station wagon zoomed past and sped down the highway.

The old man from the restaurant—from the filling station. I thought he left before the kid. Must have stopped somewhere before leaving town. Where's he going in such a hurry? He soon found out. LaBette could just make out in the far distance that the Packard had turned off the highway. He watched as the station wagon slowed and followed. *What's he doing? How's he involved?*

When the DeSoto reached the turn off, LaBette slowed. Directly across the highway was a small cemetery. He turned left and passed beneath a sign that read "Our Lady of the Prairie." The entrance was flanked by two, giant spruce trees. LaBette drove beneath the sign and turned around. He parked directly behind one of the trees.

LaBette considered his options. He could wait for one of the vehicles to leave, but which one would have the kid? *Certainly that frail old man was no match for that big guy in the Packard.* He sat and drummed his fingers on the top of the steering wheel. After five minutes, he decided he had to find out what was going on. The old farm was surrounded by trees that would provide plenty of cover. *All I have to do is get across the road and sneak up on the outside of those cedar trees . . .*

He grabbed the Luger and pulled the action back—cocking the weapon. Once he left the car, he would be exposed, but he had no choice. *This whole mess is getting out of hand.* He quickly slipped on his gloves.

He opened the door, stepped out, and crept down the short cemetery road. After looking up and down the highway, he ran across it and disappeared into the cedars. A large herd of cattle watched his every move. LaBette ignored them and snuck closer to the clearing. Before long, he heard voices—then footsteps—as if someone was running.

Once he felt he was directly opposite the clearing, he edged through the thick cedars until he had a clear view of the farmyard. He quickly located the Packard but saw no one else. He surveyed the barn, the windmill, but there was nothing else—except for the stock tank.

A car door slammed. An engine fired. *The wagon . . . old man's leaving. Where's the kid?* Tires spun on loose gravel. Then the sound of rubber screeching on pavement echoed through the small woodlot. LaBette looked behind him and saw a flash of green as the wagon passed, going west.

LaBette heard splashing. The cattle were closer than before, and their loud bawling was more noticeable than earlier. His eyes darted back and forth. *There! Over there! Something moved.*

He couldn't wait any longer. If the old man had somehow taken the kid, he felt he could easily spot the wagon somewhere down the road. He had to find out what happened to the guy driving the Packard. He stepped from the cover, now fully exposed. Then he spotted his target. A large head rose just above the rim of the stock tank.

LaBette crept closer. His eyes never stopped moving. Every sense was alert to danger. The only sound he heard was the anxious sounds of the cattle and brief splashes from the tank.

Once he was satisfied that no one else was around, he relaxed and walked over to the tank. The man's head was turned away.

"Well, well. What have we here?"

Pisant jerked and twisted his head. When he saw LaBette, he said, "Thh-th-thank God! I'm ffffreezin' to death!" He rose as if to climb out of the tank. Then he noticed LaBette's pistol and met the man's eyes.

LaBette said, "Whoa! Not so fast, there, pally. You better stay right where you are. You've got some explaining to do."

"Whaa . . . what'dya mean? Who are you? You a cop?" Pisant's voice rattled in time with his teeth. "Jesus, mister! I'm freezin' my balls off here—can I git out?"

"Nope. Not just yet. Not until you answer some questions first."

"What? I'll tell ya whatever ya want . . . jest let me git outta here, okay?"

LaBette didn't have a lot of time to waste. "Who you working for?"

"Huh? No one."

"Why'd you grab the kid?"

"Aw, geez . . . I don't know. Bait—thhh . . . that's all. Can't I—"

LaBette needed answers—quick. He looked at the barn and said, "Get out. Now!"

Pisant climbed out of the tank and folded his arms across his chest. "Cccan I ppuut my pppants on?"

"No. Walk towards the barn." He waved the Luger in that direction. "What's your name?"

"Pppiss—aannt."

"Piss Ant? Nice name. Who's in this with you, Piss Ant?" LaBette picked up Virgil's belt with his free hand.

"Uh, my friend and I—we was gonna snatch the kid's old man, but couldn't . . . ssso . . . I figgered if I grabbed the kid, I'd use 'em as bait."

"For what?"

"Kid's old man almost killed me—twice! That's why."

"What friend?" LaBette again scanned the yard.

"Mmmyy ffrriend, Llenny."

"Where's he?"

"He cchhickened out . . . went hhhoome."

They reached the barn. A number of cows had entered the clearing behind the two men and approached the watering tank. They watched the two with growing interest—expecting to be fed. "Open the doors."

Virgil did as instructed and swung the big, double doors open. Inside, stacked against the far wall, were bales of hay. More could be seen up in the loft. A long, manila rope swung from the rafters.

"Step inside," LaBette said.

Pisant shuffled ahead, clad only in his wet undershirt and briefs. He was still shivering.

LaBette spotted the end of the rope. It was attached to a cleat on the wall and ran up and through a large pulley at the top. "Stop. Don't move!" He went over to the wall and untied the rope. The end dropped and hung next to Pisant. "Go over and pick up that sawhorse over there."

Virgil did as he was told. He brought the wooden horse back and set it down. A glimmer of what was about to happen flashed in his head. "Hey! What's going on? What do you want from me, anyway?"

"Shut up! Now, go get that empty nail keg and bring it back. Hurry!"

Pisant retrieved the keg and set it down.

"Get down on your knees."

Virgil did as told.

"Now, roll over on your side—hands behind your back."

"Hey, I told you everythin' I know—honest. What're ya gonna do?"

"The truth, Piss Ant. I need the truth. You know your Bible, Piss Ant? Probably not. However, we're going to have a little Bible study class. Jesus said to the Jews, 'And ye shall know the truth, and the truth shall make you free.' Put your hands behind your back." LaBette looped the belt around Virgil's crossed hands, tightened it, and stepped on the end.

He stuffed the pistol in his trousers and tied a slip knot in the end of the rope. When finished, he draped the loop over Pisant's neck and tightened the noose. Once the noose was snug, he released the belt and grabbed his pistol. "And Jesus had more to say, Piss Ant. 'If you continue in my word, you shall be my disciples indeed.'"

"Aw, jeez, mister . . . don't . . ."

"Stand up. Now climb on the keg and step on the sawhorse."

Pisant was shaking uncontrollably now. He negotiated the upside down keg, and gingerly stepped on the thin rail of the sawhorse with bare feet. The belt sprung loose and fell away. His arms waved as he fought to balance himself.

LaBette yanked on the rope. Virgil's head snapped back—his face reddening. "And what do you suppose the Jews said, Piss Ant? 'We be Abraham's seed, and were never in bondage to any man.' You a believer, Piss Ant?"

The increased tension forced Pisant up on his toes. He gasped and clawed at the rope. It was too tight. "Ccaan't breathe . . . please?"

"That's the idea, Piss Ant. Now I'm going to tie off the rope on the wall over here." He stepped over to the cleat. "You're going to have to make sure you don't fall off that sawhorse, because . . . if you do . . . well, that'd be too bad, wouldn't it?" He tugged on the rope one more time and tied it off on the cleat.

LaBette pointed the Luger at Pisant. "Okay. I'm only going to ask you one more time. Who hired you?"

"No one . . . honest!" Pisant's voice was a raspy whisper.

"Didn't my little sermon mean anything? Why do ye not understand my speech? Tch, tch. Wrong answer." LaBette was just about convinced that the man was telling the truth—that he was nothing more than a nut case with some sort of demented vision of revenge on his mind. He's also a coward, and cowards seldom hold out very long.

"Last question. Why'd you want the kid?"

"I tol'e you. I . . . wanted . . . his old man! He was in jail so I grabbed the kid as bait." Virgil dug his fingers into the old manila rope—to no avail.

"Hmmm." He was satisfied. "'Then said the Jews, Will he kill himself?' Apparently so. Go in peace, my son. You're free now.

LaBette turned and walked from the barn. He glanced inside the Packard briefly, and trotted down the gravel road.

"Hey! You can't leave me . . . like . . . this . . . ain't human . . ." Pisant's eyes bulged. He couldn't catch his breath. He had to keep his head tilted back and to one side. He tried to reach up, grab the rope with one hand, and loosen the knot with the other—but he was cold, too disoriented by the angle of his head. He almost lost his balance.

He paused to catch his breath. *What's that?* He heard rustling from outside the door. From the corner of one eye, he saw cattle bunching up at the entrance. A trio of young heifers darted in and pranced around the floor.

"No! Noooo! Git . . . outaa . . . heeere . . . !" He struggled to raise his voice.

Soon, most of the herd pushed through. The calves scampered around the sawhorse on their way to the hay bales on the far side of the barn. Then, as if a lunch bell rang, the entire group surged ahead and headed for the tasty alfalfa.

"Go on . . . git!" Virgil watched in horror as the cattle came closer. They edged around the sawhorse. His fingernails dug into the rough sisal. He tried to lift himself high enough to loosen the tension but lost his footing. His toes wiggled in a spasm as he felt for the rough wood of the sawhorse. Finally, he rested again on the narrow perch.

One old, lame cow sauntered in. She stood quietly inside the door and surveyed the scene. Satisfied the man hanging from the rope presented no threat, she swayed over to the sawhorse and stopped.

The old cow sniffed at Pisant's bare feet, looked up at him with her large, brown eyes, and snorted a stream of snot on his bare toes. She nudged the sawhorse with her wet nose. The sawhorse rocked just a bit. Virgil couldn't see what was going on below, but felt the sawhorse tip. "Hhhey! Cut it out!" He strained to see what the old cow was up to. "Cursed cows! Hate . . . the . . . bastards!"

She raised her head, stared at the man's face, then stepped around the wooden apparatus. As she passed by, the old cow had to squeeze past another cow who had stopped in the middle of the barn. In doing so, the sawhorse dug into her side. The cow panicked and kicked at the sawhorse, hitting one leg of the stand. *Whack!* Her heavy hoof smacked against the brittle wood. The sawhorse spun away and skittered from beneath Pisant's toes. Dust rose from the dry barn floor.

Virgil was unprepared for the sudden movement and had no chance to stop the sawhorse from moving. His entire weight hung from the hay rope. He couldn't breathe and tried to grab the rope. At the same time, he stabbed wildly with his feet and toes in an attempt to find the top of the horse. It was too late. The sawhorse was out of reach.

His eyes bugged out, and Virgil focused on a clump of feathers high in the barn. Bright, yellow eyes blinked and stared back. The great horned owl soon lost interest. She let out a low *whoooo*, hopped from her perch, and spread her massive wings. She headed for Pisant but swerved and coasted out the open doors.

As Virgil's oxygen gave out, he mouthed, "My . . . name's . . . not . . ."

He jerked once, then twice. After that there was no further movement. He spun slowly on the end of the rope, empty eyes staring up at the rafters of the barn

Down below, the old cow joined the rest of the herd for an unexpected mid-day feast. The only sound heard was the *crunch, crunch* of the cows masticating, and an occasional, contented *moooo* . . ."

LaBETTE RACED DOWN the gravel road, took a quick look for approaching traffic, and ran across the highway. He headed west, putting on speed to catch up with the Ford. *Sooner or later, I'll catch up to them . . . and then, we'll end this thing so I can go home.* He checked his watch and remembered the phone call he had to make. The gray coupe tore off down the highway. LaBette didn't think he was more than ten minutes behind the old man. As long as there weren't any towns ahead, or major crossroads, he felt certain he'd catch up in no time.

Before long, the DeSoto had topped out at eighty-five miles an hour. Without slowing, LaBette passed a milk truck and a tractor with plow attached. Two automobiles coming the opposite way flashed by. Three crows pecked at the carcass of a skunk in front of him and barely managed to hop clear of the speeding car.

"Come on! Where are you?" LaBette muttered. The countryside was flat—unbroken but for an occasional farm or shelter belt. "Godforsaken country . . . who'd want to live out here?" He thought of his own home and realized how similar it was to this part of western Minnesota. "No wonder I wanted out . . ."

Soon, just above the horizon, the tops of a few buildings appeared over the unbroken landscape. "Aw, nuts . . . hope this town isn't real big." For the first time since leaving Minneapolis, LaBette now feared he might lose the boy—and the coins—and his fee! *If they turned off and he missed seeing them, or if they stopped, he could lose them for good. I'll just have to make a quick tour of the town and, if I don't see the wagon, keep driving west. And I can't forget the phone call.*

PART THREE

Quill Purdue

Twenty-Two

"HURRY, QUILL! SHE'S breathin' real hard," Charlie said.

"I am, son. There! See it! That has to be Hanley Falls just ahead." The small town rose above the plains directly ahead of the Ford. Before long they passed a set of grain elevators, and Purdue stopped at the first filling station he came to.

He rolled down his window as the attendant approached the car. "Excuse me, but we've got a bit of an emergency here. Is there a vet in town?"

"Yes, sir. Doc Haines. Best vet in the county. Keep going straight," he pointed west, "Then when you get to the four-way stop, turn right. Doc's place is about half a block on the right." The attendant ducked and looked in the back seat. "Probably best if you pull around back . . . easier to unload."

"Thanks very much."

"My pleasure. Good luck!"

Purdue pulled out and continued until he reached the stop sign. He turned right and soon located the vet's office. He pulled into a short drive-way lined with pine trees and drove behind the wood-sided building. He turned and backed beneath a low canopy and parked in front of the rear door. "Okay, Charlie. We're here. You sit tight while I go in and talk to this Doctor Haines. Be right back, all right?"

"Sure, Quill."

Purdue edged out of the car and limped to the door. He turned the handle and walked inside. "Hello? Anybody here?" The office smelled of antiseptic. A couple of dogs barked from a small room on his right. Quill walked down a long hall toward the reception area.

A woman nearly collided with him as she turned down the hallway. "Oh! My goodness! I thought I was hearing things. I'm Doc's wife, Elaine. How can I help you?"

"We've got an injured dog out back. Is the Doc in?"

"Oh, I'm sorry. He had to go to the Carothers' farm—problems with a breached cow. He should be back in, oh, I'd say thirty minutes or so?"

"Is it okay if we wait?"

"Certainly. I usually assist Doc anyway, so why don't you bring the dog in, and I'll take a look at her before he gets back."

"Thank you. My names Purdue, ma'am. Quill Purdue."

"Pleased to meet you, Quill." She reached out and shook his hand. "You're not from around here, are you?"

"No. Used to live northwest of here, out near Blue Springs in South Dakota. I'm headed home and stopped to help a young boy and his dog. Well, you'll see soon enough. Boy's name's Charlie. The dog's Taffy. I'll bring them in."

"Do you need any help?" Elaine was a large woman—broad shouldered, solid forearms. She had on a pair of overalls with a flowered blouse beneath.

"No thanks. I think we can manage." Purdue turned and walked back down the hall.

"Bring her into this first room with the table, Quill."

Quill stopped, located the room, and said. "Sure thing." He exited the small building and returned to the wagon. "Charlie? Let's go, son. The vet isn't here, but he'll be back shortly. Let's get Taffy inside." He opened the rear door.

Charlie stepped out. His shoulders slumped. He had a dour look as he gazed up at his new friend. His blue eyes were open wide for any word of encouragement about Taffy.

206

"We'll get her fixed up, Charlie. Doc's wife is a real nice lady." He leaned over and gently slid the dog to the seat's edge. "Let's see if I can get my hands under her . . ."

Taffy was limp. Her dark eyes fixed on her master as Purdue hoisted her and backed away. "Get the door for me?"

"You bet." Charlie ran to the back door and held it wide.

The old man edged sideways through the narrow opening and shuffled down the hall. Once inside the examination room, he laid the dog on the steel table.

Taffy raised her head, located Charlie, and licked the old man's hand. She struggled briefly, but Quill restrained her weak effort to rise. "Easy, girl. Charlie, why don't you step over here and try to keep her quiet. I'll go . . . oh, here she is now. Elaine, this is Charlie. Charlie, say hello to the doc's wife, Mrs. Haines."

"Hello, Mrs. Haines."

"Hi, Charlie." She noticed the worried look on the boy's face and continued, "You know, Charlie, my husband's the best veterinarian in the whole county. He'll be back shortly, and then we can see what we have to do to take care of your dog. What's her name?" She moved to the examining table and stroked the dog's head.

"Taffy."

Elaine ran her hands over Taffy's body—testing, prodding, but halted her brief exam when she reached the dog's ribs. Taffy flinched and whimpered. "Oh, I'm sorry, girl. That hurts, doesn't it?"

Charlie placed his head on top of his dog's and whispered, "It's okay, Taff. They're gonna fix you up."

Elaine straightened and asked, "What happened to her?"

Without moving his head, Charlie mumbled, "A man kicked her—hard."

"Who would do such a thing?"

Purdue interceded. "That's a very good question. We don't know yet. Why don't you and I step out, and I'll try and explain what happened. Charlie? You'll be all right here with Taffy?"

"Yeah. We'll be okay."

Purdue and Elaine left and went to the reception area. It took five minutes for Quill to explain all that had happened.

"Who was he?"

"Don't rightly know . . . matter of fact, I don't know why the boy's on the road, either. Looked to me as if the guy was going to abuse the boy—beat him up or thrash him with his belt. Charlie did say he'd never seen the man before. Soon's I get a minute, I'm going to try and find out more about where he comes from."

"Don't you think we should call the sheriff and report this?" Elaine asked. She was alarmed that the man was still loose and could possibly harm some other child.

"Yes, ma'am. I think that's a good idea."

Elaine hurried to her desk and picked up the phone. She spun the rotary dial and waited. "Jane? Elaine Haines. I'm fine. Yes, he is too. Listen, can you connect me with the sheriff's office? I don't know the number off hand. Thank you. You too." She laid the receiver on her shoulder, waited and studied Quill. *Tall, long white hair like drifted snow. Strong hands—been outside quite a bit. A contented man, but every now and then a rush of sadness fills his eyes.* The dispatcher answered her call.

Elaine spoke briefly to the dispatcher and handed the phone to Quill. "Hello? Yes, I understand Mrs. Haines told you about what happened." Quill listened to the dispatcher's response. "No, I have no idea who the man was. I left him sitting in a stock tank on an abandoned farm about ten miles west of Hutchinson. What? I don't know . . . there was a cemetery across the road. No, the boy's fine. Who?"

Quill turned away and said, "No, we have to be leaving soon. I can leave my address with Elaine, here. Yes, we're heading home. Blue Springs . . . up near Brown's Valley. P U R D U E, first name Quillan."

Purdue couldn't afford any further delays. He had to get home. "Very good. The man? He won't be going far. I threw away his keys and pulled the distributor cap. Both are in the long grass." Quill gave a description of Pisant to the dispatcher and hung up.

Elaine looked closely at the old man. "Quill? Aren't they going to want to talk to Charlie?"

Quill hesitated and said, "He's been through enough, Elaine. He's running from something, and I want to find out what before it's too late. I'm his friend, now, and he trusts me."

At that moment, Doc Haines walked through the front door. After introductions were made, he quickly went in to the examining room.

"Charlie? Hello, young man. I'm Doc." He held out his hand.

Charlie shook his hand briefly and turned back to Taffy. "Can you help her? Her name is Taffy. She's pretty badly hurt, I think."

"Let's take a look at her." He permitted Taffy a brief sniff of his hand then slowly ran his fingers over her body. By this time, Quill and Elaine had joined them. "She spit up any blood, Charlie?"

The boy blanched, and replied, "No. I don't think so."

"That's good." He put a stethoscope against her rib cage. "I think she's got a couple of bruised ribs, Charlie. I don't think they're broken, and I don't think there are any other internal injuries. I'm going to give her a sedative to keep her quiet then wrap her ribs. I'll give you some pills for her, and you'll have to keep her quiet for a few days. No hard running, just enough exercise to go do her business, okay?" He smiled at the boy and prepared an injection.

Once Taffy was sedated, Doc Haines wrapped the dog's middle with gauze and said, "Watch for any blood in her stool, son. If you spot any, bring her back right away, okay?"

Charlie looked at Purdue. "Uh, I don't know . . . where—"

Quill interrupted, "We'll be heading home, Doc. There's an old guy in Blue Springs that doubles as a vet. He'll take a look at her. You've been very kind . . . both of you."

"Give her one of those pills, twice a day, Charlie . . . until they're all gone. She'll be thirsty but keep her water intake to a minimum. And solid food only, all right?" He handed the little white pill box to the boy.

"Okay." Charlie was drained—physically and emotionally, and it showed. He stuck the pill box in his pocket.

Quill jumped in, "Guess we'll be heading out, then." He reached for his wallet, "What do I owe you, Doc?"

"Oh, five bucks ought to cover it."

"Quill? I have money . . . here." Charlie dug in his pocket and pulled out a small leather pouch with a zipper. He dug inside and pulled out a crinkled five-dollar bill. "Here."

Quill smiled.

Elaine took the bill and said, "Thank you, Charlie. It was nice meeting you . . . and Taffy. She's a beautiful golden. Take good care of her."

"I will. Thank you."

"I'll carry her out to the car for you," Doc said. He picked up the dog as if she weighed no more than a small sack of flour and walked down the hall. Once outside, Charlie ran to the wagon and opened the rear door.

Taffy was placed on the rear seat and Charlie slid in next to her. They said their goodbyes and Quill slipped behind the wheel. He took a quick look at the road map and started the car. The green wagon pulled out. Elaine and Doc waved and went back inside.

JUST BEFORE QUILL TURNED down the driveway, a gray DeSoto flew past the Haine's office, heading south. The Ford wagon turned north—in the direction of Brown's Valley.

LaBette had driven ten miles in every direction from Hanley Falls and finally sped up and down the few streets in town looking for the green wagon. Now, he knew he had lost them for good. He halted the search long enough to call Val.

"Sorry I'm late. Had a problem. No, it's taken care of. The other player . . . he's out of the game—permanently! Yeah, I'm sure. He was on some other mission of his own. No way . . . seems he didn't like the hand he was playing and folded."

LaBette listened and said, "No, nothing. I think he had a different agenda. What did you find out?" After a lengthy reply, he finished with,

"That's what I thought. What? Well, I lost him." LaBette held the receiver away from his ear, frowned and replied, "Look, don't get your underwear in a knot. I'll find him one way or another. Yeah, I got another angle. I'm coming back now, and I'll call you tonight. Don't worry, I'll get the package."

As expected, the phone call to Val shed little light on the events of the day. For some reason, the Packard guy had a bone to pick with the kid's old man and knew nothing about the coin collection. It mattered little, now, LaBette thought. *I lost them . . . could be anywhere by now.*

LaBette was furious. Val was disappointed. Five thousand bucks out the window. He was a perfectionist and, through his own carelessness, he'd let the boy slip away. "Damn it to hell! I should'a just popped the guy right off the bat. But no, I had to get cute. Nice work, Joseph!"

His only remaining option was to drive back to Minneapolis and try and pick up the trail from the Nash home. Perhaps the mother knew something, or some sort of note had been left behind indicating the boy's destination.

LaBette turned left at the stop sign and drove back toward Hutchinson. He was a long way from Minneapolis and would have plenty of time to go back over all the mistakes he made. *Who the hell is the old man? Where would he take the kid? Think, Joseph! Think!*

As always, he turned to the Scriptures for guidance. *Ye do err, not knowing the scriptures, not the power of God. Open thou mine eyes . . .*

QUILL FELT PRESSURE BUILDING in his stomach. He opened his prescription container, removed the painkiller, and stuck it in his mouth. Once it passed the back of his tongue, he waited for it to take effect. He gritted his teeth, rubbed his stomach, and took three deep breaths.

Charlie noticed Quill throw his head back to swallow the pill. "What's that, Quill?"

"Oh, I . . . uh . . . I've got ulcers, Charlie. These pills help with the pain."

Charlie was concerned. "Are ulcers serious?"

"Oh, I suppose if they are without proper medication." Quill wanted to change the direction of the conversation. He looked in the rear view. "How's she doing, son?"

"She's asleep, Quill."

"You look kinda tired yourself. How far did you travel today?"

The boy's guard was down, but he had his story well rehearsed. "Oh, I left from Minneapolis."

Time to find out about what's going on, here, Purdue mused. "Tell me, Charlie. What are you running away from?"

"An orphanage," he quickly replied.

"Is that right? And what are you running toward?"

"Huh? Oh, uh, Montana, I think."

"Why Montana?"

"'Cause Montana has cowboys and horses and stuff."

"Yes they do, but Montana's a long way away from here. Were you going to hitchhike the whole way . . . with Taffy?"

"Well, I . . . uh . . . started out riding a freight train, but . . . uh, I had some trouble . . ."

Quill noticed the boy's voice crack and wondered about his hesitancy. "Charlie? What happened, son? You can tell me. We're friends now and friends can trust each other." He waited.

Finally, Charlie opened up and recounted his experience in the boxcar. He told him everything—including the part about Willy falling from the train. He was in tears by the time he finished. "I didn't kill him, Quill! Honest! He just kinda . . . I don't know . . . he tripped, I guess. Then he was gone."

Quill pulled over, stopped and faced the boy. "Listen to me, son. It was not your fault. Whoever that guy was, he was evil . . . up to no good. Lord knows what he might have done if Taffy hadn't been there. He got what he deserved, as far as I can tell. Now, promise me you won't blame yourself ever again. Promise?" He was twisted around and had his head resting on both arms atop the seat rest, a concerned, caring look plastered on his leathery face.

"Charlie?"

"Yes, I promise. I should never have left, should I Quill?"

"Well, that depends." He chose his words with care. "Sometimes when we run from something, we wind up running into more trouble than we left behind. But, you're a brave boy, and I admire your courage, Charlie. Someday I'll tell you about somebody else who ran away only to discover how much he missed everything he ran away from. But that can wait." He studied the small face. "You're tired. Why don't you lie down and take a nap. Crawl over the seat and nestle into the rear. We've got a few hours ahead of us before we reach Brown's Valley. We'll have supper, get a nice hotel room, and then you can decide what you want to do tomorrow. That sound all right?"

Charlie thought it sounded perfect. He didn't want to be alone and Quill seemed to be a true friend . . . at a time when he needed one the most. "That sounds great, Quill. I am pretty tired." He gave Taffy a quick pat, and climbed over the seat. He snuggled in between the various bundles and before long was sound asleep.

Purdue wasn't buying into any of the boy's story. He had certainly run away but not from an orphanage. Nothing in the boy's appearance, speech, or manners indicated an orphaned child. No orphanage he had ever heard of would have permitted one of its children to keep a dog.

Nope, Charlie Nash ran away from home. *But why? What could have been so horrible, so unbearable, that he felt he had to take his dog and leave home? I'll find out why you're running, Charlie Nash, and then I'll get you back home where you belong, before . . . before . . .*

HE CONTINUED DRIVING. Mile after mile passed beneath the old Ford's worn rubber. There were fewer and fewer towns to slow him down, and he made good time.

A fox crossed the road directly ahead. Quill watched as it bounded down the ditch and across the prairie. *Beautiful country . . . sure have missed it.* The pain killers were working, but he knew he had to get his prescription refilled before too long.

Quill's thoughts were broken by a rustling from the rear. He glanced in the mirror and saw Charlie climb back over the seat and settle next to Taffy. Boy shouldn't be alone . . . shouldn't have to deal with evil at such a young age.

"Quill? I think Taffy's feeling better! Her tail's wagging!"

"That's great. son. Doc Haines said she's a tough dog. She's a great friend for you, isn't she?" He didn't add that Haines also said she was lucky the guy hadn't kick her in the head instead of her ribs.

"I think she's the greatest dog in the whole world. She saved my life, I think."

Purdue smiled and observed the surrounding countryside. They were out on the edges of the prairie now. The land was flat and unbroken. It was the beginning of what Purdue remembered as home. He recalled the wonderful change of seasons, spring storms that could be seen coming across the fields trailing dust and droplets—lightening arcing in all directions, the edge of the front as clear as a section line.

Looks like they need a good storm around here. He recalled the sound of raindrops pounding on the barn roof. *Sounded like a hundred woodpeckers.* And when the storm was over, everything was shiny and clean. Even the gravel on the roads looked new. He remembered the smell after such a storm . . . of ozone, and the earth. And when you looked around, fence wires and prairie grass glistened with clinging raindrops. *No storms coming today . . . too dry, too quiet. The fields look blown away—hope the folks around here haven't put next year's seed in the ground 'cause it won't be there come spring.* "You know anything about the prairie, Charlie?"

"Hmmm? No, not really. Just what I've read, I guess."

"Emily Dickinson said, 'To make a prairie it takes a clover and one bee. One clover, and a bee, and revery. The revery alone will do if bees are few.'"

The boy considered the poem as he stared out the window. "That's nice. But, what's,'revery'?"

"Good question. I like a man who's not afraid to admit he doesn't know something. 'Revery' means to daydream."

Twenty-Three

WHERE ARE WE GOING, QUILL?"

"Well, I'll tell you. If you're open to take a little detour from your trip to Montana, you and Taffy are welcome to come home with me to Blue Springs."

Charlie never hesitated. He felt safe and secure and enjoyed the old man's company. "You bet! That'd be neat. Where were you, anyway? I mean, were you on a business trip or something?"

"Not exactly, Charlie. I left home ten years ago . . . this'll be my first trip back." Quill barely got the words out before choking back a sob.

The boy didn't catch his friend's display of emotion. "How come? Didn't you have a family?"

Quill didn't respond right away. "My wife died many years ago. Not much to stay around for after that."

"Oh." Charlie couldn't think of anything to say to make Quill feel better, but then added, "I'll bet you still have plenty of friends left at home though, right?"

"Maybe . . . maybe not."

"Well, where have you been since you left home?"

"Oh, pretty much everywhere. Stayed with my daughter in Rock Island, Illinois, for a while, then got restless and took off."

"What'd you do?"

"Worked in the oil fields in Oklahoma for a couple of years, then drove to Florida and helped out with a citrus operation. Liked that quite a bit . . . because I was workin' with trees again." Quill passed a hand over his face and scratched his cheek. He glanced in the mirror.

Charlie looked puzzled. "What's the matter, son?"

"Oh, I was just wondering if your wife was dead and your daughter is in Rock Island, then . . . then, what's to go home to?"

Quill watched the road and didn't respond. The sudden ache in his heart had nothing to do with the pain in his gut. He knew this would be difficult enough but hadn't counted on having to explain what he was doing to an eleven-year old.

"Quill?"

"We'll talk about all that later . . . be plenty of time. I've been wondering about something though, and maybe you can help me out?"

"Sure. What is it?"

"Remember when I asked you why that guy might have wanted to grab you? The guy in the Packard?"

"Yes . . ." Charlie hesitated.

"Well, you mentioned that he said something about using you for bait. Any idea what he meant by that?"

"Nope. I don't know . . ." Charlie shivered as he recalled how terrified he was.

"Yeah, it doesn't make any sense, does it? Well, let's forget all that and talk about something else. Reach in my brown bag back behind you there, Charlie. There's a red book I'd like you to get." Quill watched as the boy turned around and rummaged through his bag.

He held up the book. "This one?"

"Yep. That's it. Know what it is?"

Charlie looked at the cover. "It's a dictionary . . . *The Oxford English Dictionary*."

"That's right. When you asked me about, 'revery,' it triggered something. Know why I carry it with me?"

"Uh, uh."

"Well, I'll tell you a little story. When I was a boy—just about your age, I think—my father gave that to me just before he left home."

"Where'd he go?"

"He went looking for gold out in the Black Hills of South Dakota. Ever hear of the Black Hills?"

"I think so . . . Isn't that where that big mountain is . . . where the presidents are?"

"That's right . . . Mount Rushmore. Anyway, my pop was having a hard time making a go of farming back then, and he heard stories about all this gold they discovered, 'Jest laying there for the pickin' like a patch a potatoes,' he said. I'll never forget the look in his eyes when he told me about it. They sparkled and shined like I'd never seen before."

Charlie moved forward against the back of the front seat and rested both arms on the top. "Gold? Real gold?"

"Yep, and he just had to go find some for himself. Only he soon found out that it wasn't quite as easy to pluck as he was led to believe. Anyway, my pop was a restless sort, and I think he just needed an excuse to get away for a while. Just before he left, he handed me that very dictionary and said, 'Quillan? If you learn one new word every day, you'll be an educated man by the time you're twenty-one.'"

"What'd he mean?"

"He meant that if I looked up a new word every day—any word—didn't matter which—and learned its meaning, and learned how to use that word, that by the time I was a grown man, I'd already have all the education I needed."

"And, did you? I mean, did you learn a new word every day like he said?"

"Yep! I'm proud to say I did. Now I plum forgot to look up my word for today though, so would you like to do the honors?"

"You bet!" Charlie opened the book.

"All right, then. Just close your eyes, turn to any page you like, and point your finger to a word. That'll be our word for the day."

Charlie closed his eyes, flipped the pages, and stabbed his finger on a page. He opened his eyes and said, "I'm in the F's. Here it is: f-l-a-t-u-l . . ."

Quill chuckled and said, "Oh, oh. I think I know what's coming."

"What's the matter?"

"Nothing. Keep going, son." Quill choked back further laughter.

"Okay, f-l-a-t-u-l-e-n-c-e. 'The presence of ex . . . excessive gas in the digestive tract.' Quill? That means a fart, right?" Charlie giggled.

"Yep. That's what it means all right. Now, use the word in a sentence."

"Hmmm. Okay, how about, 'He's full of flatulence'?"

"Pretty good. Now you know where the word 'fart' comes from."

"Can I look up another one?"

"You bet. Go ahead."

Charlie closed his eyes, turned the pages and pointed at another word. He opened his eyes and said, "I'm in the P's. p-a-l-i-d-i-n. 'A heroic champion. A strong defender.'"

"And?"

"Hmmm. Let me think a minute." Charlie looked at the back of the old man's head, glanced down at Taffy, and said, "I've got it! 'Quill Purdue is Charlie and Taffy's paladin!" He beamed and closed the dictionary with an emphatic *thump!*

Purdue was touched. Warmth filled his body. His lower lip quivered and he managed to reply, "Thank you . . . Charlie." He had to pause.

Quill rubbed both eyes and said, "You know, Charlie, it was pure happenstance that you and I met today. Furthermore, if I hadn't left my hat back at that café, I never would have spotted Taffy on the side of the road. I don't know about being your, 'paladin,' but I'm sure glad we had the chance to meet up. I was getting kind of lonely traveling by myself . . . think I needed a new friend. And there you were."

"I'm glad, too, Quill. Real glad." Charlie nibbled his lip and finished his thought. "Still, I think you were supposed to be there, Quill! I think God put you there at just the right time . . . that's what I think."

Quill was speechless. But he wasn't buying into any sort of divine providence. Not considering the scars on his own heart that had never healed. *Nope, just luck—pure and simple.*

Charlie, on the other hand was a believer. *Yep! Quill and I were supposed to meet! That's all there is to it!*

❖   ●   ❖

AFTER A LONG PERIOD of silence, Quill pointed through the side window as the red sun slowly sank beneath the horizon. "Look at that sunset, Charlie. Isn't that something?"

Charlie stared and started counting, "One, two, three . . ."

Quill joined in, "Four, five, six . . . I'll bet it takes thirty-seven to disappear. What's your guess?"

"Forty-three."

The old man and the boy silently counted as the sun dropped ever lower. When it was finally gone, Charlie said, "Guess we both lost, Quill."

"Yep. Tomorrow we'll get it right." Purdue wondered what tomorrow would bring—how he would react—what he would say. He had rehearsed the words so many times, but now that the day was at hand, he feared he'd stumble and fail.

Charlie broke the silence. "Wow! Look at that!" He was facing left. The evening glow highlighted a massive body of water below the highway.

"What's that, Quill?"

"That should be Lake Traverse. That's a man-made lake."

"Really? How'd they do that?"

"Well, during the Depression, when no one could find work, the government put everybody to work building dams and roads and such. They built the one at the end of this lake. Before the dam, the Minnesota River, which flowed through a huge marshy area south of here called Lac Qui Parle, trickled into a small river that eventually became the Red River of the North."

"What happened to that river?"

"Oh, it still runs out of the lake and flows all the way to Winnipeg, Canada."

"What was down there before they dammed it up?"

"Farms, homes, crop land, and the like."

"I hope the people all got out."

"Oh, yes. The government bought up all the property that was to be flooded. They had plenty of time to get out."

"I'll bet there are a lot of ducks out there."

"You bet. Especially at this time of year . . . thousands and thousands. You a duck hunter, Charlie?"

The boy hesitated, and lied. "Uh, no. Not really, but I bet Taffy would be a great retriever."

Quill sensed the boy's duplicity and smiled. "Yep. I bet she would too. Probably be a great upland bird dog as well."

"You mean pheasants?"

"You bet. Pheasants, sharptail, prairie chicken . . . maybe even some quail. If you hang around a while before you continue your journey to Montana, we'll take her out and see how she does. Would you like that?"

"Wow! You mean it?"

"Sure. They're all in season. I haven't been bird hunting in years. I'd kinda like that . . ." The old man stared wistfully across the lake and into the pink and blue sky.

"There's a town ahead." Charlie offered.

"Yep. About time, too. I'm starved."

"Me too. How about you, Taff? Are you hungry?" He raised her head and looked into her warm, brown eyes.

The Ford wagon drove through the town of Brown's Valley and stopped in front of the Great Plains Hotel. Quill turned off the ignition and opened the door.

"What about Taffy, Quill? Will they let her stay inside?"

"Oh, I think so. I'll talk to them and be sure it's okay. Why don't you take her across the street to that park and let her walk a bit. She's probably ready for a pee, I'll bet. I'll go in and get us a room." Quill waited to be sure Charlie could get the dog out of the car. Taffy seemed to be feeling much better. He went into the hotel.

Charlie kept Taffy on the leash until he reached the park, then unsnapped the clasp and turned her loose. She moved gingerly over the grass, found a suitable spot and squatted. She continued her survey of the ground and ducked behind an elderberry bush for further toiletry.

Charlie walked to the far end of the park and gazed out over the lake. He could see large flocks of waterfowl gliding through the twilight as they moved up and down the lake. It reminded him of his trip to Parker's Lake with his father. *Sure wish Dad could see this. If only . . . if only . . .*

Suddenly, Charlie felt a deep stab of sorrow and regret. *Wonder how mom's doing? What's going to happen to her . . . to dad . . . if I never go back?* He was conflicted by different emotions. *But, I can't go back. Remember how horrible it was . . . how mad dad was. I have a new friend now—Quill, and he hasn't yelled at me even once. No, we'll be fine as long as Taffy's okay. Just don't let anybody know the truth . . . or . . . or else they'll make me go home.*

Maybe . . . maybe if I . . . Taffy nudged his hand. "Good girl, Taff. Let's go meet Quill." He reattached the leash and went back to the car.

Quill soon reappeared. "We're all set. Turns out that the owner is an old friend. He said that Taffy was welcome. So let's get our bags and go on up to the room."

Charlie had to collect a few things that had worked their way out of his bag, but it only took a moment. Then he was introduced to the proprietor, John Smoker. Quill had briefly explained how they met and requested that his old friend not ask too many questions of the boy.

"A pleasure to meet you, Charlie. Welcome to the Great Plains Hotel. And this must be Taffy. Hello, girl." Smoker crouched and offered the back of his hand.

Charlie watched as Taffy accepted the greeting. Then he scanned the lobby. It was huge—with high, beamed ceilings, and dark woodwork. Original gas lights converted to electric, dotted the walls. In between the lights were memorabilia of the fur trade industry. "What's all that gear, Mr. Smoker?"

"This used to be a famous fur trading route for the French back in the 1800s, Charlie. They traveled up and down the rivers out here on their way to and from Winnipeg. This old hotel was established in 1866 and the traders would stay here to rest up before continuing their journey."

"Holy cow! Look at the snowshoes and all the animals and traps and stuff, Quill."

"I know, Charlie. It's really something, isn't it? Come on now, let's get our stuff up to the room and come back down for one of John's famous rib-eye steaks. Still serve those, I hope, John?"

"You bet."

Quill picked up his bag and headed for the wide stairs. "Coming Charlie? Thanks, John. We'll be back down in a bit."

"Good to see you again, Quill. Glad you're back home."

Charlie was enthralled by all the artifacts but followed Quill up the stairs. Taffy had some difficulty with the climb, and Charlie had to wait as she crept up the deep stairs. Once they reached the landing on the first floor, they found their room. It was small with twin beds and a sink. Yellow, flowered wall paper covered the walls and two windows faced west, overlooking Brown's Valley.

"Which bed would you like, Charlie?"

"You choose."

"Okay, I'll take the one over here." He threw his bag on the bed and opened it up.

Charlie placed his sack on the other bed and sat down. "Where's the bathroom, Quill?"

"Down the hall on the left."

"Okay. I'll be right back. Taffy, you stay here with Quill." Charlie left the room.

Purdue quickly went over to Charlie's bag. He hated to violate the boy's trust, but felt he had to find out where he lived. He slipped on his reading glasses and dug through Charlie's bag for something that would reveal his true identity and residence. "Sorry, Taff. Hate to be this way, but I need to find out where both of you are from."

222

Taffy thumped her tail and nosed Purdue's hand as he peered into the bag.

After a few minutes, without finding anything that would yield an address or phone number, Quill replaced the few items he had removed as quickly as possible and returned to his bed. "Nuts! Guess I'll just have to get him to open up to me, girl. Got to make sure you two stay close, though. Sure would like to get you two turned around and headed home. In due time, I guess . . ."

As soon as Charlie returned, they washed their hands and went downstairs to dinner. Taffy curled up on Charlie's bed next to his bag and watched both leave the room.

AFTER DINNER, QUILL and Charlie returned to their room. Their stomachs were full and both were tired. Charlie had borrowed a bowl from the dining room and dumped scraps of meat in it for Taffy.

"Not too much, Charlie. Remember what Doc Haines said."

Charlie slipped a pill down the dog's throat and put the bowl under the sink. She ate slowly, as if each bite was painful. She only ate half of the scraps. Charlie wrapped the rest in a wad of tissue and ran a small amount of water in the bowl. She drank every last drop.

"Think she needs to go outside before we go to bed?"

"I don't think so, Quill. She didn't drink that much." Charlie went to his bed and dug through the newspaper sack. He pulled out a change of underwear and said, "I think I'll take a bath. Will that be okay?"

"You bet! I'll keep an eye on Taffy. You go ahead."

Quill sat down on the bed next to Taffy. "What could possibly have been so horrible, girl?" He scratched her ears and stared out the window. "I wonder what happened to him . . ."

Ten minutes later, the door opened and Charlie walked in. His hair was still wet but he looked freshly scrubbed. The smell of Ivory soap trailed across the small room.

Quill rose and crossed to his bed. He removed his shoes, put his bag on the floor, and dug out a pair of flannel pajamas. He picked up a leather toilet kit and went to the door. "Be right back."

By the time Purdue returned, Charlie was fast asleep. Taffy as well. Quill covered the boy with the bedspread, turned out the light, and crawled into the other bed. He stared at the ceiling and watched as moon shadows crept into the room.

His trip home had not gone as planned, and he wondered how bringing the boy home was going to complicate things. *Maybe it will make it all easier. . . . Maybe the boy's presence will soften things somehow.*

He closed his eyes. Soon the pain would return. And soon everything would be resolved. Soon . . .

Twenty-Four

L ABETTE REACHED MINNEAPOLIS at midnight. He parked the car and entered his apartment building. He was frustrated and angry. But more than that, he felt as if he had missed something. Some tiny scrap of information had eluded him, and he couldn't put a finger on it. "You're getting old, Joseph."

He fixed a sandwich, chased it with a cold glass of milk, picked up his Bible, and went to bed. *Perhaps tomorrow . . . or the next day. I've got to get into that house . . .*

Marsha Nash was frightened beyond words at the thought of her young son out on the highway someplace—alone. Her mother was staying with her and now the two of them were discussing what to do next.

"What did Frank say?" her mother asked.

"Oh, Mother. I can't believe any of this is happening. This is all so . . . so . . . unreal."

"I know. Any chance they'll let him out . . . under the circumstances?"

"Maybe, but he won't know until his attorney talks to the judge. I'm going to call the police again." She picked up the phone and said, "Operator? Please connect me with the police department?" She looked at her mother as she waited. "Yes, Sergeant Thomas, Please." While facing her mother, she said, "Sergeant Thomas? Marsha Nash. Listen, have you found out anything more about my son?"

Marsha listened intently, and a frown soon appeared as she completed the call. "Yes, I understand. But, even once the forty-eight hours passes, then what? I see. All right. Yes, if we hear anything more, I'll let you know. Thank you." She replaced the receiver.

"What did he say?" Her mother asked.

"They're still treating this as a runaway situation. Given Charlie's note, they feel that, without a ransom note, Charlie has simply run from home. Until there is some concrete evidence of a kidnapping, there is little they can do. Lord, this is so maddening." Marsha's voice cracked as she finished.

"So, they intend to do what, nothing?" Her mother asked.

"They've notified the State Patrol to keep an eye out for him, but, until a crime has been committed, that's the extent of what they can do."

"All right, then. We'll just stay close to the phone, hope for the best, and pray."

"Charlie's so young, though. He's barely eleven, mother."

"I know, dear, but if Charlie is anything, he's persistent . . . and strong willed."

"I pray to God he's safe . . . that he doesn't run into any bad people . . ." Marsha couldn't put into words what she was really thinking.

CHARLIE WOKE EARLY just as he always did. He'd had a troubled sleep, but when he woke during the night, he was comforted to find both Taffy and Quill in the darkened room with him. He was happy to see the morning light and anxious to see how Taffy felt.

She stirred and groaned. A pat on her head from Charlie evoked a weak tail wag.

"Taffy? How do you feel, girl? Want some water?" She appeared listless.

Quill heard Charlie and rolled over. "She okay, son?"

"I don't know. She's not moving real well."

Purdue threw back the covers and went to Charlie's bed. As he leaned over to inspect the dog, a sudden pain shot through his stomach. He bent further and gasped.

"Quill? Quill? What's the matter?" Charlie put both feet on the floor and laid his hand on the old man's back. He was frightened, as Quill was in obvious trouble.

Purdue managed to say, "My pills, son. Open the bottle and get one for me?"

Charlie spotted the bottle on the bedside table, unscrewed the top and extracted a pill. He dropped it in his friend's palm.

Quill back-stepped to his bed, sat down and took the pill. He grimaced and lay back. "Thanks, Charlie. That was a bad one. I'll be all right. Why don't you take Taffy outside for a pee . . . then put her in the car. Keys are on the dresser. She'll be okay. I think she just stiffened up overnight. She's bound to be sore today."

"You sure you're all right?"

"Yep. You go ahead. I'll just lie here a minute. I'll get dressed and meet you in the dining room in a jiffy."

Charlie dressed hurriedly and led Taffy from the room. He helped her down the long flight of stairs. By the time she reached the bottom, she appeared to be moving much easier. They crossed the lobby.

"Good morning, Charlie," Smoker called.

"Oh! Hi. That was a great meal last night, Mr. Smoker."

"Thank you, Charlie. I'll pass your compliment on to the chef . . . my wife." He smiled and returned to his paper work.

After a brief walk, Charlie opened the wagon and helped Taffy inside. He returned to the hotel and entered the dining room. Quill was already seated—reading the menu.

"Feel better?" Charlie asked.

"Yes, thanks. How about Taff?"

"You were right. Think she just stiffened up."

The waitress appeared, and they gave her their orders. Charlie sipped a glass of orange juice and Quill started in on some dried toast.

The old man wiped his mouth and asked, "Tell me, Charlie. What was the name of that orphanage you were at?"

Charlie was caught off guard and stumbled a bit with his reply. "Uh, the YMCA Orphanage." He immediately looked away.

"Is that right? I didn't know the Y had orphanages. How long were you there?"

"Oh, a couple of years." The boy fidgeted and squirmed. He hated lying but had no choice.

"And before that?"

"I came from another place in . . . Duluth!"

"So, you're originally from Duluth?"

"Yes. Duluth."

"I see. And what about your parents?"

"Oh, I never knew my parents. I was an orphan when I was a baby."

"Why did you leave the orphanage?"

Charlie was ready for this question. "'Cause they weren't going to let me keep Taffy any longer."

"Yep. That might make a fella decide to leave, all right." Their food arrived and Quill forked part of his poached egg before continuing. "I am surprised that they let you have a dog at all, though. Did all the kids have pets?"

Charlie spooned his oatmeal rapidly and when he could delay no longer, said, "Oh, yes. Some other kids had dogs too. Some had cats, but they stayed on a different floor."

"Hmm. Must have been a bit . . . chaotic." Quill's eyebrows rose just a fraction.

Charlie chose not to respond, but finished his oatmeal and started in on a plate of pancakes. When he was finished, he decided to change the subject. "Where are we going today, Quill?"

Purdue smiled at the boy's dissembling. "Blue Springs, Charlie. That's where home is. It's across the lake on the South Dakota side. We'll drive north for a while. Then cross over at the dam on the far end of the lake."

"Really? We're going to South Dakota?"

"Yep. Across that big old lake is Dakota country."

"Are there Indians and buffalo?"

Quill chuckled. "Not many buffalo around anymore—sorry to say. And the Indians are mostly all on reservations scattered around the state."

Happy to have the conversation diverted, Charlie asked, "And what's at Blue Springs? I mean, you really haven't told me anything about your family . . . except about your stay with your daughter in Rock Island."

Purdue was silent. He stared out the window. A dark cloud had entered the room and settled over their table. Quill's bushy eyebrows rose and fell in time with his breathing. Deep creases etched across his forehead. He sipped his coffee and remained silent.

"Quill? Did you hear me?"

"I heard you, son. Are you finished with breakfast? If so, let's get going then, okay?" He threw fifty cents on the table, pushed back and folded his napkin. "Ready?"

Charlie was puzzled, but didn't want to make his friend mad so he didn't question him further. It seemed to the boy, however, that his new friend had secrets of his own he didn't want to share. *Maybe later . . . maybe he'll talk to me about it later . . . or I'll find out when we get to his home.*

Quill settled up with Smoker while Charlie went up to get their bags. By the time he came back down, Quill was ready to leave.

"So long, Quill. Good to meet you, Charlie. You both come back real soon, okay?"

"You bet! Bye, Mr. Smoker."

"Thanks for everything, John. I'll be in touch. Let's go, Charlie."

"Good luck, Quill. You're going to need it, old friend." Smoker watched as Quill and the boy left the hotel. His comment echoed in the cavernous lobby.

Once the car was packed, they climbed in, and Quill started the engine. "I have to stop at the pharmacy, Charlie, and get my prescription filled. Drugstore is just up the block, okay?"

"Sure. Maybe I'll come in with you and buy some baseball cards."

Quill drove a short distance, and stopped. Both got out and entered the store. Purdue went directly to the druggist, and Charlie headed to the candy section. After ten minutes, they met at the check-out, paid for their purchases, and left.

Back in the wagon, Charlie opened up a packet, pulled out the bubble gum, and declared, "Jackie Robinson! I got a Jackie Robinson, Quill!"

"No kidding? Hang on to that . . . could be worth something some day."

Charlie stuffed the gum in his mouth and managed, "I will!"

"That's neat, Charlie. Say, we haven't looked up our word for the day, have we?"

"Nope. I'll get the dictionary." Charlie grabbed the old book, blew a large bubble, and closed his eyes. He turned the pages and pointed. As the wagon pulled away from the old drugstore, he exclaimed, "M-e-t-t-l-e. Mettle. 'Courage and fortitude.' That's easy. Taffy has mettle! How's that?"

"Perfect. Yes, indeed. She certainly demonstrated her mettle yesterday, didn't she?"

Charlie hugged her tightly. "Yeah, she sure did. She's always been pretty protective and you know what?"

"What's that?"

"She can tell just by sniffing if a person is nice or not."

"Is that right?"

"Yep. She warmed up to you right away . . . but . . . those other guys . . . well, she stood right between me and them and just growled and snarled. She's really a smart dog, isn't she, Quill?"

"One of the smartest and bravest I ever saw, Charlie. You should be very proud of her."

"I am." Charlie flushed with pride. He watched the shoreline pass by and asked, "What are all those little houses?"

"Oh, fishing and hunting and vacation cottages. Ever since the lake was formed, this has turned into quite a vacation area."

"Are there fish in there, too?"

"You bet. Walleye, northern, sauger . . . lots of sunnies and crappies, too. You like to fish, Charlie?"

"Yeah, I used to take—" He caught himself before finishing.

"What's that?"

"Oh, nothing. Are we going to stay in Blue Springs?"

"I think so."

"Where?"

Time to deal with it, Quillan. "At our farm."

"Who's there?"

"My son, Cort. And his wife, Maxine." Now it was out. He knew he'd have to elaborate, but once verbalized—didn't want to.

"I didn't know you had a son, Quill. How come you didn't mention him before?"

Purdue sighed and replied, "There's a lot you don't know about me . . . about my family."

Charlie climbed over the seat and landed in front. He pivoted and sat sideways. He wanted to know more. His bright, blue eyes sparkled as he blurted, "What about your family?"

The old man stared straight ahead. *I can't do this.*

"Quill? Does your son have any children?"

Purdue couldn't look at the boy and instead snapped, "Leave it alone, Charlie!"

Quill's sharp retort hit Charlie like a pebble from a slingshot. His mouth flew open, but he couldn't speak. He shrank against the door and looked up at his friend.

"I'm sorry, I didn't mean to . . . to, but I thought you wanted to tell me about . . ."

"Listen, and listen carefully. You are welcome to come with me— you know that, but remember that you're my guest. You'll meet my family, but keep your questions to yourself. Understood?"

231

All the excitement and warmth Charlie experienced moments earlier vanished. An adult had rebuked him once again. His rekindled feeling of security and comfort was yanked away like a strong wind smacking against a dead leaf. He was crushed. *What'd I do? I thought he was my friend . . . said I could ask anything, and he'd . . .*

Charlie glanced sideways at Quill, but the old man didn't say anything. *Nothing's changed. He's just like Dad. I thought he was different but he's not.* Charlie's head drooped. He wanted to melt into the worn seat fabric but could not. The silence was too telling so he climbed into the back and huddled with Taffy.

Purdue saw Charlie leave the front and immediately experienced a massive wave of guilt and shame. *I can't help it. Why even try?* Every time he dared address the real source of his pain and agony—he failed. It had been too long . . . the scars too deep. *Why did I bother? I should have stayed with Alice. This is going to be a nightmare. Kid didn't deserve that. But . . . God, how am I going to get through this? Now I've involved a kind, innocent young boy in my mess. He's obviously got serious issues of his own . . . was just beginning to trust me, and look what I did. What's the matter with me?*

The old man and the scarred boy continued on in silence—each lost in thought and faced with decisions neither was prepared to deal with.

LABETTE KNEW HE HAD FAILED . . . failed miserably. He thought he knew what had to be done to salvage the contract. He sipped his first cup of coffee, stared at the phone, and considered his options. *I can get into the house and look for the coins . . . or find some clue about where the kid's headed. Or, I can call Val and hand back the contract. But . . . he'll never hire me again. And I need that money . . .*

He made up his mind, picked up the phone and dialed Val. "It's me. I'm at home. Call me back." LaBette hung up and finished his coffee as he waited.

In five minutes, the phone rang. "Go ahead . . . Why? Because I lost the kid, that's why! I know, I know. Calm down. Yes, I understand. I'll go in tonight. I don't know . . . if I have to, I'll take her out. Of course. A fire, explosion—something like that. Only if it's necessary." LaBette listened to Val's response.

"Here's the deal, though. If I can't find the package—if it's with the kid and there's nothing in the house to indicate where he's at, I'll have to backtrack and chase him down. That raises the ante, so you better call the money guys and tell them the price just went up by two grand. What? Can't help it, Val! What if I have to chase this kid all the way to Montana? Hell, I don't know. I told you, the old man just happened along at the wrong time. Saved the kid's heinie, near as I can tell. Okay, I'll call you later tonight."

LaBette hung up the phone. He didn't like the idea of going into the Nash house, but he had no choice. He knew the old man was in jail and wouldn't be home—the article in the paper had been specific about that. So all he had to worry about was the old lady. And without that damn dog around, he should be able to slip in, poke around the kid's room, and get back out. *But, if she wakes up? Well, too bad.* He picked up his Bible and turned to John . . .

The wood-sided Ford Super Deluxe continued north from Brown's Valley. The mood inside was sour . . . the tension unbroken. Not a word was spoken for over fifteen miles. Taffy's health had improved, and it showed in her eyes. Charlie's mood, however, had grown even more sullen.

Once they reached the dam separating Lake Traverse from the Red River, the road curved west. The dam was over a mile long—the steep spillway on the right side of the wagon dropped precipitously for a hundred feet to the river below.

Quill wanted to say something—anything to undo the damage done earlier, but could not. As they reached the end of the dam, the road forked. Quill signaled a turn south and braked.

Charlie startled the old man by saying, "I think I'll get out here, Quill."

"What? I thought you were going to come with me to Blue Springs?"

"Is Montana straight ahead?"

Purdue hesitated. "Yeess. If you keep going west, eventually you'll reach Montana, but, Charlie, what about Taffy? She still needs to rest." *Don't lose him, Quillan. You promised.*

"She's feeling better, now. We should get going, so if you'd pull over . . ." The tone of the boy's voice was firm and distinct.

Quill cruised into a small, roadside park that overlooked the dam and Lake Traverse.

Purdue took a deep breath. "Let's get out and take a little walk, Charlie. Can we do that before you leave?"

"I guess so." Charlie got out and opened the rear door. He let Taffy out, then dragged his sack over the back seat. She trotted away a short distance and squatted. Soon she was busy sniffing in the tall prairie grass adjacent to the clearing.

Quill followed the dog and stopped. He fingered a sheaf of stalks and said, "Know what this is, Charlie?"

The boy dropped his bag and shuffled over to where Quill and Taffy stood. "No. What?" He appeared disinterested, anxious to be on his way.

"It's called, wild bergamot. It's a late blooming prairie flower that somehow manages to survive everything that Mother Nature throws at it all summer long. Only the strongest manage to grow and produce flowers. This one would normally bloom in September, but I guess because of the warm weather, it sprouted late and put this small flower cluster out. Even the drought can't seem to keep this tough little bugger from blooming." He plucked a star-shaped purple flower and handed it to the boy.

Charlie opened his hand and watched as the small flower dropped into his palm. Five spoon-shaped petals rested against his skin. A breeze came up and the petals fluttered. The flower reminded Charlie of a windmill. "It's so small." He was mesmerized by the beautiful, diminutive floret.

"Yep. The Indians call this 'Wanahca'—'The Flower of Great Courage.' It has to compete with all the other wild flowers and weeds around here. They believe that the bergamot possesses some sort of magical power, and because it's so tough—so hard to keep down—they believe that if they dry the petals and sprinkle them on their food, they too will be as strong as the bergamot."

Charlie focused on the delicate flower and as he did, the petals began to wilt. "It's dying, Quill." His small voice was full of sadness.

"Yes, but if you look real close at the center, you'll see lots of tiny grains. Those are seeds. Once those are released onto the wind, they'll scatter and next season sprout as new plants. So, from one tiny flower, hundreds more will grow."

Charlie pried open the center. Minute, dark specks tumbled out, caught the breeze, and slid from his palm.

"You're a lot like the bergamot, Charlie. Strong and resilient—a little stubborn, maybe . . . but not easily defeated."

Charlie wiped his hand. The flower blew away. He considered the old man's words.

"I, on the other hand, am not nearly as strong as you. I lack the courage that you possess in abundance, Charlie." Purdue stared across the lake into the bright, reflected sunlight.

He cleared his throat and continued. "I am sincerely sorry, Charlie." His voice broke, but he continued. "I owe you an apology. I should never have spoken to you the way I did. Friends don't treat friends that way, and I consider you a friend."

Charlie was flabbergasted. For the first time in his life, an adult—and a man at that—had apologized to him. A chill ran down his back. He felt as if the hair on his neck itched. "That's okay, Quill," was all he managed to say.

"No! It's not. You didn't deserve that, but maybe after I tell you a few things about myself, you'll understand . . . and . . . perhaps forgive me." His eyes blurred as he looked down at the boy.

"If you'll postpone leaving for a bit, I'd like to talk to you. Can we go over and sit at that picnic table?"

Twenty-Five

O NCE THEY WERE SEATED on either side of the table, Quill inhaled, pursed his lips, and began his tale. "Ten years ago, I made a mistake—a bad mistake. I've been paying for it ever since."

"What'd you do?" Charlie stared across the worn planks at his new friend.

"My son and his family lived with me after my wife died. . . . We farmed together, and, even though Cort and I were very similar—both stubborn and bull-headed—we got along well enough, until . . ." Purdue pulled out his handkerchief and blew his nose. This would be difficult.

"Cort and Maxine had one child—his name was Justin. He meant the world to me, as he did them. I took every opportunity to be with my grandson, and he tagged after me all the time. Cort loved Justin more than himself and never allowed him near any of the farm machinery—and I respected Cort's concern, but Justin was so curious. . . . He always wanted to pitch in and help me with chores."

Quill held his head back and watched a few, high, fluffy clouds float past. After a moment, he continued. "When Justin was five, we bought a new tractor—a Ford, Model 8N. It was a beauty, and we were all very excited. You see, it was the first three-point hitch tractor we ever owned . . . it made our work so much easier." He lost himself for a moment in the memory of those days.

"Anyway, Justin was always after me to take him for a ride. One day as I was headed out to the orchard to do some mowing, Justin ran alongside and wouldn't go back until I stopped. I knew better, of course—but for some reason . . ." Once again, Purdue's eyes blurred, but this time, tears slipped down each cheek.

"Quill? You don't have to . . . you know, tell me if . . ."

"No. I want to, Charlie. I have to." He brushed away the tears. "I knew I shouldn't have, but I picked Justin up and put him on my lap. Cort was in town and I thought . . . well, I don't know what I thought. I let him play with the steering wheel. He was laughing—Lord, that child could laugh. I put the tractor in gear and opened up the throttle. We were having a wonderful time, and I lost track of where we were. The orchard lies on a slope—kind of steep in some areas. I don't really know what happened—maybe I wasn't familiar enough with that tractor or something, but all of a sudden we began to tip. I managed to throw Justin clear at the last minute before the tractor rolled. I was pinned. The tractor had landed on my leg."

Charlie witnessed despair and pain in his friend's face. "Quill? What happened?"

Purdue's voice was a mere whisper. "When Cort came home, both of us were in the orchard. I . . . I . . . don't remember much after that. Everything was a blur. But Justin was dead. . . . His little neck was broken when I threw him. My leg was busted up, but that was nothing."

The old man stared into Charlie's bright, blue eyes as he recalled the day. "I . . . I killed my grandson, Charlie!" Quill put his head in both hands and sobbed for a long time.

Taffy moved around the table and put her head on the old man's knee.

Charlie started to cry as well—as much for the pain his friend was feeling, for the death of his grandson, and his own, private hurt. "Quill? Quill? You didn't mean for it to happen!"

Charlie stood and walked to Quill's side. He laid his small hand on Purdue's shoulder. He couldn't find the words to express how sorry he felt.

Purdue looked up and through reddened eyes, finally replied, "What I did was inexcusable, son. I had no business going against Cort's wishes. One way or another, I caused the death of my grandson. Cort has never forgiven me for that."

"Is that why you . . . why you left?"

"Yes. It was unbearable. Cort wouldn't speak to me—hasn't since that day. It's been ten years since I left, and I'm going home to . . . to, I don't know what." Purdue had to be careful, here. "To be with my son, and make amends, I guess."

Charlie was torn now. His earlier wish to leave Quill and continue on to Montana seemed hollow and selfish. Quill had opened his heart to him, and he knew he couldn't abandon him—couldn't leave his friend. He was puzzled, however. "Why now, though? I mean, you could have come back at any time . . . couldn't you?"

"I can't answer that, Charlie." Purdue hated to put the boy off, but he had no choice. "Let's just say . . . it's time. It's time for Cort and me to somehow put the past behind us." There were no more tears. He was drained. Too much had happened in the past two days. He hadn't anticipated opening his heart to a boy of eleven—a boy he only met the day before. He felt somewhat relieved, however. He looked out over the lake.

"Look, Charlie. Look out there." He pointed to a large bird, soaring over the water. Ducks scattered as the bird cruised the open water.

"What is that?"

"That's a bald eagle, son. He's searching for food." No sooner had Quill spoken, than the eagle jolted up twenty feet, collapsed its wings, and dropped like a stone. Then its wings expanded again, and they could just see a brief ripple beneath its talons as it reached for its prey.

"Wow! What'd he just do?"

"Grabbed a duck. Cripple more'n likely." The eagle flew to the top of a dead, box elder on the shore and sat with the duck firmly clasped between its talons. "Not many of those left, anymore, Charlie."

"How come?"

"I heard it was pesticides killing them off—stuff that gets into the water—into the fish first, then the birds. Something in the chemical weakens their eggs. Eggs can't hatch properly, so no babies. It's worse for the fish-eating birds, and fish are big in an eagle's diet. Pretty soon they'll be extinct, I'm afraid."

"Then they shouldn't be using the pesticides . . . should they?"

"Nope. But try and tell that to a farmer that's barely gettin' by as it is. If he stops using chemicals, then grasshoppers and aphids and who knows what will destroy his crop. Don't know what the answer is, I'm afraid."

"How sad."

"Yes, it is."

"Will you come home with me, son? Just for a while? I don't think I can face my son alone. I need a friend with me, and right now you're the only good friend I have."

"I'd like that, Quill . . . and I'm sorry for almost, well . . . for almost leaving you. I'll stay with you as long as you want me to."

Charlie then did something entirely out of character. He leaned over and hugged the old man—tightly. He laid his head on Quill's shoulder. The back of the old man's neck smelled of a spicy aftershave. It reminded Charlie of home—of his father. He stifled an urge to sob.

Quill was moved by this touching gesture. "Thank you, son. I'm not convinced that you aren't the real paladin around here, by the way. You just don't know it yet." He patted the boy on the back and stood up. "Okay. We have a ways to go, so we better get a move on."

The three hiked back to the wagon. Charlie picked up his sack and placed it in the rear. Taffy stopped to scratch at the bindings around her middle. "I think she wants that gauze taken off."

"I suppose so, but might be best to leave it on as long as possible."

Taffy clambered into the back. Charlie sat in the front. Once the car started, Quill said, "Thank you, Charlie."

"You're welcome, Quill."

LaBette was jumpy. He hated unfinished business—loose ends were troublesome. He paced the small apartment. It was located near Loring Park—close to downtown Minneapolis—and like most of the other residences he had had, was sparsely furnished. He moved frequently to cover his tracks as often as possible.

When not on a job, his life was boring—empty. The only real rush of pleasure he felt was when he had successfully tracked his prey; picked the time, place, and method of execution, and ultimately held the contract's life in his hands. Then, and only then, was he fulfilled.

He decided he couldn't wait for the cover of darkness. He dressed in a neutral sport coat and slacks, pocketed the Luger and a pair of gloves, and left the apartment. It was 2:00 P.M. He guessed that at some point, Mrs. Nash would have to leave the house. When she did, he'd enter from the rear and have free reign to prowl about undetected. If she didn't leave, he'd just have to wait until later that night to break in. If he were discovered . . . well, so be it.

He drove to the two-story on Oliver Avenue, parked a few doors away, and settled back to wait. He had on a pair of glasses and a gray fedora. He didn't have long to wait.

Within thirty minutes, the front door opened and two women appeared. One was the Nash woman. The second he could only guess at. *Might be the grandmother,* he mused.

He watched as they climbed into a blue Oldsmobile and pulled away from the curb. As they passed his DeSoto, he ducked. Once they were gone, he left the car and walked across the street. He rang the doorbell and looked around. No one was in sight except for three kids at the far end of the block. He quickly ducked around back where he was sheltered from the neighbors, and went to work on the back door lock. He had it open in an instant.

Once inside, he moved slowly through the downstairs. Seeing nothing of interest, he climbed the stairs to the second floor and found what appeared to be the boy's room. The dresser and desk revealed nothing. He searched under the bed, the mattress, and beneath the pillow. When finished, he scanned the room and decided the closet had to be a logical spot for a boy to hide something of value. He opened the closet door, parted the clothes hanging in front, and noticed the stairs. He climbed the few steps to a small platform, and found Charlie's secret panel.

Once he had the hatbox out and its contents emptied, he realized that the kid's collection was missing. *Must've taken it with . . . this is the only place that makes any sense for a kid that age.* He put the few items back in the box and stuck the container back in the hole.

Okay, now what? Maybe the kid left a note. He went into the parents' room and, after fifteen minutes, found that nothing there would be of help.

He briefly checked two other rooms, took a fast tour of the attic, and went back downstairs. Just beneath the stairs was a small room that held a toilet, sink, and short counter with a telephone. He switched on the light. There, next to the phone was Charlie's note to his mother. He read it twice. No mention of where he was other than somewhere in Montana. *Damn! Kid could be anywhere.*

"Damnation!" Something seemed to be eluding LaBette as he reread the note. *What is it? I'm missing something . . . have been since yesterday. Wait? I've got it! The old man on the highway . . . the one who took the kid from the Packard guy. If the old man took the kid, then . . .*

He dropped the pad and turned out the light. Voices . . . LaBette froze. Women's voices . . . from the front door. *They're back!*

He pulled out the Luger and peeked around the door. Both women could be seen through the sidelights on either side of the door. They were on the porch, ready to unlock the door and enter the house.

LaBette knew he didn't have time to escape. The women would be through the front door in seconds. He pulled the door shut part way and waited. *Has to look like an accident, Joseph.* His heart raced, and he felt a familiar, pleasurable flow of warmth surge through his body. He smiled. His pulse slowed as it always did just before he went into action. *No mistakes . . . no screams. Has to be quick.*

SEYMOUR WENZEL FINISHED his lunch and drew the edge of the napkin across his mustache. He glanced at his watch and focused on the front door. *Come on, man! Time's wasting.*

Before long, Paxton Armbruster appeared, with Madeleine directly behind him. She wheeled him over to the table. After removing one of the chairs, she slid him into place. "Thank you, dear," Paxton said. "We won't be long."

Wenzel nodded at Madeline and waited for her to leave. "What did you find out?"

"Our man lost the kid . . . someplace out in the western part of the state."

"What?" Wenzel was furious. "How could he? It's just a small boy for crying out loud!"

"I know, I know, but nonetheless, the child vanished. Hooked up with some old geezer . . . our man has no idea where they went."

Armbruster held up a hand to forestall further whining from Wenzel. "However, he's going into the Nash home this very evening to search for the coins. Failing that, he may find some clue as to the boy's whereabouts."

"Sonofabitch, Pax! This guy was supposed to be the best. What happened?" Wenzel fingered his thin mustache repeatedly.

"Don't know all the details, but when my contact called about the second guy trailing the kid that complicated things. Apparently this fellow grabbed the kid—why, we don't know. Our man failed to move quickly enough to separate the kid from this second guy. The old gentleman interceded and swept the boy away."

"What a foul-up this has turned out to be!"

"Indeed."

"And what if our man finds nothing at the house?"

"I don't know. Guess we're shit out of luck then, aren't we?" Armbruster checked his watch. "I have to be in court, Seymour. Anything else we need to discuss?"

"Yes. I have another idea. Remember our discussion about the other nine coins? Where they might be?"

"Continue."

"I have the name and address of the kid's great uncle. Hedwig Mackey."

"Hmmm. Very interesting. And, if the widow is in possession of the remaining nine, you think we might be able to acquire those?"

"Why not? She lives in Chicago. When I get back to the shop, I'll call her directly. I'll cook up some cock-and-bull story and see what I can find out. If she has the coins, we'll need to send our man down there, so don't let him run off before I talk to the widow."

"I'll make the call on my way out. I have to go." He raised his hand and Madeline strode over from the bar. "Call me later. Madeline, dear, to the phone booth, if you please. I have a quick call to make, and then we can be on our way."

Wenzel signaled the waiter, paid his bill and left the restaurant. He hurried down the street to the coin store. Once inside, he left the Closed sign in place and went to his desk. He settled in his chair and picked up the phone. "Long distance, information, please. Thank you." Seymour leaned back and studied the ceiling. "Yes, I'd like the phone number in Chicago for Mrs. Hedwig Mackey." He gave the operator the address and waited.

"Can you connect me? Thank you."

Before long, the call was completed. "Hello? Mrs. Mackey?" Wenzel sprang forward in his chair.

"Good afternoon, ma'am. My name is Leonard Massimo, and I'm . . . yes, that's right—Massimo, Leonard. I'm calling from Minneapolis . . . I am the. . . . What's that? Certainly." Wenzel's voice rose to a semi-shout. "Is that better? Good. Yes, I know . . . old age deprives us of many of our senses, doesn't it. Yes, that's right—Massimo." Wenzel rolled his eyes and silently cursed the receiver.

"Does the name Heritage Coin Company help? Good, good. Now you remember. Excellent. Your husband, Hedwig, and I were dear friends for many years. I was devastated—simply devastated—to hear of his sudden passing." Wenzel tensed and raised his voice, "I said I was devastated to hear of his death! You have my deepest sympathies." Wenzel listened to her reply.

"He did? Spoke of me often, did he? How kind of Hedwig. Of course we corresponded frequently and whenever he visited his relatives here in town, he always made a point of stopping by." Wenzel smiled . . . pleased with how his subterfuge was progressing.

"Well, I'll get right to the point, Mrs. Mackey." He stroked his eyebrows. "Excellent. Now then, in deference to your sad circumstance, I wanted an appropriate period of time to pass before contacting you. Your nephew, Charlie Nash, stopped in recently for an appraisal on two 1943 copper Lincoln head pennies." Wenzel hoped that this might trigger something in the old lady.

"Yes, you are familiar with these coins, are you, Mrs. Mackey?" Wenzel sighed and held the receiver away from his ear.

"Yes. A delightful child. Very bright, indeed. Now then, Hedwig indicated in one of our many conversations that he was also in possession of the remaining nine pennies that were originally minted." *Careful, Seymour.* He waited and held his breath.

"Oh, how well I recall just how secretive Hedwig could be. Oh, no. He trusted me implicitly, but you see it was his fervent desire that, uh . . . I'm sorry, but I must be a bit un-delicate here, that in the event of his . . . demise . . . he wanted me to contact you to ensure that the remaining coins were properly and fairly sold. For your future security and comfort, don't you know?" Wenzel listened to her reply.

"He was concerned that you should have nothing to worry about financially, Mrs. Mackey . . . you know how thoughtful and farsighted Hedwig was. At any rate, I promised your husband that I would contact you and offer my services should you decide to sell the remaining nine, you see." He held his breath.

"Oh, yes. I think I know what you are referring to. Hedwig did disclose the true origin of the coins to me—that is, how he came to possess them. Oh, yes, but alas, with age comes memory loss, Mrs. Mackey." *Careful, don't blow it . . .*

"Of course, dear lady. I will be just as circumspect in our conversation as I was with Hedwig. Yes, he did. Let's see, as I recall . . ." *Come on You old bat, open up!*

Wenzel pressed the receiver to his ear until it hurt. *Bingo!* He wrote as he listened. "Yes, that's right . . . your brother-in-law. Now I remember. Yes, yes . . ."

Her brother-in-law . . . worked on the press . . . stole coins . . . didn't dare sell . . . too much stress. Suicide! "Oh, my! I am sorry for you. Now it's all coming back to me. Yes, most understandable. I'm sure the poor man suffered greatly . . . guilty conscience and all. What's that? Oh, I'm sure Hedwig paid his widow—your sister—a handsome price. When was that? 1945. I see, I see." Wenzel had difficulty restraining his glee.

He was so excited he had to urinate. He clutched his crotch in agony. He struggled to control his voice. And then, as if a needle had pricked his fattened head, he gasped. "Ahem! Excuse me. Would you mind repeating that? All nine?" *Oh, no!*

Wenzel collected himself and in a much lower, tone, replied, "Yes, I think that's a wise decision. I said, I THINK THAT'S A WISE DECISION." His tone was filled with anger. "As long as you are situated financially, that's a, uh . . ." he choked out the words, "a perfect place for the coins. If that was Hedwig's wish, then certainly you are doing the right thing." *Noooo! How could you?*

"When did you say they were coming for the coins? End of the week, you think . . . ? Maybe Friday. I see." *There's still time, Seymour!*

"Well, very good, Mrs. Mackey. Hedwig would have been proud of the way you've handled this. I think, given the history of the coins, that the Smithsonian is the proper home for them. Of course, what they are paying is a fraction of their worth, just a fraction, but Hedwig would be pleased nonetheless."

Wenzel was almost through. One more question. "I trust the coins are in a safe place until they can be handed over, Mrs. Mackey? Excellent! Yes, the wall safe, of course. I recall Hedwig mentioning that he liked keeping the coins close at hand—so he could admire them at his leisure."

Get rid of her. "Well, it certainly has been a pleasure speaking with you. As I said, Hedwig was a dear friend, and I shall miss him terribly. All the best to you, Mrs. Mackey. Good bye."

Wenzel slammed down the receiver and ran to the bathroom. When finished, he again picked up the phone to call Armbruster. *A piece of cake,* he muttered to himself. *All he has to do is get there before the Smithsonian representative, present some sort of fake identification to gain entry, and the old bat will open up the safe for him.* He thought he had it all worked out. *But? If she refuses? Well, that's why we're hiring this guy.*

Wenzel punched numbers into his adding machine as he waited for Paxton's secretary. When finished with the tally, he whistled and jotted down the figure. "Holy mackerel!"

"Oh! I'm sorry. I was speaking to myself. Seymour Wenzel, here, calling for Paxton. Yes, I know. I have a very important message for him. Please tell him: 'Pull back our man. He has to go to Chicago! Call me right away for details!' Got that? Very good. Thank you."

Wenzel rubbed his hands and leaned back in his chair. "Maybe we don't need the kid's pennies after all. On the other hand, if I had all eleven . . ."

A customer knocked on the window and shielded his eyes as he peered in.

"Go away, you putz! I'm closed for the day—maybe for good." He smiled, stroked his tiny mustache with both fingers, and studied the numbers scribbled on his notepad.

Twenty-Six

THE NARROW, TWO-LANE HIGHWAY wound around the western perimeter of Lake Traverse. Charlie was mesmerized by the beauty and character of the hilly land that rose away from the valley of the twenty-mile long lake. "I don't think I'd ever want to leave this place if I lived here."

"I know. It's something to see, isn't it?" Quill replied. The hilltops were a mixture of light and dark brown. The darker sections had been worked recently, and the others bore the remnants of small grain stubble. Bottomlands held copses of varying sizes left untouched and teeming with wildlife. Charlie spotted numerous deer standing near the edges. Small critters darted across the hills. Some of the land still contained standing corn and whenever the station wagon approached these sections, pheasants by the score scampered along the edges.

Charlie pointed. "Hey! Lookit all the pheasants!"

Taffy nudged him aside and gazed at the colorful birds, one ear cocked, with her tail beating a steady tattoo against the seat back. She definitely liked looking at the big birds.

"You'd love to get out and chase those, wouldn't you, girl?" Then Charlie turned to the old man and said, "How much farther, Quill?"

"Oh, just a few miles." Purdue grimaced as the pain in his gut worsened. *Dammit! Each bout now seemed to last a bit longer—the pangs, deeper.* He threw back two pills this time, hoping to kill the ache in half the time. Sweat formed on his forehead. He gritted his teeth.

"Are you okay, Quill?" Charlie hated to see his friend in such obvious agony and wondered why the pills weren't more effective.

Purdue whispered, "I'll be all right in a minute." *Please. I need more time. . . .* Another wave struck, and he had to brake as his eyes closed.

"We can stop for a while if you want, Quill."

"No, that's okay. That's better." He shook his head and wiped his brow. *That was a tough one.* He accelerated and crested a small hill. "Look, Charlie! There's Blue Springs straight ahead."

As the green wagon coasted into the small village, Charlie tallied the few buildings. First was a filling station with an old, rickety sign above that read, Curly's Blacksmith and Livery. The remainder included a Lutheran church, post office, the Red Horse Saloon & Eatery, an Ace Hardware, and an A & P Grocery. Half a dozen small houses were scattered up and down both sides of the highway. A small, brick school building sat by itself down the street.

"Not much to look at, is it, son?"

"No, but I think it's neat. I've never seen a blacksmith shop before."

"Hah! And I reckon you still won't, either! Old Curly Rafferty refused to take that sign down—said it was 'nostalgic.' Funny old coot, but a good friend . . . wonder if he's still around?"

Purdue stopped in front of the single pump and got out. He stretched and studied the familiar landmarks that had been a large part of his life. An unexpected twinge of excitement and joy surged through his veins. He inhaled deeply of the warm, dry autumn air.

"Can't ya see the sign?" An older man—half-hunched over stepped outside and pointed to a hand-painted sign to his left: PUMP YER OWN DAMN GAS! "Darn fools! I suppose you want me to crank that pump, do ya?"

"Curly? Is that you?"

The old gent tugged at his spectacles and stepped closer. When he was three feet away from Quill, he threw his head to one side, looked up, and scanned what seemed to be a familiar face.

"Purdue? It can't be! By Jesus . . . it is! Quillan Purdue! As I live and die . . . we all thought you was goners. Cort wouldn't never tell us what happened to ya, so we just kinda figgered you fell off the edge of the world one day. I'll be damned. Come 'ere!"

Purdue stepped closer, and the old man wrapped two thick arms around his back and pulled him in. "Damn, I'm glad I lived long enough to see you again, Quillan."

Quill chuckled. "Thanks, Curly. Me too." Both men had tears in their eyes. They stood apart and clasped hands. "You look wonderful, old man . . . you really do." Quill said.

"Aw, don't gimme that crappola! Look the same as always 'cept I'm about six inches shorter all the way around." The two old friends laughed and patted the other's arm. Curly looked past Quill and said, "Who's that?"

"Oh, I almost forgot. Come here, Charlie." Quill beckoned to the boy.

Charlie and Taffy strode over to the two men. Taffy sniffed Curly's greasy overalls and wagged her tail. "Curly? I'd like you to meet my very good friend, Charlie Nash. Charlie? Shake hands with Curly Rafferty."

Curly grabbed Charlie's small hand and shook it with a finger-crunching grip that belied the old man's appearance. Charlie looked down. *His hand's bigger than both of mine,* he thought. He smiled at Curly's obvious enthusiasm and vigor. "Nice to meet you, Mr. Rafferty."

"What's this 'mister' bullcrap? You call me Curly or I'll take a ball-peen hammer to yer toes!"

Charlie laughed. "Okay, Curly. And this is my dog, Taffy. I think she likes you."

"Haruumph. Got no use for dogs, myself. She is pretty, though. What's all that shit wrapped around her gut?"

Quill interceded. "In spite of Curly's gruff exterior, he also passes as the local vet around here, Charlie." Quill interjected. "And he loves dogs—honest."

Curly ran his hands over Taffy's head and looked directly into both eyes. She displayed no sense of concern.

Quill said, "She was kicked by a real nasty fellow yesterday, Curly. Vet said she'll be okay, but he clipped her pretty good."

"Hope you pounded the crap outta the guy, Quillan?"

Purdue smiled. "He got the message, Curly."

"Good. Ain't never had time fer folks that was mean to dogs—or any other critter for that matter . . . even if I don't have no use for 'em myself." He scratched behind Taffy's ears. "Let's take a good look at you, little girl." With considerable effort, he stooped and ran his fingers over and around the dog's mid-section. Taffy winced slightly, but continued to let him touch her.

"Don't think she's busted up inside, son. Lucky, though. A good kick in the ribs can do considerable damage. She must be a tough little bugger!"

"Thanks for looking at her," Charlie said.

"My pleasure. Hey! Let's go next door, and you can buy me a beer, Quill. You drink beer yet, Charlie?"

"No. I'm not old enough." The boy laughed at the idea.

"The beer don't care how old ya are. Hell, I had my first one when I was eight! How old ya think I am, anyway?" Curly's voice echoed down the highway.

"Gee, I don't know . . . seventy maybe?"

"Hah! See there, Quillan? Hell's bells, son, I'm eighty-five! Outlived three different wives . . . and I'm lookin' for a fourth!" Curly smiled—displaying no more than ten teeth total. "Come on. I'm thirsty."

"Charlie, why don't you get Taffy a drink from that faucet over there and we'll meet you inside." Purdue threw an arm across Curly's shoulders and the two old friends headed for the Red Horse Saloon.

"So, how they hangin', Quill?"

Quill chuckled. "Same as always, old man. Low and lonesome."

As they entered the bar, Curly turned to Quill and, devoid of any humor, said, "Where'd ya find him, Quillan?"

"It's a long story, old friend, but I picked him up on the highway down the other side of Hutchinson. Same guy that kicked Taffy was about to beat on Charlie. I stepped in."

"No shit? Sounds like the boy's pretty lucky you came along."

"I'd say it works both ways, Curly. He's a good kid, and I'm fortunate to have him with me."

"Not real big, is he? Don't look no bigger 'n' a pound a soap after a hard day's wash."

"No, but he's a tough little guy. Small for his age, but wiry. And his dog is very brave."

They sat at the bar and Curly called out, "Maggie! Hey, Maggie! Ya got a couple of payin' customers here."

A small woman appeared from a storeroom and walked down the length of the bar. "Keep your voice down, you old fool. I hear you. What'll it be?" She looked from one to the other and stopped at Purdue. Her forehead creased, and her mouth fell open.

Curly laughed. "You look like you seen a polecat, Maggie!"

"My, my, my. As I live and breathe! Quill Purdue! God, it's good to see you again, Quill." She leaned over and grabbed his head. After a long look into his eyes, she pulled him close and kissed him long and hard.

Purdue was touched. "Maggie. I've thought of you often."

"I should hope so." She dried her eyes and blew her nose. "Curly? Why didn't you tell me Quill was coming? I would have liked to clean up a bit." She patted her gray hair, and straightened her dress.

"Aw heck, Maggie. Give it a rest, will ya? You two had yer chance years ago. Now it's my turn. Too late for both of ya now."

"Oh, I don't know about that, Curly. Geez, it's good to see you, Quill."

"Thanks, Maggie. You too."

"All right. Enough. How about that beer? Quillan?"

"Lemonade for me, Maggie."

"You bet. Coming right up. Quill Purdue . . . honest to goodness . . ." Maggie stepped away.

"Looks like things have changed around here, Curly."

"Got that right. Hell, last summer, whole place was crawling with Beaners. See the resort down the way?"

"Yep. Spotted that on the drive in. Nice looking place."

"Yeah, 'cept it fills up with city folks from all over the place—Sioux Falls, Fargo, God knows where. And that campground they got? Hell . . . boats and motors and all kinda shit goin' on."

"Well, that's progress, I guess."

"Progress, my ass. You know how many times I got stiffed on gas in the old days? Could count on one hand—my left . . ." Curly held out his left with two fingers missing and continued, "This many . . . in one year! Hell, now I'm about ready to take down my sign I get burned so often!"

Charlie entered with Taffy. They walked across the planked floor kicking sawdust and peanut shells. He glanced around and saw a large, smiling bear backlit next to a Hamm's Beer sign. A flashing sign above the bar mirror pictured a northern lake. "From the Land of Sky Blue Waters," appeared briefly, vanished, then flashed again.

A large jukebox stood at one end of the bar. Curly spotted the boy in the mirror and called out, "Hey, Maggie! Another cold one for Charlie!"

Maggie replied, "Who's Charlie?"

"Come here, son. I want you to meet another old friend. Maggie, say hello to Charlie Nash and Taffy."

She reached over the mahogany and extended her hand. "Hi, Charlie. Any friend of Quill's is a friend of mine."

Charlie shook her hand and replied, "Thank you. It's a pleasure to meet you."

"Nice boy, Quill. What'll you have, Charlie?"

"Do you have Cherry Coke?"

Maggie laughed. "City boy, I'll bet. Sorry, Charlie. It's just plain Coke out here."

"That's fine." Charlie noticed Quill's lemonade and was relieved. Walking into the saloon brought back painful reminders of the last time he was in a bar.

"How about something to eat, son?" Curly asked. "It's almost lunchtime, and I'm hungry enough to eat a skunk!"

"Sure. Could I have a hamburger and fries?"

"You bet. Quill?"

"Ham and cheese on rye for me Maggie. Easy on the mayo."

"Curly? The usual?"

"Yep. 'N'other one a them flat steaks and a mess a fries, Maggie." Curly replied.

"Be right up. You boys enjoy yourselves."

"Say, Charlie. What you doin' on the road alone, anyway?" Curly asked.

Purdue noted the boy's discomfort and tried to intercede, "He's taking a sabbatical, Curly."

"A what? You and yer high-faluttin' words. Speak English, will ya?"

Charlie jumped in. "I ran away . . . from an orphanage."

Curly studied the boy closely and frowned. "You did, did ya? How come?"

"Uh, they, uh . . . they weren't going to let me keep Taffy anymore."

"That right? How come they let ya have her in the first place?"

"I already had her when I went there."

Maggie returned with their drinks. Purdue felt that Charlie had suffered enough scrutiny. "Here's your Coke, Charlie. How about a toast? Here's to Curly . . . and hoping he finds wife number four—soon!"

Curly and Charlie both laughed and the three clinked glasses. Taffy curled up beneath Charlie and napped while the three chatted. Curly didn't pursue Charlie's history, but accepted the boy as a friend of Quill's.

Charlie broke the silence. "How come the town is called Blue Springs?"

Quill turned to Curly and said, "A great question. You see, it's this way . . ." He smiled as he sensed Curly's growing discomfort. "Old Curly here was one of the first to settle here. How old were you, Curly? Twenty . . . twenty-one?"

"Who cares? Whatever he says next is pure bull crap, Charlie."

"Hah!" Quill snorted. "Nothing but prairie around here back then. A few sod-busters settled around here and set out to plow up the ground. It was almost impossible—the soil was nothing but a thick mat of com-

253

pacted blue stem roots. Most of these folks couldn't afford John Deere's new plow . . . what'd they call that, Curly? The 'Singing Plow.' Right?"

"You're tellin' the story, so ya might as well keep flappin' yer gums."

Quill laughed and continued, "So . . . our friend here, being an enterprising sort, knows that all these farmers are going to need lots of work done on their broken-down plow blades, their wagons, and their tools. Curly opens up his blacksmith shop and before long people are standing in line outside his door. He decides he needs to create something unique . . . a trademark, if you will, that would set him apart from any other smithy in the county."

"Go straight to hell, Quillan!"

"This is where it gets good, Charlie . . . What do you suppose he came up with as his trademark?"

"I don't know. What?" Charlie asked. His eyes were wide with curiosity by now, and he was enjoying the byplay.

"Robin's-egg blue buggy springs! That's what." Quill chuckled—relishing the re-telling and knowing that his old friend still appreciated the humor in spite of his protestations.

"Huh?" Charlie was puzzled.

"You see, back in those days, a large part of Curly's business was installing new springs on horse-drawn buggies and wagons. They were nothing more than bands of steel clamped together in the shape of a diamond. He thought that if he painted them a distinctive, hard-to-miss color—something other than the traditional, black—everyone would know where they came from. Other folks would notice, and pretty soon Curly would have more business than he could handle. That about right, old man?"

Curly scowled and remained silent.

"Yeah . . . but why that color?" Charlie asked.

"He bought what he thought was barrel of gray paint. Gray was pretty distinctive when everyone else was using black. But the container was mismarked, and Curly didn't notice that it was light blue instead of gray."

"Well, why didn't you send it back, Curly?" Charlie asked.

Quill jumped in. "Cause Curly's color-blind! He never noticed!"

"What'd he do?" Charlie looked from Quill to Curly.

Purdue stifled a laugh and continued. "He went ahead and painted half-a-dozen springs. When the owners came to pick up their wagons, they complained about the color. Said the springs looked like the belly of a speckled trout. Curly argued with them, of course—he's a stubborn old goat. And too cheap to throw the paint away, he kept using it. Tried to convince the farmers they would somehow learn to like that robin's-egg blue." Quill slapped Curly on the back and howled with delight at the telling.

"Yeah, well, it woulda been a great idea 'cept for that crappy paint color," he muttered. He was smiling by the time Quill finished the story.

"The fella that opened the mercantile down the street had a sense of humor, though—he hung out a sign on each end of town declaring this 'The Village of Blue Springs.' The name stuck . . . in spite of Curly's efforts to change it."

"Well, I like the name, anyway, Curly."

"Thanks, Charlie. I do to."

Their food arrived. Quill and Charlie ate while Curly had another Schmidt. He worked a few peanuts as best he could, then attacked the abused flat steak. Surprisingly, his ten teeth did it some justice. Soon lunch was over, and Quill knew they had to be leaving.

"I'll take the bill, if you please, Maggie." Purdue said. He gave her a ten dollar bill and said, "Keep the change."

"Will you be staying around here now, Quill?" Maggie asked. Her green eyes sparkled.

"Yes. I'm back for good, Maggie. It was great to see you again. Take care of yourself."

"I will, Quill. Stop in again . . . soon, okay?" She leaned over and kissed his cheek.

Quill wasn't sure how to answer her so he simply said, "Let's go, Charlie." He slid off the stool.

"Thank you."

"You're welcome, Charlie. You come back too, you hear?"

"Bye."

"Curly, I owe you for gas. You coming or staying?"

"I'm staying. I got to try and convince Maggie here that she'd be a perfect number four. 'Course that may be difficult now that you're around again, but what the hell . .\/." He smiled at Maggie. Then he said to Quill, "I'll add it to your bill, now that you're back."

Purdue hugged the older man and said, "Thanks, Curly. Stay well." He slipped a five-dollar bill into his hand and said, "I better pay you now. See you soon, old timer. Watch out for him, Maggie." Purdue winked at her and turned away. His eyes glistened.

"I will."

"So long, Charlie," Curly called. "You're traveling with a mighty fine fella. Pay attention to him, and yer bound to learn something."

"Bye, Curly."

Maggie rested her elbows on the bar. She and Curly watched the three leave. When the door closed, she sighed and said, "God, I loved that guy! I never should have let him get away, should I, Curly?"

"Nope. But what the hell, there's still me, Maggie girl. How 'bout you and I take a tumble in the back room?" Curly laughed.

Maggie threw a towel over his head.

Outside, Quill led Charlie to the grocery store. Fifteen minutes later they left with three bags full of food. "Hate to just drop in on Maxine without bringing groceries."

They piled into the wagon. Charlie said, "I liked your friends, Quill."

"Thank you. I've missed them . . . missed being around here. Curly was like a father to me after my dad left home. Forgot just how much I—" He couldn't finish.

Before he could catch himself, Charlie blurted, "Then how come you left?"

"I had to. No matter how hard I tried to apologize . . . to, to beg Cort's forgiveness, he wouldn't talk to me."

"I'd of forgiven you, Quill."

Purdue blew his nose. "You would? You sure about that, Charlie? Once a fella stuffs a ton of anger in his gut, it's awful hard to get rid of it.

256

Cort was full of bitterness . . . and I was loaded down with guilt, I guess. We just couldn't talk to each other. After my leg healed, he . . . he, well, he asked me to leave."

"Just like that? You left your family?" All of a sudden, Charlie realized that his question could have been directed at himself.

"One thing I've come to realize over these past ten years is that it's much easier to hate than it is to forgive, Charlie. And my son, Cortland, truly hates me. . . . I only hope . . . I hope that somehow he'll forgive me before—" Purdue realized he had said enough.

"Before what, Quill?" Charlie waited for Quill's answer, but the old man remained silent.

Twenty-Seven

LABETTE FINGERED THE LUGER and waited for the front door to swing open. Marsha Nash and her mother were talking, but LaBette was unable to hear what they said.

After a minute or so, Marsha turned away and trotted back down the sidewalk to her mother's car. She opened the door and retrieved her purse.

LaBette had the opening he needed. He stepped from the tiny room and ran through the kitchen to the back door. After slipping outside and carefully closing the door, he walked through the backyard and up the alley. He passed three houses, looked for a suitable pass-through to Oliver Avenue and, without hesitating, walked back out to the street.

The women had entered the house by the time LaBette reached his car. He started the engine and pulled away, frustrated and angry that he had failed to find the coins. The only clue as to the boy's whereabouts seemed to be finding the old man who picked him up near Hutchinson. "Like looking for a needle in a haystack," he muttered.

By the time LaBette reached his apartment, he had resigned himself to having to live with his first contract failure. The boy—and his coins— could be anywhere by now.

The phone rang just as he removed his coat. He picked up the receiver. "Hello? No. Nothing. Went through the house top to bottom . . . no safe anywhere I could see, but I found the kid's hidey-hole. No coins, though. What? Yeah, I agree. I'm afraid we're out of luck, Val."

LaBette was sitting down by now with one elbow on the small, metal table that served as a kitchen table. Suddenly he stood. "What? Hang on while I get a pencil." He laid the phone down, walked over to a small dresser and opened a drawer. He returned with pencil and paper. "Go ahead. Yep. Marie Mackey. Got it. What's the address? Okay. So I'm to show up as a representative from the Smithsonian. No problem. No idea where the safe is, though. No, not to worry. If I can get my foot in the door, I'll make her open the safe. I know. No witnesses. It'll be a piece of cake. What time is it?"

LaBette looked at his watch. "I can catch the Hiawatha Limited at 7:30 tonight and be in Chicago in the morning. If the Smithsonian guys aren't due until Friday, I'll be a day ahead of them. Aw, hell, Val. She's an old lady. I'll tell her there was a miscommunication back in Washington. I'll make up something. How much? They said I could name my price? Well, well. I'm assuming these nine pennies are worth something if the Smithsonian is interested in them. Okay . . . tell them twenty-five thousand for all nine. Right. I'll call you when I get back. I will. You can count on me, you know that, Val. Goodbye."

LaBette hung the phone up and looked down at his notes. One notation made his eyes blur: $25,000.00! That was a very large fee. He had three hours before he needed to be at the Great Northern station downtown. Plenty of time to get ready and take a short nap. He went to his closet. *Now, what would a guy from the Smithsonian look like . . . ?*

Purdue turned off the blacktop onto a gravel road. He and Charlie were going west, and as they drove away from the lake, the land became more undulating. Large, flat expanses of pasture and prairie grass filled the landscape.

Charlie soon noticed large herds of cattle grazing across the countryside. Horses mingled with the cattle, and his excitement mounted. "Holy cow! This is just like I imagined it would look."

"It is something to see, isn't it? From one of these hilltops, you can see for twenty miles or so."

"Are we almost there?"

"Yep . . . matter of fact, the land on our right is ours—least ways we pay the government to graze our cattle on it. Cort owns about six hundred acres—the rest is rented."

Charlie was incredulous. "You mean you have cattle . . . and horses?"

Purdue laughed. "Of course. What'd you think we did out here?"

"I don't know. Grow corn and stuff, I guess."

"Well, yes, we do grow corn and small grains like wheat and oats, but it's mostly grown to feed the cattle. We also put up huge amounts of hay. Well, you'll see soon enough. Here we are."

Quill braked and turned north on to a smaller gravel road. A sign at the entrance declared, PURDUE CATTLE COMPANY—POLLED HEREFORDS. A smaller sign beneath in the shape of an apple read, HILLTOP ORCHARD.

"What does 'polled' mean?"

"It means 'hornless,' Charlie."

"Like they never grow horns?"

"That's right. The cows and calves mostly stay out on pasture from the time they're born to market. It'd be a lot of work to bring in all the calves just to dehorn them."

"But why don't you want them to have horns?"

"Cows aren't too bright. We don't want them to hurt themselves or any of the others in the herd. They stay out of trouble better that way."

"That's really neat!"

They drove up the hill and, before long, saw a white, two-story farmhouse at the end of the drive. Charlie observed two large barns on either side of the house. Smaller equipment sheds, a granary, and corn crib sat adjacent to the larger barns. A long, front porch faced the yard with a clear view to the south and west.

The driveway curved in front of the house. A white, picket fence stood in front of the porch. To the right and left of the short walkway was a pair of flower gardens. Perennials, long since dead, displayed brown stalks with faded tufts. The annuals—pansies and mums among them—still held multi-colored flowers. Patches of overturned, dark soil gave evidence of fragile bulbs dug and stored inside for the long winter ahead.

Quill had a brief flash of his wife, Sarah, crouched over her beloved beds—carefully trimming and weeding her pride and joy. His heart heaved at her memory, but then lightened as he took in what was once his home—his former life.

"This . . . this is really, uh, beautiful, Quill." Charlie tried to take everything in with a quick scan and failed. There was too much to see in every direction.

"Thanks, Charlie. I have many fond memories of this place." He switched off the ignition and climbed out. As he closed the door, he stretched and looked out over the landscape. A warm rush passed from his head to toes. *God, this feels good . . . I only hope . . .*

The front, screen door creaked open, and Purdue turned back toward the house. A young girl with blond braids stepped out and held the door open for her mother.

Quill's mouth fell open. Tears filled his eyes as he gazed on the small girl. He shifted to the tall woman in the rear. "Max . . . Maxine? I, I didn't know . . ."

Maxine Purdue took her daughter by the hand, walked across the porch, down the steps, and across the concrete. "Quill? I'd like you to meet your granddaughter, Sarah. Honey, this is your grandpa."

Purdue crouched, then with some effort, knelt. He couldn't speak. He choked back additional sobs and simply stared at the beautiful, little girl. Finally he collected himself enough to say, "Hello, sweetheart. I'm very happy to meet you." He extended his arm with palm open.

Sarah looked up at her mother for direction. After Maxine nudged her forward, she took three timid steps and clasped Quill's moist hand. Both grandfather and granddaughter stared at one another for thirty seconds.

Sarah finally said, "Hello. Who's that?" She pointed to Charlie who had left the car and was standing quietly with Taffy at his side.

Quill gathered himself, turned, and said in a low voice, "Come here, son."

Charlie walked to Quill's side. Taffy trotted ahead and greeted Sarah. She wagged her tail and leaned against Sarah's trousered leg.

"Maxine, Sarah . . . I'd like you to meet my friend, Charlie Nash."

"Hello, Charlie," Maxine said.

"Hi," Sarah intoned.

"Hello." Charlie looked at his boots, unsure of what to do next.

Maxine strode to her daughter's side and extended her hand. "That's a beautiful dog you have, Charlie. What's her name?"

Charlie clasped her hand and said, "Taffy. She's a golden retriever."

While Sarah petted the dog, Maxine stepped around them and after Purdue rose, gave him a big hug. "I'm so sorry, Quill. This has to be very hard for you. I wish I could tell you that things have changed, but . . ." She kissed his cheek and looked into his eyes.

Quill whispered, "You named her . . . Sarah . . . I didn't know . . . Alice never told me."

"Yes. I . . . I'm sorry. Cort insisted . . . he, well . . . he wanted it that way, Quill. I wanted to write you soon after she was born, but he wouldn't hear of it. She's been a blessing . . ."

He looked down at his granddaughter who by now was running across the grass with Taffy. "She must be . . . what? Eight or nine?"

"Nine."

"She looks like you, Maxine. Same slender build, big blue eyes, same wavy hair." Purdue wiped his eyes. "She's simply the prettiest thing I've ever seen."

Charlie sensed that Quill and Maxine needed time alone, so he followed Sarah across the yard toward the apple orchard. Row after row of trees loaded with red fruit blanketed the south-facing slope for as far as he could see. Soon Taffy and Sarah were running from one tree to another—playing tag. Charlie watched . . . happy to see how much better Taffy was feeling.

They came back towards him and stopped. Sarah was breathing hard as she asked, "What's the big bandage for?"

"Oh, she got kicked in the ribs a couple of days ago, but I think I can take it off now. Come here, girl." Charlie knelt and began removing the gauze. He unwound the entire wrap and crumpled it up into a ball which he then tossed for her to chase.

Taffy bounded away, mouthed the soft bundle, and tossed it in the air. Sarah giggled with delight and said, "Can I do that?"

"Sure. Hold out your hand to her. Here, Taff!" She ran over and presented the ball to Sarah, who accepted the prize, spun, and threw it into the ankle high grass. "She'll do that all day long if you want her to."

"How old is she?"

"Two and a half."

"I used to have a dog."

"Really?"

"Her name was Shelly. She died a while back."

"Oh. I'm sorry. What happened?"

"Pack of coyotes got a hold of her. My dad said she never had a chance. She was smaller than Taffy, but she could run like the wind. Dad used her to help round up our cattle."

"Gee, I would've liked to see that. She must have been real smart."

"She was. Smartest dog in the county, my dad said."

Charlie noticed a man had joined Quill and Maxine. From his vantage, he assumed it must be Quill's son, Sarah's father. "Is that your dad?"

"Yes. Come on. He'll want to meet you." She grabbed his hand and led him away.

As the two children approached the adults, Charlie heard Quill's son say, "I knew you were coming . . . Alice called. I also know the reason you're here, but it doesn't matter . . . nothing's changed." His voice was hard—chilled—with a sharp edge that did not invite further comment.

"Alice promised she wouldn't tell," Quill said. His voice trembled.

"I made her. Had to be some reason for you coming back—now." Cort finished with, "I can't turn you and your friend away, but know this one

thing: what I said to you ten years ago still stands. You're not welcome here."
He brushed past Quill and marched toward his daughter and the boy.

"Sarah? Who's that with you?"

"This is Charlie . . . and Taffy."

Cortland Purdue stuck out his large hand and said, "Hello Charlie and Taffy. I'm Cort Purdue."

Charlie shook his hand. The man's grip was firm. He looked up and realized that Quill's son looked a lot like his father, except for the color of his hair. He had the same angular face with high cheek-bones, was just as tall and rangy, with long arms. Cort was wearing jeans, cowboy boots, and a blue, checkered shirt with the sleeves cut off at the elbows. Thick, curly hair poked from between the V of the collar. He wore a similar Stetson as Quill, and his face was the color of caramel candy.

"Hello. It's nice to meet you." Charlie said.

"Where you from, Charlie?" Cort's tone was reserved—his look questioning.

"Minnesota."

"How'd you and Quill meet up?" He was checking the boy over from top to bottom.

Quill interceded at this point. "We met on the highway over near Hutchinson, Cort. Charlie was traveling west, and we became fast friends. He was headed for Montana but agreed to stay with me for a while. I thought we could stay in the guest room . . . the one with the twin beds." Quill turned toward Maxine and added, "That be all right, Maxine?"

"Certainly, Quill."

"I got chores to finish," Cort said abruptly and turned away. "Sarah, why don't you show Charlie around. He'd probably like to see the calves. Stay out of the hay loft."

"Yes, Dad. Come on, Charlie!" She tugged at his arm and the two of them plus Taffy walked towards the barns.

"You have new baby calves?" Charlie asked, somewhat sheepishly.

"Well, no. Beef calves are born in the spring. Most are out with their mammas, but there's always some orphans. Cows sometimes die or they just reject a baby for no reason. We also have a colt in the barn. It was born late, in July, so it's not very big yet. I named him Starlight 'cause he was born under the stars."

"A baby horse? You're so lucky."

Cort watched them leave, spun—showing his broad back and strode toward the machinery shed.

Maxine gave the old man a sympathetic look and said, "Come inside, Quill. Let's get you situated." Maxine threw an arm over Purdue's shoulders.

"I better get these groceries in the house, Maxine"

"Groceries? You didn't need to do that."

"I know, but I wanted to. Not much of a guest if I show up empty handed, especially when I bring my own company." He opened the wagon's rear door and hauled out three bags. Maxine took one and he carried the remaining two.

Once inside the house, Quill looked around. He was pleased to see that nothing much had changed except for the piano in the parlor. The two shelf units flanking the fireplace still held all of his books. "Place looks good, Maxine. Feels good, too. Lots of love here, I'd say."

"Thanks, Quill. We all love it here . . . I'm sure you know that. I never got to tell you, but . . . it was very generous of you to sign everything over to us, by the way. You didn't need to do that, you know.

"Yes, I did. Until recently, I never really thought I'd be back here, to tell you the truth. It does feel good, though . . . like home." He tested the air. "Hmmm. Bread . . . or pie?"

"Both. Today's my baking day. Your timing was excellent. Here, let me take those." She had set her bag down and helped with his two. "Have a seat, Quill. Want a glass of lemonade?"

"Please." Purdue sat at the wooden table and gazed out the kitchen window to the orchard and beyond. "Always was my favorite spot in the house."

"Me too." Maggie said as she prepared the pitcher of lemonade.

"How are the trees?"

"We still get a decent crop every year, but no one could make them produce like you did. Cort has replaced a few every year. I think in spite of what he says, he has kept on with it for your sake, mostly."

Quill was happy to hear that. "Looks like they're about ready to pick, Maxine."

"It's funny, but as you said that, you sounded just like Cort. He said those very words a few days ago." She finished storing the food and handed Quill his glass. She poured one for herself and sat across from him.

At that moment the kitchen door slammed and Cort entered the kitchen. Without saying anything, he strode to the sink and washed his hands. When finished, he turned, leaned back against the sink, and folded his arms. "What do you know about the boy?" He asked.

"Very little, actually. I know he ran away from home—not an orphanage as he pretends. I know he's troubled, afraid of something, and afraid to get too close to anyone. And I also know he's lucky to be alive." Purdue then told them about Charlie's harrowing experience on the train followed by the kidnapping on the road.

"Oh, my God! That poor child! Thank the Lord you happened by when you did, Quill." Maggie exclaimed.

"I think so. Not too sure what that guy's plan was. Charlie hasn't told me much at all, but I want to find out what that nasty guy meant by, 'using him as bait.' Something's screwy about that . . . almost as if he wasn't the real target at all. I need to find out where he ran from, but so far I haven't been able to discover where his home is. That's why I need to keep him close, so nothing more happens to him. I hope you don't mind if he stays with us?"

"Certainly not. He can stay as long as he wants. If he has a family, though, they must be worried sick about him."

"Yes, and that's why I wanted to find out where he lived—so I could call his parents. Sooner or later, I'll get it out of him—once he trusts me enough, I think."

"Can you trust him?" Cort asked.

Quill remembered his son had very little tact—particularly when speaking to his father. "Still get right to the point, don't you?" Quill jerked forward. He clutched his stomach with both hands. Pain ripped through his side. He stabbed at his pocket for the pills, unscrewed the top and swallowed two.

Maxine rose and went to his side. "Quill? Can I do anything?"

Purdue closed his eyes and held his breath. He whispered, "It'll pass in a minute, dear."

Cort observed his father's agony with apparent disinterest. He poured a glass of lemonade and sipped it quietly.

Quill leaned back and took a deep breath. "The answer to your question, Cort, is yes. I trust the boy implicitly. I guess I shouldn't be surprised that you question my judgment in people."

"I had to ask, what with Sarah, and all."

"I'm sure you did. You've nothing to worry about. He's a great kid, and I'm honored to call him a friend."

"He seems very nice, Quill. Sarah took to him right off the bat. And, that beautiful dog of his . . ."

"Maybe you should notify the sheriff," Cort volunteered.

"Considered that, but I feel it would violate a confidence we've built up, Cort. He's beginning to trust me. Besides, if he refused to tell the sheriff where he's from, they'd lock him up in a home someplace . . . and who knows what they'd do with Taffy. The boy's hiding something—some terrible hurt, and I want him to talk to me about it when he's ready."

"I hope you know what you're doing," Cort said. He finished his drink, put the empty in the sink, and left the kitchen.

"Cort needs to learn something about compassion, Maxine."

"He does have a big heart, Quill—just like you. He hides it better— that's all."

"Maybe, but I would have thought that the passing of time might have . . . I don't know . . . softened him up a bit."

"Quill, I'm glad you came back. I think Cort is too—in spite of how he acts." She laid he hand on his arm and squeezed it tightly.

"Hmmm. I don't know, Maxine. If I'd of known about Sarah, I might not have come back. Doesn't seem right . . . somehow." His eyes filled with tears.

"She's your granddaughter, Quill. She should be given the chance to meet her grandfather." Maxine hesitated. Then, her eyes filled as well. She felt compelled to ask, "How long?"

Before Purdue could answer, the children burst threw the kitchen door. Both were breathless. Taffy followed and skidded to a stop against Quill's legs.

Quill wiped his eyes. "Whoa! Slow down, you two or you'll bust a gasket!"

"You should see the calves . . . and, and the colt, Quill! They have a baby horse, and his name's Starlight!"

"Is that right?"

"This is the neatest place I've ever seen in my life," Charlie exclaimed.

The adults smiled and Maxine said, "Looks like we're going to have to get you a cowboy hat on our next trip to town, Charlie?"

"Really? Honest? A cowboy hat? Like Quill's? Do, uh . . . do you think that I could—"

Maxine interrupted, sensing the boy's embarrassment. "Yes, I'm sure that Sarah would be happy to let you ride one of her horses, Charlie. Have you ever ridden before?"

"Uh, well, my friend took me to a riding stable one time, but we just rode around in circles."

Sara said, "It's easy. Once you get the hang of it. You can start out on Pumpkin . . . she's real gentle and not too big."

"That'd be swell, Sarah. Thank you."

Maxine rose and said, "Come on, Charlie. I'll show you around the house. You'd probably like to see where you and Quill will be sleeping. Sarah, honey, why don't you stay here with your grandpa?"

Sarah smiled shyly, and said, "Okay." She pulled out the chair next to Quill and sat down.

Charlie followed Maxine from the kitchen. He soon discovered that the house was a perfect square. The parlor was on the right of the front door adjoining the living room. The dining room on the left. All the floors except the kitchen were hand-laid hardwood planks. The kitchen was covered in linoleum. Cast-iron radiators dotted many of the walls, steam fed by a coal-fired boiler in the basement.

Upstairs were three bedrooms and a bathroom. Maxine directed Charlie to the first room to the left of the landing. "Here's where you'll be staying, Charlie. Bathroom's over there. We finally got indoor plumbing a few years ago. Then there's Sarah's room, and over here is our room."

Charlie walked into the bedroom. It contained twin beds on the north wall, a small dresser between two windows, and a small closet. Charlie walked to the windows and looked out at the barns, corrals, and an old chicken coop. "This is real nice, Mrs. Purdue. It reminds me of . . ." He caught himself before finishing the statement.

"Please, call me Maxine, Charlie. What does it remind you of?" Her eyebrows arched, hoping to pick up a clue.

"Oh, I don't know . . . just a picture I saw once, that's all."

"I see. Well, let's go get your stuff from the car and get you situated before dinner. How's that sound?"

"That'd be great, uh . . . Maxine."

Downstairs, Quill and Sarah were quizzing each other. Sarah promptly lost her shyness and blurted out, "Why have you been gone so long?"

"Well, I'll tell you, sweetheart. Many years ago, before you were born, I decided it was time to see some of that great, big world out there. I'd lived here all my life and never been anywhere. Your mom and dad could take care of the place, so I just took off one day, and I have been traveling all over ever since."

"I saw pictures of you . . . and Grandma. Mommy keeps them in a drawer. You look like Dad . . . 'cept your hair's white."

Purdue smiled. "It wasn't always white, you know. Used to be the same color as your dad's."

"Are you going to stay here for good?"

"I hope so, Sarah."

"That's good! I like having you here . . . and Charlie too." She had made up her mind. "Dad said you planted all the apple trees when he was a boy, but no one thought they'd grow. How come you thought they would?"

"Hah!" Quill was pleased to hear that his son had spoken of him to Sarah. "I used to do a lot of reading, sweetheart. And it seemed to me, that because there were no other orchards around here, that there should be at least one. I read that the climate . . . do you know what that means?"

"The weather?"

"Yes. Wherever there's a large body of water, like Lake Traverse, the climate near that water is different . . . milder—not so cold. It's called a micro-climate. So, I thought if that was true, I should be able to grow apple trees here because we're so close to the lake."

"Dad says we have to start picking real soon. Will you and Charlie help?"

"Of course. I'd like nothing better."

She moved closer and touched his suspenders. "Why is my dad so mad at you?"

This caught Purdue off guard. He hadn't been around children for many years, and had forgotten how totally honest they could be. Her awkward question was unsettling. He studied her closely, not sure how to answer. Finally, he inhaled and asked, "What have your parents told you about Justin, sweetheart?"

"Justin? Mom said he died in a tractor accident when he was five. I never saw him."

"Yes, I know. What did your dad tell you?"

"He doesn't talk about Justin much."

"Well, your dad is mad at me because . . . because I was driving the tractor when Justin was killed." There, he said it. Time to quit ducking the issue. He waited for her reaction.

Sarah considered Quill's confession and concluded, "Yes, but it wasn't your fault, was it?"

"Well, yes, it was, sweetheart. You see, your dad asked me not to let Justin ride on the tractor and I . . . I let him ride with me anyway. Your dad had every right to be angry with me."

270

"I bet you felt real bad about that, didn't you?" She touched his cheek and looked deep into his eyes.

Quill couldn't help himself. He lost control, and tears poured down his cheeks. His lower lip quivered, and he had to put a hand over his mouth. His broken heart filled with regret and sorrow. *I've missed out on nine years with this sweet child . . . and now . . . ?*

"Don't cry, Grandpa. I'm not mad at you, and I don't think Dad is anymore, so it's okay for you to be here. Honest!" She laid her head on his shoulder and threw both arms around his neck.

Maxine heard the last of their conversation from just outside the kitchen. So did Charlie. Maxine put a finger to her lips and motioned him to the front door. Once outside, she said, "Let's let them alone for a bit, shall we?"

"Sure. I think Quill is really happy to be here, Maxine. I hope that, uh, Cort will maybe think it's a good thing he's here too."

"I do too, Charlie. I do too. Let's get your bags, okay?"

Sarah went to the counter and took a tissue from the box. She returned and handed it to Quill. "Here, Grandpa."

Purdue took it and wiped his eyes. "Thank you, honey. I'm sorry I haven't been around here for you."

"That's okay, Grandpa. You're here now, and I love you."

"I love you too, Sarah . . . more than you'll ever know . . ."

Twenty-Eight

SHERIFF GIL MCILHENY tossed the paper on the bar and yelled, "Hey, Mal! How about a cold one? I'm off duty." He opened the Wednesday edition of the *Minneapolis Star*, and found the article he was looking for.

Tucked away on the back page of the out-state edition he read, "Lockhart Man Found Hanged in Barn." It mentioned that an anonymous caller had alerted the sheriff's department and, "When Sheriff Gil McIlheny arrived on the scene, he discovered one Virgil Pisant hanging from a rope in a barn. McIlheny told the *Star* that he knew Pisant, and the man had been under a great deal of stress recently. Consequently, with no indication of foul-play, his death was immediately ruled a suicide."

Mal set McIlheny's beer down and said, "Well, I guess old Virgil couldn't take it anymore, huh, Gil?"

"I guess. Good riddance, I say. He just made my life a lot easier."

"Wonder what happened to Lenny, though? No one's seen him around, either."

"Maybe the Weasel did the same thing as Piss Ant—we just haven't found him yet. Who cares, anyway?"

"No one I know," Mal replied.

McIlheny sipped his beer and thought back to the day before. *Sure looked like suicide . . . still don't know what happened to his keys though. And the missing distributor cap?* McIlheny convinced his deputies to look past those two items and sign the report. *If it wasn't suicide, whoever did it sure did the world a big favor. Wonder who the old guy was who phoned it in?*

He finished his beer, threw a quarter on the bar and stood up. "Gotta go, Mal. See ya soon."

"Take it easy, Gil."

McIlheny left the bar and climbed into his patrol car. He scratched his head and stared through the windshield before turning the key. *Probably should have followed up and tracked that guy down, but hell, I'm not about to waste one more minute on this, and for sure, I'm not driving all the way to Blue Springs, South Dakota, just to thank the guy.* He turned the key and drove away.

THAT EVENING, THE PURDUE family and their guest, Charlie Nash, sat down to a supper of fried chicken, mashed potatoes, gravy, garden peas, and apple pie. They ate in the dining room seated at a round table. Charlie and Sarah sat next to each other and chatted to themselves. Taffy lay between both, her head popped up as each in turn passed table-scraps to her. They thought the adults hadn't noticed, but they had.

Quill sat across from the children. Cort and Maxine on either end. "The chicken is wonderful, Maxine. You guys gave up on raising your own, though, I see."

"Yes. Cort and I decided it was easier to buy them from the Johnsons down the road. I hated cleaning them . . . not to mention the killing."

"I stopped and visited with Curly and Maggie when I went through town. Can't believe old Curly is still hanging around. He'll live to be a hundred."

"Is he still chasing Maggie around?" Maxine asked.

Purdue laughed. "Yes, and she just ignores him."

"I still say you and Maggie would have been perfect . . . Oh, I'm sorry, Quill. I didn't mean . . ."

"That's okay, Maxine. No harm done."

Charlie and Sarah both overheard the short byplay, and Sarah piped in, "What about Grandpa and Maggie?"

"Eat your supper, Sarah," Cort said. He gave his daughter a stern look and then turned his attention to their young guest. "Tell me, Charlie. Where were you going when you met up with my . . . with, Quill?"

Charlie finished chewing and replied, "Montana."

"Is that right? I understand you left an orphanage?"

Charlie looked at Quill.

"I thought it would be all right to tell them, Charlie . . . hope that was okay?"

"Yes. I don't mind." He continued to eat.

"And why did you leave?" Cort asked.

"They said I had to get rid of Taffy . . . and I wouldn't do that, so I left."

"And how long had you been there?"

Maxine intruded. "Cort, let the boy eat." She pursed her lips and raised her eyebrows.

Cort waited, then continued, "That's a real nice dog you have there, Charlie. Does she hunt?"

"Yes, I got to take her duck hunting once, and she did real good . . . brought back every duck that was shot." He blurted it out and immediately regretted his brag.

"Who'd you go hunting with?" Cort asked.

"Oh, uh, one of the, uh, the man who ran the orphanage took us." Anxious to change the subject, he added, "Would it be all right if she sleeps in our room?"

"Certainly, Charlie." Maxine said. "Do you have food for her? If not, we still have some of Shelly's left, and I set her bowls out for you in the kitchen."

"Thank you."

"Now, who wants pie?" Maxine rose and began clearing the plates.

Charlie pushed away, picked up his plate, and followed her to the kitchen.

"Here's the dog food, Charlie." Maxine said.

Taffy trotted over and waited. Charlie filled one with water and the other with dry food. Maxine mixed in a few table scraps, and Charlie set the bowl down. As she always did, Taffy ate slowly—deliberately.

"Thanks, Maxine. You have all been really nice to me and Taffy."

"You're welcome, Charlie. We enjoy having you here. Sarah doesn't get to be with too many children around here. One of the shortcomings of living out in the country, I guess."

"I think I'd love living here . . . so would Taffy."

"Maybe, but it can get pretty lonely sometimes . . . especially in the winter." She finished slicing the pie and handed two plates to the boy. Maxine carried two more, and they went back to the dining room.

"When can we get another dog, Dad?" Sarah asked.

Cort looked at his wife, then back to his daughter. "I don't know, honey. Soon as we find another cattle dog, I guess. Not many breeders around here. Probably have to go all the way to Sioux Falls to find one, I think."

"Used to be a fellow up near Buffalo Gap who raised border collies, Cort. He still around?" Quill offered.

"I don't know," Cort answered abruptly. "Think I'll pass on the pie, Maxine," just as his wife was about to go back to the kitchen for the last piece of pie. "Gonna take a walk down to the orchard and check out the apples." He stood and looked down at Charlie. "Be interesting to see how your dog does on pheasants, Charlie."

"I think she has a real good nose."

"Well, maybe we'll try and get out one of these days and check her out. I'd like to eat some pheasant this winter, wouldn't you, Maxine?"

"Yes. That's such a nice change from chicken and beef."

"That'd be great," Charlie said.

Cort studied the boy for a bit longer and left the dining room.

"Mind if I tag along?" Quill asked.

"Suit yourself." Cort replied, without looking directly at his father. "Soon as you're finished, Sarah, you can take Charlie with you and feed the calves." He walked to the front door and left.

Quill finished his pie and said, "Thank you, Maxine. That was delicious. Glad to see those McIntoshes haven't lost any of their flavor." He picked up his plate and carried it to the kitchen. "You kids have fun." He opened the door and trailed after his son.

"Can we be excused, Mom?"

"Yes. You two go ahead. I'll clean up."

Sarah led Charlie by the hand, and they ran to the barn. Taffy trotted ahead, eager to investigate the strange four-legged animals with the strong scent.

As they approached the barns, Taffy stopped. Her nose high, she stared at the corn crib. She flicked one ear—her left so that it stood up above her head. Six or seven pheasants were scrabbling around the perimeter picking at loose pieces of corn. Her tail straightened and she froze.

"Look, Charlie! What's Taffy doing?"

"Looks like she's pointing, kind of. Saw that in a book one time." Charlie stepped next to her and together they edged toward the crib. The pheasants sensed their presence and stopped eating. Two roosters cackled and poised to fly.

Almost in slow motion, Taffy slowly inched forward. When she was within twenty feet, the roosters leapt in the air and the entire flock flew away. She gave chase for a short distance and returned—her tail wagging with pleasure.

"Good girl, Taff."

"Looks like she'll do great, Charlie."

They opened the barn door and slipped inside.

"What do we have to do?" The calves bunched up against a short barricade. Their strident and constant *maa-a-a*s echoed through the barn. Taffy stepped close and reached out to sniff at one of the bolder heifers. Her left ear again poised as if she were raising a flag. One of them snorted and blew snot in her direction. Taffy jumped back and laid both ears flat in alarm.

Sarah laughed, as did Charlie. "I think she's afraid of 'em," he said.

"She'll get used to them. I'll bet she'd be a good cattle dog, Charlie."

"You think so?"

"Sure. She's not too big, she's fast, and probably real smart." Sarah retrieved a two-wheel cart and a shovel. She handed the shovel to Charlie. "Here. Open up that chute over there and fill the cart with sileage. I'll get the oats."

Charlie wheeled the cart over to the door beneath the silo, opened it, and began shoveling. He wrinkled his nose at the pungent odor emanating from the bin—a warm, moist combination of chopped corn stalks and molasses. The calves brayed loudly as they smelled food. Once he had the cart filled, he returned.

Sarah opened the gate. "Bring the cart in here, Charlie." She held it open and kneed the calves away.

Charlie slipped in, not quite as confident among the milling animals. "Taffy, Stay! Now what?"

"Put a scoop in each of those pans over there and I'll do the oats."

After the feed had been distributed and the calves had jockied for position, she picked up a pitchfork and said, "Here."

"What do I do with this?"

Sarah laughed. "Haven't you ever pitched manure before?"

Charlie laughed, even though embarrassed. "Nope, but it looks like I'm going to learn."

"Put it in the cart. I'll shovel what you can't get." The two cleaned up the pen and Sarah wheeled the cart out side. "We have to dump it over there on that pile. Dad will pick it all up with the tractor." Once the cart was emptied and hosed clean, Sarah led Charlie out and over to an adjacent barn. Once inside, she said, "Now if you'll climb up to the loft, you can throw down some straw bales."

"Is it okay . . . I mean, your dad said not to climb into the loft didn't he?"

"He just meant that he didn't want us playing up there. It's all right—go ahead." Sarah replied.

Charlie located the ladder on the wall and started climbing. Taffy barked and pranced beneath the ladder. "I think she wants to climb up here." Once he reached the deck, he asked, "How many?"

"Three of the hay, three of the straw."

Charlie looked around. "How do I tell which is which?"

"The hay is green, the straw is . . . straw color."

It wasn't much help, but Charlie made a guess. He pulled the bales over to the edge and kicked them over the side. Taffy jumped away as the first one fell and landed with a loud WHUMP! A cloud of dust and debris billowed across the floor. Five more followed. Then he climbed down.

Sarah was loading the bales on a larger hand cart when Charlie reached the bottom of the ladder. When all six were loaded, they wheeled the cart back to the other barn.

She reached in her pocket and pulled out a small knife. The twine snapped as she applied the sharp blade to one bale.

"You have a pocket knife, too?" Incredulous that a girl would carry such a thing, he took out his own and copied her.

"Sure! It comes in handy for lots of things around here. Now, just chuck layers of the straw into the pen. I'll put the hay into their manger."

Charlie started throwing slices of straw into the pen. Afterwards, Sarah filled their trough with fresh water. Before long they were finished.

"There! All done. Thanks for your help."

"It was fun." He stood, leaned against the top rail of the pen, tilted his head, and asked, "How, uh . . . how do you tell the boys from the girls? They all look the same to me."

She checked to see what he was looking at. "Oh, dad castrated the boy calves last spring. Now they're steers."

Charlie looked puzzled, but kept further questions to himself.

Sarah spotted his obvious embarrassment. "Their testicles, Charlie. Dad cuts off their testicles so they don't turn into bulls." She giggled. "You don't know much about cattle, do you?"

"What . . . I mean, how . . . ?"

"That's another use for a pocket knife . . . but it has to be sharp."

"Doesn't it hurt?"

"I suppose so."

"Holy cow! But, I don't understand . . . how do the momma cows have babies if there aren't any bulls?"

"Oh, we have a bull—Hawley. But he's the only one. They'd fight all the time if there were two of them. Hawley is in a pen in the other barn, but don't go near him. He's mean!"

"I won't, that's for sure."

"Come on. Let's see where Dad and Grandpa are."

QUILL CAUGHT UP WITH CORT in the orchard. He approached and said, "How do they look?"

His son had a large apple in his hand and was cutting it open. He pried a few seeds out and turned them over in his hand. After inspecting each, he handed them to Quill.

Quill picked one up and turned it over. "Don't see any white . . . seeds are all brown. Looks like they're ready, Cort."

Quill waited for a reply, but his son remained mute. "I'm glad you kept the trees. I was afraid you might cut them down."

Cort considered his father's statement and finally replied, "Surprised myself, really. Guess I kinda grew attached to 'em over the years." He took a bite from a slice and chucked the rest into the grass. The sun was creeping below the far horizon. "Never tire of that view."

"It is pretty, isn't it?" The sky was pink and orange and purple. There wasn't a breath of air. "How many are left, Cort?"

"Of the trees? Pretty close to four hundred. I've replanted some of the older ones that weren't bearing anymore."

Quill was pleased. Maybe there was hope. "Cort, I need to try and talk to you. This is as good a time as any, I think." He inhaled and contin-

279

ued, "I want you to know just how sorry I am. I've lived with my mistake all these years and . . . and, I'll go to my grave full of guilt and remorse for what happened."

Cort didn't respond . . . didn't look at his father. Instead, he moved away and sat in the grass—knees up, arms across both.

Quill sat down next to him and continued. "I know you hate me. What I did was wrong, and I accept full responsibility. I just hope that . . . I don't know . . . maybe for Sarah's sake, that you'll find a way to forgive me." His voice broke.

Cort spoke at last. "You know, they're still some old-timers around here that believe you spent tons of money on some magical, new-fangled fertilizer for these trees. I try to tell them that the night you dumped all those truckloads around here, that it was nothing but sheep manure." He paused and looked over at his father. "Funny how they seem to want to believe something different."

Purdue wasn't sure where his son was headed, but he was heartened that Cort was even speaking to him. He remained silent.

"I'm a bit like those old-timers, I guess. I've chosen to believe that you intentionally ignored my request. Why, I don't know. I've thought about it for ten years too, and I don't know that anything you can say will make much difference."

"Do you have any idea how much I loved that boy, Cort? I mean, really loved him? We did everything together. You had taken over the farming operation, and I just kind of puttered around . . . Justin was with me all the time. I can't tell you exactly why I let him on the tractor that day. I don't know why. All I do know is that if I could change any of what happened, I would. But I can't."

They heard the children approaching. Quill quickly added, "I'm tortured by Justin's death—and so are you . . . but for different reasons. You've become bitter and hard." Quill stood and walked around in front of his son. "Look at me, Cort. Please?"

Cort raised his head and, for the first time in ten years, looked directly into his father's eyes.

"I've thought about this a long time, and I'll only say it once. Give yourself the gift of forgiveness—not for me, but for yourself . . . and Maxine . . . and most of all, for Sarah. Life's too short, Cort. Don't waste it!" Quill stepped around his son and greeted the children.

WHEN QUILL WENT TO BED that night he felt he was home—at last. He turned down the covers and discovered a ten dollar bill on the pillow. He smiled as he knew immediately who had left it there.

Charlie watched from his bed. Taffy was curled up on the far end— already asleep. It had been a long day, but Charlie was content—at peace.

He thought of his bedroom back home—of his green and yellow bedspread with the funny tufts, of the red vinyl chair in the corner where he'd poked holes with his knife after a particularly rough encounter with his father. He missed his room, missed his own home, missed his mother and grandmother, but somehow through the bond he was developing with Quill, he was beginning to feel wanted—needed even. He couldn't put it into words, but somehow he felt partially responsible for helping his friend find his way home. He believed that it was important that he stay for a while . . . for Quill. Somehow, something had to be worked out, but he wasn't sure what that was.

Quill broke the silence in the small room. "Hmmm. I wonder who put this on my pillow? Can't be the tooth fairy . . . don't have many teeth left. . . . Maybe it was Taffy? No, I don't think so. Charlie? You leave this here?"

"I just thought I should help pay for my share of the food and gas and stuff."

"Thank you, son. I appreciate the gesture. You sure are the thoughtful one, aren't you? Someone has taught you well, Charlie Nash. Oh, I almost forgot. We didn't look up our word today, did we?"

"No. I'll get the dictionary." Charlie hopped out of bed and picked up the well-used book. He sat on the edge of the bed and began leafing through the pages.

"Do me a favor, son. Look up the word, 'veracity.'"

"Huh? Okay."

Charlie paged to the V's and asked, "How do you spell it?"

"V-e-r-a-c-i-t-y."

"Got it. Veracity. 'Adherence to the truth. Truthfulness.'" He looked across the small space. Quill was staring at him, his forehead creased as if he were about to ask a question. "Oh, yeah. Let's see . . . how about, a person should always . . . that's a hard one, Quill. A good person . . . a . . . aw, gee, Quill. I don't think I can use it in a sentence."

"Sure you can. Think about the meaning. Think about what it means to you. . . . Good night, Charlie. I'll see you in the morning." Purdue rolled over and faced the wall. Soon he was snoring.

Charlie stared at his friend for a long time. He considered the old man's words, about what Quill might have meant. Suddenly he tensed . . . as if a sign had been plastered to his forehead. *Does he know? What does he know? Veracity . . . truth . . .*

He closed the book, turned out the light, and crawled into bed. Moonlight filled the room. He stroked Taffy's side. Her tail thumped once, then twice. Charlie closed his eyes and wondered what he should do next. *Tomorrow . . . Plenty of time . . .*

Twenty-Nine

O N THURSDAY MORNING, October 10, The Hiawatha Limited pulled into Chicago's Union Station at 7:00 A.M. LaBette had spent the previous evening dining alone and then retired early to a small, but comfortable sleeper compartment.

He skipped breakfast when he arrived. It had long been his belief that much of his skill lay in his ability to tap into every one of his five senses at will. A full stomach dulled one of those. *Plenty of time to eat—later,* he reasoned.

LaBette carried a satchel containing little but a change of underwear, a map of Chicago, and the Luger. He was dressed in a very conservative gray suit, silver tie, and black fedora. He had glasses on once again, and sported a moderate mustache. He hailed a cab and gave Marie Mackey's apartment address.

He sat back and took in the sights. Chicago was one of his favorite towns. *So much to see . . . so much to do. Maybe I'll retire here instead of Minneapolis . . . weather's better. More people—easier to fit in. Commuter and elevated trains going every which way. Hell, with all the new planes flying now, I might just fly to the Caribbean when it turns cold.* He liked that idea.

The yellow cab pulled over and stopped. The driver flicked the meter and said, "Three-fifty, bud."

LaBette was feeling generous and gave him a five. "Keep it." He picked up his satchel and left the cab.

As the cab pulled away, he glanced up and down the street, and then craned his neck at the tall apartment building. He adjusted his tie, pulled his hat down, and entered the building. Once inside, he checked to find Mackey's apartment number, took the elevator to the seventh floor and got out. The hall was empty.

He rehearsed his plan. *Gain entry, force her to open the safe, pop her in the head, and leave. Shouldn't take more than five, ten minutes—max.*

Marie's apartment was directly across from the set of elevators. He took four steps and rang the bell.

After thirty seconds, the door opened and a small, white-haired lady asked, "May I help you?"

She spoke with an accent . . . French, he surmised. LaBette cleared his throat and said, "Yes, Mrs. Mackey?"

"Yes. I'm Marie Mackey."

"Oh, good. Then I have the correct apartment." As he spoke, he opened the satchel and stuck one hand inside, fingering the Luger. "My name is Schrader, Albert Schrader. I'm with the Smithsonian, and I believe my office arranged for a pick-up of certain coins from you. I realize I'm early, but . . ."

"Oh, dear! I'm afraid there's been some mistake, young man. Two of your people were here yesterday afternoon. They took the coins with them. I don't understand . . ."

A voice from inside the apartment called out, "Who is it, Marie?"

LaBette was startled as much by what Marie said as by the voice coming from the apartment. *Choose . . . quick. Could be more than one . . . that means trouble . . . too messy.*

Still another voice said, "Marie! Come on dear, it's your turn."

"I'm sorry. My Thursday bridge group is inside. Perhaps you'd like to come in and call your office?"

"No. That won't be necessary. Typical bureaucratic snafu, I expect. I won't trouble you any further. If nothing else, I had a nice trip to Chicago. Have a nice day, Mrs. Mackey." LaBette tipped his hat, closed the satchel, and turned away. The door closed behind him. He was seething. His retirement fund had just taken a serious hit and was slipping away like melted snow.

When he left the building, he headed for a corner phone booth. Once inside, he deposited the required coins and dialed Val's number. He didn't have to wait long. "It's me. No. I was too late! I don't know. They came early, I guess. Either that or the old bat got her days mixed up. I guess so." LaBette leaned against the window and watched the traffic pass by.

Suddenly he straightened. "What? Repeat that." He listened carefully. "You mean that since the Smithsonian now has the nine coins, the other two would probably triple in value? Why? Of course! Out of circulation. So the kid's two are worth—what? The Lord does indeed provide for those . . . never mind. *I've got to find that kid before the trail gets too cold.* Right! I'll take the . . . let's see . . ." He checked his watch.

"I can catch the 10:30 Zephyr and be back tonight. I'll call you when I get home. Right. Good bye." LaBette replaced the receiver, picked up his satchel, and left the booth.

He flagged the first passing cab and directed the driver to the train station. I've got to find that damn kid!

ON THAT SAME THURSDAY, Charlie woke to the sound of a tractor engine. He opened his eyes and looked over at Quill. He glanced at the dictionary. He was still disturbed by Quill's questioning look the night before. He had no chance to think it through, however.

"Charlie? You up yet?" Sarah poked her head in the door. She was whispering.

"Hi! Yeah, I'm up. That your dad down in the yard?"

Taffy leapt from the bed and went to greet the young girl.

"Yes. Hi, Taffy." Sarah knelt to enjoy a wet kiss. "Come on and get dressed. We're picking apples today, and I get to skip school!" Sarah's voice was excited and anxious. "Hurry up, lazy bones!"

"I'll be right down." He threw back the covers and headed for the bathroom. By the time he returned, Quill was awake. "They're going to start picking, today, Quill."

"I figured he would." He yawned and stretched. He hadn't slept well and had had to take two pills during the night. "You go ahead. I'll be there in a few minutes."

Charlie finished dressing. He decided a clean pair of dungarees was in order, so he emptied his pockets of loose change, his pocket knife, and Taffy's name tag, and quickly threw them all into his bag—except for the knife. He went downstairs two steps at a time.

Maxine had breakfast ready. Sarah was already eating.

"Good morning, Charlie. Did you sleep well?"

"Yes. It was great." He paused and added, "I hope it's all right, but Taffy slept on my bed last night."

"Of course it's all right. Shelly used to sleep with Sarah too. Don't worry about it . . . the bedspread can always be washed. Say, speaking of that, would you like me to wash any of your clothes today?"

"Uh . . . I don't have too many, but that would be great."

"Well, just set whatever you have on the end of the bed. I've also got to go to town today . . . maybe I could pick up a few things for you?"

"Sure. I've got money."

Maxine smiled. "Okay, we'll settle up later. Maybe I can find a hat for you, too. That sun can get pretty hot out in the orchard. You're going to help with the picking, aren't you?"

"You bet! I've never done it before, but I can learn."

"Well, it's a big job, and we can sure use your help." She filled his plate and set it in front of him. "I hope you like French toast?"

"My favorite. Thank you."

Sarah finished and watched Charlie eat. She smiled at him with her chin resting on two, small fists. She had on a blue shirt beneath her overalls.

286

Her hair was pulled back in a ponytail, and it bobbed up and down each time she spoke. "Did you know who your parents were, Charlie?"

"Sarah! Maybe he doesn't want to talk about that." Her mother said.

"That's okay. No, I went to the orphanage when I was a baby. My parents died in a car accident."

Maxine stood behind the boy and shook her head from side to side at her daughter.

Sarah noticed her mother's gesture and didn't pry any further.

"Oh. That's too bad. Come on, Charlie. Hurry up!"

He finished eating and asked, "How come you get to skip school?"

"All the farm kids do this time of year. We have to help with the harvest and stuff. You know how to pick apples?"

"No. Not really." He chugged his milk, wiped his mouth, and stood up.

"I'll take that, Charlie." Maxine reached for the plate and took it to the sink.

"Come on. I'll show you," Sarah said. "It's easy."

"Thanks for breakfast, Maxine." He followed Sarah to the back door, and stopped. Taffy had hung back. "Wait. I have to feed Taffy first." He picked up her bowl, found the food in the cupboard, and filled it up.

"Give her some of this," Maxine said as she scraped the dishes into the bowl.

Charlie set it down and waited for Taffy to eat.

Sarah grew impatient. "She's a slow eater. Shelly used to gobble everything in five seconds."

Maxine couldn't remember when her daughter had been as animated, as excited about anything as she was about having the boy and his dog—and Quill, around.

Taffy finished, slurped water for a bit, and they were ready.

Maxine watched them leave and stacked the dishes in the sink.

"Good morning," Quill said, entering just after the kids left.

"Oh, Quill! I didn't hear you come down. Hungry?"

"Not terribly, Maxine. Just a small portion is fine."

287

Maxine studied her father-in-law. He didn't look well. Dark shadows hung beneath each sunken eye. "Tough night?" She had a worried frown.

"Yes." He wanted to change the subject. "Understand it's picking day. Cort and the kids already out?"

"Yep. You know Cort. 'Burning daylight' and all that. Wonder where he got that from?"

"I know." Quill smiled as he remembered how hard he used to work.

Maxine put a plate in front of him and sat across the table. She sipped her coffee. "I'm going into Brown's Valley today. Thought I'd pick up some clothes for Charlie. He really didn't bring much with him, did he?"

"No. I've been through his sack. He's traveling pretty light."

"He seems a bit happier than when he first arrived."

"Yes, I think so too. But, the boy is carrying a burden of some sort. He trusts me, and I'm confident that with just a little nudging, he'll open up and tell me what happened back home."

"I think you're right. I hope so, Quill. If he has a family, I'm sure they're worried sick by now." She paused, struggling with how to phrase her next question. "Quill? When are you going to tell him about . . . you know."

He wiped his mouth and stared out the window. "I don't know, Maxine. This has all come on me rather suddenly. Honestly, I was hoping I wouldn't have to . . . that once he told me the truth, we could work it out, and he'd return home without . . . without finding out."

"And what about Sarah?"

"Oh, Lord, Maxine. I don't know. She was such a surprise. I'm having a hard enough time . . . I never expected . . ." Quill grasped his stomach as a new wave of pain hit. He gasped and clutched the edge of the table.

"Quill?" Maxine stood and went to his side. "Quill? What can I do?"

"Nothing . . . dear." But, after another jolt of pain, he said, "My pills . . . upstairs . . ."

She ran from the kitchen and took the stairs two at a time. She retrieved the bottle and raced back down to the kitchen. "Here. How many?"

"Two. My God . . . I can't stand this . . ." Sweat poured from his hairline. He took the pills and swallowed.

"Glass of water?"

"Yes."

After a few minutes, the pain subsided. "It's getting worse . . . and more frequent," he said

Maxine wiped his head. "I'm so sorry, Quill. I wish . . . I wish there was something we could do." She sat back down. "How long do you have?"

"The last doctor I went to thought a couple of months. That was a month ago."

"Do they know what it is?"

"An aneurism. Specifically, an abdominal aortic aneurism."

Maxine was weeping. She covered her mouth with a dish towel. Quill reached across and touched her wrist.

"Maxine, don't. Please."

"I'm sorry." She blew her nose and wiped her eyes. "How did they find it?"

"Started with a backache. Went to a chiropractor for a while, but he couldn't help me. Apparently this type of aneurism in men my age is easily disguised as simple back pain. I can stand quite a bit of pain, but finally it got so bad I went to the emergency room. The doctor felt my stomach and found it."

"Can't they do anything? Operate? Remove it?"

"I was told that the surgery for something like this is very experimental and unbelievably expensive—more money than I've seen in a lifetime. Even then there's no guarantee."

"Quill? Maybe we could . . . you know . . . mortgage the farm!"

"That wouldn't begin to cover it, Maxine—it's that expensive. This is a wonderful little farm, but isn't worth that kind of money. Besides, I'd never permit it. No, I'm afraid it's my time to go. I've come to accept that, and it's okay. Doctor said it would happen quick, so that's a blessing, I guess."

She was unsure of how to pose her next question. "Lord, this is hard . . . how will you know when . . . you know?"

"Towards the end, blood flow is interrupted to the lower extremities. The aneurism gets bigger and blocks blood flow in the aorta. He said my toes would turn blue."

Cort heard everything through the screen door in back. He entered and said, "You have to tell Sarah. I won't do it." His voice broke as the words left his lips.

He spun around, took four steps and left. *BANG!* The screen door slammed shut.

❖ ● ❖

ONCE LABETTE RETURNED to Minneapolis on Thursday night, he immediately called Val.

"Finding them won't be easy. I know, but I still think I've missed something. Maybe it'll come to me in the morning. I'll be in touch."

The following day, Friday, LaBette discovered the article in the *Minneapolis Star* about a suicide west of Minneapolis. He jotted down the sheriff's name and sat back. He nibbled on the pencil for a few minutes, then bolted upright.

"Of course! What's the matter with me? What's the first thing the old man would have done after he left the guy in the Packard? He'd either find a vet for the dog or call the sheriff and report the guy—or both!" He picked up the phone.

"Information? Yes, I'd like the number of the sheriff's office in . . . uh, McCloud County. What? No, I don't know the city . . . Hutchinson, maybe? I'll wait." LaBette paged through his Bible and turned instinctively to the Book of John. "What's that? Got it. Can you connect me, please. Thank you."

After a few more seconds the dispatcher came on the line. "Hello? Yes, I'm calling from the *Minneapolis Star* . . . following up on the suicide your people investigated a few days ago. Pardon me? Oh, yes, of course. Donaldson . . ."

He picked up the paper and continued, "Out State Edition, that's right. Any word on who your 'anonymous caller' was? Why? Oh, you know how we newspaper folks are . . . always curious. No? That's too bad. Well, thanks for your time. Goodbye."

LaBette hung up. "Damn!" The sheriff's department had no further information on the caller. *That leaves only a vet—or doctor. If they even stopped . . . and if they gave a forwarding address.*

At this point, LaBette knew he would have to pack for a long trip and head west. One after one, he'd visit every veterinarian and doctor's office within a hundred miles of Hutchinson until he found the right one—if indeed there was a right one.

He had one more call to make. "It's me. No luck. I have to go out there and start knocking on doors. I know, but it's the only lead I have. If the dog was hurt bad enough, I'm sure the kid would have insisted on taking it to a vet—or a doc, even. It'll take a while, I know that. All right. I'll call when I have something to report."

LaBette loaded the DeSoto with everything he thought he'd need in the way of equipment, weapons, and disguises and left town that same day. He didn't reach Hutchinson until after 5:00 P.M., so he booked a room at a hotel in town.

He began his search in earnest on Saturday. After visiting the local veterinarian and three physicians—most of them closed for the weekend—he drove west. His first stop in Hanley Falls was at Doc and Elaine Haines. He was too late. The office was closed. A sign read: OPEN MONDAY THROUGH FRIDAY—9:00 A.M. TO 5:00 P.M.

"Dammit! Can't anything go right with this contract?" He knew that most of the other clinics and vets would probably also be closed until Monday. He dug out a Minnesota map and drew an arc around Hutchinson. He then circled the towns of Montevideo, Willmar, Granite Falls, and Olivia.

"Okay . . . I'll have to hit all these bergs on Monday. Have to check them out anyway. Looks like I spend the weekend in downtown Hanley Falls. Hope they have a movie theater." The thought angered him, but the idea of twenty-five thousand dollars made it worth the discomfort. He climbed in the DeSoto and headed for the only hotel in town.

THE PURDUES ALONG WITH their mysterious young guest began picking apples that first morning—Thursday. Charlie proved to be a quick study. Cort showed him how to hold the apple in his hand and twist the stem from its branch. After a while, Charlie seldom tore off the following year's bud spur as he plucked the red fruit.

Cort positioned the tractor between the rows of trees. A flat-bed trailer was attached and loaded with empty crates. All but Quill filled their canvas picking bags, dumped the contents in crates, and went back for more. Three-legged ladders were moved from tree to tree. Quill tried to keep up but tired easily. After a couple of hours, he went inside to lie down. Guilt forced him up and out again.

Quill chose to take control of the sorting and washing operation in the apple shed. Culls were thrown into a huge bin for cider, and the rest packed for shipment.

The family took brief breaks for lunch and lemonade, but worked from dawn to dusk. By Saturday, Charlie's hands were blistered and every bone in his body ached. But he never complained, and sleep came easily each night. The Pudue family no longer questioned him about his background. He was grateful for that.

Taffy fully recovered from her damaged ribs and spent each day either in the orchard chasing apples thrown by Charlie or Sarah or stalking pheasants near the corn crib.

Before long, word had spread, and a number of neighbors appeared to help with the picking.

Charlie was amazed at how that many people so freely gave of their time. "Why are they doing this, Cort? I mean, why are they helping?" Charlie asked Saturday morning after nearly a dozen people had arrived to help.

"That's what neighbors do around here, Charlie." Then he laughed. "Besides, there isn't another orchard within a hundred miles of here. As payment for their help, they get to take as many apples as they want home with them."

These long days at the Purdue ranch were some of the happiest of Charlie's brief life. Each one passed quickly. One blurred into another.

❖ ● ❖

QUILL'S CONDITION STABILIZED, but his ill-health did not go unnoticed by his granddaughter, Sarah. One day she asked Charlie, "What's wrong with Grandpa, Charlie?"

He too was concerned, but accepted what Quill had originally told him to be the truth. "He has ulcers. In his stomach. Sometimes the pain gets pretty bad. That's why he takes those pills all the time."

"Will he get better?"

"I don't know. I hope so." Charlie decided that when he had the opportunity, he'd question his friend further.

Produce trucks from Sioux Falls began arriving on Saturday evening and would return each day to pick up the crates of apples until the harvest ended. Charlie helped Cort load the produce truck late each day. The remaining day's harvest was stored in the root cellar. One day after the truck was loaded and sent on its way, Charlie and Cort went into the apple house to grind the culls in the cider press. By then the bin was almost full.

Cort turned the crank while Charlie fed apples into the hopper. Mason jars were filled with the sweet juice and set in empty crates.

"Cort? Can I ask you something?" By now, he and Cort and been with one another enough that Charlie felt more comfortable in his presence.

"Sure, Charlie. Fire away."

"How come you still hate your dad?"

Cort stopped turning the crank. He looked directly at the boy. He didn't reply right away. A frown creased his forehead. "I don't know if I can answer that, Charlie. You . . . you do know what happened with Quill and my son, Justin . . . don't you?"

"Yes, but that was such a long time ago. And, well, it was an accident, wasn't it?"

"It was." Cort began turning the crank again—slower than before. "Charlie . . . you're only what? Eleven? Maybe when you're older . . . when you have children of your own, you'll understand how painful it is to . . . to lose a child." He paused.

"More than that, though, a farm is a dangerous place for a child . . . and my . . . and Quill knew that. That's why I never let Justin near any of the equipment . . . that goes for Sarah as well."

"But, Maxine said that Justin loved Quill . . . that he followed him everywhere. Quill hates himself for what he did, Cort. He's the nicest man I've ever met. I don't think he has a mean bone in his whole body. Can't you forgive him . . . someday?"

"I honestly don't know, Charlie. I've tried. Believe me, I've tried. Maybe . . . maybe someday. Now let's finish this cider and go have supper."

The boy's pleas for forgiveness echoed in Cort's ears. *Can't you forgive him . . . ?*

PART FOUR

Red Sky in the Morning

Thirty

O
N MONDAY MORNING, LaBette rose early and left town. He spent the entire day canvassing the towns circled on his map without finding a trace of the boy or the old man. None of the doctor offices or veterinarians he visited had ever heard of his quarry. By the time he returned to Hanley Falls, the veterinarian's office there was again closed. He had to spend yet another night in the small town's only hotel. Frustrated, he knew he was running out of chances to find the boy. If he struck out with the vet idea, he was uncertain what his next move should be.

He was at the Hanley Falls Clinic when they opened Tuesday morning. Posing as a cop from Minneapolis, LaBette entered the small office. Elaine greeted him as he closed the door. "Hi, there," he said.

"Hello. Can I help you?"

LaBette stepped to the counter and opened his wallet. "Name's Donaldson. Minneapolis Police Department." He flashed the badge and quickly flipped the wallet closed.

"You're a long way from home." Elaine studied the man closely. Something seemed out of place—maybe it was just having a Minneapolis cop in her office. "What can I do for you?"

"I'm looking for an older gentleman and a young boy who may have stopped here last week with an injured dog? Medium dog—tan in color."

Elaine was even more alert now at the mention of Quill and Charlie. *Why would he be after them?* "Why are you looking for them?"

LaBette immediately sensed that the woman knew who he was inquiring about. Like a ferret smelling blood, he wasted no time. "Police business. Were they here?" His question was at once accusatory and curt.

Elaine decided she didn't like the man and chose to lie. "Nope. Sorry. Now if you'll excuse me, we're in the middle of surgery." She turned to leave the counter, hoping he would take the hint and leave.

Instead, LaBette tipped his hat back and leaned on the counter. "Lady, do you know that withholding information in a kidnapping case is a felony?"

Elaine snapped back, "Kidnapping! That's absurd!" Too late, she realized her mistake.

"So, they were here!" *Finally. I knew it . . . sooner or later . . .*

"Look. I don't know why you're looking for them, but I can assure you that that nice old man . . ."

LaBette cut her off. He was so close . . . "Kid's name was Nash, right? Charlie Nash?"

Elaine sighed, and resigned to her blunder, said, "Yes."

"Now we're getting someplace. Old man say where they were headed?" He held his breath.

"No. Now if you'll excuse me . . ."

"Not so fast, lady. I'm sure you have a file on the dog and its owner, right?"

"Yes. But that's private. Aren't you supposed to have a search warrant for something like that?"

"You did work on the mutt, right?"

Elaine began to worry that this man was not everything he presented himself to be. "Yes. The dog had been kicked in the ribs. We did what we could for her and they left." She tapped the counter top with her fingernails and then ventured, "Could I see your badge again?"

LaBette had heard enough. "Sure." He reached in his coat and pulled out the Luger. "Here's my badge!" He pointed it at her chest.

"Oh, my God!" She put her hand to her mouth and gasped. "Please! I've told you everything I know."

"Is that right? Get the file!" As he waited, he slipped on his black gloves. He grabbed a tissue from the box on the counter and wiped it clean.

Elaine opened the file cabinet, found the file, and dropped it on the counter. "Here."

LaBette scanned it quickly. *Owner: Charlie Nash. Injury: kicked in side. Bill paid by: Quillan Purdue.* No home address. He closed it and stepped around the counter. "You have but one chance to live . . . and that's to tell me the truth. Where were they going?" He pointed the gun at her head.

Elaine didn't hesitate. She was trembling. "Blue Springs. Someplace in South Dakota. That's all I know, honest!"

"Very good, my dear. See how good it feels to unburden your soul with the truth?" He pulled out the silencer and screwed it on the end of the barrel.

"Oh, no! Please? I won't say anything, I promise!"

"Who's back there?"

"My . . . my husband."

"Move." He directed her down the hall to the surgical room. He pushed her forward into the small room.

"Hi," Doc said. "I'm all done . . ." He looked up and saw first the pistol—then LaBette. "What the hell?"

"Hush, my children. All is right with the world now." He shot Elaine in the back of the head with a soft *pop!* from the Luger.

Haines ducked but he had no chance. The second bullet struck him in the neck as a second *pop!* echoed in the tiny room. The Haines were dead within seconds.

"'Verily, I say unto you, The hour is coming, and now is, when the dead shall hear the voice of the Son of God: and they that hear shall live.' The Gospel according to John."

LaBette stepped to the table and pointed the gun at a tabby cat that Haines had just spayed. He pulled the trigger. *Pop* went the pistol for a third time. "Bye, bye, kitty. Guess your nine lives are all used up."

He unscrewed the silencer, put it and the pistol in his pocket, wiped the door knob clean, and left the office.

"Well, well," LaBette said as he climbed into the DeSoto. "Blue Springs it is, then . . . let's see where it is on the map. Got it!" He started the engine, took off the gloves, and pulled away from the curb. He turned the car around and headed north—toward Blue Springs.

THE DAYS AT THE RANCH passed quickly, and each day Quill's health deteriorated. He tired easily—knew he was running out of time. His death was imminent, and he had accepted that. He was filled with regret, however, at losing nine years with his granddaughter, Sarah.

Somehow, he had to prepare for the inevitable—telling Sarah, and perhaps Charlie, about his condition. He was unsure and frightened about how they would react. *I don't know if I'm strong enough for this*, he thought.

The time spent at the farm had been wonderful, but Charlie still had not opened up as he hoped he might. After the night he prodded Charlie with "veracity," the boy had never mentioned the word again. It was almost as if he knew that Quill suspected the real truth and was afraid to discuss it. *Have to force it, somehow . . . some way.*

ON TWO SEPARATE OCCASIONS during that week, Cort took a break and escorted Charlie over to the corral. He saddled up Pumpkin and gave the boy his first riding lesson. Charlie was thrilled. He had his western hat by now, a straw lid he quickly formed to look like one worn by Tom Mix. He still didn't have any cowboy boots, but knew he would buy a pair at the first opportunity.

The apple harvest was completed by the end of the week, and the children spent all day Saturday riding horses around the ranch property. After a couple of spills, Charlie found that once he relaxed in the saddle, he could set the horse comfortably. With Taffy trotting ahead, he and Sarah rode through the pasture and down to the fields below the orchard. It was a dream come true for an eleven-year-old city boy. He was a cowboy riding the range with his dog and new friend.

ON SUNDAY, OCTOBER 20, Quill begged off going to church with the rest of the family and stayed home. He sensed that it was almost time for Charlie to go home, so he vowed to find out where the boy lived—one way or another.

While Charlie and the rest of the family were at church, he again opened up the boy's bag. This time he dumped the entire contents out on the bed. One of the first items to spill out was Taffy's tag. "Well, well. What have we here, Taff?"

Taffy wagged her tail in response, then jumped on the bed.

Quill slipped on his reading glasses and studied the tag. "I knew it! You two did have a home, and it's in Minneapolis. Come on, girl. Let's go phone home," Quill said as he fingered the tag and headed downstairs.

Quill picked up the receiver and waited for the operator to come on the line. "Operator? I'd like to place a call to Minneapolis." Quill gave her the number and stroked Taffy's head as he waited.

"Hello? Is this Mrs. Nash? Is your son Charlie Nash? No, no. Nothing's happened to him. He's fine, I assure you. Mrs. Nash? Are you all right?" He waited for the boy's mother to collect herself, and continued, "My name is Purdue, Mrs. Nash, Quill Purdue, and your son has been with me since he left home. Yes, I'm sure you've been worried, and I would have called sooner, but Charlie refused to tell me where he was from. He ran from home because he was scared, Mrs. Nash—frightened by something that happened back there that caused him to leave, and I've been attempting to get him to open up to me. What? No, he was hitchhiking when I picked him up and now he's staying with me and my family in South Dakota." Purdue listened intently.

"Yes, I think he's almost ready to return home. Charlie is a wonderful boy, Mrs. Nash, and we've become fast friends. He's had a terrific time out here and so has Taffy. I would expect that some time in the next day or so, you can come out here and pick him up. What's that? Your husband? Certainly. No, he's at church right now, but I promise I'll call again soon and give you directions. I just wanted you to know he's safe and in good hands." Quill didn't know what more to say.

"Yes, I know you do. We have all grown to love him as a member of our family. Certainly. It's a long drive, but I promise I'll call again soon. I will. Take care. Goodbye."

Quill replaced the receiver. He had decided not to elaborate on the boy's horrendous experiences on the road. *Plenty of time for that . . . later.* He knew what he had to do next. The only question was how to get the boy aside and . . . and what? *I can't force it out of him.*

"Whew! That was difficult, Taffy. Time for you and Charlie to get back with your family, girl."

Quill heard the front door open. He quickly pocketed the tag and sat down at the table.

"Wasn't much of a sermon," Cort said.

"Sermon? All he did was quote the Scripture, for Pete's sake!" Maxine replied.

"I thought he was yucky!" Sarah said.

"Reminded me of someone I saw on television, but I can't remember who it was." Charlie replied.

"Wish we had television." Sarah said.

"I'm sure you do," her father replied and smiled as he did.

"Who was yucky?" Quill asked when they entered the kitchen.

"Oh. Hi, Grandpa!" Sarah ran to Quill and threw open her arms.

"Hello, Sweetheart. How was church?" He hugged her tightly and didn't want to let go.

"It was the strangest thing, Quill." Maxine said. "We had a new preacher today . . . Reverend Douglas. Not at all like Reverend Stevens."

The family moved into the kitchen.

"What happened to Stevens?" Quill asked.

"Apparently he was called away for some sort of family emergency," Cort answered. "Funny, none of the parishioners knew anything about it, though."

"Must have been very sudden," Quill replied. "What about Curly? He hears about everything that goes on in that town."

"Nope. Not even Maggie. She cleans up and gets the church ready for Sunday service, too. She never heard a word."

Quill observed that Charlie seemed strangely quiet—pensive almost. He watched as the boy headed for the stairs. "Charlie? Are you okay?" Quill called.

"Huh? Oh, yeah. I'm fine. I need to go upstairs for something. Be right back."

Quill turned to Maxine and shrugged his shoulders. She did the same. "I'll get dinner started," she said. "Sarah, will you help?" Maxine put on an apron as she spoke.

"Sure." She had on a yellow dress, white socks, and black Mary Janes.

"You look like a princess, this morning, Sarah," Quill said.

Sarah beamed at the compliment. Other than her school dress, she seldom wore anything but bib overalls with a boy's shirt beneath. "Thanks, Grandpa, but I better go change clothes now." She skipped out of the kitchen and went upstairs.

"Can I talk to you for a minute?" Cort asked Quill.

"You bet. Out on the porch?" Quill followed his son through the front door. They sat next to each other in matching wicker armchairs.

Cort wasted no time getting right to the point. "I've been thinking about what you said a while back."

"What's that, son?"

"About telling Sarah."

"Go on."

"I changed my mind . . . I think I should be the one to tell her that you're . . . dying."

Cort's voice broke as he finally spoke the one word he had been avoiding.

"I see. Why?"

"I don't think it's fair for you to have to be the one. It's going to be hard enough for her as it is."

Purdue considered what he had just heard. He didn't reply for a long time. "That's very courageous of you, Cort, but are you sure? I've had plenty of time to come to grips with this thing, and I may be better able to explain it to her . . . in a more matter-of-fact manner."

"Maybe, but I've thought about a lot of things since you returned, and while I wish none of this was happening. It is, though, and I need to deal with it. I need to help Sarah understand why you came back when you did."

He drew in a deep breath and continued, "And maybe if I do this, it will help me get past everything else I've laid at your feet for the last ten years."

Quill couldn't believe what he was hearing from his son. He was buoyant—giddy almost. "What happened . . . ? I mean, why now?"

"Something you said after you first arrived—about forgiveness. It struck a chord, I guess. That and a conversation I had with Charlie a while back."

"Charlie?"

"He's an amazing young boy—a lot like . . . like Justin, really." Cort rubbed his face and continued, "He said he'd never met a nicer person than you . . . said you didn't have 'a mean bone in your whole body.' I just figured that if an eleven-year old could come to that conclusion about you in so short a time . . . well, I don't know. But I thought about it and concluded that I probably overreacted and forgot all about what the Lord teaches us about forgiveness." Cort cleared his throat. "Anyway, this has been going on long enough."

Quill turned to face his son. He laid a hand on his son's arm and left it there. "Cort? What happened between you and me probably had to happen. You and I are too much alike in many ways. I can honestly tell you that if our roles were reversed, I am not certain I wouldn't have acted exactly the same. Does that make sense?"

"Yes. But it still doesn't excuse what I've done—how I've behaved. I've seen how much Sarah cares for you. And, because of me, because of my anger, she's not been able to be with you—to love you—until now. We've all suffered more pain over Justin's death than we needed to. I'll have to live with that, Dad, but . . . but, I want to make it right with you before it's . . . too . . . late." Cort's eyes misted. He covered his mouth with one hand, and gripped his father's with the other.

"Cort . . . don't. Please. It's okay. You reacted in the only way you knew how. But that was then. Now you have been blessed with a second chance . . . you have Sarah and what you just said about forgiveness is all I've prayed for these many years. Thank you for that, son."

Cort stood and walked to the dark screen surrounding the porch. After a few seconds he turned and said, "I am so sorry, Dad. Can you forgive me?"

Quill stood and went to his son. "I already did. Besides, It's I that needs forgiveness—not you." He threw both arms around Cort and hugged him tightly.

Cort laid his chin on his father's shoulder. His quiet cry was a final release . . . a combination of an ultimate lament for his long dead son and relief at having his own father in his arms.

Maxine appeared in the doorway to call both for dinner. When she saw them embracing, she backed away and returned to the kitchen. Her heart filled with joy at seeing two people she loved finally make amends. *Thank you, God.*

"Where are Dad and Grandpa?" Sarah asked.

Maxine blew her nose and said, "They'll be right along. Let's get the food on the table, shall we?"

Father and son stood apart and looked at one another as if seeing the other for the first time. "When will you tell Sarah about your illness, Dad? Or should I?" Cort asked.

"Soon, but I think it should come from me, don't you?"

Cort hesitated, then nodded. "Probably. It won't be easy for either of us, I'm afraid. She's grown very attached to you."

"I know. I should tell Charlie first, I guess. I'll let you know when, son. In the meantime, I want you to know that I'm at peace, now. What I hoped to accomplish by coming back has happened. Finding Sarah here was an unexpected bonus, and while my heart is filled with regret at not sharing more of her life, at least I've had this much time with her."

"How, uh . . . do you know what to expect? I mean, how will it happen?"

"Doctors said it likely would be sudden. The pain would shift to my back, bruises will appear, and once the aneurism enlarges further, my toes will turn blue. When that happens, the end will be near . . . maybe a day or so from that point."

Quill noticed that his son was having trouble dealing with the subject of his death and said, "Don't, Cort. It's all right, honest. I've had a great life and now that I'm here . . . now that you and I are finally speaking to each other—I'm fulfilled." He patted his shoulder and finished with, "Come on. Let's go eat." The two men walked back into the house together.

Charlie came downstairs at the same moment Quill and Cort returned from the porch. He didn't say anything but continued on into the kitchen. Something from the morning's sermon, coupled with Quill's interest in the idea of truth, weighed on the boy's mind. *They've been so nice to me . . . I wish I didn't have to lie about . . .*

"Charlie? Everything okay?" Quill called out.

"Yeah, I'm all right," he replied in a small voice. He went into the kitchen and asked if he could help with dinner.

"Thanks, Charlie but we're all set. Let's all go into the dining room," Maxine replied.

The Purdues, along with their guest, sat down for a quiet lunch. A broad smile crossed his face as Cort said grace.

For the first time in days, Quill ate almost a full meal. He was almost glowing he felt so happy. Even his complexion had changed—instead of the normal wan, slack tone of his face, he had more color in his cheeks.

Charlie was distracted and remained silent. While the rest of the family thought the preacher's words lacked substance, to Charlie, the preacher's sermon struck a chord that he could not shake. *If they really knew why I was on the road,* he reasoned, *they wouldn't have opened their home—their hearts, as they did. They probably just feel sorry for me.*

306

The word, "veracity," buzzed like a swarm of flies. He was a liar. The Purdues . . . Quill . . . deserved better. *What do I do? If I tell them the truth, they'll send me home. Maybe . . . maybe it's time. And what about Mom? How is she doing? She has no idea if I'm okay* . . . Charlie picked at his food.

Cort broke the silence. "Charlie? I was thinking that now that the apples have all been all picked, maybe you'd like to bring Taffy out pheasant hunting?"

Sarah jumped in with great enthusiasm and asked, "Can I go too, Dad?"

"Oh, I think so, sweetheart. How about it Charlie? Would you like that?"

"Sure. That would be neat," he said with little enthusiasm.

Maxine glanced at Quill and raised her brow.

He gave a slight shrug back and tried to glean from Charlie's expression what might be going on. "Boy, that sounds like fun. I'd sure like to join you three if I could. Probably can't do much walking, but I can post. That be all right, Cort?"

"You bet! We'll all go—even Mom," Cort added, glancing at Maxine.

Charlie had just about made up his mind and was about to blurt out the truth when Quill jumped in with a question that caught the boy off guard.

"Ever fire a shotgun before, son?" Purdue waited for the boy's response.

"No! I almost did, but . . ." His mood changed as if a curtain had been raised on a new day.

"Well, seems to me a young fella that's eleven years old ought to be taught how to shoot a shotgun. Still have that old single-shot twenty around, Cort?"

"Yep. Been saving it for Sarah, but she's got a ways to go yet. Like to carry a shotgun on our hunt, Charlie?"

"Huh? Really? Boy would that be cool! Hear that, Taff?" He looked down at his dog and smiled. "We get to go hunting together!" Charlie's animated reply was not lost on the Purdues.

"Okay, then. We'll have to have a little lesson in gun safety before we go. Why don't you kids help clean up and, uh . . . Dad and I'll get everything ready?" For the first time in anyone's memory, Cort had referred to his father publicly as 'Dad.' Quill and Maxine noticed. So did Charlie and Sarah.

They all pushed away from the table and headed in different directions. Maxine and the children began clearing the table, while Quill and Cort went in search of the shotguns and ammunition.

Charlie decided that his declaration to the family could wait until later.

"Mom? Isn't Dad still mad at Grandpa?"

"No, I don't think so, Honey. I think your father has managed to leave the past behind. I have a hunch that you had something to do with everything—and Charlie, too. Your father is a good man and in spite of that gruff, hard exterior of his, he loves us all a great deal. I think he finally realized that if he didn't shed his bitterness, that maybe he'd never have another chance to get close to his dad before . . ." She hesitated.

"Before what?" Sarah asked.

Maxine carefully considered her answer. "Ten years of anger is long enough, Sarah. Your grandpa is old, and . . . well, he won't be with us forever, you know." The words stung as they left Maxine's mouth, but she felt her daughter, and Charlie, needed to hear them.

"He's not that old," Sarah said. "I bet he lives to be a hundred. I know he's been sick, but—"

Charlie jumped in. "Maxine? What about Quill's ulcers. Will they get better?"

"I don't think so. But I don't know that much about it. Come on now—let's get these dishes done so we can go hunting." Maxine had already said more than she intended.

Thirty-One

EVERYONE EXCEPT MAXINE gathered behind the house. Cort had set up half a dozen cans on fence posts as shooting targets.

"Charlie? This is a twenty-gauge, hammer-type shotgun. Come here, son."

The boy stepped close and stared at the weapon. His heart pounded as Cort handed him the gun. It was heavier than he thought it would be. He was nervous and didn't want to make a mistake.

"You have to open the gun, 'break it,' like this." Cort flicked the lever on top, and the gun opened. "You slip the shell in here—then close the weapon. Now this is important: Whenever you are walking with the gun—when you aren't actually hunting—I want to see the gun open, like this. Understand?"

"Yes," Charlie replied—his voice shook as he spoke.

"Once the gun is loaded, you have to close the barrel," Cort took the gun back and snapped it shut. "Now, to fire it, you have to cock the hammer—like this." He pulled the hammer back with his thumb. "The shotgun can't fire unless the hammer is cocked, understood?"

"Yes."

"Okay. Turn this way and put the gun to your shoulder." He positioned the boy so he was facing away from the group. "Snug it in your shoulder there real tight. Now lay your cheek against the stock. That's it. Now, cock the hammer. Yep. Just like that. Aim at one of those tin cans and cover it with that front bead on the barrel. That's right. Keep both eyes open, son. This isn't a rifle. Good! When you're ready, squeeze the trigger."

Cort stood back and watched the boy. "Lean forward a little . . . that's it."

Charlie squeezed—just a little. BOOM! The gun fired and recoiled. His shoulder ached but he didn't let on. The tin can flew off the post and landed in the pasture. "I hit it!" He started to turn toward the others.

"Hold it, Charlie! Always be sure where you're pointing the end of the gun. Pretend like it's loaded—even if it isn't. Point it either at the ground or the sky—nowhere else. That's important!"

Charlie dropped the barrel until it pointed at the ground. "Like this?"

"Yes. Now, break it open. The empty shell will eject."

He broke the gun and the empty flew past his cheek. "Can I do it again?" He was excited.

"Sure. Here's a shell. You load it."

Charlie took the shell, turned away from the others, and dropped the shell into the chamber. He looked at Cort who nodded, and then snapped the gun closed. Once it was against his shoulder, he cocked the hammer, aimed at another can, and fired. BOOM! A second can spun off a second post. This time he was prepared for the impact and the recoil didn't hurt quite as much. He lowered the barrel, ejected the shell, and with a huge smile of his face, turned to his audience. Finally, he could now say he had fired a shotgun. He was thrilled.

"Way to go, Charlie!" Sarah said.

"Good job, son. Looks to me as if you're ready. Think so, Cort?" Quill asked.

"Yep. Just one more thing. Pheasants aren't like cans, Charlie. They jump up and fly away from you, so the gun has to swing with them. You'll have to lead them just a bit—even more the farther away they are."

"What do you mean?" Charlie asked.

"Lead means the distance you move the end of the barrel ahead of your target so that, by the time the pheasant gets there, your shot is too."

"Oh. I get it."

"If you put the gun up and point it without swinging with the bird, you'll miss. But don't be concerned. It takes a while and even the best shots miss—right, Dad?"

He winked. "Yep. I remember when Cort first started—took him months before he hit his first bird!"

"Nah! Not that long! Did it?" Cort laughed along with the rest. "Okay. Get Taffy and let's pile into the truck. Maxine! We're ready!" he called. "Dad, you and Maxine can ride in front, the kids and dog in back."

Maxine came from the house and once everyone was loaded in the truck, Cort drove out of the yard past the orchard. He was headed for a low-lying field of corn west of the farm. "You know," he stated as they passed the apple trees, "We picked over 1,000 bushels this year, Dad."

"No kidding!" his father said. "That has to be some kind of record, doesn't it?"

"Well, if the stiffness in my arms and back are any indication, I'd say so!" Maxine intoned.

"It's still a lot of work for you guys, isn't it?"

"Yes, Quill, but it's pretty neat, actually. There's something about those trees . . ." Maxine said.

"I think that unlike anything else around here, the trees mirror all four seasons of our year. Kind of like a barometer of Mother Nature's different moods." Cort added.

"I'm glad you both feel that way. Your mother thought I was nuts, you know."

"Yeah. I remember." Cort said. "But, she always pitched in and helped. She never complained."

Quill looked at his trees as if he could see his wife standing beneath one of them.

"She knew they were yours, Dad. And she knew how proud you were that they did so well."

Quill felt a surge of warmth rush through his chest. "She would have been a wonderful grandmother, wouldn't she?"

"Yes she would have, Quill." Maxine replied.

As they approached the field, Quill noted that Cort had left a dozen rows of corn standing in strips that ran the length of the field. "You left strips of corn standing, Cort? That's a great idea. Much easier to hunt this way."

"I figured I could always cut the corn later. Besides, it leaves a little food not only for the pheasants, but also for deer." He drove to the far end and stopped. "Okay. Here we are."

The adults piled out of the small cab and walked back to the truck bed. "Dad, if you and Maxine cover this end of the field as we walk toward you, there's bound to be some birds that fly out here. I'll take the kids and go up to the other end. We'll walk down the north edge first. Oops! Wait a minute—change of plans. One of you will have to drive us down to the far end and bring the truck back here. Otherwise we'll have to walk it twice."

"I'll drive you back there," Maxine said.

"Sounds like a plan." Quill retrieved his shotgun and stood aside.

Cort sat on the passenger side of the truck while Maxine climbed behind the wheel. She turned the truck around and pulled away.

"Good luck, Charlie," Quill called. "Have fun, Sarah!"

The kids waved as they passed by. Taffy hung her head over the edge. Her tail moved constantly, and her left ear was waving high as her nose gathered in the abundant scent.

Once Maxine reached the far end of the field, she parked the truck. Cort, Charlie, Sarah, and Taffy climbed out. "Have fun, kids!" she said.

"We will," Sarah called.

"Put this leash on Taffy, Charlie." Cort said. "Just until we get into the corn. Then you can let her off."

"Here, Taff!" Charlie attached the lead and picked up his gun. The three of them hiked over to the nearest rows of corn as Maxine drove back down the length of the field to join Quill.

Taffy quickly caught fresh scent and strained at the lead. Her tail beat against Charlie's legs. "She's really excited, Cort," He said.

"There's lots of scent in here. I don't think you'll have to worry about her, Charlie. She's plenty birdy. One more thing, Charlie. We only shoot roosters. Taffy's bound to flush hens in here, but let them go. Okay, now let her go. Let's see what happens."

Once free of the leash, Taffy darted forward and veered to the right. Then did an abrupt about-face and headed back to the left weaving between the stalks. They could see numerous pheasants darting between the rows. Suddenly, Taffy skidded to a stop and pointed her nose into the breeze. She extended her tail, raised her right leg and left ear at the same time—and froze!

"By God, she's pointing! Even her ear, for crying-out-loud! Look at that, Charlie! You've got a pointing retriever, I think. All right, load your gun, close it . . . now cock it, and step close to Taffy. The bird will jump as you get close to her. Go ahead, son."

Sarah stood next to her father. Neither moved. Both watched as Charlie closed the gun, cocked it, and moved in.

His heart was pounding, and he couldn't breathe. When he was ten feet from the dog, he heard something startling. *WHIRRR!* A loud cackle followed. Then a large rooster burst into the air. The bird sported a long tail and flew straight up for twenty feet before leveling off. Charlie watched the bird without raising his weapon.

"Shoot, Charlie! It's a rooster!" Cort called.

Charlie didn't react fast enough. He did manage to get the shotgun to his shoulder, but he had trouble locating the bird, and at the last moment, felt reluctant to shoot.

Realizing that the boy was too late, Cort casually brought his double barrel up, aimed, and fired. *BANG!*

Charlie jumped at the sound! He realized what happened even before the shower of feathers and dust erupted, and the bird folded and dropped into the corn. Too startled to move or speak, he forgot to release Taffy. She couldn't restrain herself, however, and sprang forward. Within seconds, she pounced on the bird and raised her head. The rooster hung limply from her mouth.

The boy finally gathered himself and remembered to break the gun open before doing anything else. When Taffy trotted back to Charlie's side, he held out his hand and said, "Drop, girl!" She opened her mouth and the still warm bird fell into Charlie's outstretched hand. Taffy immediately began spitting feathers. Charlie noticed and said, "A little different than ducks, huh, Taff? Good girl!"

"I'll be damned!" Cort now knew that both Taffy and Charlie had more than a passing interest and familiarity with hunting. *Either that or the dog is the most natural hunter I've ever seen.* "That was very impressive, Charlie. That's quite a hunting dog you have there, son."

"Thanks, Cort. She did good, didn't she?"

Sarah walked over and began petting Taffy. "Good girl, Taffy. Wow, Charlie! That was something! But why didn't you shoot?"

"I . . . I don't know. It all happened so quick," he lied.

"That's all right. Happens to everyone. Deer hunters call it 'buck fever.' Lots to think about, and if you're unsure, best not to shoot until you are. Next time . . ." Cort added.

"Come, on. Let's keep going. There're plenty more in here." He picked up the bird and put it in the back pouch of his jacket.

Taffy started off and soon was quartering the strip. She never got more than thirty yards in front of Charlie—she didn't need to as the corn was full of fresh scent. Before long, she stopped again and nosed into a stalk.

Charlie closed the gun and pulled back the hammer. This time he thought he'd be ready. He stepped in and raised the gun. Another rooster jumped up. He raised the gun, found the bird but once again couldn't shoot.

BANG, BANG! Cort hit the bird with his second shot. The bird tumbled to the ground and immediately started running.

"Fetch, girl!" The bird had been winged, and Taffy gave chase. All three watched as she chased the bird from one side to another. Suddenly she spun around, dove, and trapped the bird. She ran back and sat next to Charlie. He took the bird and handed it to Cort who quickly wrung its neck.

"Ugh! I don't like to watch that," Sarah said.

Charlie shrunk back. A sudden vision of the small, green-wing teal

314

from Parker's Lake filled his head. He felt sorry for the rooster, just as he had for the teal.

Sarah's father stuffed the bird in his pocket. "Okay, let's keep going, kids. We still have plenty of corn left to walk." Cort wondered about Charlie's failure to shoot but said nothing.

Charlie waved at Taffy, and she bounded ahead into a new patch of the brittle, golden stalks. Cort and Sarah followed close behind Charlie, who hurried to keep pace with his dog.

A pair of eyes watched the group's every movement from a hill just south of the cornfield. Unknown to Cort, Charlie, and Sarah, LaBette—Charlie's relentless pursuer—lay motionless in a patch of tall, blue stem grass, peering through the scope of his favorite rifle—the Springfield. The long-barreled weapon tracked the progress of each bird hunter as the trio moved down the rows of standing corn.

LaBette lay well hidden. He had selected a position on top of a small hill, six hundred yards south of the corn field. He scanned the field with the optic, identifying each of the group down below. The crosshairs settled on the girl's small back . . . then rose to her head. Blond pigtails bounced and waved. The crosshairs parted her hair.

The sniper felt a familiar rush of pleasure as he steadied the Springfield. He moved the weapon slightly to the left and covered the boy. Sporting a straw cowboy hat, he carried a weapon of his own.

It's going to be so easy, LaBette thought. "All right, my children, now we are playing in my sandbox!" he whispered.

Caught up in the moment, he was suddenly back in France. . . . The targets below were uncovered—out in the open, and wearing Nazi uniforms. *The French will praise my prowess! Five kills in one outing!*

LaBette lowered the weapon, wiped his eyes, and the uniforms vanished. He raised the rifle once more. The small, tawny dog moved through the scope. He followed its movement.

That cursed dog! I can't get close to the house with that mutt around. I need to know that I can surprise them. Take the dog out, Joseph!

He paused. If he shot the dog, what would they think? He had to be sure they wouldn't suspect anything other than an errant shot fired by one of a group of deer hunters he had spotted earlier. *What to do? Wait! Go check the house—now!*

He edged back beneath the brow, knelt first, then stood and ran down to the DeSoto. Knowing he had plenty of time before they returned, he chose to drive to the house and search for the coins.

LaBette jumped in the car and turned it around. He sped back down the highway to the driveway and drove to the house. If anyone happened to stop by for a visit while he was there, he'd simply stay inside until they left.

The front door was open so he walked in. The Luger was in his pocket. He was convinced that the boy had brought the coins with him and probably stashed them in whichever room he was staying in. LaBette ran up the stairs, found Charlie's room, and began searching.

He went through the newspaper bag, looked under both mattresses, under pillows, in the dresser drawers, in the closet—everywhere—but didn't find the coins. They weren't in his room. *Where then?*

He spent the next thirty minutes searching the entire house. He was careful to put everything he touched back in its proper place, and when he was satisfied the coins were not in the house, he left. He stood outside and looked at all the barns and sheds. *Damnation! He could have stashed them anywhere! Wait! The old man's car!*

Ten minutes spent searching the Ford Custom Wagon yielded nothing. There was nothing on or under the seats or in the glovebox or on the back deck. "I'll bet the brat's got them in his coat or stashed them in one of the barns," he muttered.

He climbed back in his car and drove back to his original spot on the road. Once he repositioned himself on the hill, he knew what he had to do. He'd have to confront the entire family, including the boy, and force him to reveal his hiding place.

But first, the dog had to go. Above all else, his plan to gain access

316

required subterfuge—deception, and he had to be able to get close without the dog raising any alarm.

He crept through the grass on his belly and raised the Springfield. The hunters had covered over half the field by the time LaBette returned. He noticed they walked east to west, and their progress brought them closer to his position as they shifted laterally. All he had to do was wait until they were close enough, pick out the dog, and then take her out.

LaBette was anxious to fulfill the contract and return home, but he knew he must endure awhile longer. *Tribulation worketh patience, Joseph.* The end was in sight. He'd wait until they were working the last strip of corn. He ran one hand over the worn stock of the Springfield lovingly, as if he were caressing the flank of a lover. The sensation warmed his loins.

Crowned with glory and honor; that he by the grace of God should taste death for every man. Labette smiled and waited.

Thirty-Two

B Y THE TIME CHARLIE, SARAH, and Cort reached the end of the field on the first pass, Cort had shot three roosters. Twenty yards from the end, one last group rose—three hens and a rooster.

The three watched as Maxine and Quill raised their guns. The rooster flew to the south and both fired. It crumpled and dropped. Charlie sent Taffy to pick it up. "Who shot it?" Charlie yelled.

Maxine and Quill looked at each other and shrugged their shoulders. "Don't know," said Quill. "Probably Maxine. . . . These old eyes can't see so good anymore."

All five took a break and chatted about how well Taffy had done. Maxine had brought along lemonade in a large Mason jar, and she passed out paper cups of it.

Taffy flopped in the grass adjacent to the field. She was panting heavily and her tongue drooped from a corner of her mouth.

"I've got a jug of water in the truck, Charlie. Let's give her some before she gets too hot. She's been working pretty hard," Quill offered.

Charlie laid his gun down in the grass. He and Quill walked over to the truck. Taffy got up and followed. Charlie located the full Mason jar, cracked the lid, and let her slurp from the jar.

"Pour some in your hat, son. Be easier for her that way," Quill said.

Charlie filled his hat and held it for her to drink. She finished almost the entire jar. "Good girl, Taffy. You were great." Charlie turned to address his friend. "Quill, I, uh . . . I need to tell you something." Concern and sadness filled his voice.

Quill put his arm around the boy and said, "What's up? Here, let's sit on the tailgate." They both sat down—Quill kept his arm around Charlie. "What's going on, Charlie? Why so sad?"

Charlie hesitated, and then blurted, "I . . . I couldn't shoot at the birds, Quill!"

"Why not?"

"I don't know . . . uh, something happened before . . . when I went duck hunting." Charlie then went on to talk about the crippled teal, how he watched it die in his hands and felt nothing but sadness over its death. "I just don't think I want to shoot a bird—or any animal, I guess."

Quill smiled, just a bit, and said, "And . . . ? That bothers you? That you don't want to kill something?"

"Yes." Charlie turned to look in his friend's eyes for direction. "I don't like seeing animals suffer."

"Hmmm. Charlie, do you know who Albert Schweitzer is?"

"What? Yeah, isn't he some kind of scientist, or something?"

"He's a doctor, actually, and one of the brightest minds the world has ever known. He won the Nobel Peace Prize just a few years ago, 1952, I believe. He was a great humanitarian and a philosopher. He said, 'The sympathy that a man feels towards every living creature is what truly makes him a man.' I'd say you are in pretty good company, son. Don't worry about it. I respect you for your compassion, and hope you never lose what you are feeling right now. I don't think you should try to kill anything if you don't want to. Someday, as you get older, you'll come to understand that there is a difference between just killing, and hunting. Out here, we only shoot what we intend to eat—we don't just kill for sport. There's a big difference. But for now . . . well, just enjoy watching Taffy work. That should give you plenty of pleasure, okay?"

"Okay. Thanks for understanding, Quill."

"You're welcome. Now, let's get back before they all wonder what we're doing."

They walked back to the others and neither said a word to anyone about their conversation. Maxine drove them back down to the other end and they worked the next patch to the south. Cort killed two more roosters. As they came to the end, Taffy froze directly in front of her master. Charlie crept close and saw the multi-colored pheasant crouched next to a corn stalk. He stamped his foot and the bird rose. The sun caught the reds, blues, and greens of the bird's feathers at just the right angle. Charlie thought it was the most beautiful pheasant he'd seen yet—and the biggest.

He set the twenty-gauge against his shoulder, followed the bird's flight, but once again, refrained from pulling the trigger.

BANG! Cort's gun fired and the bird fell.

Charlie released Taffy, broke the gun, ejected the live shell, and cradled the gun in the crook of one arm. He held out his other to receive the bird from Taffy. "Drop, girl. Good job, Taff."

"Why didn't you shoot, Charlie?" Sarah asked.

Cort stepped closer and asked, "You okay, son? Is your shoulder sore or something?"

"Yeah. I guess my shoulder is a little sore. I think I'll just carry the gun and work with Taffy, if that's okay, Cort?"

"Of course it is," Cort replied. He wondered if the boy's decision not to shoot had something to do with his conversation with Quill earlier, but chose not to press the matter.

Quill and Maxine walked toward them. The old man had just as big of a smile on his face as the boy. He draped an arm over the boy's shoulders, leaned close, and whispered, "I'm proud of you, son. I . . . I'm sure glad I . . . was here . . ." Quill sniffed and finished with, "Anyway, I'll never forget this day, Charlie . . . and neither will you, I'd guess."

"Let's take one last pass and call it quits," Cort said.

Maxine drove them back and then returned to the far end of the field to join Quill. They watched as the three moved down the rows. Two more roosters were shot, five hens flew out, and when they were fifty yards away, Taffy froze on another point.

"That young dog's amazing," Quill commented.

"Yes, and Charlie's so proud of her," Maxine said.

"She's going to sleep well tonight."

"We all are, Quill."

Just then, they watched as Taffy disappeared into the corn as a rooster took flight. They heard two shots as Cort fired. The bird was untouched and flew right at them.

"Your shot, Quill," Maxine said.

As the bird approached, it veered to the north and leveled off. Quill raised his gun. Before he could pull the trigger he heard a scream coming from the field in front of them. He lowered the gun and looked toward Cort and the children. "What—?"

LaBETTE WAITED UNTIL THE GROUP of hunters was directly below his position. He looked through the scope and found the dog. His line of fire was at a thirty-degree angle. The dog was in the open, free of the maze of cornstalks. *Perfect!* It was on point. He had a clear shot. He lined up the crosshairs just behind her shoulder.

TAFFY LEAPT FORWARD—to her right. As LaBette tugged on the trigger, the rooster exploded from the cover of the standing corn. Cort fired at the startled bird. *BANG! BANG!*

Poof! The thirty-caliber round left the Springfield, but LaBette had flinched at the sound of both shots from below. The bullet passed beneath Taffy, slammed into a chunk of limestone, and burrowed into the soft earth. A small chip flew off the rock and struck Taffy just below her ribs on the left side.

She gave a slight yelp. Then, in mid-flight, she twisted as the small fragment entered her stomach. Taffy landed on her side with a thud, and lay still. Blood puddled beneath her.

Charlie and Cort never heard Taffy's cry of pain. They were focused on the retreating bird and waiting for Quill or Maxine to shoot.

Sarah heard a slight *buzz!* as a second chip of stone whizzed past her ear. She swatted at the invisible insect. Then she noticed Taffy, and shrieked *EEEEKK!* Her yell was so piercing and shrill, that her mother and grandfather heard her from the far end of the field.

Charlie turned around. Sarah had her hand over her mouth and pointed at the dog. Charlie twisted and saw Taffy. She wasn't moving! He ran to her and laid his gun down in the dirt.

"Taffy? Taffy? Come on, girl! Get up . . . please?" He gasped as he realized that his dog was badly hurt.

He turned to Cort who knelt next to him. "Cort? She's bleeding, Cort. What happened to her?"

"I don't know, son, but she's hurt bad. We have to stop the bleeding." He took off his shirt and pressed it against her stomach. "MAXINE! BRING THE TRUCK! HURRY!"

Taffy didn't move. Her eyes were open but unfocused. Her chest heaved. Charlie was frantic! Confused, frightened and unsure of what he could or should do, he laid his cheek next to Taffy's and whispered, "Please, God. Please . . ."

AT FIRST LABETTE FEARED he had missed, but when he saw the dog go down in a heap, he knew he hadn't.

LaBette kept the scope trained on the scene below. The dog wasn't moving. Must have been a clean hit. He saw the pool of blood and knew his shot had been true. He lowered the weapon and slithered back from the edge of the hill. Once he was below the crest, he stood, shouldered the weapon, dusted off his shirt and trousers, and walked back down to his car.

He would have preferred killing all of them right there and then, but knew that wouldn't secure the coins for him. *After all,* he thought, *let's not lose sight of the real purpose of the mission, Joseph.* He recited a comforting passage as he put the rifle back in the trunk, climbed in the car, and drove away.

MAXINE AND QUILL DROVE UP next to the other three. Both jumped out. Quill said, "What happened?" He looked down at Taffy's still form. Her rib cage moved up and down, but there was no other movement or sound except for her heavy breathing. Her tongue hung limply from her open mouth.

"Don't know, Dad." Cort looked up but kept his hand over the wound. "Sarah screamed, we looked down, and there she was."

Charlie raised his head. In spite of the heat and an afternoon in the hot sun, his face was ashen. He was petrified—frozen with fear! "Quill? Please, Quill . . . can you do something? She's hurt real bad, I think."

Quill knelt down and removed the blood-soaked shirt. He felt for the wound. "She's got a hole in her belly . . . 'bout the size of a dime." He replaced the shirt. "Keep pressure on it, Cort. We've got to get her back to the house and call Curly."

"Charlie, put your hand over mine. Now, when I slide mine out, you press hard, okay? I'm going to slide my arms under her and pick her up. Grab her head, Dad. Go ahead, Charlie . . . that's it. Okay, let's go." He slid his bare arms beneath the dog and lifted her up.

With great care, he laid her down on the tailgate. "Climb up, son. Sarah and I will ride back here with you. Let's go, Maxine."

Sarah and Cort climbed up into the truck bed while Maxine and Quill got in the cab. Maxine started the engine, put the truck in gear, and crept forward. She turned around, and drove back to the farm house.

Once they reached the house, Cort lifted Taffy out and took her into the kitchen. Maxine threw down an old horse blanket, and they gently set her down.

"I'll call Curly," Quill said.

Charlie felt numb. He was in shock! How could this have happened? Taffy—one minute so alive and full of energy, and now she looked as if she were drawing her last breath. He couldn't speak, but just sat next to her with his hand on the bloody shirt—holding it in place as if her life were in his small hands. Sarah sat down next to him. She was crying—quietly, steadily.

Cort and Maxine sat down at the table. They tried to console Charlie, but the words had little effect.

"Curly's very good with animals, Charlie. He's patched up many of our cows over the years, hasn't he, Cort?"

"You bet! He may not look like it or act like it, but he cares about animals more than anyone I know. She'll be in good hands, son."

Charlie never looked up. He held the cloth tight to her side. *Please, God . . . don't let her die. She's my best friend in the whole world . . . I can't lose her.*

Quill returned and said, "Curly will be right out. Said to keep pressure on the wound and don't let her drink anything. How's she doing?" He sat at the table.

"She's hurt real bad, Quill," Charlie answered. "It's all my fault. If I hadn't left home, she'd be all right. I never should have taken her with me."

The three adults looked at one another, but didn't press the boy about his startling admission.

Plenty of time for that later, Quill thought. *It's a start, though. Sure hope his dog makes it—for his sake.*

Sarah had heard Charlie's words as well, but didn't say anything. Instead she asked, "What happened, Dad?"

"That's a good question, sweetheart. I don't think I know. I shot twice at the pheasant . . . then you screamed, and we saw Taffy lying there."

"Dad? Maxine? Either of you see or hear anything?"

Quill replied, "Just Sarah's scream. I didn't hear any other shots, if that's what you mean."

"Me either," Maxine volunteered. "I did hear a few rifle shots earlier, probably someone out hunting deer, but nothing right then."

324

"I suppose it could have been a stray bullet, but most of the hunters around here are pretty careful where they aim. Besides, with all the shooting we were doing, they had to have known we were out there."

"Could she have fallen on something, Charlie?"

"Huh? No, I don't think so. But maybe . . . when she gets in the corn rows I can't always see her."

"Possible, I guess. Maybe she ran into a sharp corn stalk or something. Maybe Curly will have an idea after he looks at her." Cort said.

There was very little conversation after that. Maxine fixed a pitcher of lemonade and everyone but Charlie drank a glass while they waited.

Curly arrived ten minutes later. He didn't bother knocking, just stuck his head in the door and yelled, "Hey! Where is everyone?"

"In the kitchen, Curly," Maxine replied.

The old blacksmith entered the kitchen. He was carrying a black satchel that appeared to be heavy, for he tilted to one side as he walked. He went directly to Charlie and said, "Scooch over, young fella. Let's have a look at your friend."

With some effort, he knelt down and then put on a pair of reading glasses. He pulled back the blood-soaked shirt and inspected the wound. "Roll her over, son . . . gently."

Charlie did as he was told. Curly ran his eight fingers over her body and stopped. "Another wound right here, behind her shoulder. Whatever it was, passed clean through. Question is: What'd it hit on the way?" Taffy was whimpering by now—a steady, low, mewing sound.

Charlie had a hard time breathing. His mouth was dry and his lips were plastered to his teeth. *A second hole!* Saliva collected between his thin lips. "Taffy? It's okay . . . I'm right here. We're going to fix you up, I promise."

Curly looked at Quill. His thick eyebrows bowed and he shook his head.

She was still bleeding—from both the entry and exit wounds, but not as heavily as before. "Don't look like it hit an artery, Charlie. That's good. But I can't tell what kind of damage it did to her innards. Sorry, Boy . . . but that's the truth of the matter."

Curly opened her mouth and inspected her gums. They were pale—almost white. "She's crashing, son. It doesn't look good. Even if I were a surgeon, which I'm not, I couldn't do much for her." He hesitated before continuing.

"Listen to me, Charlie! Whatever hit her could have struck any number of vital organs—intestine, liver, stomach, kidney—and if it did, she's in serious trouble."

The old man reached over for his bag. He removed a package of gauze and dabbed at both wounds. "Looks to me like it was a twenty-two . . . maybe a rock chip. Any of you folks carry a twenty-two today?"

"Just shotguns, Curly . . . and all our shots were in the air." Cort replied.

"Don't matter, I guess. Probably some kid out plinkin' varmints, and if so, he'll never own up to it." He glanced at Quill. "She's sufferin', Quillan."

He took a deep breath, and laid a large hand on Charlie's shoulder. "Son? This is one of those real bad moments in life when a decision has to be made."

Charlie's eyes bulged. He slowly moved his head from one adult to the other. He settled on Maxine.

Her eyes were wet, and she ran to the boy and hugged him tightly. "I'm so sorry, Charlie."

He barely heard her words. All his thoughts were on Taffy. *She's the best dog in the whole world. I love her so much . . .*

"Quill? Why don't you, me, and Charlie go out on the porch?" Curly volunteered.

Curly stood up and picked up his bag. He reached down and with great difficulty, pried Charlie loose from his dog. "Come on, son. Sarah there can watch Taffy for you."

Quill followed both out to the porch. The two old men sat and faced Charlie.

"Do you know what I think we should do, Charlie? What I think is best for your dog?" Curly looked at Quill for support.

"Charlie? Look at me. Do you trust me?" Quill asked.

Charlie raised his head. His eyes were glazed; his mind, numb. He barely managed a weak, "Yes . . ."

"Then you know that I wouldn't want you to do anything that wasn't right, don't you?"

Charlie realized what they were telling him he ought to do. He saw red! What did they want to do to his best friend—his dog, Taffy? "No, Quill! NO!" He screamed.

"She's in pain, son, and it isn't right for her to suffer like that." Curly added.

"NO! Please! We can make her better, Quill! We have to try! Please!"

"Charlie, listen to me. Curly has seen lots of injured animals over the years and he knows what he's talking about. Taffy won't recover, son. We . . . we have to put her down . . . and soon. Let's not let her suffer any longer. . . . Remember what you told me about the crippled teal, Charlie? How you hated to see it suffer?"

Before Charlie could reply, he heard Sarah's shrill voice from the kitchen, "DADDY?"

Cort appeared in the doorway and stepped out on to the porch. He didn't say anything—he didn't have to.

Charlie glanced in his direction, puzzled by Sarah's shout. Then he spotted the rifle in Cort's right hand—hanging against his leg. The boy's mouth opened—a strangled, bubbling sound came from his lips. Finally, he managed to shout, "NOOOO! YOU CAN'T!"

Thirty-Three

CHARLIE BOLTED PAST CORT and ran back to the kitchen. He was fully alert now. He slid across the linoleum and put both arms around his dog. "I won't let them . . . you're going to be fine, aren't you girl!" The three men returned to the kitchen.

Charlie blurted out, "I . . . I remember when she was a puppy . . . she cut her lip real bad. She was bleeding a lot, and the vet sewed her up. Can't you sew her up, Curly?"

"If that's your decision, yes, I can." He didn't sound convincing, however. Curly opened his bag, withdrew a brown package and laid it on the floor. "Look, son, she's bleeding inside. This will stop the blood from oozing out, but won't fix what's goin' on in her guts. Are you certain this is what you want?"

"Yes, I am!"

"And if she's bleeding inside? Curly? What happens to the blood?" Maxine asked.

"If she lives, it might eventually all be absorbed into her system. But, if, as I suspect, some vital organ has been ruptured . . ." He looked at the boy. "She'll still likely bleed to death." He waited for Charlie's reaction.

"Please, Curly? We have to try!" Charlie pleaded.

He nodded and said, "If this is what you want, then I'll stitch her up for you."

Charlie's heart skipped. He wiped his eyes and asked, "Will it hurt?"

"Not much. I doubt she'll feel it." He unwrapped the brown folder, revealing a series of surgical instruments. Curly used a sharp pair of scissors to remove the hair around both wounds. Then he fingered a curved needle and what looked to Charlie like a pair of narrow, hook-nosed pliers.

"Hold her head steady so she doesn't jerk." Curly began stitching the wounds. Each one only required six stitches to close. He snipped off the loose threads and replaced the instruments.

Curly closed the bag and stood, arching his back. "That's all I can do for her, son. Maxine, do you have an eye-dropper? Or turkey baster?"

"Yes."

"Charlie, fill the dropper with a little sugar water and every hour or so, put a few drops on the back of her tongue. She'll likely dehydrate, but that's the least of her problems. Good luck, son. I'll call in the morning."

"Thank you," Charlie said. His voice was barely audible.

"You're welcome. Quill? Can I talk to you a minute?"

The two old men walked back out to the porch. When they were alone, Curly said, "'Course you know that puttin' them stitches in's about as useful as making beds in a burning house, don't ya?"

"I know."

"If she makes it through the night, she's got a chance—a slim one. It'll be a miracle, though."

"Yes. But it's his dog. We can't just take her out and shoot her, so it's his call."

"Kids and women—their hearts are bigger 'n their brains sometimes."

"I know. Tell me, is there a chance the bullet could have hit something that wouldn't be fatal?"

"Slim . . . but I suppose . . ." Curly rubbed his stubbly chin, thinking. "You know, come to think of it, the spleen is down there. If it hit that and nothing else . . ." He scratched his head now. "Possible, I guess. If so, spleen don't do nothin' anyway. It'll bleed plenty, but if she don't bleed out before all's said and done, the blood would reabsorb into her system."

"Well, there's hope then, right?"

"Not much, I'm afraid. I'd say the odds are about one in twenty, Quill. If it is the spleen, though, then everything we're seeing now would look just like a fatal shot. Can't say more 'n that—not being a surgeon an all."

"Well, thanks for all your help, old friend." Quill patted Curly on the shoulder.

"Anytime, Quillan. Gotta go now. Who knows what blamed fool robbed me blind while I was futzin' out here today . . . forgot to lock up."

Quill smiled and watched him stump down the porch steps. He would miss his old friend. Quill noticed that clouds were building in the west and the wind had picked up. "Looks like a change in the weather, Curly."

The old man paused before getting into his truck. "Yep! 'Bout time, too. Radio said it's gonna cool off over the next few days. Front movin' in. Wouldn't be surprised to see some rain in a couple days—or snow, maybe." He climbed into the truck, waved and drove off.

Quill closed the door and went back inside. It had been a long day—especially the afternoon—and he was tired.

Once he had returned to the kitchen, he said, "If you folks don't mind, I think I'll go lie down for a while. You be all right, Charlie?"

The boy didn't hear at first, then he slowly turned his head and replied, "Yes. I'm gonna stay here with Taffy."

Cort stood and said, "Sarah? I'll take care of the calves tonight if you want to stay with Charlie."

"Thanks, Dad."

"I'll get supper ready," Maxine offered. "Quill? You need anything?"

"Nope . . . Oh, Cort! I was going to help you clean the birds . . ."

"Don't worry about it, Dad. Only takes a couple of minutes for each one. You go lie down." He nudged his father out of the kitchen and left the house.

Charlie and Sarah sat with Taffy for another two hours. They chatted only briefly . . . neither one wanted to discuss what her chances for recovery really were.

Charlie silently beat himself up for putting his companion in harm's way. *If he'd only left her at home—or stayed home myself—she wouldn't be injured.*

He prayed harder than he ever had in his whole life. *God, I promise that if Taffy gets better, I'll find a way to get home and learn to live with Dad . . . and, and, I will go to church every Sunday, and say my prayers, and, and . . . please, please?*

Praying only seemed to make him feel worse—guiltier, if that was possible. He was certain that he had never felt so frightened, so unhappy in his entire life.

"Charlie?"

"Huh?"

"I'm praying for Taffy."

"Thanks, Sarah. Me too. She doesn't look too good, does she?"

"No, but you know what?"

"What?"

"Shelly looked a whole lot worse. She was all torn up and bleeding everywhere. Taffy just looks like she's resting. I'll bet she's mostly tired from hunting and after a good night's sleep, she'll be lots better."

"Maybe . . ."

"She did great, didn't she?"

"Yep! Your dad said he'd never seen a young dog do as well."

Cort returned. He washed up and said, "Dad still upstairs?"

"Yes. Do you want to go get him while I set the table?" Maxine replied.

"Okay." When he entered Quill's room, he noticed his father was still asleep—at least he thought he was. As he turned to leave, he heard a groan.

"Dad?" He rushed back and leaned over the bed. He reached out and laid a hand on his father's chest. "Dad? You okay?"

Quill didn't respond. His eyes remained closed. Another groan rose from his throat.

"What can I do? What do you need?" Cort's face was etched with concern.

"Pills . . . on table . . ." Quill mumbled.

Cort opened the bottle and shook out two white pills. He went to the bathroom to get a glass of water. "Here, Dad."

Quill opened his eyes—they were red and streaked with thin white and blue lines. "Hurts pretty bad, son." He tried to lift himself up but failed.

"Here. Let me help." Cort lifted his father's head, put the pills on his tongue, and let him sip from the glass.

Quill's head fell back to the pillow. He gritted his teeth as the pain in his gut struck again. After a minute, he said, "I'll be all right, now. Don't think I can eat right this instant, though. Think I'll just lie here for a while. How's Charlie?"

"I don't know. Pretty torn up by all this, I think. Sarah's been with him. Neither of them has moved. Dog's still breathing, but I still think we should have put her down. It's going to go hard on him if she dies during the night."

"I know. You and I would have done it, but Charlie's only eleven." The pills took effect and the pain lessened. "You hear him talk about 'home'?"

"I did. Think he's ready to open up?"

"Maybe. Probably depends on what happens to the dog, I'd bet. If she dies, more than likely he'll clam up like a barn door in a strong wind."

"Either way, Dad . . . uh, the kids have to be told about you're . . . you know." Cort could feel his eyes fill—he needed to stay strong, but as the end drew near, he was losing control.

Quill patted his arm. "Don't, Cort. It's going to be all right—honest. I told you that having seen Sarah, and having this brief time with you has made everything worth while. We all would like to go back and change the past, but that's just not possible. I'm at peace, son. And I want you to be as well."

Cort sucked in a big chunk of air, wiped his eyes, and said. "Maybe you'll feel like eating later?"

"We'll see. Go down and be with your family. I'm all right."

"Okay." Cort stood and left the bedroom.

After he left, Quill again was smacked with pain, and he rolled over and faced the wall. The pills were losing their effect. He buried his face in the pillow and groaned.

WITH GREAT RELUCTANCE, Charlie left Taffy's side long enough to eat supper with the Purdues. He had little appetite and finished before the rest of the family. Conversation was minimal—centered for the most part on where the stray bullet came from—if indeed it was a bullet.

"No other explanation, Maxine. After supper, I'm going to drive around and talk to some of the neighbors—see if anyone was out hunting today, or one of the kids took out a twenty-two."

"That's a good idea, Cort. It almost had to be someone from around here."

"Sarah? Do you want to come with me?"

She glanced at Charlie and realized that he was preoccupied. She decided to join her father. "Okay."

"Good, let's get going then. We shouldn't be gone for more than an hour or so, Maxine."

Cort and Sarah left and Charlie took that as his opportunity to go back to the kitchen.

Taffy appeared much the same as she had after Curly left. Her breathing had evened out, but her eyes remained closed, and other than an occasional whimper, she didn't move.

Charlie opened her mouth and squirted water from the eye dropper on the back of her tongue. Her gums were still pale.

Maxine came over and knelt beside the boy and his dog. She felt Taffy's stomach. "Seems to be a build-up of fluid—Curly said there would be."

"Is that blood?" Charlie voice rose.

"Yes. But, we can hope that it was only the spleen that was damaged, remember? If so, then all this blood will get re-absorbed just like Curly said."

Charlie was trying his best to remain optimistic, but he had an overriding fear that because he had been living a lie with the Purdues—because he had chosen not to tell them the truth about his background—he and his dog were being punished.

Quill entered the kitchen. "How's she doing?"

"Oh, hi, Quill. About the same, I guess. You hungry?"

"I could eat a little something, Maxine. I'm feeling a mite better now."

Maxine rose and went to prepare a plate of food.

Charlie couldn't remain silent for another second. He had to speak out. "Quill . . . Maxine . . . I have to tell you something."

Maxine set Quill's plate down and knelt beside the boy. "What is it, Charlie?"

He stroked Taffy's soft cheek, stood, and sat at the table. Maxine sat down next to Quill.

Charlie looked into both pairs of eyes in turn, and with great difficulty said, "Quill, you remember the word you asked me to look up a week ago? Veracity?"

"Yes I do."

"Well, I know what it means. It means 'truth—honesty.' I thought for a long time how to use it in a sentence . . . just like all the other words we look up, but I couldn't. I think I know why—because it made me feel so bad." His lower lip quivered, and his small, blue eyes misted.

"Go on, son," Quill encouraged.

"I think that because I haven't been honest with you that . . . that God is punishing me now. He knows how much Taffy means to me, and . . ." He couldn't finish.

Maxine rose to go to him, but Quill put out his arm, holding her back.

After what seemed like minutes, Charlie continued in a very low voice. "I didn't run away from an orphanage. I ran away from home." Once he said the words, he immediately felt better.

"Oh, Charlie! What could have been so horrible at home?" Maxine asked.

"My dad. My dad drinks . . . all the time, and, and . . . well, he went to jail, and it was my fault." Once the words came out, he was glad. "He hates me now, and I just thought it was better if I left. He'll never stop drinking, and I guess I couldn't stand being around him any more." He stared at Quill.

"Let's clear something up before we go any farther here, son. About God—He doesn't work that way at all. God doesn't punish people for their mistakes or choices . . . He's always around for us—in good times and bad. Didn't you know that?"

"That's right, Charlie," Maxine added. "We should all try to tell the truth just because it feels better to do so—not because we are afraid of some kind of penalty or retribution from God. That's what makes him our God—because he loves us and cares about us, no matter what."

Quill observed the boy's reaction and decided they had to proceed slowly. His heart was filled with gratitude that his small friend decided to finally come clean—that he didn't have to pull the truth from him before it was too late. *One less obstacle to deal with*, he thought. *If I can just hold on a while longer, maybe we can get him back home and he won't have to deal with any more sorrow.*

"Think I'll eat while we talk," Quill said. He cut a slice of meat and stuck it in his mouth.

"You're not mad at me?" Charlie asked.

"No? Why would I be?" Quill chewed the meat and swallowed with some difficulty. "Besides, I knew you weren't from an orphanage."

"You did? How?"

"Well, for starters, I think I told you that I couldn't imagine any home for children that would allow pets. Secondly, you didn't look, act, or speak like a child raised in an institution. And third? Taffy's name tag."

Charlie eyes opened their widest—as did his mouth. "You mean you all knew? Cort? And Sarah? And you, Maxine?"

"Yes, Charlie. We knew—at least we were pretty sure. It wasn't until Quill—" Maxine halted.

"Uh, I have a confession to make Charlie."

"What's that?" the boy asked.

"I went through your bag—more than once—looking for something that would indicate where you were from. I finally found Taffy's tag a short while ago. I'm sorry for snooping, but we felt your parents would be worried sick over your disappearance."

"But still . . . in all this time . . . you didn't say anything . . ."

"We thought you'd tell us when you were ready." Maxine said. "And you did."

Charlie couldn't believe that the entire family had remained silent. He realized that they probably were aware of even more. "Then . . . if you know where I live, then—"

Quill took another bite and chewed for a bit. "Yes, and as long as we are dealing with veracity here, I have to tell you that I've spoken to your mother." Quill waited for the boy's reaction.

"You have? What did you tell her?"

"I wanted to be sure she didn't worry about you any more than she had to. I told her you were with me—with my family—and I'd take good care of you until you were ready to return."

"Was she . . . is she, okay?"

"I think so, but she misses you terribly—so does your father, from what I can gather."

"Dad? He's in jail."

"Nope. He got out because of your leaving. Something to do with a suspended sentence until sometime later. He's just waiting for me to call and tell him to come pick you up."

Charlie's eyes clouded, and he lowered his head. "I can't go back, Quill. You don't know what he's like."

"Maybe you should tell us, then. You sure had your own good reasons for leaving, but maybe if you talk about it, Maxine and I—and Cort, and even Sarah—can help."

Charlie looked doubtful. He nibbled his lip and looked down at Taffy.

Just as Charlie was about to reply, they heard a knock at the front door.

"I'll go see who that is," Maxine said. It was getting dark now, and she glanced at the clock. "Awfully late for visitors. Cort and Sarah should have been back by now." She left the kitchen.

Quill continued to eat. Both he and Charlie could hear snatches of the conversation coming from the front hall.

"Oh, hello, Reverend . . ."

"Make it a point . . . visit members . . . parish . . ."

"How nice . . ."

"Is this . . . good time . . . ?"

"Unfortunately . . . Cort . . . Sarah . . . not here . . . and . . . guests."

"Oh, is everything . . . ?"

"Yes . . . an accident today . . . dog has . . . injured . . ."

"I see . . . perhaps another . . ."

"Yes. That would be . . ."

"Next day . . . or so?"

"Fine. Maybe . . . call first . . . be sure . . . home."

"Of course. Good evening . . . Purdue."

They heard the door shut and Maxine returned to the kitchen. "What an odd man he is."

"That the new preacher?" Quill asked.

"Yes. Sounds like he plans to stay awhile. He's trying to make personal calls on all the parishioners. Kept looking over my shoulder . . ." Maxine shuddered as if a cold wind blew against the back of her neck. "Sure hope Reverend Stevens returns soon."

Maxine sat down. Charlie had just begun to tell them his story when they heard the front door open again—then shut.

"What in the world?" Maxine stood, but before she could move, footsteps sounded from just outside of the kitchen.

337

Thirty-Four

H E'S CREEPY!"

"I know. He's different than Reverend Stevens, but let's hope he won't be around very long." Cort said.

Father and daughter entered the kitchen. Sarah hurried over and knelt next to Taffy. "How is she? Any better?"

"Don't think so," Charlie replied.

"I gather you ran into Reverend Douglas?" Maxine asked.

Cort removed his coat and hung it in the back hall. "Yeah. Said he was making the rounds so he could get to know the congregation." Cort twirled his finger near the side of his head.

Maxine smiled and nodded. "Yes, I agree."

"About what?" Sarah inquired.

"Nothing. Say, is there any of that apple pie left?" Cort moved to his father's side and laid a hand on his shoulder. "Feeling better?"

"A bit . . . thanks, Cort. Piece of pie might hit the spot, Maxine."

"You bet. Charlie? Sarah?"

"No thanks," both kids replied in unison.

"So, what did the neighbors say?"

"None of them were out today, Dad. Must have been strangers, I guess. Think I'll take one of the horses out in the morning and ride around the area—see what I find." Maxine set a plate in front of her husband who was seated by now. "Thanks, honey."

Charlie remained silent—unsure whether of not he should continue. He caught Cort's eye and said, "Uh, Cort . . . I have something to tell you."

Cort swallowed, wiped his mouth, and said, "Go ahead, Charlie."

"I haven't been, uh—truthful with you. I mean about—uh—where I came from."

Cort looked at Quill, then Maxine. Both nodded. "I see. And you've decided that you need to what? Get it off your chest?"

"Yes. I didn't come from an orphanage. I ran away from home."

Sarah's eyes widened knowingly. She leaned forward to look at Charlie, who had moved down to the floor near her and Taffy. "Charlie? You have a mom and dad . . . and a house, and everything?"

"Uh, huh." He quickly repeated everything for Cort and Sarah.

"Charlie, thank you for being so forthright with us. That took a great deal of courage to admit the truth," Cort stated.

No one spoke. The Purdues didn't press the boy for more information, even though they all wanted to.

"Charlie? Look, son," Quill said. "You don't have to tell us any more if you don't want to."

"No . . . that's okay. I think I want to. You've all been so nice . . . it feels like I should tell you what happened . . ."

FOR THE NEXT HOUR and a half, Charlie told the Purdues everything—starting with the car accident. He left nothing out and did his best to convey how frightened he was when he and his father ran into the car. The shooting incident left them all wide-eyed and amazed.

When Charlie was finished, he sat back and closed his eyes. *There. It's out. I'm glad I told them. Now I don't have to lie anymore.* He waited for someone to speak.

Maxine left the table and went to Charlie's side. She cradled his head in her arms and said, "You've been through a living nightmare, Charlie. No boy your age should have to deal with all of that. I, for one, don't blame you for leaving home."

"Maxine's right. Near as I can tell, your father chased you away . . ." Cort immediately realized what he had just said and looked toward his father. He continued, "Understand this, though, Charlie. Your father did not intentionally set out to hurt you. He's . . . well, he's sick. He's one of those people who can't drink. He just hasn't figured that out yet."

Quill joined in. "Cort's right, son. I daresay that he probably feels pretty bad right now about what happened. He knows why you left—even if you never told him or your mother. None of us ever sets out to hurt the people we love, Charlie. Sometimes things just happen. If you remember, I told you that I left home because Cort and I couldn't talk to each other anymore. And . . . and because of that, we lost ten years together that we can't get back—ever."

Charlie watched and listened. "You think I should go home, don't you?"

"That's up to you. Just like it was your decision to leave. Just like it was your decision to tell us the truth." Quill's response hung in the room like a spider dangling from its web.

"Charlie, you don't have to decide anything tonight," Maxine offered. "You can stay here as long as you like. You'll know when it's time to call your parents. In the meantime, you're always welcome here. I think you know that."

"Yeah. It's fun having you here. Taffy has to get better, anyway." Sarah offered.

Cort said, "Tell you what . . . it's been a long, tiring day. Let's get to bed. Plenty of time to figure out what to do tomorrow—or the next day."

"That's a good idea. I'd like to go upstairs, now. Charlie, will you help me?" Quill asked.

"Sure," Charlie said. He stood and helped the old man out of his chair. He held his arm, and together they left the kitchen.

"Good night, all," Quill called over his shoulder.

"Night, Grandpa." Sarah ran to give him a hug and a kiss.

Once they were in their bedroom, Charlie helped Quill to his bed. He watched as his friend sat down and lay back. A grimace crossed his face.

"You okay, Quill?" Charlie had a worried expression on his young face.

"Yes. I wanted to explain something to you in private, though."

Charlie sat on the edge of Quill's bed. He waited for the old man to continue.

"People react differently to liquor, Charlie. Some just can't handle it—no matter what. I don't know your dad, but I bet he's a decent man— otherwise you wouldn't have turned out to be the great young man you are." He watched the boy's reaction.

"Yeah, but if drinking makes him so . . . so, mean and stuff, why doesn't he just stop?"

"He can't. Something happens with some people—can't rightly explain it any better than that. Listen. People drink for different reasons— some 'cause it tastes good, others 'cause they like how it makes them feel. Others? Well, lots of folks drink to hide some sort of pain. I suspect that's your father's case—but I don't really know."

"What kind of pain, Quill?"

"Oh, I don't know. Maybe someone died—maybe he doesn't like the way his life is going . . . his job, or marriage. Could be just about anything."

He paused to catch his breath and continued. "After Justin died, I started to drink too much, too. Used to spend most of my time at the Red Horse in Blue Springs."

Charlie couldn't believe what he was hearing. *Not Quill!*

"Cort wouldn't talk to me, and I couldn't deal with the pain of losing Justin. So, I drank to forget. By the time I left home, I was pretty far gone, Charlie."

"What happened? I mean . . . why, when . . . ?"

"I'm not proud of this, son, but just like your dad, I got in some trouble down in Oklahoma." The memory hurt. Purdue didn't want to continue—but he knew he had to.

"I wound up in jail—for three months."

"You did?"

"Yep! Most humiliating experience of my life, too. When I got out, I said, 'No more booze.'"

Charlie studied his friend's face and said, "Then maybe my dad . . . ?"

"You think about that. Don't be so hard on him, son. Just remember what happened to Cort and me. All right? Don't let that happen to you. I'm going to get some sleep, now. Hand me those pills?"

Charlie opened the bottle and Quill took two. Charlie helped him with the glass of water.

"Thanks, Charlie. By the way, I'm very proud of the way you handled yourself today?"

"What do you mean?"

"Oh, not every young man would have owned up to what you did—about killing critters, and all. You have a big heart, son. Now, get some rest, okay? I'll pray for Taffy before I go to sleep."

"Thanks, Quill. I will too." Charlie left the room and went back down to the kitchen.

Maxine had just finished cleaning up. "Charlie? Do you want to stay down here tonight with Taffy?"

"Yes, if that's okay?"

"Certainly. I'll get a blanket and pillow for you. Be right back."

Charlie filled the eye dropper and dispensed the fluid once again. Taffy's eyes were still closed, and she wasn't moving. The whimpers he heard earlier that evening had stopped. He felt her belly and thought it seemed swollen, but he wasn't sure. *You have to get better, Taff . . . You just have to!*

"Here you go, honey. Let us know if, well . . . don't be afraid to wake us up if you need anything."

"Okay. Thanks, Maxine . . . for everything. You and Cort and Sarah have been great to me and Taffy. I'm sorry about lying to you and all that." Charlie's voice shook.

"No need to apologize. We've loved having you here—you know that. I just keep trying to put myself in your mother's place, though, Charlie.

She's probably terribly worried. I'm just glad Quill's called her so she knows you're all right."

"I'll call her as soon . . . as soon as Taffy . . . you know . . ."

She stroked his head. Her eyes glistened. "Get some sleep. I'll see you in the morning."

"Good night." Charlie lay down next to his dog and pulled the blanket over his lower torso. He turned so he could look directly into Taffy's face.

A single light remained on over the sink. Charlie stared at his dog for a long time. He prayed for her recovery and listened to the sound of a rising wind as it blew against the old farm house. After thirty minutes, he finally fell asleep.

Taffy hovered between life and death for the balance of the night. Charlie woke more than once from bad dreams, and saw that that there was no change in the dog. If anything—maybe due to the poor light—she looked worse.

Maxine came downstairs twice during the night to check on the boy. Each time she entered the kitchen she found him asleep—the blanket lay crumpled next to him as if he was having a restless night. She covered him up, patted the dog and whispered, "Get well, dear Taffy. Charlie is going to need you by his side . . ."

In the morning, Sarah was the first family member downstairs. She came into the kitchen and sat next to Charlie. She looked into his face for a long time without speaking.

As if sensing her presence, Charlie woke with a start. "Huh? What's the matter?"

"Nothing. It's me."

Charlie rubbed his eyes and checked on his dog. "She looks the same, Sarah."

"Yes, but that's good, Charlie. Curly said if she made it through the night she'd have a good chance, didn't he?"

"Yeah. I better give her some water." He filled the eye dropper from a small bowl and opened her mouth. He stared at her gums. "Look, Sarah! They look kinda pink, don't they?"

She pressed her head against his and eyed the dog's gums. "Oh, yes! They really do! She is going to get better, Charlie, I just know it. I prayed for her really hard, and God is going to help her get better."

Maxine entered. She wrapped the sash on her blue robe and said, "Any change?"

"We think so. Her gums have more color," Charlie said.

Maxine knelt for a close look. She wasn't certain this was true, but said, "Oh, I think you're right. Good!" She stood and began preparing breakfast.

"I'm going to go tell Quill!" Charlie said.

"I'll go with you," Sarah volunteered.

"Uh, maybe we should let him sleep awhile." Maxine had checked on Quill before coming downstairs, and he didn't appear to have done very well during the night. His face looked pained and drawn—as if he were losing his strength.

"Why don't you two go take care of the calves? I'll keep an eye on Taffy for you."

"Charlie?" Sarah looked at him and waited.

"Okay. Let's go." Both left through the back door. The sun was barely up and hung just below a heavy layer of slate-gray clouds. Everything in the farm yard had an orange and purple cast to it.

"Look at that sun rise, Sarah." Charlie said as they started out.

Sarah faced east and said, "Dad always says, 'When the sky's red in the morning, farmers take warning.'"

"Like it's going to rain or something?"

"Or something, I guess . . . It's getting colder, too. Let's hurry."

The two kids raced to the barn and threw open the door. Sarah said, "Listen!"

They both turned and faced the driveway. A door had slammed and they heard a car starting up.

"Who's that?" Charlie asked.

Sarah looked puzzled. It was unusual to hear cars anywhere near the farm with the half-mile driveway to the road. "I don't know. Come on!"

They ducked inside the barn and closed the door.

Thirty-Five

LABETTE'S FRUSTRATION MOUNTED with each passing hour. Ever since he arrived in the Blue Springs area, his plan had been thwarted in one form or another.

It had been difficult enough trying to blend in with the rural environment without drawing attention to himself. Every time he tried to get close to the Purdue farm, something or someone interrupted his plan.

First it was all the damn neighbors stopping to pick apples! The produce truck appeared daily, but never at the same time. Then the old guy from Blue Springs popped in and out, and the girl was going back to school. *Need to have all of them together if I'm going to do this right . . .* Now he worried about an approaching storm. Radio said lots of rain for the next forty-eight hours.

He was watching the house from a hidden spot along the drive when the two kids came out and ran to the barn. He knew the girl would probably be going to school soon, so he ran down to his car and backed down the driveway. He was going to have to force his way into the house and that concerned him. *Somehow, I've got to go in when everyone's at home. No loose ends, Joseph. Patience.*

He turned east toward Blue Springs. As he approached town, an old pick-up passed and slowed. The driver waved. LaBette ignored the friendly greeting—he was preoccupied.

They that wait upon the Lord shall renew their strength: they shall mount up with wings as eagles: they shall run, and not be weary; and they shall walk and not faint.

THE KIDS FINISHED SARAH'S chores in twenty minutes. As they closed the barn doors, the sun had disappeared—swallowed by a thick bank of clouds. Both cast glances down the driveway but saw nothing as they ran back to the house.

"Smells like rain, Charlie!"

By the time they came into the kitchen, Sarah's father had already begun eating breakfast. "Good morning! You two are up and about early."

"We think Taffy's better, Dad."

"That's great! I think that if she makes it through the day, that she'll be just fine."

"You really think so, Cort?" Charlie asked.

"Yep! Seen it in cows more than once. Animals have this strange ability to heal themselves that we humans don't have. Can't explain it, exactly, but I know it happens."

Charlie was encouraged, and, for the first time since Taffy was shot, he felt stirrings of real hope. He sat down to breakfast.

"I've been thinking of something you said last night, Charlie—about that guy who grabbed you."

At that moment, Quill shuffled in. "Good morning, all."

"Quill! I think Taffy's going to make it! Look, she's breathing easier and I think she tried to open her eyes!"

"Oh, Charlie! I'm so glad. Let me have a look-see." He came close and knelt down. After lifting one eyelid and checking her gums, he said, "Yep! I do believe she's doing better. Boy, that makes me feel good." He stood with some difficulty, wavered just a bit until he caught his balance and sat down.

"You okay, Dad?"

346

"Yeah . . . feel kinda queezy's all." He wanted to divert the family's attention. "What was it you asked Charlie when I came in?"

"Oh! I had been thinking about the guy who nabbed him—wondered about whether or not Charlie had seen him before."

"Kinda noodled about that myself, but forgot about it with everything else that was going on. Charlie?"

Charlie was eating but stopped chewing mid-bite. He considered the question for a bit, swallowed, and said, "No. I don't think I ever saw him before."

"Well, it's almost as if he was waiting for you or something . . . that business about, 'using you for bait.' What do you suppose he meant by that?"

"I don't know . . . never had much chance to think about it, I guess."

"He didn't look familiar?"

"No, not really."

"What'd he look like?"

Quill interceded with, "Like his face was on backwards."

They all laughed, and Cort continued his questioning. "How about his car—seen that before?"

Charlie thought long and hard, remembering the old, blue coup. He set his fork down and took a drink of milk. "Maybe . . . I don't know. It was a Packard, I think."

"Yep, it was a Packard, all right," Quill volunteered.

"What about the car your dad ran into? What was that?" Cort was reaching and knew it, but his curiosity wouldn't allow him to leave it alone. Something didn't add up.

"It was dark . . . and it all happened pretty fast." He closed his eyes and tried hard to remember the other car that night.

"Did the guy say anything to you, Dad?"

Quill considered Cort's question and replied, "No, I don't think so. I was kinda anxious to get Charlie out of there, so I had him undress and jump in an old stock tank. I pitched his keys, pulled the distributor cap and chucked that, too. Then we took off."

"Hmmm. Very strange."

They all heard the front door open and a voice call out, "Anyone home?"

"In the kitchen, Curly," Maxine replied.

Curly sauntered in. "Morning, All. Had to deliver a truck part to Johnson down the road so I figured I'd stop and check on our patient. How's she doing?" Curly knelt next to Taffy.

"Doing better, we think," Cort said.

After a thorough inspection replicating Quill's, Curly said, "I'll be damned. Color looks good . . . even saw a bit of a glint in her eye. Looks like you musta prayed pretty hard last night, son." Curly smiled showing a few teeth.

"I did. You think she's gonna make it?" Charlie's voice rose with hope.

"Think so. Like I said, if she made it through the night her chances would be lots better. Whatever it was that hit her must of nicked the spleen and nothin' else. Amazin'! She'll probably wake up pretty soon and be mighty thirsty, but I'd go easy on the water, son. Soon as she's standing on her own, give her something to eat and git her outside for a spell." Curly rose to leave.

"Thanks, Curly—for everything!" Charlie said.

"You're welcome, Charlie, but I've a hunch that the Almighty had a hand in this and had more to do with her hanging on than me. Gotta go. Big storm coming later today."

Curly stepped close to Quill, patted him on the shoulder, and said, "Look a bit under the weather yourself there, Quillan." A concerned frown creased his forehead.

"Had a rough night, Curly. Say hi to Maggie for me, will you?"

"You bet. See ya all later." Curly left the kitchen. The front door slammed shut as a gust of wind blew across the yard.

"Something to eat, Quill?" Maxine asked.

"Maybe just some toast and jam, Maxine. Thanks."

Maxine checked the clock on the wall and said, "Sarah? You better get dressed for school, honey. I'll drive you down to the bus when you're ready."

Sarah gave her mother a woeful look and replied, "Do I have to go, Mom?"

"Yes. You've missed enough school this month. Go on now—hurry up."

Sarah pouted just a bit, then ran upstairs to change.

Charlie finished eating and sat down next to Taffy. As soon as he started stroking her head, he heard a faint, thump! His heart pounded. He watched her tail. Once more, she lifted it a couple of inches before it flopped back to the linoleum.

"Taffy? You awake, girl?" He leaned close to her ear and gave her a kiss.

As soon as he did, she whimpered—then groaned. Her eyes opened and focused on her master. "Look! Her eyes are open! Quill! Cort! Look!"

Everyone smiled. Maxine laid the back of her hand against Taffy's cheek. "Oh, Charlie. I'm so happy for you!"

He was so happy he wanted to shout and jump up and down. *Thank you, God! Thank you! Thank you!* He hugged Taffy and felt his entire body tingle with excitement.

Cort turned on the radio. A station out of Aberdeen was broadcasting storm warnings for eastern South Dakota and western Minnesota. He and Maxine leaned close to the radio.

"*High winds and heavy rain are forecast for today and tomorrow. Stockmen's warnings have been posted. There is the possibility of localized flooding in low-lying areas. Temperatures are expected to drop throughout the day and the rain may turn to sleet or ice by Tuesday morning. Stay tuned for further details.*"

Cort turned the volume down and said, "Well, it looks like the drought's finally over. All this rain's going to create problems, though."

Maxine said, "Wonder how much we'll get?"

"They didn't say, but sounds like quite a bit over the next two days. Sure glad we got all the apples picked."

"What do we have to do?" Maxine asked.

"I'm going to have to ride out and see if any of the cows need to be brought in. If so, we'll have to try and get them into the barn."

"After I get Sarah off to school, I'll go with you. Saddle up Buttercup for me?"

"You bet." Cort threw on a heavy coat, hat, gloves, and left the kitchen.

Sarah reappeared—ready for school.

"Here's your lunch, sweetheart. Don't forget, you have 4-H after school, so I'll pick you up at 5:00, okay?"

Sarah was despondent. She wanted to stay with Charlie and Taffy. "All right."

Charlie reached for Taffy's water bowl, lifted her head and let her dip her tongue in the tepid water. She took a couple of laps and lay back with her eyes closed.

"Bet she sleeps most of the morning, Charlie," Quill volunteered.

Charlie patted Taffy's head and stood up. "Maybe I'll ride down to the bus with you, Sarah."

"Yeah! You can wave at my friends. Let's go."

She ran to Quill, threw her arms around him and gave him a kiss on the cheek.

"Bye, sweetheart. Have a good day." He barely managed to get the words out as the true significance of the day struck him like a sock in the jaw. *Now that Charlie had finally opened up and revealed everything, I have to call his parents. It's time for him to go home.* He watched both leave. His heart ached for what had been lost—time with his granddaughter.

"Need anything, Quill?" Maxine asked.

"Nope. Probably go back and lie down, though. Don't feel so good, Maxine. Got to make a phone call first, though."

Maxine smiled, knowingly. "Yes, I guess you do." She followed the children out the front door.

Quill picked up the phone and waited for the operator to come on the line. "Long distance, please. A Minneapolis number." He unfolded a scrap of paper from his shirt and gave her the number.

After a long wait, he sat up and said, "Mr. Nash? Quillan Purdue calling. Yes, he's fine. It's time, Mr. Nash. Charlie's ready to go home. I think the sooner you can get here, the better. I'm sorry. Can you repeat that?"

Quill felt a sudden rush of pain in his lower back—pain like nothing he had experienced! He gasped, and the phone slipped through his fingers. *Thunk!* It landed on the counter.

It took every ounce of strength he had to straighten and pick up the receiver. "Mr. Nash? You . . . still there?"

Purdue took a deep breath. "Sorry. I've got to go lie down, but I just wanted to tell you that you have a fine boy in Charlie, but . . . well, I'm sure I'm not telling you something you don't already know, but you've got some fences to mend."

Quill grimaced as another wave of pain shot through his mid-section. "He's got a heart as big as the sun, Mr. Nash, but it's been broken too many times." He listened with great difficulty. "Good. I'm glad to hear that. You've got a tough road ahead of you, but if you're determined, you can lick it! That's wonderful." Quill leaned back and clawed at his back.

"I'll give you directions. Do you have a pencil handy? It's about a six or seven hour drive, I guess. Bad weather coming, but you shouldn't run into it until later in the day. Ready? Once you reach Brown's Valley . . ."

Quill completed the call and hung up the phone. He managed to make it to his bedroom before collapsing. He knew the end was near. The tips of his toes were a faint blue, and the aneurism protruded noticeably as it pulsated with each beat of his heart. The pain in his gut now equaled that in his back. *Couple of days . . . maybe three at the most . . .*

His greatest concern was his inability to hide the pain and obvious ill-health from Charlie and Sarah. *She has to be told, but how do I do that without Charlie finding out?* He hoped he could mask how he really felt long enough for Charlie's dad to arrive. Once the boy was gone, he could break the news to Sarah—a task he dreaded but knew had to be done.

He heard footsteps on the stairs and rolled over to face the wall. He heard Charlie enter and crawl into bed. *Boy has to be exhausted . . . hope he sleeps for a few hours . . .*

Maxine dressed for the change in weather and left the house. She and Cort would spend the balance of the morning checking on the cattle. If need be, they'd toss a rope over any that looked weak, and lead them back to the shelter of the barn.

The house was quiet—except for a strong wind that blew from the West. The shutters on Quill and Charlie's room rattled a steady beat against the wood siding. The old man suffered in silence—sleep eluded him . . . but not the boy. Charlie fell into a deep slumber almost as soon as his blond head hit the pillow.

Quill's ears were ringing from too many pain pills, but he thought he heard the sound of someone pounding on the front door. He tried to lift his head from the pillow to hear better, but couldn't be certain it wasn't just the wind. *Maybe a neighbor stopping by for a visit . . . Either way, not much I can do about it . . .*

LaBette knocked on the Purdues' front door for a full minute. The wind tugged at his hat. He pulled it down and looked around. *Truck's still in the yard. Maybe they're out in one of the barns.* He leaned into the wind and went around to check all the outbuildings.

Too many to keep track of on this job . . . have to start eliminating a few to simplify matters. He returned to the front door and knocked again. Still no answer. He gave up and decided to come back later.

As he climbed into the DeSoto, he had a sudden inspiration. The girl! Once he had her, the rest of the family would do whatever he asked. As a group, he knew they would otherwise be more difficult to control all at once. But if their precious daughter were missing. . . . *And the King said, divide the living child in two, and give half to the one, and half to the other.*

He checked his watch and decided he had plenty of time before school let out. He smiled as he pulled out of the yard. *Be on my way back home tonight, I'll bet.*

Thirty-Six

ORT AND MAXINE MADE two separate trips back from the pasture with four cows in tow. They unsaddled the horses, rubbed them down, gave each a helping of oats, and bedded them down in their generous box stalls. When the cows were locked in the barn in a large pen opposite the orphan calves, they returned to the house.

"Still think that looked like someone was lying there," Cort said as he hung up his coat.

"You've been reading too many of those mystery novels, I think. You're imagining things."

"I don't know, Maxine. That sure wasn't a deer bed we saw up there."

"Okay, then explain to me why someone would intentionally stalk us and then shoot Taffy? Makes no sense."

"I know. Still . . . I wonder if somehow it's connected to Charlie . . . that guy who grabbed him or something."

"Quill left him in a stock tank, Cort. How would he ever find us out here, and why?"

"I don't know, but it bothers me. If someone made me sit naked in a stock tank, I'd be plenty mad. It might motivate me to look for that guy."

"Maybe. Come on. Let's have some dinner. Why don't you check on your dad while I fix us something to eat?"

Cort left and went upstairs. Maxine went over to Taffy. She stroked the top of her head. "How you doing, girl?"

Taffy opened her eyes, spotted Maxine, and wagged her tail. She opened her mouth and licked Maxine's fingers.

"Thirsty? Here. See if you can take a drink." She moved the water dish closer and helped the dog reach it. "Good girl! Let's see what I've got for you to eat."

She went to the ice box, took out a plate of cold chicken, and cut a few small pieces.

Taffy sniffed the morsels, licked for taste, and accepted the food. Maxine watched her eat. "By golly, you're going to be just fine, aren't you?" She stood and cut more of the chicken for dinner.

Cort returned with Charlie. "How's Taffy?" he asked.

"I just gave her some water and a little chicken. I think she's doing great, Charlie. Do you want to try taking her outside for a bit? She's probably got to go to the bathroom."

"Sure. Come on, Taff." He crouched and helped her stand. He stood over her and gently lifted her to her feet. Her knees buckled once, but then she regained her balance. They all watched as she took a few tentative steps. Charlie led her to the back door, and outside.

"Amazing," Cort said. "Never would have guessed that."

"I know. Thank goodness, too. Enough sadness around here as it is."

Charlie and Taffy returned, and she found a new spot beneath Charlie's chair to lie down. She went back to sleep in an instant.

"Be a while before she's back to normal, I think," Cort offered. He studied the boy as he sipped his coffee. He looked thoughtful—concerned. "Something on your mind, Charlie?"

"Uh? Oh, I was just thinking that Quill doesn't seem to be getting any better. I know he's hurting a lot even if he doesn't complain. But you think he should see a doctor or something?" Charlie nibbled his lower lip and glanced from Cort to Maxine.

Cort didn't know how to respond. "I think you should go talk to Quill, son." It was the best he could do.

Charlie had been alarmed by Quill's appearance, but after hearing Cort's words, he trembled. "What . . . ?"

Maxine turned from the stove, wiped her hands, and went to the boy. She put her arm around his shoulders. She had hoped to offer words of consolation, but they wouldn't come. Too distraught to speak, she bent and kissed the top of the boy's head.

The mood in the small kitchen changed quickly. Charlie knew . . . For the first time since he met Quill, he knew. Like a clap of thunder, the reality of his friend's condition rang in his ears. He stood up and shook his head from side to side. His eyes were wide with fright.

He looked to both Purdues for some indication that he was mistaken—that what he heard them say meant something else. But the looks on their faces said it all. "Nooo!"

Charlie ran out of the kitchen and took the stairs two at a time. He tore into the bedroom and knelt next to Quill's bed. The old man wasn't moving. "Quill? Please, Quill . . . wake up?" he whispered.

The old man lay face up. His breathing was shallow—labored. His face was colorless. If he heard the boy's pleas, he didn't respond.

Charlie put both elbows on the bed, folded his hands, and closed his eyes. *Please, God. Not Quill! Please don't let him be sick . . .*

He focused on Quill's eyelids—willing them to open. The boy sat unmoving for over twenty minutes. "Quill? It's me, Charlie," he whispered again. He reached out and touched his hand. Very gently, he stroked the veins as if they would break at his touch.

Quill opened his eyes and fixed on the boy. The old man's lips were parched, but he managed to ask, "Water?"

Charlie ran to the bathroom and returned with a glass. He held it to Quill's lips as he sipped a small amount.

"Thanks, son." He noticed the concern stamped on the boy's face. "What's the matter, Charlie? Taffy okay?" His voice was barely audible.

"Quill? Remember that word, 'veracity'?"

"Yes. What about it?"

"It's your turn, Quill. Please?" Charlie bit his lip as he waited for the old man to reply.

"Oh, Charlie! I'm sorry. I was hoping that you wouldn't . . . I didn't mean any harm, Charlie. I just felt you had been through enough, and . . . well . . ."

"What's the matter with you, Quill?" Charlie's voice quaked with each word.

The old man lifted one hand and covered both of Charlie's. He looked directly into his blue eyes and said, "I'm dying, son."

Quill's words hit the boy like a runaway locomotive. *No! How can that be? Quill was sick, but . . . dying?* It was incomprehensible. Hadn't he just lived through the horror of almost losing his dog? And now this?

"But . . . you said it was ulcers . . ." Tears filled each eye.

"I know. I'm sorry. I was hoping that you wouldn't find out until, well, I just didn't think you needed to deal with this, that's all. Now listen to me, Charlie."

The eleven-year old strained to hear something positive. "What, Quill?" was all he could manage.

"I've known about this for some time. I have what's called an aortic aneurism. It's in my stomach. I'm near the end now, son, and there's nothing that anyone can do."

"Can't they operate or something?" Charlie's voice rose in time with his heartbeat.

Quill stared hard at the boy. Anticipating Charlie's question, he replied, "Out of the question, I'm afraid. Surgery for this condition is highly experimental, very risky, and expensive beyond belief. It's not an option." Before Charlie could protest, Quill put a finger to the boy's lips and continued.

"I'm at peace right now, Charlie. Really." A tender smile formed on his lips. An enduring, gentle look filled his lined face. "Thanks to you, I've been able to spend time with a granddaughter I didn't know I had, and Cort and I have patched things up to the point where our relationship is stronger now than it ever was."

356

"Wha . . . why? What did I do?" The words tumbled out.

"You became our lightening rod. Something you said to Cort made him think about all the time we'd wasted. Somehow, your being here softened his heart and allowed him to unburden his soul . . . and to forgive." He paused to catch his breath.

"Spending these weeks with you made me realize how much I have missed the love of my family—and friends like you. I was all locked up inside, but you helped me open up. Thank you, Charlie—for being my friend."

Charlie refused to give up. His mind was racing—so was his heart. "Quill, I'll bet my dad can find the money for your operation—he knows lots of people." His eyes lightened with hope.

"Oh, Charlie! Thank you for that, but I couldn't let him do it, son. Besides, I was told that there are only a handful of doctors in the country capable of performing such a surgery."

"I don't care. We have to try, Quill! There has to be a way!" He grabbed the old man's hand and squeezed it—hard!

Quill was losing strength and knew he had to convince the boy that there were no viable options. "I want you to understand something, Charlie." He spoke with great difficulty through clenched lips. "My wife died many years ago, Charlie. I think I told you that, didn't I?"

"Yes."

"Do you believe there's a Heaven?"

"Yes." His lip trembled. So did his hands.

"So do I. And I believe my wife, Sarah, is waiting in Heaven for me right now. I want to be with her, son—and that's very comforting to me. I have no regrets about how I've lived my life. I still have to carry the burden of Justin's death with me, but that's tempered by knowing that God gave me a granddaughter. I think this was his way of providing a new start for Cort and Maxine. Another child to love and cherish—to help them over the pain of losing Justin."

"Please don't give up yet, Quill?" Charlie begged.

"Do you remember that little, purple prairie flower I showed you? The bergamot?"

"Yes."

"Well, I'm kinda like that flower—I've had my time in the sun." The old man patted Charlie's cheek and lay back. "I'm tired now, son." He closed his eyes.

Charlie watched Quill's labored breathing. When he was certain that the old man was just resting, he stood and backed away. He sat on the edge of his bed and stared out the window.

It was 2:30 P.M. Large rain drops smacked against the window. He turned and looked at Quill. *There has to be some way to . . . I have to call home . . . have to get Dad to do something. Wait! What could he do? Maybe Mom. She could call someone. But, what will I say? Will she understand? There's no time . . .*

The rain pounded against the house. Charlie struggled to come up with an answer, but there didn't appear to be one.

ONCE THE RAIN BEGAN, Cort left the house to make sure the livestock were all secure and to move the tractor into the shed.

Maxine kept an eye on Taffy and tried to stay busy. Thoughts about Quill's condition kept intruding, and she wondered how Charlie would deal with his friend's death. *And what about Sarah? She'll be devastated . . . she'll never understand. Dear God, if ever we needed your comfort and strength . . .*

She heard the front door open. Male voices. *Who could that be? Curly?*

Cort and a large man she had never seen before came into the kitchen. Taller than her husband, with graying, short-cropped hair, he was dressed in khakis, a brown hunting coat, and a hunting cap. He smiled as Maxine waited for an introduction.

"Honey, this is Charlie's father, Frank. This is my wife, Maxine."

Maxine covered her mouth. "Oh my gosh! Really? How? Who . . . ? I'm sorry, but I'm confused . . ." She reached out and shook his hand.

Frank removed his hat and stepped close. "I'm pleased to meet you, Maxine. Quill called early this morning. I've been on the road all day . . . probably broke every speed limit to get here."

Cort smiled. So did Maxine. "Charlie'll be so surprised. I don't think he knows you were coming."

"Where is he?"

Cort and Maxine exchanged glances. Cort finally said, "Maybe we better have a chat before you see your son. Please, have a seat."

Frank frowned. "Is anything wrong?"

"Oh, no. Charlie's fine . . . it's just, well . . . please, let's sit."

For the first time since entering the kitchen, Frank spotted Taffy asleep beneath the table. "Taffy? That you, girl?" He knelt and ducked low.

At the sound of a familiar voice, Taffy opened her eyes, slowly rose, and crept toward Frank's outstretched hand. She sniffed and licked his palm.

"What happened to her?"

"We don't really know, to be honest with you." Cort went on to explain how she came to be injured.

Frank listened intently. Concern filled his handsome face. "For God's sake! And you don't know where the shot came from?"

"Nope. But she's very lucky to be alive. Curly, our friend who doubles as the vet around here, thinks the bullet or fragment must have passed through her and maybe just nicked her spleen. That's the only way he figures she could have lived through this—that and your son's prayers, I guess."

Frank sat on the chair and said, "I'd really like to see my son."

Cort didn't hesitate. "Did my father tell you anything about his condition?"

"What do you mean?"

"My father's dying. He has only a few days left . . ."

"Oh, no. I'm so sorry. What is it? His heart?"

"No. It's called an aortic aneurism. It's in his stomach."

"Not operable?"

"I'm afraid not—at least not for him. Surgery for this sort of thing is experimental and terribly expensive."

"And, you folks . . . I don't mean to pry, but isn't there some way . . . ?"

"Dad wouldn't hear of it. Besides, even if we mortgaged the farm, it wouldn't be nearly enough."

"How expensive is it?"

"Forty, fifty thousand."

"Good Lord! Does Charlie know?"

"He's with Dad now. I expect he does know."

Frank ran a hand over his head and sighed. "Listen, you folks have been very kind to take Charlie in, but I have to tell you, I really don't know much about what's happened . . . other than he hates me for what I did . . . for my behavior. What did he tell you about why he left?"

Maxine jumped in. "Everything. He finally opened up to all of us. It was very courageous and I'm sure very difficult for him. He's been through a lot . . . and now, to have to deal with Quill's death? Well, he's going to need all the support and love you can give him."

Frank considered what Maxine had said. "Then he probably told you the real reason he left? About my drinking?"

"Yes." Cort said.

"What else?"

The Purdues chose to recap for Frank everything they knew about Charlie's experiences. They didn't leave anything out.

Frank was speechless. He stood and walked to the sink, then turned and leaned against the edge. "I don't know what to say. Sounds to me like I owe your father a great debt of gratitude, Cort. If it weren't for him I hate to think of what might have happened." He tried to comprehend everything he had just heard. "Packard, you say? It was a Packard I hit that night."

Cort and Maxine stared, then exchanged looks. Cort said, "Well, I think that clears up that mystery."

Plenty of time to digest it all later, Frank thought. *Think! What's missing here? I have to do something, but what?*

At that moment, Charlie came downstairs. He had heard voices from the stairs, but refused to believe the familiar sound of . . .

Father and son spotted one another at exactly the same moment. Charlie stood transfixed, as if he were dreaming. "Dad? Dad? How . . . ?"

Frank opened his arms and knelt down. Charlie rushed across the kitchen and crashed into his father. He buried his head against Frank's broad chest.

Anguish filled his father's face as he mumbled, "I'm so sorry, Charlie. Can you ever forgive me?" He held the boy away and looked deeply into his eyes. "Charlie? Charlie?"

"I thought . . . I thought you hated me because of—"

"Never! None of what happened was ever your fault, Slugger. It was me, and only me. Honest. You were never to blame and I need you to believe that." Frank's voice quavered, but his apology was sincere and cleansing.

Once again, the boy leaned against his father.

Taffy rose and came over to be with her master. She nuzzled between the two and rested her head on Charlie's arm.

"Look, Dad. It's Taffy!"

"I know, Slugger. Cort and Maxine told me about her injury. I'm sure glad she's okay."

"She's a fighter, Dad! And you should have seen how great she was hunting!"

"I knew she was a great hunting dog, Slugger. You forget I saw her work at Parker's Lake."

"Yeah, but this was pheasant hunting. Me and Cort and Maxine, and Sarah and Quill . . ." Then he remembered his friend upstairs—dying, and sadness once again filled his heart.

"What's the matter, Charlie?" Frank asked.

"It's Quill, Dad. He's going to die unless he has an operation but it's too expensive and—"

"Whoa. Slow down, Slugger! Cort and Maxine told me about your friend's illness. Sounds to me like we owe him just an awful lot." *That's it! Of course!* "Maybe there's something that we can do . . ."

Charlie's voice rose. "You mean it, Dad? What?"

"Let's go sit down. You folks might want to hear this, as well," Frank said to the Purdues. He turned back to his son. "Let me ask you something, Slugger. You still have those coins Uncle Hedwig gave you, or did you leave them at home?"

"No. They're upstairs in my bag. Why?"

"Well, Aunt Marie called while you were gone. Apparently there's two pennies in that collection Uncle Hed gave you that are worth a lot of money." He quickly told the history of the coins and finished with, "So she sold the remaining nine to the Smithsonian. That means that the only two left in circulation are the two in your collection."

"What? Really?" Charlie paused then as he remembered Wenzel's offer. "Wait! The man in the coin store said he'd give me three hundred dollars—that was all!"

Frank took out a scrap of paper and studied it. "Who said that?"

"The man in the store Uncle Hedwig told me to see."

"Mr. Massimo?" He read from his paper.

"No. He's dead, Dad."

Frank frowned. "Hmmm. Something doesn't add up here . . . Aunt Marie said that a Mr. Massimo called her just last week. Anyway, rest assured, the coins are worth a a lot of money, Slugger." He watched his son's reaction.

Charlie beamed. Then the reality of what he heard struck. "Then maybe we can sell them and—"

"Maybe, but first things first. I have a good friend, an old teammate who's a surgeon at the University of Minnesota Hospital. I need to find out about this operation, and if there's anyone there qualified to perform it." He looked at Cort. "Can I use your phone?"

"Of course. But we couldn't ask you to pay for this . . ."

Frank looked at his son. "Charlie? Any problem with spending part of your fortune—and Marie indicated it would be a fortune—for your friend's operation?"

"No. Please! Call your friend, Dad!"

"Let's find out if it's even possible before we all get our hopes too high." Frank rose and went to the phone. He picked up the receiver.

"It's a party line, Frank." Maxine offered. Her heart seemed to rise and land somewhere in the back of her throat.

"Operator? Yes, I'd like long distance information, please. Minneapolis. University of Minnesota Hospital. Please charge the call to Kenwood-4

4743—a Minneapolis number. Thank you. I'll wait." Frank gave his son a wink of reassurance as he waited.

Charlie observed a side of his father he had seldom seen. He seemed calmer—more confident and in control, somehow, a take-charge kind of man without the rashness alcohol added. It was comforting, and he really wanted to focus on that, but he couldn't. He was too worried about Quill. *What if the doctor wasn't available? What if they were too late? Could they still get Quill to Minneapolis in time?*

The rain had turned to sleet as the temperature dropped. Ice pellets slapped against the kitchen windows which had begun to fog up. Frank heard intermittent static on the line as ice built up on the thin phone line leading from the house. He was having difficulty completing the phone call.

Charlie chewed on his lower lip and stared out the window. *What about the storm? What if they couldn't drive through it . . . ?*

Thirty-Seven

LABETTE PARKED IN FRONT of the small brick schoolhouse just south of Blue Springs at exactly 3:30 P.M. The orange school bus waited directly in front of the DeSoto. The windshield wipers scraped across the cold glass as he waited for the Purdue daughter to appear with the rest of the children.

He had it all worked out. One of many false license plates he carried had been mounted on his car. He didn't worry about being recognized, for, by the time he finished his task, he'd be long gone. By the time anyone connected him to the deed, it would be too late. Like a wisp of wind, he'd swoop in, pick up the prize, and vanish into the storm.

Twenty or more children of various ages ran from the school—ducking against the pelting sleet. They piled onto the bus. The doors closed, and it pulled away. *Where's the girl?* He knew he would recognize her but she hadn't appeared with the others. *Must be staying for some sort of after school event. No problem. He put on his hat and got out of the car.*

364

Frank Nash held the receiver close to his ear. "Bill? Frank Nash? I'm fine. No, we're all right, but I've a huge favor to ask of you. Are you familiar with an abdominal aortic aneurism? Uh huh . . . yes, I understand that, but we were led to believe that some sort of operation can be performed. What's that? Sorry, static on the line. Is this something you've done? No? Who then? Dr. Lillydale. Well, here's why I'm asking . . ."

Frank described Quill's condition and did his best to convey the urgency of the situation. "No, I'm afraid I don't have his medical history. I can get that for you, I think. I'm out west now with the patient—on a ranch near Blue Springs, South Dakota. Yes, we'd have to get him there right away, I understand that. No, I'm well aware of the cost. We have enough to cover it, so that's not a problem. Hang on . . ." He covered the receiver.

"Cort? You know the name and location of Quill's last doctor?"

Maxine opened a drawer and took out a notepad. "Here it is." She handed it to Frank.

"A Doctor Nordstrom. Fairview Clinic, Rock Island, Illinois. Here's the number . . ." He waited. More static. "What? Oh, good. Call and get what you need from them. What else? Okay, I can do that. I'll call you back as soon as I can. Thanks a million, Bill. I won't forget this. I understand. Goodbye."

Frank hung up the phone. "He said he'd contact the only surgeon qualified for such an operation—a Doctor Lillydale. He stressed just how risky and untried the operation is. Said they have to open up the aneurism and insert some sort of tube made of a material called 'Dacron.' It's a fabric of some sort and apparently the only thing the artery will accept without clogging up. Sounds like it replaces a portion of the artery so blood can flow as it should."

"So it's doable?" Cort asked, hopefully.

"Yes, but he cautioned that it would depend on Quill's general health and what his previous doctor has to say. Dr. Lillydale has performed this particular operation only a handful of times, so the risk is very high." He refrained from repeating his friend's other comment about how dangerous the surgery was—as well as the expense. He had been told that the success rate was no better than fifty percent. Frank would make sure that Quill understood the risks.

"What's next?" Cort asked.

"I need to talk to your father and look at his feet. Then I'm to call my friend back. If we get the green light, then we have to get Quill to Minneapolis as quickly as possible. Can I see your father?"

"Yes, of course. Charlie, will you take your dad upstairs?" Cort asked.

Charlie grabbed his father's hand and led him from the kitchen. "Come on, Dad."

Frank and his son climbed the stairs to the bedroom. Quill had his eyes closed when they entered. Charlie pulled his father close and said, "Quill? Can you hear me, Quill? My dad's here, Quill."

They waited for a response. Finally, with great effort, the old man opened his eyes and tried to focus on Charlie. "Hey, Charlie! Who's that with you?"

"It's my Dad, Quill. You called him, and he's here, and he's going to help you get better!"

"Whoa! Slow down, son." He raised his arm to extend a hand.

Frank moved close and gripped it firmly. "Mr. Purdue? I owe you a great debt of gratitude." He smiled down at the old man.

"Better start by calling me Quill, young fella, and it's I that owe the debt. Don't know how I'd of managed all this without your son. He's an amazing boy and you should be very proud of him."

"I am . . . I truly am. I'm just beginning to realize a great deal about my son, thanks to you and your family."

"Glad to see you made it . . . what with the storm and all."

Charlie could no longer contain his enthusiasm. "Dad! Tell him about the operation!"

Quill looked from Charlie to his father. A puzzled look called for further explanation.

"Seems we know a doctor in Minneapolis that has done the sort of operation that you need, Quill. Need to check a few things, though."

"What? But . . . the money, and . . ."

"I've got the money, Quill!" Charlie said. "My coin collection. It's worth tons of money!"

"What coin collection?"

Charlie rattled off the history of the pennies and finished with, "See! It can be done, Quill."

"I couldn't ask that of you—or your dad. Besides, I don't think I could—"

Frank interrupted. "There's still time, Quill, but just barely. We'll have to get you to Minneapolis as soon as possible. I have to tell you, though, that the doctors stress that this operation is very rare, and the risk, substantial."

Quill considered all that had been said and studied the joy plastered across the boy's face. *It's not possible . . . is it? Lord? Am I dreaming?* "I, uh, don't know what to say . . ."

"You don't have to say anything, Quill. I assure you that Charlie's coins are worth a great deal of money, and whatever the operation costs, it won't put a dent in it. Now, as time is critical, I have to check on a couple of things and call the doctor back." Frank leaned over the bed and continued, "Do you mind if I look at the aneurism first?"

Quill tried to pull his shirt up and failed. Frank helped him as Charlie watched. They both stared at the bulge that pulsed on the old man's stomach. Frank ran his fingers over it, measuring its size.

"Okay. Now let's look at your toes." He sat down and pulled off Quill's socks. All ten were a light blue color. "Any feeling when I touch them?"

"No, not yet."

"How about there?"

"Yes, I can feel that."

"Okay. I have to make another call and report this to my friend, Doctor Bill Profitt. You rest easy. If they give us the green light, we'll get you loaded up and hit the road as soon as possible. Need anything right now?"

"No. Thank you. I still can't believe this is happening, though. Pinch me, will you, son?" Quill smiled at his small friend.

Charlie laughed for the first time in what seemed like years. He gave Quill a slight tweak on the back of his hand. "There! Now do you believe it?"

"Yes. Thank you, Charlie. You too, Frank. If I could just hang around for a short while to see my granddaughter grow up some . . . that would be so . . ." He couldn't finish. Tears welled up and he failed to choke them back.

"Rest, Quill. Charlie, why don't you stay with your friend for a while?"

"Okay."

Frank left the room. It was completely dark outside as he made his way back downstairs. Once in the kitchen, he walked directly to the phone and picked up the receiver. He held it to his ear, waiting for the operator. He heard nothing but a steady buzz. He held it out to the Purdues with a puzzled look on his face.

"Oh, no! Not again." Maxine said.

"Damn. Every time we have heavy wind, the phone goes dead. It won't come back on until much later. You'll have to drive into Blue Springs. Curly has the only phone that ever seems to work during one of these bad storms."

Frank hung up the phone and grabbed his coat. "Where's he located?"

"Can't miss him. Curly's Livery is right next to the Red Horse Saloon," Cort said. "Be careful, Frank. These roads get pretty greasy."

"Okay. I'll be back as soon as I can." Frank put on his hat and left the house.

The Purdues embraced. "I can't believe this is happening," Maxine said.

"Yes. But it is," Cort mumbled. "Let's go up and see Dad."

They walked into the bedroom and found Charlie sitting next to Quill.

"Dad? I . . . I . . ."

"Come here, Cort."

Charlie rose and stepped aside as Cort sat on the bed.

"Seems as if the Good Lord has a change of plans for your old man, doesn't it?"

"I'm so excited right now, Dad. When you first came back, well . . ."

"I know. I had myself convinced that the best thing for all of us was for me to just check out and accept the inevitable. Now, after spending time with you and Maxine and Sarah, I don't know. I'd like nothing better than to be here for her, to try and make up for all the time we've lost."

"Do you feel strong enough for a trip to the Cities?" Cort asked.

"I think so. Besides, what do I have to lose? The Almighty has intervened in some mysterious way and brought the Nashes into our lives. I think I want to see where this leads. Don't you?"

"Yes, we do." Cort leaned over and hugged his father. "I love you, Dad. Stay strong . . . please?"

"I love you too, son." He patted his back and concluded with, "Now why don't you all let an old man rest up a bit? Huh?" He smiled through a cloud of tears.

Once all three were back downstairs, Cort said, "I need to see to the calves. You guys want to help?"

"Sure!" Charlie said. "Where'd my dad go?"

"Phone's out. He went into Curly's to call from there. He'll be back soon."

"Oh, okay. I can let Taffy out at the same time."

"I'll help for a while. Then I have to go pick Sarah up from school," Maxine said.

They put on heavy coats and parkas and left the house. Taffy tested the weather and with some difficulty, negotiated the steps. Charlie waited for her to do her business, ducked into the fierce wind, then took her to the barn to join Cort and Maxine.

Thirty-Eight

LaBette pulled into the yard and stopped. He noticed the pickup parked in front of the house. Lights were on inside. He looked to his left and saw that the door to one of the barns was open. Lightning flashed and thunder clapped. He grabbed the Luger and stuck it in his pocket. *It's time to end all this, Joseph.*

He stepped from the car and turned away from the wind. With one hand on his hat, he trudged to the front door, entered the porch and knocked. He waited for someone to respond, but there was no answer. He knocked again. Still nothing. *The barn . . . probably chores . . .*

He retraced his footsteps from the porch and down the steps. The wind howled and now carried with it large flakes of snow. He leaned against the blow and headed for the barn. A powerful yard light illuminated the yard, and another one above the barn highlighted the snowflakes as they tumbled horizontally.

LaBette removed the Luger and held it behind his back as he approached the barn. With his other hand, he drew back the door and stepped inside.

Charlie and Maxine were feeding the cattle. Maxine doled out feed while the boy broke apart leaves of straw for bedding. Cort was busy pitching manure with the three-tined fork. Taffy lay on the cold floor watching Charlie. The cows and calves bawled loudly, masking LaBette's entrance.

Taffy tensed. Her hair stood up behind her neck as she sensed the stranger's presence. She stood with her ears laid back and then a low, menacing growl rose deep in her slender chest. Charlie heard her before the others. He turned and with a surprised look on his face, said, "Oh, hi!"

Maxine heard his voice, and she and her husband stopped what they were doing to face the door.

"Reverend Douglas! What brings you out in weather like this?" Maxine asked.

LaBette's stiff, white collar stood out against the black of his raincoat.

"Oh, well, you know, God's work is never done, is it, now?" He smiled, moved his right arm and pointed the gun at Cort. "I have your daughter."

Maxine's hands flew to her face. She couldn't comprehend what she heard. "What? What do you mean?"

"Who are you?" Cort asked. "And what do you want?"

"Drop the pitchfork, Mr. Purdue." He took a quick look around the interior. "Where's the old man?"

"He's inside—in bed. He's sick . . . uh, he's dying." Cort said.

"Good. Now, I can assure you I mean no harm to any of you—if you do exactly as you're told." Taffy's growls turned to snarls. "And if you don't restrain that dog, young fellow, this time I won't miss!" He pointed the gun at Taffy.

Charlie ran over and grabbed her collar. He was frightened and the man's word's struck home. "It was you? You shot her?"

"Yes, indeed. Sad to say, it was not a killing shot. I don't miss very often." His threats had found their mark. All three froze in place, unsure of what to do or say.

Charlie face filled with hate. "I remember you now. You, you came to the house . . . the encyclopedia salesman . . . but you looked different . . ."

"Very good. You have an excellent memory."

Before he could think, Charlie blurted out, "If I was bigger I'd beat the crap out of you for what you did!"

"Is that so?"

Cort interceded. "What happened to Reverend Stevens, and what did you mean about our daughter?"

"Ah, yes, the good Reverend. Currently his new congregation is of a different sort—mostly slimy, scaly types with fins, I imagine. He had a regrettable accident and is resting at the bottom of Lake Traverse." LaBette paused to let his words register as he intended. "As for your daughter, I have her in a secure place . . . however, if I don't return to her, or if you decide to get heroic and do something foolish, you'll never see her again—alive." He waited for the words to sink in.

"Oh, my God! Sarah! No, please. She's just a child."

"Nonetheless, understand that her life is in your hands. If you cooperate, and if the boy here tells me what I want to know, she'll be returned to you unharmed. If not . . . ?"

"I don't understand . . ." Cort said.

"Of course you don't. Verily I say unto you, If a man keep my saying, he shall never see death. Neither shall the child—if you follow my instructions."

LaBette edged closer to Charlie, never losing sight of Cort as he posed the greatest threat.

"Now then, my children . . . down to business. This boy has something I want . . . something I need."

Charlie was terrified, angry, and confused. All he could see was the pistol pointed at Taffy.

"Don't you want to know what it is I seek, boy?"

"No, er, yes . . ."

"Good! That's a start. Do you have any idea how far I've come? How long I've been chasing you? You certainly have made my task a difficult one, but ah, the ultimate reward far outweighs any inconvenience. Sooner or later, my time always comes, and now it is at hand. Let's get started. Time's a wasting, as they say. Where have you hidden the pennies?"

"Huh? What . . . How'd you know?"

LaBette cut him short with a wave of his hand. "Never mind. The pennies—two to be precise, stamped 1943. Pure copper, I was told."

"You can't have them . . . they're for Quill . . . for his operation . . ." Charlie blubbered.

"Please, don't make this any more difficult than it has to be. If you don't tell me where the coins are, I'll have to pry it out of you. Trust me, kid, it won't be pretty. Now where are they?"

Charlie looked first at Maxine, then Cort. Neither spoke.

LaBette stepped away from Charlie, raised the pistol, aimed and shot one of the calves in the forehead. *BANG!* The sound reverberated through the barn as if a clap of thunder somehow erupted inside.

All three watched in horror as the calf fell over. An older cow bawled and nudged her dead calf.

Taffy leaped towards LaBette, snapping her teeth and snarling. Charlie hung on to her collar with both hands.

"That's just for starters. Are you beginning to sense the gravity of this situation?" He looked at the boy.

"Still not talking? All right then . . ." He raised the pistol again. *BANG!* The cow staggered and fell on top of the heifer. Now the entire herd was in a frenzy over the gunshots and smell of fresh blood.

Taffy barked and tugged to get loose. She snarled. Her teeth clicked like a pair of castanets.

LaBette pointed the gun at the dog.

"No! No! I'll get the pennies. They're in my bag!" Charlie shrieked.

"Oh, really? I don't think so. You see, I've been through the entire house—your bag included. Yes, while you were out hunting the other day. I couldn't find the coins, however. If I had, we could have avoided all this messiness. So, that means you have stashed them someplace else. Where?"

"They have to be there. I haven't touched them since I left home."

"Oh, dear. We're going to be like that, eh? Perhaps one of you can convince the boy just how much he's endangering your daughter's life?" He nodded to Sarah's parents.

"You have to tell him, Charlie!" Maxine screamed. "Tell him now!"

Charlie was frantic. His face flushed, and he stammered, "They were in a folder, and I put it in my bag when I left home. If, if they're not there, then, I must've lost them someplace. Maybe they fell out . . . Quill's car!"

"Nope. Already looked in the old man's car." LaBette waited.

Charlie was scrambling to make sense of the man's words. "The other car, or the boxcar, or . . . I don't know . . . Please, you have to believe me!"

LaBette aimed at another cow. *BANG!* Then at a calf. *BANG!* He pointed at Cort. "You're next. Best get the kid to talk, I think."

Dammit to hell! What if the kid lost them? LaBette was just beginning to think that the boy actually didn't know where the pennies were. He began to panic, and that was unlike Der Teufel.

OUTSIDE, FRANK PULLED into the yard and stopped. He jumped from the Buick and ran to the house. As he reached to open the door, he heard a loud CRACK! He turned toward the barn. A strange, dark clad man was pointing at something . . . He shielded his eyes and stared in disbelief. *He has a pistol!* The muzzle flashed, followed by a second *CRACK!*

He opened the door and ran inside. "Charlie! Charlie!" He checked the kitchen then ran upstairs. "Quill! Wake up."

"Huh? What . . . ?"

"Quill, there's a man in the barn with a gun . . . he's shooting. Where is everyone?" Frank was trembling as he leaned over the old man.

Quill never hesitated. "Help me up . . . the window. Quick!"

Frank managed to get the old man over to the window. From there, they could both look directly into the barn.

"The preacher. It's the preacher. Under my bed . . . a rifle. Shells are in the closet—top shelf. Hurry!"

Frank dropped down and strained to find the weapon. He grabbed it and handed it to Quill. "Here! I have to get down there!" He turned to leave.

"Wait! Open the window!" Purdue said.

Frank heaved the sash open. Purdue knelt down, hefted the weapon and rested it on the sill. *How far? Yes, yes! You walked across there thousands of times . . . three hundred paces . . . and the wind . . . ?*

Frank ran out of the room. He tore downstairs. The front door was still open. He slammed against the porch door, hit the ground running and slipped. Both feet went out from under him, and he landed on his back. WHUFF! All the wind in his lungs escaped. He couldn't breathe. *Get up! You have to get up!*

He pushed up from the mud to all fours and shook his head. He could still see the preacher in the doorway. The pistol was up as if he was ready to fire again. *NO!*

Frank stood and ran to the barn. Just as he reached the doorway, LaBette sensed movement, turned, and re-aimed at the stranger.

As soon as LaBette moved, Taffy tore from Charlie's grasp.

"Taffy! No!" Charlie screamed.

Too late, the golden retriever bit into LaBette's thigh just before he pulled the trigger.

"Owww!" LaBette shrieked. He pulled the trigger. BANG!

The bullet tore through Frank's jacket and gouged a deep groove in his upper arm. In spite of being hit, he never slowed from his all-out run to the barn. Momentum carried all two hundred pounds of the former football star towards the black-clad shooter. He slammed into LaBette—chest high with his good shoulder.

Both men went down in a heap. Frank hit his head on the concrete floor, however, and didn't move.

"Dad!" Charlie screamed. "Dad!' He ran to his side.

Taffy released her grip and backed away, barking and snapping.

LaBette stood and staggered toward the door. He leaned against the jam, and aimed at the boy. Everyone froze as they realized what was about to happen.

As he stepped forward, he applied pressure on the trigger. Then, CRACK! It sounded as if he had fired.

Charlie staggered—his eyes flared. His body felt numb.

LaBette jerked backward and slammed against the door frame. The pistol wavered, slipped from his hand, and clattered to the floor. His mouth opened and a trickle of blood oozed across his lower lip. He tried to speak, but only gurgled dark blood. He raised a hand to his neck as if he had been stung by a bee.

A small hole appeared on the right side of his white cleric's collar. He held crimson fingers up and stared at the blood dripping from each digit. His eyes widened in surprise and horror as he realized what happened. He looked beyond, toward the house—at the lighted window on the second floor. LaBette shook his head and saw a face . . . the old man . . . *A sniper?* The muzzle of a rifle pointed in his direction. *No! It's . . . not . . . possible . . . I should've . . .*

LaBette's legs folded. He slid down the door jam to a sitting position. His eyes never left the face in the window. The pistol lodged beneath his thigh, out of sight.

Maxine raced over and shouted, "WHERE IS MY DAUGHTER?" She grabbed the front of his coat and shook him back and forth. "TELL ME!"

Blood seeped from the hole in LaBette's neck. He shifted his gaze, focused on Maxine, and smiled. His words were garbled. Pink bubbles formed between his lips. Maxine heard him say, "And . . . the third beast . . . had . . . a face . . . as a man." Blood continued to flow down the front of his black shirt.

"Please, please! Where is Sarah?" Maxine was hysterical. She looked around for Cort who had picked up the pitchfork as the only weapon in sight. "Cort? He has to tell us . . ."

Cort rushed over, leaned the fork against the door, and knelt by LaBette. He felt for a pulse. "He's still alive, but just barely. HEY! CAN YOU HEAR ME?" Cort shook LaBette's shoulder.

His lips parted. Cort put an ear close. "I am the voice of one . . . crying . . . in the . . . wilderness . . ." He waited but there was no further response—just a vacant stare and a slight smile.

Charlie lifted his father's head and called out, "Dad? Dad? Are you all right?"

Frank opened his eyes. He shook his head and waited for the nausea to pass. After a few seconds, he sat up. "I'm okay, Slugger. How about you?"

"I'm fine. You saved our lives, Dad. You and Taffy both." Charlie beamed with pride but then remembered that Sarah was missing.

"Help me up, Slugger." He covered the wound in his arm with his free hand.

Then Charlie saw the blood on his coat sleeve. "You're hurt! You've been shot!" The boy stared at the blood and his mouth fell open.

"Easy, Charlie. I'll be okay."

Maxine was crying steadily. She covered her mouth with both hands.

"Take it easy, honey." Cort said. "We'll find Sarah, I promise." He had no assurance whether his words were true or not but knew he had to restore calm. "Come on . . . let's get into the house and see how Dad is. Frank? You make it all right?"

"Go ahead. We'll be right behind you."

Cort escorted Maxine from the barn. Frank and Charlie shuffled past the still form of Joseph Tenavie.

Taffy growled and stopped next to LaBette. The hairs on her neck stood tall. Charlie heard a scraping sound, turned, and saw that LaBette had picked up the Luger and had it in his lap. The man fumbled, then wrapped bloody fingers around the grip. He raised his arm toward Charlie.

"DAD!" Charlie's scream was carried by the wind.

Frank's reaction was instinctive. Unaware of Sarah's plight, he pushed Charlie aside. Then he jumped forward and grabbed the pitchfork. LaBette leveled the pistol for one final shot!

With one great lunge, he drove all three steel tines through the preacher's neck. Blood spurted from a perfect row of new holes and spilled over LaBette's Bible, which slipped out from inside his coat. The killer's eyes were open—but sightless. Pinned against the wooden barn door, Der Teufel was dead!

Frank booted the gun away, and with one last, emphatic thrust on the fork, released the handle. The wooden shaft quivered briefly, settled, and was still. Frank turned away, put his good arm around his son, and left the barn with Charlie.

Taffy stepped close to the impaled body. She retreated as LaBette's legs jerked in a final, involuntary spasm. Satisfied he could do no further harm, she came back and sniffed once, limped a few steps away, and squatted in the yard. When finished, she hurried to catch up with her master.

Rain turned to snow as Charlie, his father, and Taffy reached the house.

Thirty-Nine

O H, GOD, CORT! What about Sarah?" Maxine sobbed and clutched her husband's jacket.

At that moment, the Nashes entered the kitchen. "What about Sarah?" Frank asked. "What did he say?"

"He said he had her someplace, and if we told him what he wanted, he wouldn't harm her. If not . . ." Cort left the rest unfinished.

"Who was he?"

Cort blurted, "We don't know. He said he killed Reverend Stevens, and took Sarah from school. We don't know what he did with her. I suppose he walked in dressed as a man of the cloth, gave some excuse to take her out, and . . . I don't know."

Maxine's eyes widened. "You don't suppose he's already . . . ? Dear God, no! Cort?"

"Honey, please. That isn't helping us find her." He hugged his wife until her sobbing eased. "Charlie, go check on my dad, okay?"

Charlie ran out and up the stairs. He found Quill slumped against the wall beneath the window. Snow was blowing in. "Quill!" He ran over, closed the window, and touched the old man's arm.

Quill opened his eyes. "Help me up, son."

379

Charlie helped his friend back into bed. Charlie saw the rifle and said, "Quill? You did that? I mean, you shot that guy?"

"Did I hit him?"

"Yes. But he shot my dad, and he has Sarah someplace. He wouldn't tell us where, Quill!"

"Oh, no!" Quill's face paled as he realized that by shooting the preacher he eliminated any chance of finding his granddaughter. "What have I done?"

"You had to, Quill. He was going to start shooting us. He already killed some of the cattle and also Reverend Stevens. After you shot him, he still almost shot . . . me. My dad had to stab him with the pitchfork."

Purdue took a moment to digest the boy's words. "Why though. What did he want?"

Charlie looked down. "My coins. He wanted two of my coins."

Quill studied the boy and realized something else had happened. "And? You said you'd give them to him, right?" He waited. "Charlie?"

"No, well, sort of . . . I think I lost them, Quill. He said he searched the house and my bag and your car and didn't find them. Wait!" He ran to the closet, pulled out his bag, and dumped the contents on the bed. He sorted through the mess, turned, and said, "They're not here! I lost them someplace. I don't know where . . . maybe the boxcar, or that guy's car . . . I don't know, Quill." Charlie's head dropped.

"Easy, son. Doesn't matter. Main thing now is to find Sarah. Go on down and see what's going on, okay?"

"All right. I'll be back in a few minutes." Charlie left the room. His head was spinning. *Without my coins, Quill won't be able to have his operation . . . And what about Sarah? If she's . . . ?* He shook with terror as he realized the implications of what he was thinking. He returned to the kitchen.

"Oh, Frank! You've been shot!" Maxine just said as she noticed Frank's blood soaked arm.

"Yeah, guess I have. Don't think it's too serious, though."

"Cort, help me get his coat off." Together they removed his jacket. Cort tore away his shirt sleeve and inspected the wound.

"Pretty deep gash, Frank. Go get the first-aid kit, honey."

When she returned, they bound his arm with gauze and gave him four aspirin for the pain. "That should hold you," Cort said.

"Yes. Thank you. Now what about your daughter?" Concern filled Frank's face.

"We have to call the sheriff." Then Cort realized they couldn't. "Damn! Phone's down. We have to get to Curly's! Charlie, how's Dad?"

"He's all right, I guess," Charlie said. His voice was weak.

"What's the matter, Slugger?"

Charlie struggled to speak. "I lost the coins, Dad . . . Sarah would be safe if I hadn't lost them, and now Quill won't—"

Maxine cut him short. "Charlie, don't. You can't blame yourself for any of this. It isn't your fault. Besides, we don't know anything, yet. Even if you had the coins, well, he might have shot us all, and we'd still never . . ." She couldn't finish.

"Come on, we're wasting time," Cort said. "Charlie, you and your dad stay here. We've got to get to a phone and start looking for Sarah." He and Maxine prepared to leave.

"Wait a minute!" Frank said. "What about his car? Maybe . . . ?"

Cort raced out of the house before Frank could finish speaking. He skidded to a stop next to the DeSoto. He opened the door and peered inside. The backseat was empty except for a suitcase. He backed away as Maxine joined him. She was out of breath.

She saw the look of disappointment on her husband's face. "The keys, Cort! Check the trunk!"

Cort grabbed the keys from the ignition, backed away, and ran to the rear of the car. He fumbled with the keys and dropped them in the mud.

"Hurry, Cort!"

Once he had retrieved the keys, he found the right one, inserted it in the lock, and the trunk lifted. He opened it all the way. His heart was racing. One quick glance by both parents filled their hearts with despair. The trunk was empty except for a couple of bags and a gun case.

Cort didn't pause. "Come on! Get in the truck!"

Frank and Charlie stood at the door to the porch. They saw Cort shake his head. "Damn!" Frank said. He waved at them to go ahead. He and his son went back in the house.

Cort and Maxine piled into the pick-up and drove off into the falling snow.

"What if they don't find her, Dad?"

"I don't know, Slugger. I don't know about much of anything right now." Frank was feeling lightheaded and weak. "Come on. You can fix me something to eat." He put his good arm over his son's shoulder and led him back to the kitchen.

THE PURDUES RACED TOWARD Blue Springs. Curly was just closing up when they arrived. After a brief explanation of what happened, Curly picked up the phone and placed a call to the sheriff.

Within twenty minutes, he and half a dozen deputies together with Curly, the Purdues, Maggie, and two other local residents gathered to form a search party. One major concern was that the man who had impersonated the preacher might have had an accomplice. If so, he could be holding Sarah with him and might be moving around in another vehicle. They'd have to stop and search every car and truck in the area.

The Minnesota and South Dakota Highway Patrols were each notified and roadblocks were set up fifty miles in every direction. With that covered, every deserted building, parked auto, and truck had to be checked. Residents of homes and farms were asked to allow a search of their outbuildings. Because manpower was limited, the search would take hours.

Curly and Cort went down to the school and searched every inch of the building—including the bus parked outside. They found no sign of Sarah Purdue.

When they returned to Curly's, Maxine looked up as they entered—hope written across her distraught face. Maggie hugged her tightly. Sarah was still missing.

A DEPUTY WAS DISPATCHED to the Purdue farm to secure the crime scene. Once he spoke with Frank, the local doctor was called to patch up his arm. The deputy remained on site and was in constant contact with the search party. As each hour passed, the news reported to the Nash's was grim. There was no sign of Sarah.

THE COMMAND POST HAD been moved to the Red Horse Saloon. Cort and Maxine sat with Curly and Maggie waiting for news of their daughter. At 11:30 P.M., the sheriff returned with one of his deputies. The Purdues scanned his face for a hopeful sign but only saw defeat.

"We've searched everywhere, Cort. I'm afraid we're running out of options."

Maxine blanched. "You can't give up . . . you just can't!"

"Maxine, I'm sorry. We'll spread out even farther, of course, but we've got to reassign some of our men to other duties . . . same with the Highway Patrol guys." He turned to leave.

"What about the church, Fred? You checked that, right?" Curly asked.

Maxine's face brightened. "Yes, of course! The church!"

The sheriff turned to his deputy. "Harold? You cleared that already?"

"Yep! One of the first buildings we checked. Sorry, Maxine."

"What about the parsonage? Tucked away behind the church, most don't even know it's there," Maggie offered.

When it was discovered that no one had checked that particular building, orders flew and men were dispatched immediately. Within seconds, they all raced from the saloon out into the raging storm and across the street.

"Please, God? It can't be too late . . ." Maxine uttered as she fought to keep her balance on the slippery road.

Frank and Charlie were in the upstairs bedroom with Quill when they heard the front door open. All three held their breath, waiting for word of Sarah. It was 12:30 A.M.

"Grandpa? Grandpa? It's me, Sarah! Where are you? Charlie?"

Footsteps pounded on the stairs, and, seconds later, Sarah bounded into the room. Her parents stood at the base of the stairs and held hands.

Sarah threw herself on Quill's bed and hugged him tightly.

Quill was speechless. Tears rolled down his cheeks. He thought if he hugged his granddaughter any tighter he'd smother her . . . but he refused to let go. *Thank you, God! Thank you, thank you . . .*

Frank and Charlie looked at each other, stepped close and held each other's hand. Neither could speak.

Sarah pulled back from her grandfather, turned around and asked Frank, "Who are you?"

"This is my dad, Sarah," Charlie said with pride in his voice.

She looked from father to son with genuine interest. "Hi! You look like Charlie."

"Hi, yourself," Frank said. He glanced down at his son. "Yes, I guess so. We're all glad you're safe, Sarah."

"Me too. That man was scary. You know what he said, Charlie?" She moved close and looked into her friend's eyes.

"No. What?"

"He came into school and said Dad was hurt and that I had to go with him!" Memory of the phony preacher made her shiver. "Then he took me to the reverend's house and tied me up and put tape over my mouth and . . ." She couldn't finish.

Charlie took her hand. "Yeah, but you're safe now, Sarah. Just pretend it was all a bad dream. That's what I do sometimes."

She sniffled. "I'll try."

"Everyone's safe now," Quill said. "Let's try and forget all about that man. We're together again and that's all that matters."

Cort and Maxine entered the small bedroom just as Quill finished speaking.

A frown appeared on Charlie's face. He looked at his dad and said, "What about Quill's operation? Without the coins . . ." The room was silent. No one had an answer.

Finally Frank spoke. "I don't know, Slugger." He looked over at Quill, who shook his head and smiled.

"It's all right, Charlie. Really. Let's just let Nature run its course. I think this was in the Lord's plan all along, anyway." Quill hugged Sarah tightly. But, then he realized, *She doesn't know!*

Sarah turned her head, looked up at her grandfather, and asked, "What are you talking about, Grandpa? What's the Lord's plan?"

She was the only one who had no idea about his illness—he had never had the opportunity to talk to her. He looked first at Maxine, then Cort. Both shook their heads.

"I have to tell you something, sweetheart. I should have done it some time ago."

Sarah had a puzzled look on her face.

Charlie's heart stopped. "No! You can't . . . Dad? Please, there has to be a way . . . ?"

"If I could have a moment with Quill, alone, please?" Frank requested.

Maxine took Sarah's arm. She was reluctant to leave. Then Charlie and the Purdues left the small room. Frank moved to the bed and sat down.

"Here's what I've been thinking, Quill. I have a small mortgage on the house, and we have quite a bit of equity built up. I think the bank would give me a second mortgage that would cover the operation." Silently, he hoped the bank would concur. . . . He wasn't certain, however, as his business had suffered lately. He held up his hand to halt the old man's protest.

"I couldn't let you do that." Quill said.

"Yes you could . . . and you will. Charlie would never forgive me— or you—if we didn't proceed." He smiled. "Listen, I'm still young enough. I can repay it in a few years. I'm not worried about that, Quill. Please. For Charlie's sake . . . and Sarah's?"

The room was quiet for a long time. Quill's eyes misted. He was weak, and the roller coaster of emotions was taking its toll.

He inhaled, blew the air from his lungs, and said, "Only if you promise me one thing."

"What's that?"

"You have to promise me that you've had your last drink . . . ever!" He focused on the large man sitting next to him.

Frank smiled and without hesitation, replied, "That's easy. You have my word." He extended his arm, and the two men clasped hands. They remained that way for long while.

"Get some rest, Quill. We're leaving first thing in the morning." Frank stood, winked, and left the room.

Forty

EVERYONE SLEPT SOUNDLY that night, except Quill. All the energy he had expended getting out of bed to shoot LaBette had taken its toll. He was worn down and had little strength left to fight the pain in his back and stomach. Try as he might, he couldn't mask painful groans during the night.

Charlie heard his friend cry frequently but felt helpless to do anything except pray and wait for daylight. He heard Sarah come into the bedroom more than once to check on her grandpa. Charlie stayed quiet during her visits.

Frank camped out on the sofa in the living room and managed a few hours of sleep with the aid of numerous aspirin.

EARLY TUESDAY MORNING, friends and neighbors began arriving at the Purdue farm. It had snowed throughout the night. Six inches of heavy, wet snow covered the ground and roads, and it was still snowing. Fortunately, the snow was too heavy to drift much, which proved to be a blessing because a strong Northwest wind that blew in carried with it thirty-degree temperatures.

Everyone gathered in the kitchen at 7:00 A.M. Plans were made for the journey to Minneapolis. Charlie and his dad would drive their Buick. The Purdues would all travel behind them in Quill's Ford Custom Wagon.

Once Maggie Albright heard of Quill's illness, she asked if she could ride along.

"Of course, you can, Maggie." Maxine said. "Cort's going to put the back seat down and lay a mattress in the back for Quill to lie on. You and Sarah can ride back there and take turns tending him."

Once Sarah had an idea of the seriousness of her grandfather's condition, she never left his side. Her mother insisted she eat breakfast before going back upstairs. Sarah bolted a few bites of food and left the kitchen.

Quill moved in and out of consciousness. He was crashing, and only sheer will and determination would keep him alive during the journey to Minneapolis.

Sarah took his hand and said, "You just have to get well, Grandpa. You just have to!" She squeezed his bony fingers, waiting for some sign of recognition. "Grandpa? Can you hear me?"

There was no response. Sarah stroked his forehead and brushed back a few strands of white hair. She felt helpless, and her small body sagged with sadness.

Cort and Charlie came into the room. "Time to get ready, sweetheart. Mom has your suitcase packed, but you better go check to see that you have everything."

Sarah gave Quill one last hug and left the room. She was distraught and couldn't find words to express how worried she was.

"Got all your stuff packed, Charlie?"

"Yes. I guess so." Charlie couldn't stand to see his friend so ill and weak.

"Why don't you take your bag downstairs? I think your Dad is loading the car."

Charlie glanced at Quill, picked up his bag, and left. Taffy limped alongside.

"Dad? Can you hear me?" Cort called.

Quill's eyelids flickered but didn't open. He groaned just a bit and one hand twitched.

"You have to stay strong for me, okay? We've come too far to have it end like this. Sarah needs you. I need you. The family needs you back here all in one piece. Hang on, Dad. Please?" Cort's eyes drained at that moment.

Try as he might, he couldn't stop crying. All the emotion of the past days seemed to boil over like a kettle of hot stew. He knelt and lay his head on his father's chest. He could hear his heart thump. "Keep that ticker going, old man. We're in this thing together."

Downstairs, Curly arrived with the sheriff. "Driveway's plowed out . . . so's the highway." Curly said. "Quill ready?"

"I think so, Curly. Cort's with him now. We need to get one of the mattresses from his room down." Maxine replied.

"No problem." Curly left the kitchen.

"Mr. Nash? You'll be following me all the way to Brown's Valley," the sheriff announced. "I've arranged for a plow to clear the road ahead of us. Cort will follow you and a highway patrol car will bring up the rear."

"That's great, Sheriff. Can't thank you enough for all you've done." Frank said.

"Our pleasure. The Purdues are good friends, and we'd all like to see Quill back here again. Now, once we reach Brown's Valley, I'll have to go back across the river, but the sheriff of McCloud County will meet us there and escort you all the way to the Cities."

"Quill's barely conscious, Sheriff. We'll need some help getting him down to the car." Frank said.

"Whenever you're ready. Plenty of help outside. The Johnsons have already started butchering the dead cattle, and there's others to help."

Maxine was busy filling a basket with sandwiches and drinks. "I'm ready whenever you folks are."

By 8:30 A.M. everything was ready to begin the journey. A team of men carried Quill down and loaded him in the back end of his wagon. Sarah climbed in back and lay down with Quill. Maggie joined them while Cort and Maxine sat in front.

Curly stood next to Cort. "Don't worry about a thing, Cort. I'll be out here morning and night to feed the cattle and check on the place."

"Thanks a million, Curly." He reached through the window to shake his hand. "Don't know what we'd have done without you."

"Just be sure you call when you have news of Quill's operation, okay?"

"You bet. So long, old friend."

Frank started the Buick. Just as he was ready to leave, Charlie said, "Wait! I forgot something." He opened the door and ran back into the house. He returned minutes later with Quill's dictionary tucked under his arm. "Okay. All set."

Charlie rolled down his window and shouted, "Bye, Curly."

"Bye, bye, Charlie. You come back real soon, ya hear?"

"I will."

They swung in behind the sheriff's car and the caravan pulled out of the farm yard. Charlie turned for one last look. The white farm house seemed to meld into the snow-covered fields beyond. Horses in the pasture raced along the fence pacing the automobiles as they drove away. Charlie waved.

In spite of the plow clearing the road ahead of them, progress to Brown's Valley was slow. Gil McIlheny was waiting when they arrived. After brief introductions, he climbed back in his car and followed a Minnesota State Highway plow truck toward the Cities. The trip east would take six and a half hours.

Quill regained consciousness a few times during the journey. He spoke briefly to Sarah and Maggie, then drifted back into a dream-like state. Cort and Maxine kept their concern for his fate to themselves in deference to Sarah.

The nine-year old maintained a steady stream of chatter with her grandfather. The fact that he couldn't hear her much of the time did not diminish her energy. She held his hand and patted his shoulder as a constant reminder of her presence.

Maggie lay next to him holding his other hand and occasionally wiping his forehead. It seemed to her he was feverish, and her concern grew with each passing mile.

They nibbled at the food Maxine prepared, only to have something to do during the tedious trip to Minneapolis.

Cort wondered how much more difficult the trip would have been without the plow or the police escort. The roads were still slippery, but at least they didn't have to worry about passing other cars. As it was, the drive felt like it took forever. He reached over and squeezed Maxine's hand. "This is going to be a long day, honey."

"Yes, I know." She lowered her voice. "If your dad comes through this . . . we'll have much to be grateful for."

FRANK AND CHARLIE SPENT the time reliving the boy's experiences during the past weeks.

"You sure have had one whale of an adventure, haven't you, Slugger?"

"Yeah, I guess I have. Best part of all, though, was meeting Quill and his family . . . and, having you come to pick me up." He smiled at his dad.

"Your mother and grandmother are sure going to be happy to see you."

"Me too. I missed them . . . and I missed you too, Dad."

"You'll never know how sorry I am about everything, Charlie. I promise you that you'll never have to be afraid of me again. I'm done drinking, son—forever."

"You mean it, Dad?"

"Yep! Having you gone and spending time in jail taught me a valuable lesson. I think I've been given a second chance at being a better father . . . and husband. Your mother has put up with a lot too, you know."

"I know." He studied his father's profile. "How come you got out of jail, anyhow?"

"The judge felt that under the circumstances, I should be with your mother. I still have to go back and finish my sentence, but that won't be so bad."

"Sure wish I hadn't lost my coin collection."

"You know, Slugger, sometimes these things happen for a reason. Besides, what would you have done with all that money, besides pay for Quill's operation?"

"Hmm. I don't know. Buy a new pair of hockey skates and a shotgun some day. Give some to the Purdues and maybe buy a ranch when I'm older . . . out near Blue Springs. That'd really be neat, wouldn't it, Dad?"

Frank smiled. "Yes, it would, Charlie."

"I could have horses and lots of dogs . . . No, Taffy would probably be jealous. No more dogs." He turned and looked over the seat back. "Isn't that right, girl? No more dogs—just you."

Taffy slapped the seat back with her tail and closed her eyes.

SHERIFF MCILHENY WAS PREOCCUPIED. Something about the people behind him was puzzling him. He had been thinking about it ever since he met the caravan at Brown's Valley. *Something about one of these cars . . . that old Ford Wagon back there. An old man . . . and a kid. I swear I saw or heard about it or something. Where? When? Wait a minute! Blue Springs! Of course.* He slapped his forehead in disbelief, then picked up the hand mike and called his dispatcher.

"Mike, do me a favor. Dig out the file on the Virgil Pisant case. I'll wait." *What was that guy's name?*

"Go ahead. The original call from Hanley Falls . . . yeah, from the vet who was killed. What'd it say the guy's name was? Purdue? Quillan Purdue? No kidding?" McIlheny smiled and sat straight in the seat. "Nope. That's all I need. Thanks."

What do you know about that? If that don't beat all. This old boy did me a huge favor. Better make sure I get him to the Cities as fast as possible. He blinked his lights at the plow to speed up.

They reached University Hospital at 3:30 p.m. McIlheny shook Charlie's hand and said to his father, "I think we have all the pieces to figure this mess out, Mr. Nash. We'll be in touch after a bit."

Frank wasn't sure what the sheriff was talking about, but replied, "Sure. No problem."

"Good luck. Hope everything turns out for your friend back there." He climbed in the cruiser and pulled away.

Orderlies rushed out with a gurney and unloaded Quill. They wheeled him into the emergency room, and, after a brief exam, he was hustled up to the surgical floor. Frank signed the necessary papers as payee of the hospital bill, and by the time he was finished, joined the rest of the group on the fourth floor.

He stepped out of the elevator and was immediately greeted by his friend, Dr. Bill Profitt who separated himself from the family to meet his old teammate. "Frank. Good to see you again."

"Likewise, Bill. Can't thank you enough for setting all this up. What's next?"

"Let's step into the conference room," he said to the adults. You kids want to get a bottle of pop or something?"

"Come on, Sarah." Charlie said. "I've got money."

She hesitated, reluctant to leave her grandfather.

"You can see him before the operation, sweetheart. I promise," Maxine offered.

Charlie took her hand and led her away.

Once in the small room, Dr. Profitt said to Cort, "I don't need to remind you how serious your father's condition is. He has what's called a 'pulsatic aneurism.' Think of it as a balloon: When small it's hard to blow up, but as it gets bigger it inflates quite easily. The bruises on his back and flank are typical—they're called, 'Grey Turner Sign.' Unsightly, but in themselves, relatively harmless. We have to run a number of tests to determine his general health, and if Dr. Lillydale gives us a green light, we'll proceed immediately."

"What kind of tests?" Cort asked.

"For starters, we need to check his heart . . . to make sure it can withstand a very aggressive, grueling operation. Routine blood work is necessary as well, but the main thing is to be certain he's strong enough to endure the surgery."

"Assuming you proceed, what happens?" Maxine asked.

"Dr. Lillydale will cut open the aneurism, remove part of it, and insert a piece of Dacron to act as a substitute for part of the artery. It's a very delicate procedure with tremendous risk, as you know. Blood has to be rerouted during the operation and once the material is sewn in place—the new tube, if you will—blood will re-enter the artery and flow as it normally does."

"And then?"

"He'll be given blood thinners to prevent clotting. Then we watch, wait, and pray."

"For what?"

"For acceptance, more than anything. Many times the body will reject foreign materials. Infection takes over and then . . . well, one thing at a time. If he survives the operation, his chances will improve dramatically, and then with care and a healthy lifestyle, we will add years to his life expectancy."

"What exactly are the odds here, doctor?" Cort waited.

"I won't kid you. Fifty percent . . . at best." He paused for the words to register. "Okay. If there are no more questions, I need to scrub. I'll be assisting Dr. Lillydale. Know this, though. Your father is in the hands of one of the foremost vascular surgeons in the country. That in itself is a huge plus. Now try to relax as best you can. We'll keep you apprised of the operation as we go along." Dr. Profitt left the room.

"Oh, my." Maggie said. "I had no idea. How long has Quill been living with this?"

"Don't know for sure, Maggie. Probably for some time, at least as far as the pain's concerned. I think the last doctor he saw in Rock Island told him he had a few months left. That's about all I know." Cort said.

Charlie and Sarah returned with their bottles of Coke. "What did he say?" Charlie asked.

"They're going to run some tests and then if everything looks all right, they'll begin the operation." Frank replied.

"Can we see him before, uh . . . you know?"

"I don't know if he'll be awake, but I would think so, yes." Maxine replied.

"Good. I have to tell him something," Charlie said.

DR. PROFITT RETURNED in thirty minutes dressed in blue scrubs. The room was quiet as he entered. "We're all set. His heart is strong, and other than the fact he's running a bit of a fever, everything else came back positive."

"Where is he, doctor?" Cort asked.

"They're wheeling him into the operating room right now. If you'd like to see him, we'd better hurry." He stepped aside and allowed the family to pass. "This way. He's awake and somewhat lucid. Oxygen tends to do that."

They all walked down a hallway and turned left. Quill's gurney had been halted in front of the double doors to the operating room. Sarah ran ahead and stopped next to her grandfather.

"Hi, Grandpa!"

Quill had an oxygen mask on and all could see that his color had improved. He opened his eyes and looked across at Sarah. The nurse pulled down the mask. "Hello, sweetheart."

"You're going to be all better, aren't you?"

"I sure hope so, honey. You know why?"

"Why?"

"Because you and I have a lot to talk about. And you promised you'd take me riding on Pumpkin. I wouldn't miss that for the world."

"I love you, Grandpa."

The old man's eyes clouded. "I love . . . you . . . too, Sarah."

Cort and Maxine edged close. "Dad? We'll all be waiting for you, all right?"

Quill nodded. He was tiring. "Where's Charlie?"

"Right here, Quill." Cort drew him in until he was head high with Quill. "You know what?" Charlie asked.

"What?"

"We didn't look up our word for the day." He held out the dictionary.

"You remembered to bring it! I forgot, but you didn't."

"We have to go now," the nurse said and prepared to pull the mask back on.

"Wait! Here, let's look one up." Charlie turned to a spot already marked. "Let's see . . . okay, I've got it: 'Best Friend: A person you know, love, and trust. A person with whom you dare to be yourself.'"

Quill smiled, and two large tears crept from the corners of each eye. "But . . . that's two words, Charlie."

"I know."

"And . . . ?"

"Oh, yeah. Hmmm. Quill Purdue is Charlie's best friend . . . forever." Charlie closed the book and crossed his arms. The book snuggled against his chest.

"Thank you, son. Take care of the dictionary for me, okay?"

"I will. Wait!" Charlie stepped back then forward again and leaned close to whisper in the old man's ear. "Quill I never knew either of my grandfathers and, uh . . . well, I just want you to know that I—" He couldn't finish.

Quill struggled to say, "I know, Charlie. I feel the same way." He smiled briefly.

"We really must go," the nurse said.

"I'll see you later, Charlie . . . and Sarah."

"You promise?" Sarah asked.

The nurse slipped the mask back on. Quill reached out and both children grabbed hold of his hand—three hands nested as one until the doors opened. Then they had to let go. Quill was wheeled into the brightly lit room. A dozen doctors and nurses were standing with palms turned upward, waiting for their patient.

The doors closed with a *swish,* and Quill was gone.

Forty-One

THE OPERATION TOOK six hours. Doctor Profitt or one of the nurses came out every hour to update the family on their progress. When it was all over, Quill was taken to the Intensive Care Unit. His life hung in the balance for a long time.

The doctors' concerns about Quill's body rejecting the Dacron tube appeared to be justified. Blood flow to his lower body was impeded for a time, and they were concerned they might have to go back in and try another material. That option was ruled out in the end as it was decided that Quill couldn't withstand a second operation.

ONCE QUILL HAD BEEN MOVED to the ICU, everyone decided to leave and go to the Nash home to rest. Cort and Maxine stayed in the guest bedroom next to Charlie, while Maggie and Sarah slept on the third floor in another bedroom.

Charlie was happy to be home, but his concern for Quill dogged his every waking moment. He returned to the hospital each morning with the Purdues.

Frank stayed at home to arrange payment of the hospital bill and catch up on work. His conversations with his bank proved more difficult than he imagined. With interest rates high, banks were not as eager to lend money for second mortgages as he had initially thought. He had neglected his business over the past year, and a number of clients had taken their business elsewhere. The bank suggested he shop around for another source of money to cover the hospital debt.

ON THE SIXTH DAY after the operation, Monday, October 28, Quill opened his eyes for the first time since he had been wheeled into surgery. He was out of danger, and, from that point forward, his progress was remarkable. He regained his strength within days, and the nurses had all they could do to keep him in bed.

Once Cort and Maxine realized that Quill was out of danger, they decided they needed to get back to Blue Springs to take care of their farm. Sarah pleaded to stay with the Nashes, but she lost out and prepared to leave with her parents. Maggie would remain behind and accompany Quill home with Frank and Charlie when he was ready to travel.

On Tuesday morning, Cort, Sarah, and Charlie went outside to get the old Ford Wagon ready for the return trip. They opened the back door and slid the mattress out so the backseat could be folded up. The mattress would be stored in the Nash garage until Cort could collect it.

Sarah crawled in to release the latch, and as she did so, had to reach down between the flat back and the wheel well. Suddenly she exclaimed, "Hey! What's this?"

She peered down into the narrow space, then stretched her slender arm as far as she could reach and pulled out a small, dusty package. She turned it over in her hands, wiped off accumulated dirt and dust, then turned to face Charlie and Cort.

Charlie's eyes flew open. "Sarah! You found it! My coin collection!"

"What? You've got to be kidding!" Cort exclaimed.

Sarah beamed and handed it to Charlie. He unfolded it and exclaimed, "They're both here! Look, Sarah! My two pennies!"

WENZEL HEARD THE DOOR TINKLE and looked up. Two serious-looking men dressed in gray suits entered and approached the counter. He put on a smile and said, "Gentlemen? How may I be of service?" The swarmy smile spread beneath the pencil-thin mustache.

"Seymour Wenzel?"

"At your service."

"You are under arrest."

Wenzel's smile vanished like a night crawler about to be plucked by a robin. "There must be some mistake. I can assure you that I run an honest business here. And who, might I ask, has filed a complaint?"

"You're coming with us, Wenzel. Anybody else here to close the store for you?"

He finally realized the seriousness of their intent, and meekly replied, "No."

"Give me the key, then put your hands behind your back."

"What, uh, er, is the charge?"

"Conspiracy to commit murder . . . for starters."

Wenzel blanched—worse, he felt his bladder pre-release. He held it as long as he could, but by the time the cops had him in the back seat of the police cruiser, he lost control. "Oh, dear . . ."

It took the detectives less than an hour to convince Wenzel to open up. Veiled references to life at Stillwater Prison—living with the general population—went a long way toward eliciting his cooperation. He folded like a cheap suit.

Paxton Armbruster and his trusted assistant, Madeline, were arrested later that same day. In time, after scouring Armbruster's extensive files, the police discovered a phone number for Dominic Portebello—aka, Val; aka, Little Dom; aka, the Bull; aka, Potbelly Dom. They hit the jackpot when they nabbed Portebello. It would take months to unravel his involvement in a long list of unsolved homicides in the Twin Cities, as well as in Chicago. For the first time ever, the police, and subsequently the FBI, had a tie to the Minneapolis mob, and a parade of family members would eventually have their day in court.

Portebello was placed in a new witness protection program and became the government's star witness for the prosecution.

Charlie's involvement was kept quiet—for his protection. But behind the scenes, the police made certain that he and his family understood the true import of how he had helped take down a number of vicious criminals.

FRANK NASH COMPLETED the remainder of his sentence later that winter. He met and became friends with the Reverend Vernon Johnson, who had started a local chapter of Alcoholics Anonymous. He attended regular, weekly sessions with the group and was responsible for helping a number of individuals deal with their disease. He never had another drink.

Seven months after returning home, Charlie returned to the Purdue farm in Blue Springs with his father and mother. Charlie was to be the best man at a wedding—Quill's. He and Maggie had decided to get married and had built a small cottage over-looking Quill's orchard.

The wedding was held outside on a glorious day in late May when the apple blossoms were in full bloom. Quill's daughter, Alice, and her husband were also there. Sarah walked down the aisle dressed in a pink party dress and wearing a garland of ivy with honeysuckle sprigs. She scattered apple blossoms that fluttered in the warm breeze and beamed with excitement.

Curly escorted Maggie behind Sarah and many later said they spotted tears dripping from his crusty eyes. He denied it. "That's a bunch of crappola," Curly said later.

Cort and Charlie waited next to Quill as the bride approached. Quill had completely recovered by now and had gained fifteen pounds. He thought he had never been so happy.

The service was brief, and when it was over, the assembled guests sat down to a full meal in the front yard. Charlie finished quickly and went to the barn to check on a new colt born two weeks earlier.

Sarah came running out of the house looking for him. "Charlie! The phone! It's long distance!"

He poked his head out of the barn and yelled back, "Over here, Sarah!"

"You've got a phone call!" She cupped her hands as she yelled.

Charlie ran back to the house. He was breathless by the time he picked up the receiver. "Hello?" He listened and said, "Oh, Hi, Uncle Tom! What? They did? Wait a minute 'til I get Dad." He laid the receiver down and said, "Sarah! Hurry! Go get my mom and dad . . . and Quill, please?"

He waited until everyone was assembled. "Okay, Uncle Tom. Go ahead." His mouth fell open and the receiver slipped from his hand.

Frank bent and picked it up. "Tom? Charlie's in shock, I think. What? Will you repeat that for me? Holy Moley! Forty-seven bids? No kidding. My, my, my. Good old Uncle Hedwig. Right. Thanks for calling, Tom. We'll be back in a few days. Charlie's staying for a month. I'll see you when we get home." Frank hung up the phone. Father and son looked at each other and smiled. Neither spoke. Eyes wide, the boy simply stared at his father.

Quill ultimately broke the silence. "Well? How much?"

Charlie shuffled over as if in a daze, pulled his friend down to eye level, and whispered in his ear.

Quill straightened. His eyes sparkled. A sharp whistle escaped his lips. "Better go get your dictionary, Charlie. We've got a new word to look up . . ."

Outside, Taffy sauntered over to the orchard and lay in the shade beneath one of the blossoming trees. She gazed down the hill to the pond below. Her nose tested the wind, and she cocked one ear high as a small flock of green-wing teal coasted overhead with their wings set. They circled the pond once, then twice, and settled quietly in the middle. Heads erect— alert for danger, they surveyed the familiar water. Satisfied that all was as it should be, they relaxed and began preening. A young male in full color broke from the group and swam toward shore. He peeped once, then again, and ducked into the rushes.

Taffy studied the ducks for a few moments, relaxed her ear, rose, shook twice, and trotted back to the house.

Epilogue

O N MAY 21, 1956, the only two remaining 1943 Lincoln-head copper pennies from an original twelve minted at the Philadelphia Mint, were sold at a private auction by Sotheby's in New York City. They were purchased at auction by a private party for a then record $723,000.00—from an anonymous bidder.

Edwin H. Dressel, the former superintendent of the Philadelphia Mint, had retired to Gulfport, Mississippi. When contacted by the press, he remained adamant in his conviction that the twelve coins had never been minted.

Charlie's two coins were never seen in public again . . .